Warning
This work is written for a mature audience and includes scenes depicting graphic violence, blood and gore, sexual assault, substance addiction, alcoholism, mental illness, suicide, and other possibly triggering content.

NIGHT'S REIGN

NIGHT'S REIGN
Curse of the Fathers, Book One

Daan Katz

Daan Katz

Copyright © 2022 Daan Katz

February 2022

www.daankatz.com

Cover Design: www.etherictalesnedits.com

Map and Logo: www.lisawitmond.com

All rights reserved. No part of this document may be used or reproduced, transmitted, or stored in a retrieval system in any form or by any means without the prior written permission of the author, not otherwise circulated in any form of binding or cover other than that in which it is published and without a similar condition being imposed on the subsequent purchaser.

This is a work of fiction.

All characters, locales, and situations in this publication are fictitious, and any resemblance to real people, alive or dead, is purely coincidental.

NIGHT'S REIGN

A FLOUNDERING PRIEST. A WOMAN IN A WHEELCHAIR. AN ANCIENT CURSE.

On the run from a cursed king and his army of assassins, priest Niels Bosch seeks sanctuary in rural Briscona. What he gets is a barrage of intimate and unsettling questions from his new cantor, Beldenka Nadinov. Questions he can't risk answering.

Accompanied by his friend and bodyguard Mikhandor, and Bel's protector Leks, the pair set out to challenge the mad king. But Bel has a dark secret of her own — a secret that could endanger the entire mission.

When Niels unearths the chilling truth and realises there's much more at stake than just his life, it's too late to turn back. He must lift the curse and end Night's reign forever.

Review by Christiana Matthews, author of "Flowerface"

I greatly enjoyed Night's Reign. If you enjoy beautiful prose, engaging characters and impressive world-building, this is the book for you.

The wheelchair using heroine is independent and sassy, paired with a diffident, awkward hero who doesn't quite know how he got cast in that role and isn't sure he can handle it. The dark secrets in his past result in a band of assassins hunting him, thrusting him and his lady into some very cool adventures.

Add in a mysterious otherworldly guardian, a family of in-laws shrouded in political intrigue, beautifully described backgrounds and some delightfully creative curses, and you have a winner of a book. Read it. You won't be disappointed.

Review by L.C. Cunningham, author of "The Witch of Lichley Lane: and Other Disturbances in Lichley Town"

A great story with a novel take on the chosen one!

Two good viewpoint characters here, but my favourite was wheelchair bound Bel. She is snarky and cutting and has real grit as a character, something I enjoy reading and a nice contrast to nice-but-sometimes-hopeless Niels.

There are two narratives going on here, and I found myself being very into the backstory. The story also picked up pace in the back half and the final chapters are where it shines the best (as any good story should!).

Review by L.R. Friedman, author of "Descend"

I just put down Night's Reign a few days ago after devouring it in about 48 hours. Daan did an incredible job with this novel and I'll share a few of my favorite things about it:

- There was a really unique cast of characters throughout the book and no one was one-dimensional. The book is divided in parts which really helped organize the different storylines so they played together beautifully once they merged. For me, sometimes it can get overwhelming when there are a ton of characters to juggle - not with this book. They were introduced in waves so it was easy to follow and keep the storylines and who's who straight.
- I LOVED Bel. I'm always a fan of a strong female character and she was a wheelchair rocking badass. Daan's way of capturing her strength and telling her story over the course of the book was really well done.
- The book also dealt with mental health which I always love addressed in fiction. I felt like it made the characters rich and relatable. I could see how the characters internal struggles drove their

choices throughout the book.

If you are looking for a great dark fantasy read, I definitely recommend picking up Night's Reign and diving into this beautiful world created by the very clever Daan Katz.

To Lisa and Robin
May you never lose your magic

CONTENTS

Prologue	1
BRISCONA	5
Chapter One	7
Chapter Two	15
Chapter Three	23
Chapter Four	29
Chapter Five	37
Chapter Six	46
Chapter Seven	56
Chapter Eight	67
Chapter Nine	79
Chapter Ten	89
Chapter Eleven	94
Chapter Twelve	101
Chapter Thirteen	110
Chapter Fourteen	120
Chapter Fifteen	129
Chapter Sixteen	139

Chapter Seventeen	148
Chapter Eighteen	157
Chapter Nineteen	166
Chapter Twenty	177
Chapter Twenty-One	185
INTERLUDE	191
Interlude I	193
SENKERLAND	203
Chapter Twenty-Two	205
Chapter Twenty-Three	215
Chapter Twenty-Four	224
Chapter Twenty-Five	233
Chapter Twenty-Six	241
Chapter Twenty-Seven	253
Chapter Twenty-Eight	264
Chapter Twenty-Nine	272
Chapter Thirty	280
Chapter Thirty-One	288
Chapter Thirty-Two	300
INTERLUDE	307
Interude II	309
EBARU	315
Chapter Thirty-Three	317
Chapter Thirty-Four	326
Chapter Thirty-Five	336
Chapter Thirty-Six	345

Chapter Thirty-Seven	354
Chapter Thirty-Eight	362
Chapter Thirty-Nine	370
Chapter Forty	379
Chapter Forty-One	386
Chapter Forty-Two	395
Chapter Forty-Three	405
Glossary	417
A Word of Thanks	423
About the Author	425
By Daan Katz	427
Step into Daan's Worlds	429
Last, but not Least	430

MAP OF BRISCONA

PROLOGUE

Promise

night's reign
repels starlight
ghetto girl dies alone
another addict giving birth
to hope

The grey stones of the temple had taken on a greenish hue, and the air smelled stale. Where were the candles? And why had the fountain gone dry? Surely, the gods had not forsaken this place? This was holy ground. Why was there no priest?

Time became a fluid thing as Shansi imagined herself back in Naz's strong arms. She clung to him as he held her and kept her from falling. His voice, warm and seductive as always, soothed her fears. The sweet scent of his skin comforted her. The luscious taste of his lips increased her longing for him.

Her excited moan turned into an agonised wail as pain shot through her abdomen again and forced her to her knees. Why could she not have been born a boy? In a reflex, her hand went to the medallion she wore on a delicate golden chain around her neck. Worth a fortune, yet utterly useless. If only she'd been able to sell it.

She rubbed the stupid tears from her eyes with the back of her hand, and forced herself to her feet. She had to be strong. For the child she was about to deliver into this world.

Please, good Goddess, I can't do this alone.

A faint noise, like a breath of wind, made her look up, and a beam of sunlight guided her eyes to the large statue. Gods be praised, it was still there and more magnificent than ever. As she set out towards it, another contraction made her double up on the floor again. Was this her punishment?

If only Baba hadn't gone missing. If only Naa hadn't died. And Mam. Asra and Siana. The useless tears came again. Shansi bit her lip. She sniffled. Wiped her eyes once more.

"Holy Gods! Be strong for once. Blazing. Be. Strong." She crawled closer to the statue of the Goddess, until finally she could touch it.

"Bring it on." Her voice sounded raw. Broken. Her womb cramped again. Hit by a bout of nausea, she swallowed the bile that rose in her throat. Her breath came in short, ragged bursts. A sudden cold made her shiver. Her legs started to tremble.

When the pain subsided, she tried to sit up, but almost immediately the next wave of pain crashed into her. In a vain attempt not to cry out, she dug her nails into her skin. Gods, but this was savage! How could any woman survive something as fierce as this? She closed her eyes. Bit her lip bloody. Dug her nails yet deeper into her skin. Gasped for breath.

For how long she lay there, on the cold stone floor, whimpering in agony, she couldn't tell. For once, there was no time. No hunger, no thirst. Not even the all-consuming need for a fix that had been the driving force behind almost all of her actions since little Siana died in her arms. If only she could have saved her sister.

If only she could have stayed with Naz. He had been good to her. He'd always provided her with the good, clean stuff. Not the rubbish on which she'd been surviving after she had left him. If only things had been different. If only his family could have approved. If only...

But all her if-onlies mattered not one bit. She was going to die today, and her child would become a retarded, sickly person. If it lived.

"Child."

Shansi opened her eyes and looked up. Someone was approaching. A woman.

"Are you..." Her voice cracked. "Are you the Goddess?"

"No, child." The woman came closer. "Just her servant. I was sent to attend to your needs. Drink some." She supported Shansi as she offered her a small cup of water. Then she wiped her face with a cool, damp cloth. "Is that better?"

Shansi nodded. It wasn't much. A shot of *Saffire Tease*, or even *Hog Flare* would have been considerably better, but that was not an option. She had to think about her baby. In all honesty, she should have been doing that since the day she discovered she was with child, but she'd been too selfish.

More contractions. More pain, ever more unbearable. The nausea came back with such force she threw up. Another shiver ran down her spine. Her legs started trembling anew, and worse than before. She grasped at her swollen belly, writhing. A suffocated wail escaped from her lips.

The woman stayed by her side and tried to make her as comfortable as possible. Though it brought little relief, it was still better than having to go through this nightmare alone.

Just when she thought she couldn't take any more, her baby was born.

A beautiful boy with golden eyes and copper skin. Just like his father.

She must have lost consciousness then, because next she woke up in a real bed, between soft silken sheets, in a cool, well-ventilated room. The lady from the abandoned temple sat on a chair beside her. The child, her child, lay in a basket.

"My son..." She barely had the strength to whisper. "Is he... is he...?" She couldn't bear to finish the question. She knew the answer already. He would die and she, his own mother, was to blame.

"He is weak, but I'm confident that he will pull through. I gave him the medallion. It will give him the strength he needs. Was it your father's?"

She shook her head. "My grandfather's. His wife and other children died from the pestilence. Long before I was born. My mam..." She closed her eyes. So tired. Even just breathing took almost too much effort. "Mam was his only remaining child. But she's dead too, now. They all are."

"I see. I'm sorry." The woman was silent for a moment, then asked, "What will your son's name be, dear?"

"Moradin."

It had been Naa's name, and it seemed fitting that her son should be named after him. "Can I..." The nausea found her again and made her cut off her words. She shivered with cold. Black specks swam in front of her eyes.

"Child!"

The woman stood bent over her, felt her forehead, her pulse. "Stay with me, girl. Stay with me!"

"Cold," she said through chattering teeth. "Naz." She grew colder still, and weaker. "Naz..."

Naz took her in his arms. "Don't be afraid." His body felt warm against hers, and his voice sounded more alluring than ever. "Nothing will hurt you."

"No!" a woman's voice cried out in the distance. "Don't you die on me. Don't..."

BRISCONA

CHAPTER ONE

Vision

> dragon
> seeks sanctity
> flickering flame kindles
> tiniest spark illuminates
> blind eyes

   Niels sat down on one of the wooden benches and smoothed his blue priestly robes. The familiar scent of incense and burning candles, and the susurrant sound of water made him feel at peace with himself and the world. It always did. The Sanctuary was his home. Far more so than the little cottage just across the street. Though his fatigue didn't leave him, now that he was alone, he could at least rest for a little while. He folded his hands in his lap and closed his eyes.

   When the heavy wooden door opened and a ray of sunlight caressed his face, he woke from his slumber. The door fell shut again, but as far as Niels could make out, nobody had entered. He was about to get up when he heard something. A soft *shhh-shhh* sound that he couldn't identify. Then he made out a moving shape in the dimly lit hall. He squinted. A woman in a wheelchair, a small birdlike creature — was that really a dragonet? — perched atop her shoulder. For a moment, he wondered what to do, then decided to just wait and see.

   With a confidence that astounded Niels, she went straight to the altar, where she said the ancient blessing over the Sacred Candles; softly, so he could not hear it, but he saw her lips form the words he himself recited every morning.

"Blessed are you, Queen of the Worlds, who kindles the Light of Life in the human soul." Next, she went over to the Fountain of Renewal, where she chanted the blessing over the Holy Water in a clear, melodious voice. She dipped in a finger and brought it to her lips.

Not wishing to disturb the woman in her devotions, Niels remained seated, and observed her as she prayed to the Goddess. He watched, and wondered. Who was this young lady, who radiated a peace and fortitude he could only hope to ever achieve?

When she had finished her prayers, she wheeled her chair over to where he still sat gawking at her.

"So here you are." Her strong voice belied her frail appearance. "I'm Bel. Beldenka Nadinov. Cantor. And you, I assume, are our new priest."

"Niels Bosch." Holy Gods, but she was gorgeous! Her ivory skin contrasted beautifully with those short mahogany curls that framed the most delicate face he had ever seen. And if that alone wasn't enough, she spoke in a most delightful northern accent. He felt like a schoolboy again and hoped she couldn't see the blush that crept up his face. "I arrived yesterday."

"So I heard. I'm sorry that I couldn't be at the welcome reception last night, but I had previous engagements that could not be rescheduled." She scrutinised him, head to toe. "And here I thought they would send us another old bloke who would either die or go senile in the next five turnings."

"That bad?"

"Usually, yes. And quite understandably so. These are the Barlows, which equals the end of all civilisation. Nothing ever happens here. I do hope you're not married?"

"Beg pardon?" Did she really have to be that forward? Or was she just winding him up?

She shrugged. "Because it would be unfair to your wife and children. Every child, and every woman deserves better than to spend their lives in this gods-forsaken outpost."

"If..." he searched for the right words to say, "if you're feeling that way, then why are you here?"

"I'm weird like that. I happen to enjoy the solitude. Peace and quiet, and all that. Besides, everyone here knows me, which means fewer stupid stares."

Niels nodded. "I can appreciate that. In fact, that's exactly the reason why I am here. I opted out."

That was true enough and sounded far better than saying, I'm on the run because some deluded soul wants me dead and has been chasing me for close to twenty turnings.

"So," Beldenka's eyes bored into his, and he bent his head, "no wife or children then?"

"No."

"You're not very forthcoming, are you?"

"Should I be?"

"It would be nice."

"Hmm." What could he say? He hated small talk. That, and life had taught him it was best to keep his distance. No need to provoke fate.

"Are you thick, or what? We'll be working closely together for the next few turnings. Preferably longer. I'm sick to death of having to adjust to one new priest after another." She sounded every bit as annoyed as he himself felt. "I hate working with strangers. It drains my energy."

Niels took a deep breath. Getting angry now would get him nowhere. "I apologise. But I fail to see why I should be obliged to talk about myself. I am a priest."

That sounded lame.

"So what? Do you think being a priest exempts you from being human?"

"Priests listen. They don't talk about themselves."

"What a load of dragon dung! The old priest Gharbani was quite chatty. So were the other priests I worked with."

He sighed. He had hoped to find peace here, but even though he was probably safe from his lunatic stalker for the time being, his new cantor seemed intent on making his life torture.

"I am not them. And if you'll excuse me now, I need to go home and have lunch."

Beldenka raised an eyebrow. "It's pretty late to be having lunch, wouldn't you say?"

"I fell asleep."

"You..." She stared at him with an intensity that raised the hairs on the back of his neck. Finally, she shook her head. "Of course. You must be tired. Take the rest of the day off. Go home. Rest. Settle in. I'll see you again tomorrow. Then we will talk." She turned her chair and went as quietly as she had come.

Niels suppressed a yawn as he got to his feet. Taking the remainder of the day off wasn't a bad idea. He had not unpacked yet. Not even one box, and his furniture stood randomly scattered throughout the house. Slowly, head bent, he walked out of the building. Once outside, he straightened his shoulders, strode over to the statue of the Goddess and raised his hands in a silent prayer.

He pushed the heavy black leather sofa, the only decent piece of furniture he currently owned, against the wall. Tired already, he sat down to survey his work. Two boxes unpacked. Mostly kitchen stuff. Good. At least he would be able to fix himself a proper meal. Now, if he put that wobbly kitchen table and those two mismatched chairs against the wall opposite the worktop, he'd even have a place to eat his meals. It was a start.

With a pang of regret he remembered his beautiful home in Tan'Rabu, with the long gauze curtains that filtered the harsh glare of the tropical daylight, and the buzzing fans that spread a welcome breeze in the almost unbearable heat inside. He'd had beautiful, well-crafted furniture, and slept between soft silken sheets. He had been living a dream there. A dream that ended in a nightmare on the day Zia died.

His vision momentarily blurred, he forced himself up from the sofa. He blinked once, then let his gaze wander the room. The dark oak table, which had clearly seen better days, would still make a fine desk. If he put it over there by the window, he could watch the chickens frisking about in the garden when his work threatened to overwhelm him. He needed to unpack his books as soon as possible. But that meant he'd have to assemble his bookcase first, and right now he couldn't face the effort involved.

Most of his clothes were still in his travel bags, getting wrinkly and smelly. But he hadn't found his clothes hangers yet. So much work, and so little energy.

And what if... but no! He should not allow himself to think like that. He was safe here. *The end of the civilised world.* Was that not what Beldenka had called the Barlows? Surely, King Hanassan and his cronies would never think to look for him here, in this gods-abandoned settlement.

He didn't bother to lift his feet properly as he shuffled into the kitchen to pour himself another cup of tea. Everything took too much effort. As he sank down in his sofa, the thought came to him, unbidden. What if that madman finally found him? So what if that sorry creature killed him? Would it really be all that bad? At least it would all be over. No more running. No more fear. No more looking over his shoulder.

The more he thought about it, the more convinced he became that he'd been wrong, coming to the Barlows. If he were a man, he would pack up and go. He would find the king and either deal with that madman's grandiose delusions and blood-lust, or die trying. Yes, he should do that. But not today. Next sevenday, he promised himself. Next sevenday. So tired. He closed his eyes and drifted off to sleep.

Darkness greeted him when he opened his eyes. His neck and back ached. Not even forty and already he felt like an old man. What was worse, he behaved like one. Sleeping his days away. What was he thinking?

He rubbed the sleep out of his eyes, got up, stretched, and went over to the kitchen where he fixed himself a simple meal of bread and cheese.

As he sat at his kitchen table, the unpacked boxes stared at him from the living area. So much unpacking still needed to be done. Books, clothes, knick-knacks and more random stuff. He'd hardly started unpacking and already he felt like he was drowning in the chaos. Even just thinking about the mess made him want to go back to sleep.

One bag. He would empty just one of his travel bags out and put those clothes in the wardrobe. Then, he should go do something fun. He grimaced. Do something fun. It was the very last thing he wanted, but it might help.

Three pairs of pantaloons. All of them black. Ten shirts. Eight white, the other two blue. Socks and underwear. His gi, which he hadn't worn in far too long. He stroked the fabric with his fingertips before he put it on the shelf. Memories of the many hours he spent training put a melancholy smile on his face. He sat down on the creaky bed and rested his head in his hands.

No. He needed to get out of the house and engage with people, whether he liked it or not. He needed to get fit. It could mean the difference between life and death.

Lacklustre, he took off his robes and got dressed in a pair of pantaloons and a shirt. His sports bag, filled with arbitrary bits and bobs, lay in a corner of the bedroom. He dumped the contents on the floor. He stowed his gi, a pair of bamboo slippers and a towel in the bag, put on his helmet, and made for the door. He'd better jump on his velo before he got the chance to change his mind.

Yesterday, on his way to the Barlows, he'd spotted a training centre in a neighbouring village, Ambleville. Yeleksim's Gym. Though it didn't look all too reputable, it was probably the only one in the entire region.

The dressing room was cleaner than he'd anticipated. The lockers were equally clean and only one had a damaged lock. Just one other man was on the mat, practising forward rolls. A tall, muscular fellow with unruly platinum-blond hair and charcoal eyes.

Niels froze. "You!"

The man grinned so broadly, Niels thought his teeth would fall out of his mouth. "Who else, your Holiness?"

"And here I was hoping... oh, never mind. I guess I'm supposed to spar with you then."

"You guessed right. And before you object, let me tell you this: There won't be any others tonight. I made sure of that."

Mikhandor Faylinn. Erl. Insufferable, arrogant otherworldly individual, and utterly devoted to his job, which happened to be bodyguard. Niels' bodyguard. Not that Niels had ever asked for one, but Erls were a peculiar people. They had their own rules and stuck to them no matter what.

"I should have known. How did you know I would be here tonight? And, while we're at it... are the king's minions on my trail?"

"You should know by now, young man, that it is my sacred duty to know where you are, and what you are planning to do next. My job description tells me to always be two steps ahead of you, remember?" Pompous arse! Always so full of himself. "As for the king and his confederates, I can't be entirely sure, but I don't think so. Not yet. Who knows, we might be able to spend a couple of uneventful turnings here."

"That would be a first." Some people would give anything to have an exciting life. Niels would be just as happy if his life weren't quite so interesting, even if only for one or two turnings.

"Kata?"

Niels nodded. "Sounds good to me."

As they went through the forms, Niels felt the tension drain from his body, the worry flee from his mind. The effects would not last, but it was good to just *be*. He needed this. It was one of the few things that kept him sane.

Three steps forward, half a turn left, grab your opponent's right hand and pull him closer...

Sparring with a man almost twice his size, and throwing him as easily as if he weighed no more than a bag of flour was exhilarating. It made Niels feel as if he could take on the world and conquer it. Without even breaking a sweat.

Mikhandor was more than just a bodyguard and it was unfair to think of him as a big-headed bastard. Throughout the turnings he had been a friend, a tutor and a combat trainer. A good one too. Firm and demanding, but never harsh or cruel.

"Feeling better now, my friend?" Mikhandor asked when they were back in the dressing room.

Niels nodded.

"So, we shall be training regularly again, won't we, your Holiness?"

"Yes, we will. But let us build it up slowly. I'm not fifteen any more."

"I don't care about your age. Even if you were a crippled old man, I'd still expect you to show up for your training three out of every seven nights. Unless you want more, of course."

"You're a cruel, relentless son of an Erl."

"Thank you." Mikhandor inclined his head. "Three times a sevenday it is, then. But don't worry. I won't beat you up too badly. Not at first, anyway."

Niels stuffed his gi back in his bag. "A crippled old man, eh? So you would still teach me how to fight if I were in a wheelchair?"

"The question is irrelevant, but yes. Absolutely. I can't see why not."

"But don't you think that would be cruel?"

"Quite the contrary. I think it would be cruel not to teach a disabled person how to defend themselves. They would probably need it even more than most able-bodied persons."

That made sense. Perhaps he should...

"Are you going to invite that cute cantor of yours to come train with us?"

"Am I *what?* Are you out of your mind?"

"She's cute though, isn't she?"

"Oh, will you shut up?" Embarrassment and amusement warred inside his head. Niels shook his head and smiled as amusement finally won the upper hand.

CHAPTER TWO

Fever

hedgehog
grim harbinger
augurs mind-melting heat
dragonbreath quenches evil flames
and rules

Getting up in the morning was never easy but now, with stiff, burning muscles, it was even harder. His own stupid fault for allowing himself to grow soft. Niels kept his eyes closed and tried to go back to sleep. In vain. His bladder reminded him there were other bodily functions that needed to be taken care of.

As he relieved himself, he heard a knock on the door. Erl's balls! Visitors? At this ungodly hour? When he was still practically naked? For one moment he hesitated. Then he decided to just open the door. Whoever it was would sarding well get what they had asked for. A grumpy, half naked priest.

Moments later he stared at a small figure in a wheelchair and his bravado melted. He felt the heat rise to his cheeks as he stammered, "B-Beldenka?"

"Well, well. Good afternoon to you too, Mister Sexybutt." With a mischievous grin on her face she looked him up and down. Several times.

Mister Sexybutt. Right. As if things weren't bad enough already.

"I... Come in. I was just getting dressed." He fled into his bedroom and stood there, hyperventilating, head pressed against the cool wall. Gods, this was awkward. That woman!

The way she had looked at him! How could he ever face her again? And to think he would have to work with her. Closely. Day by crashing day.

Breathe, sard you! Calm down.

She'd seen him in his smallclothes. So what? That was hardly different from seeing a man in his bathing suit. He could live with that. He had to. Man up. Grab a pair of pantaloons and a shirt. Put them on. Better yet: Put on your robes. Look professional. Comb your hair. Shaving can wait. Now go see what the lady wants.

He stepped back into the living room, trying his best to look more confident than he felt. It didn't work. "S-sorry about that," he began, "I... I..."

"No. I should apologise." Beldenka didn't look very contrite, and her voice sounded as firm as it had the day before. "I showed up at your door, uninvited, knowing full well that you had to be exhausted still. That was inconsiderate of me."

Niels didn't know what to say. He'd expected her to make fun of him, or something even worse than that. Instead, she offered her apologies, even if they might not be entirely genuine. The words seemed sincere enough, but how could anyone be that confident when apologising?

"That's, uh... no harm done. Let's just forget about it. Can I get you something to drink?"

"Water would be good. Thank you."

"I hope you don't mind if I fix myself something for breakfast. I only just... but I'm sure you figured that out already."

Stupid cabbage head! He should not have brought that up again. He opened the *kooler* and rummaged inside to hide his discomfort. Milk, eggs and butter. He had a new bag of flour in the storage cupboard, so he could make pancakes. That was breakfast sorted then. But he'd better get Beldenka that glass of water first.

"So, what brought you here at this early hour?"

Beldenka raised her eyebrows. "Early? It's shortly before noon, Niels. I was in the House of Prayer and didn't see you there, so I thought I would come and see how you were doing. I thought maybe you got stuck unpacking and I could lend you a hand."

That late already? Had he slept away most of the morning? Not good. "You? Help me? But you are..."

"Yes. I am a cripple." The words sounded harsh, yet there was no rancour in her voice — or none that Niels could detect. "That doesn't make me needy or anything. I live alone. Well, with little Zilla here." The way she looked up at the scaly thing almost made him believe she was reading its thoughts. "I run my own household, drive my own *karr*, do my own shopping, and earn my own silvers. Is there anything there that suggests incompetence?"

"My apologies. I didn't realise... I mean, I just never knew anyone in a wheelchair before."

"That's alright. It always takes people a little getting used to. I promise you won't notice the chair any more once we've been working together for a while. I'm pretty good at making people forget about that."

With that personality of hers, Niels didn't doubt it.

"You're not from around here, are you?" Her name, her accent, and even her looks suggested she originated from one of those cold, inhospitable northern countries.

"Ingravia. But I left when I wasn't even ten turnings old yet, and haven't been back since. Not once."

There was a story there. Maybe something to do with her chair? Yesterday, she'd accused him of not being forthcoming. Now, he wondered about her willingness to share. Could he ask? She might not take to that very kindly. But he was curious. Had she always been in a wheelchair? Or was her disability caused by an illness or accident? Or even — the gods forbid! — an assault. Ingravia was rumoured to be a harsh country, with crime being its prime profession.

"The dragonet?" He'd never seen a real dragonet before, and used to think they were a myth. Until yesterday.

"Zilla." She looked up at the creature and smiled. "I admit to having a soft spot for dragons and their little cousins. That has to be my Ingravian heritage, and I do hope it's the only one. Everything you might ever have heard about Ingravia is true, and worse than that, I assure you. Your turn. Where are you from?"

"Beldenka, you know the answer to that question already. I am a priest."

She rolled her eyes. "You're a priest? Really? I hadn't noticed yet. When you opened that door, I could have sworn that you..." She broke off and bit her lip. What had she been about to say? "Sorry." Her voice was barely above a whisper. "You're from Ebaru then?"

"Yes." He didn't feel obliged to tell her that he was adopted by a Darsian family and grew up in Dorhedde. The less anyone knew about him, the better. "And it's not the tropical paradise people think it is. Hidden from the tourist industry, there is poverty, narc abuse and crime to rival the Ingravian, uh... culture."

Beldenka looked as if she saw water catch on fire. "The other priests never mentioned this."

"That doesn't surprise me. Most honestly don't know. Others prefer to ignore it. I could not."

In an instant, his mind took him back to Ebaru, where he stood at the graves of the poor, with his great-granduncle, barely able to take it all in. The memory of the enormous losses and the pain they caused, made him shudder. His face contorted into a grimace as he relived the overwhelming grief that came with his new knowledge.

"Niels?" Beldenka had rolled up close to him, too close. She put a hand on his arm and, in a reflex, he flinched back.

"Sorry. I didn't mean to make you uncomfortable."

"Ghosts of the past." He shook his head. "So you wanted to help me unpack. I suggest we get started. Though, to be honest, I have no clue how."

"Well, that's easy. Just grab the nearest box and open it."

Niels looked at Beldenka first, then at the box, and finally back at Beldenka again. He folded his hands behind his back to prevent himself from scratching his head. "But shouldn't there be some sort of system to it?"

Beldenka laughed. An enchanting, melodious laugh. "This *is* the system, Niels. One box at the time."

Box after box they unpacked, and as they did so, Niels put everything away. Not everything found a permanent home yet, but surprisingly much did. Beldenka was far more capable than Niels would have thought anyone in a wheelchair could be. She helped assemble the bookcase and, though he hated to admit it, she was more proficient with his tools than he himself was.

"It's easy," she said when he asked her how she had gained those skills. "I live alone. When something breaks, I repair it. I don't have the time or patience to sit around and wait for the repairman to come all the way from Ambleville. Besides, I don't want to spend an unholy amount of silvers on these guys either. So I bought me some good machines, and earned the investment back ten times over already."

"But is this not much harder for you than for able-bodied people?" The moment the words were out of his mouth he wanted to hit himself. How could he be so insensitive?

Beldenka, however, didn't seem offended. She just shrugged. "From what I see, it's quite a bit harder for you than it is for me. Here, give me this." She pointed at a screw, "and the machine. You are hopeless."

He knew he wasn't the best handyman around, but he liked to think he could at least manage. Yet here he was being called hopeless by a diminutive woman in a wheelchair. That was sobering.

"It can't be *that* bad," he tried.

"Well, maybe I could teach you." She looked at him first, then at the nearly finished bookcase and shook her head. "Then again, why go through all this trouble? I'll be around almost every day, and I actually like this stuff."

Niels' mouth fell open. "You do?"

"Yes." She hummed a cheerful tune as she continued her work on the bookcase. Every now and then, she got out of her chair and sat on the floor, or stood on wobbly legs. Sometimes, she even walked a couple of uncertain steps.

"I hope you will not think me incredibly rude, Beldenka, but would you mind telling me why you're in that chair?" They sat on the sofa with a cup of tea. "You see, I always assumed people in wheelchairs could not walk at all, but you just proved me wrong."

"This is a mistake many people make, Niels. Don't worry about it. You know better now." She sipped her tea and looked at him over the rim of her cup.

The silence stretched. Was she going to tell him, or did she not want to talk about her ill fortune? He wanted to understand, but he couldn't in good conscience press her into sharing information she wasn't ready to divulge yet.

"I walked like everyone else. I ran, I danced, I played. I was this child who could never sit still. I wanted to become a ballet dancer when I grew up — a prima ballerina, no less — and I was doing quite well. My father and mother were proud of me, my brother and sisters adored me, and my friends envied me."

She fell silent again. Took another sip of her tea. Niels did not speak. But he listened to the silence. A silence that told a story all its own. A story of pain, and loss.

"I had a cold. No big deal. When you grow up in Ingravia, you learn not to pay too much attention to minor nuisances like these. You don't want to be seen as weak."

She bent over and placed her cup on the table. Twisted a lock of her hair around her finger, let it go, and did it all over again. And again.

"My cold got worse, and I ended up in the hospital. The doctors couldn't figure out what was wrong, and decided it was probably this mysterious virus that had been killing people left and right lately, so I was placed in isolation. The doctors and nurses, and even the cleaners, all wore protective gear when they had to enter my room. I was allowed one visitor a day, but behind this glass wall only. There was never any direct contact."

Beldenka shook her head. "No hugs or kisses for little Bel. Nobody held me when I cried. It was wretched. But I pulled through. Only, when I was finally allowed out of the bed, I could not walk any more. I hated it. Hated life. Hated my legs for letting me down so badly."

She wiped her eyes with the back of her hand. "The doctors assured me my strength would come back if I kept doing my exercises, so I exercised like a manewolf on Oracle. Nothing happened. Except for the bad that came with being a cripple. I lost my friends. My brother and sisters avoided me. Papi and Mumi hid me away. The prodigy had become an embarrassment. My future had been destroyed. I knew I would never dance again."

"That is harsh."

"This is Ingravia. Be strong or die. Since I hadn't had the decency to die, I became a *Reject*." She balled her hands into stiff fists and sat up straighter. "So I fought even harder. I exercised more. I dragged myself around the house to get food and drink whenever I wanted it. I pulled myself up by the shelves of my father's bookcase, so I could reach his best books. And over time, I got at least some strength back."

"You dragged yourself? You were not even given a wheelchair?" Niels shook his head. And here he thought his younger years had been unpleasant.

"I knew that wheelchairs existed of course, but not in Ingravia. In the end, my parents decided to send me to a boarding school in Suttbron, Senkerland. I was not allowed to come back home. Ever. And this was the lovingest thing they could have done for me." Her posture relaxed. "So now you know my story, and there is no need to talk about it ever again."

Niels nodded. "Thank you for your trust. More tea?"

"Yes, please."

When Niels sat down again, Beldenka said, "Now that you know pretty much everything there is to know about me, I think this is the time for you to share your story."

"I am just a simple priest. I don't have a story." He couldn't afford to have people prying into his past.

"And you really want me to believe this? When you've come to work in the Barlows of all places? I told you yesterday, and I'm telling you again, we only ever get old blokes here. Since you are hardly old, there's got to be a story and I deserve to know it."

"I was born. I grew like any other boy. I went to primary school. Then I went to secondary school. After I finished school, I went to the seminary. I graduated. I became a priest. There. That's my story."

"My, my! Aren't you prickly? What is this thing that you're so desperate to hide? What's the worst that could happen?"

"I could be killed. *You* could be killed." The words were out before he knew it, and there was no taking them back now.

Beldenka stared at him. She said nothing. Niels closed his eyes in an attempt to hide the panic that threatened to overtake his thinking. He concentrated on his breathing, the way Mikhandor had taught him.

A warrior needs to keep his calm under all circumstances. Control your breathing, and you control your mind.

"So... you are on the run." He thought he detected a small tremor in Beldenka's voice. "Either you're being paranoid, or you really are in danger. I don't know what's going on, but since you don't seem insane to me, I will believe you."

She sat up straighter. "Well, if there is anything Ingravia has taught me, it is that you don't run, and you don't hide. You fight. And you know what? I don't fear death, and neither should you."

"I don't fear my own death, Beldenka, but I have seen too many people die. Because of *me*. Have you any idea what that does to a man?"

"Look at me, Niels." She put a hand on his arm. Again. He wasn't sure whether he liked that or not. "We are going to the House of Prayer now. We're going to sing the blessings together, and after that, we'll start working on this moon's liturgies. I refuse to be intimidated."

CHAPTER THREE

Highroad

guileless
hero takes flight
despised child remembers
rebel rises to challenge past
failures

Working alongside Beldenka was unlike anything Niels had ever experienced before, and truth be told, it was disconcerting. Her confidence only emphasised his awkwardness and the way she looked at him made him feel exposed. It was as if she were analysing his every move, his every word.

"Niels Bosch," she said. "Niels Bosch. Such an unusual name for a priest."

He was beside her and covered her mouth with his hand before he even realised what he was doing. "Erl's balls! Not here, Beldenka! Never here." He let go of her, and took a few steps back, ashamed of his rash reaction.

The dragonet flapped its wings and hissed at him. Beldenka reached up and soothed the thing with gentle strokes and sweet whispers. Only when the creature had calmed down did she turn her face towards him.

"Niels?" Her verdigris eyes studied his face. She didn't seem shocked or offended, so maybe he hadn't completely ruined everything in his stupid panic.

"I apologise, Beldenka, for being such a lout, but for the love of the gods, don't ever do that again. No private talk in here. In fact..." He hesitated. He'd been about to say, no private talk at all, but that wasn't going to work. Not with this woman. He shrugged. "I'll explain later."

Beldenka sighed. "Oh, well. Back to work then." She leafed through her sheets again, then held one up. "How about this one?"

"Mother of mankind." He hummed the first line. "Yes. Good choice, I think."

Beldenka smiled. "Am I allowed to say that you have a good singing voice?"

Niels felt his cheeks flush. "Allowed, yes. Though I would prefer for you to refrain from complimenting me."

"Ha! I can see that." She giggled like a schoolgirl. "You may be a bit paranoid and overly secretive, but this shy boy charm really becomes you. I could get used to that."

Was this revenge? Or did she just enjoy embarrassing him? "Zinnir's eleventh finger! Will you stop this?"

"Are you always this sweary?" Did he hear laughter in her voice? Did she think this was funny?

"It's one of my bad habits. And you? Are you always this pissing annoying?"

"Well, yes. That is one of *my* bad habits. My father used to warn me that my tongue would get me killed one day, and in Ingravia this might well have been true, but this is good old sleepy Briscona, where nothing ever happens."

"Beldenka!" Niels gave her what he hoped was a stern look. Getting yourself killed was not a laughing matter. He remembered the fire, back in Ebaru. Though he had been able to escape, with little more than the clothes he'd been wearing, not all of them had been so lucky.

"Ona's big tits! I can't torching say anything in here, can I? Don't you have any sense of humour?"

He shook his head. "No. But I see you're already beginning to understand why I am such a sweary brute."

She turned her chair abruptly and wheeled away. Was she angry? Upset? Was it a call of nature? He had absolutely no idea, so he picked the score up again and tried to concentrate on the notes. It didn't work.

The memories flooded his mind, and it was almost as if he were back at campus. The roar of the flames resounded in his ears again. He could sense the enormous heat, smell the petrol. Taste it, even. He stood nailed to the ground, holding his travel bag, unable to move. Unable to think clearly. Then Mikhandor appeared out of nowhere, or so it seemed, tossed him over his shoulder and carried him to safety.

Half of an hour passed, and Beldenka hadn't returned yet. Should he go looking for her? A simple piddle shouldn't take that long. But if she was angry or upset, she likely would not want to see him. He shook his head. Why did people always have to be so difficult?

He picked up the Holy Book. Not surprisingly, it fell open at the Prophecies. It usually did.

> *"And when he returns to the Land of the Sun, he shall know grief beyond comparison, and his soul shall find no peace. His enemies shall always be near, seeking to take his life. Yet, though many shall fall around him, his life shall be spared, for he was chosen by the Goddess Eylah herself..."*

He had read the words countless times, and still they made him shiver. As a boy, he had rebelled against them, unable to believe. Not wishing to believe. Who in his right mind would have chosen a life like that for himself? The pain, the grief, the fears. The enormous responsibility.

Why should he be the Chosen One? Why not someone else? It wasn't fair.

These days, he knew. Life was not fair. A man could not simply choose his own destiny. That wasn't the way the world worked. Sor was created by The Lady, and she determined her people's destiny. Within that framework, a person had free will. Stepping outside of her plan was not an option.

Some people were more important for The Lady's purpose with Sor than others, of course. If you were lucky enough to be born a commoner, pretty much all of your choices were truly your own, and your fate in life depended largely upon your own behaviour and that of others around you.

Niels didn't have that luxury. Every priest was essential in The Lady's plan, and Niels had come to understand and accept that in him some exceedingly important prophecies would have to find their fulfilment. If he failed, the world would suffer and it would be centuries, if ever, before another man could take his place and repair what he had left broken.

Bel lay under the duvet, curled up in a ball. Bawling like a baby. And why? Only because of that oaf priest with his stupid fears and weird sense of humour — if one could even call it that. What was wrong with that man? What was wrong with her?

This was ridiculous. She'd been through so much worse and never batted an eye, and now she was crying. Over little more than nothing. She should grow some fangs and get on with life. There was absolutely no reason to be so upset.

And why should she care anyway? The man wasn't her lover. Nor was he her friend. Just a priest. A colleague. Not even her superior. They were equals. And if he was behaving like a manewolf's arse, she had every right to treat him as such.

She dried her eyes. Breathed deeply. And the tears just came again. As if the repressed pain of all those turnings finally forced its way out.

This wasn't about Niels, she realised now. This was not Cantor Beldenka Nadinov crying over nothing. This was little ballerina Beldenka Nimblefoot losing the use of her legs. Losing her future, her family, and her home. Talking to Niels about her childhood had unlocked emotions that had always been lurking there, neatly hidden away behind the polished façade of a woman who was always in control.

Niels had somehow disarmed her, and that was the scariest thing. Scarier even than being exiled.

Niels Bosch, her great-grandmother's tits! That wasn't his real name. It couldn't be. No priest had a Darsian name. What was up with that? Was he hiding his true identity because someone had it in for him? Someone who wouldn't hesitate to kill others who got in his way? Had he upset some Ingravian High Lord? She had to find out. Maybe, she could arrange a meeting with Mumi. Or better yet, go see Leks.

She dried her tears once more. She was ready to face the world again. Almost. But first, she needed a good soak in the bath, clean clothes, and a meal. Then she would go back to the House of Prayer and get on with business as usual. She would show that priest what she was made of.

"Ah, you're back." Niels got up from the bench and walked towards Beldenka, who somehow looked more delicate than before. Vulnerable, even. Was it something in the way she moved? "Were you angry with me, or upset?" He searched her face. Her eyelids seemed swollen. Had she been crying? "What did I do wrong?"

"You silly man. You really are clueless, aren't you?" To his surprise, she smiled at him as she spoke those incriminating words. As if she were not really insulting him.

"I'm afraid so, Beldenka, but I honestly did not mean to hurt you. I was only trying to lighten the mood a little, but I'm starting to think I inadvertently made everything worse." He was hopeless with women. He should have gotten himself a wife, and fathered a giggle of children turnings ago already, but with his people skills he should consider himself lucky if he ever got married at all.

"Don't flatter yourself. This was not about you. Now, shall we just continue where we left off? Minus the stupid banter?" Without waiting for him to answer, she reached for her sheet music.

"Beldenka, I was about to go home. It's getting late." His stomach made a growling noise, and only now did he realise he should have eaten hours ago. That was another of his many failings. He forgot to eat and drink.

"And you haven't eaten anything since lunch, have you?"
"I was studying the Scriptures."

It was the third hour after midnight, and he hadn't slept for even a moment. Or maybe he had dozed off a few times, but it certainly didn't feel like it. He had been tossing and turning all night long, memories of his childhood assaulting him.

It was yet another reason why he hated to talk about his life. The danger was bad enough on its own. Having to deal with the memories was even worse. Why could he not just forget everything and start over? A whole new life. Was that too much to ask for?

Yet here he was. Stuck in the middle of nowhere with a cantor who was clearly determined to drag it all out of him. All the gruesome details. And if that alone weren't bad enough, there was Mikhandor too.

Mikhandor. Sometimes he longed for the days when he didn't know about the man's existence. The days when he was just a little boy. Loved by his parents, admired by his brothers, adored by his little sister, and despised by the rest of the family. He never figured out why they had hated him so much. Not that any of it mattered now. He would probably never see them again anyway.

Back then he had thought his life was bad. He shook his head at the innocence of the child he once was. Such a foolish little boy. That life had been idyllic. And he'd lost it all the moment he boarded that *draken* to Ebaru.

But how could he have known? How could any of them have known?

CHAPTER FOUR

SECRETS

thief yields
mighty dragon
limp knight shields lame warlord
combat master travels the world
beyond

She had to stop herself from turning around and staring after the big blond bloke that left Yeleksim's Gym. Where had she seen that guy before?

"Bel, my pretty, what brings you to my dark den?" Leks grinned from ear to ear as he bent forward and leaned on the counter.

"Who is the blond demigod?" She couldn't help herself. She just had to know.

"Weird chap, that one. Calls himself Mig Felling. Pays me quite handsomely to have the gym to himself three nights a sevenday, so who am I to say that's not his real name, eh?" He scratched his armpit. "A drink, sweetie? Got some excellent booze here."

Bel smiled. "No booze for me, Leks. Not this early. You should know that by now. But a kaw brew would be nice."

"Course I know, but it was worth a try, eh?" He reached for the copper kaw pot. "A perk it is then. Here you go, sweetheart."

"Thanks. That smells good." She held the mug in both hands, and inhaled the dark brew's strong aroma. It reminded her of home. A home she once loved. Before she became a Reject.

"I need some intelligence, Leks."

"Don't you always?" He reached for a cloth and started wiping the worktop. "What's it this time?"

"This new priest. You do know old Gharbani died last winter, don't you?"

He nodded, poured himself a mead beer and hefted his horn, though Bel knew that was just for show. She'd only ever seen him drink water.

"Well, this new guy... I think he might have gotten on the bad side of some High Lord."

"A priest? Ruffling... Nah, that makes no sense, Bel." He shook his grizzled head.

"I know, but here's the thing. He goes by a Darsian name and insists people have been killed because of him. Many people, even. What's that sound like to you?"

"Hmm." He massaged his temples with his fingertips. "Weird. Utterly weird, that. And you certain sure the guy's not been bitten by a red fire beetle?"

"I don't think I ever met a saner person than him." She took a sip of her kaw. "So what am I to think?"

"I'd think it might not be entirely safe to be around him much. That's my two silvers."

"Ah, but that's not an option, as I'm sure you understand. So I need to know more. Especially seeing that he's not exactly forthcoming."

"Course the man's tight-lipped. You would be too, if you were walking in his slippers."

Bel nodded.

"What's he look like?"

"I managed to sneak a portrait of him. Got it on this *marble*. Can I use your *logatome?*"

"Always, deary. Always." He hobbled to his office, his prosthetic leg never quite in sync with the rest of his body, and Bel followed him on silent wheels. She attached the marble to the tome, waited for the connection to take effect, then pressed her thumb to the reader on the screen and said, "Cantorbel logging. Unlock image swearpot."

"Swearpot?" Leks crackled a laugh. "You call your new priest Swearpot?"

"You should hear him. I honestly never met any cleric as sweary as him. You'd think a priest would..." a soft *ping* drew her attention back to the tome. "That's him."

"Ah, no! No, no, no. This can't be true." He shook his head slowly. "Bel, sweetheart, I'm sorry. Really am."

"What? What's wrong?" Leks never denied her anything.

"Can't do this. The blond giant, Mig. He, uh, he also pays me to keep out of his client's business. And promised to pay me in a different kind of currency if I broke trust with him." He looked at his remaining fingers and let out a long breath. "Seven's my lucky number, you know. So... yeah."

Bel felt the blood drain from her face. "That's nasty! You'd think that kind of thing only happened in Ingravia. Or maybe Antoria, but not here." A shiver ran down her spine. "So, our new priest is somehow under the protection of this Mig bloke. That actually makes a sinister kind of sense." Now she knew where she'd seen the giant before. He'd been loitering about in the proximity of the House of Prayer.

"Uh, Bel... not to be an old fang, but I'll have to tell Mig you wanted info on his man. He may not be too happy about that. But my contract..." He took his eye out, cleaned the lens and popped it back in. The message was clear.

"Oh, Leks, I'm so sorry. If only I'd known. I'd never have troubled you." She gulped the rest of her now lukewarm kaw down. "That flaming priest! I'm gonna go tell him some things he won't want to hear. I'll make his ears burn. And he can torching well introduce me to his oversized friend, too. I will get to the bottom of this whole blighted business."

"Bel, Bel." He actually took a swig of his beer. "Better be real careful, young lady. You don't want to end up like me now, do you?"

"Do I look like I'm bothered?" She turned her chair and wheeled out of the building, muttering curses under her breath.

A few yards out, she turned and rolled back in, straight into Leks's office. "Forgot this." She yanked the marble free. Then she took the old man's bearded face between both hands and pressed a gentle kiss on his forehead. "Don't you worry about me, *Ded*. I'm a big girl. I can take care of myself."

She found Niels exactly where she expected him to be. On a bench in the House of Prayer, the Holy Book opened in his lap. Though he looked at her as she came closer, he didn't say a word.

"We need to talk. Now." She was done playing games.

"Beldenka?" He looked adorable with that confused look in those gorgeous golden eyes of his, but that would not save him from her ire.

"You heard me. Now, do you want me to spell this out for you? Right here? Or would you prefer to talk in the privacy of your own home?"

He stood up. "Come with me."

He walked at a gentle pace, back straight, head held high, face unreadable.

"I'll make us a tea," he said, "and something to eat."

"You're stalling, your Holiness." Try though she might, she couldn't keep the sarcasm out of her voice. Torching priest didn't even seem to hear it.

"I'm just hungry." He actually managed to sound surprised as he rummaged in his kooler.

"Yes, and I am the Queen of Dragons, but guess what? It won't help you one bit. We're going to talk, whether you like it or not."

"The Queen of Dragons? You? I thought that was just —"

"For Zinnir's sake! Don't you understand sarcasm, Niels?" What in the Dragonmother's inviolable name was wrong with that man?

"Oh. Sarcasm. I see." He placed two cups of fresh mint tea on that ugly wooden crate that served as a low table. "So what is it that's bothering you so much, Beldenka?"

He went back into the kitchen area and returned with a ceramic bowl filled with figs, bite-sized lumps of goat's cheese, and nuts. At least he knew a thing or two about good food.

"Your friend Mig, or whatever his real name is. The big blond mountain ape. He threatened my friend Leks." The thought alone was enough to make her want to roast that big bully over a nice hot bonfire.

"What are you talking about?" Niels stared at her, his eyes wide with confusion. "Mig would never do such a thing."

"So you're calling Leks a liar?" She'd known Leks forever, and had never caught him in a lie. Not once. She trusted him with her life.

"I don't even know this Leks, Beldenka. All I am saying is that Mig—"

"Into the Pit of Doom with your Mig! And quit calling me Beldenka. It's Bel. Just Bel." If she were a dragon, she'd be spitting fire now. Zilla started screeching, and flapping her wings in a response to her agitation. She rolled over to the window, anxious to put some much-needed physical distance between herself and Niels. Best not give Zilla the chance to attack, like she had done that day when... No! She shouldn't think of that.

Zilla, please! I need you to calm down. We both need to calm down. No more violence. Ever. Well, maybe I'll let you have some fun with this Mig guy. Later. But not Niels, you understand? Not Niels. He's just stupid. Not bad.

The silent heartbeats dragged by, until she heard Niels approach on slippered feet. Felt a hesitant hand on her free shoulder.

"Bel... I apologise. I don't want us to fight. I hate discord. Obviously, this Leks means a lot to you. Can you tell me who he is? Please?"

She turned her chair and followed Niels back to the sofa.

"Leks is a sweet old man who, through no fault of his own, fell foul of the wrath of some Minor Lords when he was younger." No need to tell him that one of these was her own father.

"Early on in his career, they had removed his left eye and replaced it with a *okular*, so that he could serve them better. When they didn't like the results of his hard work any longer, they... It cost him a leg, three fingers, and a couple of teeth. Then he was exiled. He's been living in Ambleville for, dunno, fifteen turnings or so, and owns Yeleksim's Gym."

"Yeleksim's Gym." Niels nodded. "I see. So that is the connection."

They were both silent again, but now the silence felt different. More relaxed. Bel was glad for it. She didn't understand why she had to lash out at Niels so often, and it made her feel awful. She didn't want to be that kind of woman.

"Mig," Niels said after a while, "has been looking out for me ever since I was a baby. He's older than most people would think."

Something clicked. The man was a *Transient*. "From which world? And why?"

Niels gasped. "You are too observant for your own good."

"So people have been telling me my entire life. Which world?"

"I apologise, Bel. I am not at liberty to tell you. Like it or not, but the danger is real."

"So this is why your friend pays Leks to have the Gym to himself three nights a week, and threatens to maim him if he even just dares mention your name." She felt the heat of the anger colour her cheeks again. In a reflex, she raised a hand to calm Zilla before the dragonet could start fluttering again.

Niels made a face. He shook his head slowly. "Mig takes his duty maybe a little too seriously at times. He probably even thinks it's his fault when I as much as fart. But he is not malicious. He will not hurt anyone if he can at all avoid it — which might be one of the reasons why I'm always on the run."

"Won't hurt anyone if he can avoid it? This doesn't sound so reassuring."

Niels shrugged again. "It's the best I can give you."

"You're not going to tell me his real name, are you? Or yours." She silently cursed the priest's secretiveness. How was she ever going to be able to work properly with someone like him, who trusted nobody? And how indeed could she trust him, if she didn't even know who he really was?

"My real name is Niels Bosch." He sounded so sincere, Bel almost believed him. Almost.

"No priest has a Darsian name."

"Look Bel..." His shoulders drooped. "I was adopted. Now, can we please not talk about this any more?"

Bel nodded. She felt stupid now, and insensitive. The poor sod looked positively miserable. He'd probably had a pretty rotten childhood. She really should leave it alone now, so as not to upset him even more. And yet... "I need you to introduce me to your friend Mig."

"That's easy enough. You can come with me to the gym tonight, if you like. Mig already suggested he was interested in training you."

"What? This man doesn't even know me." But one look at Niels' face told her Mig knew exactly who she was. "What kind of training?" If they thought she was interested in Deep Thought or some such twaddle, they were mistaken.

"Combat training."

"No. You are mocking me. This is not funny!"

Niels shook his head. "I would never mock you, Bel. Never. Mig said it would be cruel not to teach a person in a wheelchair how to defend themselves."

"I can't. This is madness! I'm just—" She broke off. Would it really be possible for her to learn how to fight? With these useless legs of hers? The prospect was strangely appealing. "Fine. I'll come with you. Also, which High Lord have you pissed off?"

"High Lord?" He looked as incredulous as he sounded. "What makes you think... Oh, I see. Well, you're wrong. I never had anything to do with any High Lord. Not as far as I know, anyway."

Way to go, Bel. She'd done it again. Jumped to conclusions. When would she ever learn? The man didn't know any High Lord. He'd probably never even met a Minor Lord. What had she been thinking?

The world was more than Ingravia. And hadn't Niels himself said that the criminal syndicate in Ebaru shouldn't be underestimated? Would it be too far-fetched to think there would be an active gangdom in other parts of the world, too? Like Darsrijck perhaps, or Senkerland? Or even here, in pastoral Briscona?

That was an uncomfortable thought, but could she afford to close her eyes to the truth? When Niels had already told her that he was a dangerous person to be around?

She suppressed a shiver. To hide her discomfort, she bent over and took a small lump of cheese from the bowl. "Are you sure your Mig wants to train me?"

"Positive."

"How does he know I'm not a dangerous criminal? I'm Ingravian, after all." She was only half joking. If they knew who Natoniev Nadinovik, the reputable businessman, really was... Or worse, if they knew what she had done... They might just change their minds.

"He does not." Niels looked as stoic as he sounded.

"Yet he still wants to train me? Isn't this a bit reckless?"

"He's not taking any chances. Not really. He has vetted you, I'm sure."

"He did *what?*" The nerve of that man! Vetting her. As if she were cattle.

"He vets everyone he thinks I'll be in close contact with. Of course he can never be entirely sure about anyone, but if he thinks a person is safe, they most likely are. Mig is seldom wrong. He is a good judge of character."

"Dragon's breath! The audacity of this man! I... I will..." She could think of a thousand things she would want to do to him, but the man would just laugh in her face. He was a flaming giant, and she a tiny little thing with legs that couldn't even support her own weight. No match for Niels' Transient protector at all.

"It's not arrogance, Bel." Niels was trying to appease her. "He is only doing his job. Mig has to keep me safe. I may not like it, and you don't have to like it either, but there is nothing we can do about that, so we might as well accept it."

Easy enough for him to say. He had known the man his entire torching life, so he didn't know any better. She, on the other hand, could well do without nosy people prying into her past.

Some secrets were best kept.

CHAPTER FIVE

Obsessed

killer
prowls in darkness
dragon humbles giant
exile and tribe of lords unite
for life

The door opened noiselessly and Mikhandor stepped into the room.

"Young lady," he said in his dulcet voice, "out with you. I need to talk to my friend here. Alone."

Niels held his breath. He might be a bit of a dork, but even he could see that Bel wasn't going to like being treated like that. And sure enough, she turned her chair. Slowly. Very slowly.

Then, even slower, she rode up to where Mikhandor stood, and didn't stop until her knees touched his legs. She looked up at him. Her face, her entire posture showed not even a hint of insecurity.

"You," she said as she pricked a slender finger into his stomach, "are the most impudent, boorish person I've met in my entire life." Her voice, sweet and soft though it sounded, held a clear threat. "I don't care where you come from or how important you may think you are — or how old for that matter — but remember this: You are a guest in our world."

She stared at him, the lines of her face hard and uncompromising, until he took a few steps back and looked away from her.

It was the weirdest thing. Niels had never seen anything like it. Nobody messed with Mikhandor. Yet, here was Bel. Tiny, disabled Bel, intimidating him with nothing but her voice — which she had not even raised — and her eyes.

"Is uh... is the lady always like this?" Mikhandor looked at Niels. His voice sounded hushed.

"The lady," Bel said, "is standing right in front of you, you asinine animal, and she has the mental faculties to speak for herself. In case you hadn't noticed — it's only her legs that aren't working."

Niels could not blame her. Mikhandor was blundering, and making things worse with every word he said.

"You heard the lady, Mig. She has a name too, by the way."

Mikhandor stood scratching his head, looking from Niels to Bel and back again. He took a deep breath, opened his mouth and said... nothing. This same behaviour repeated several times over until finally he found his tongue.

"My apologies, young lady. I am Mig, Niels' personal trainer. Pleased to meet you."

"Beldenka Nadinov, cantor." She jutted her chin out and held Mikhandor's gaze, never flinching. "Your apologies are accepted. This wasn't so hard now, was it?"

"If you say so, Miss." He took another deep breath, opened his mouth and, again, shut it without saying another word.

"Tell me everything you know about me. And don't even try to pretend that you haven't vetted me, because Niels here told me just now you did exactly this."

Niels swore under his breath. He could already see this escalating, and that was the last thing he needed.

"I... uh, I shall make us some more tea. And Mig, Bel knows you are more than just a personal trainer, so there is no need to pretend. Also, I invited her to come train with us tonight, as you so kindly suggested the other day."

He went out into the garden to pick some fresh mint, and feed the hens. But even more to simply be alone for a few moments. The animosity between Bel and Mikhandor made him nervous. He wondered if he could do anything to make them get along better, but as always in situations like these, his brain drew a blank.

"Cha-caw, cha-caw! Come chickies, come to Niels." He scooped a handful of grains and seeds from the barrel and held it out. Soon enough, the stately white Lady Lilia came up to him and gently picked some grains out of his hand. Then Miss Molin came running, and finally Young Yoli. Mr LeCock kept his distance, as Niels had already come to expect.

When Niels came back in, Mikhandor was seated in the wing chair. An ugly, threadbare thing, but large and comfortable nonetheless. Bel sat a good three arm's lengths away from him. They were, however, conversing more amicably than before.

"... know who he is. Of course I do. It is my job to know."

"And you still don't think I might be a dangerous killer?"

Mikhandor laughed. "No, and neither is your father. Though he certainly works hard to make people believe he is."

Now that was interesting. A man who wanted people to believe that he's a merciless killer. What kind of man would that be?

"What makes you think so? Haven't you seen what he did to Yeleksim Bogrovik?"

Yeleksim Bogrovik? The owner of Yeleksim's Gym? Bel's friend Leks? Niels couldn't believe his ears. Did she just imply that her own father had tortured and mutilated this poor man? Bel definitely had more secrets than Niels had previously thought.

"It's hard to miss that, Miss Nadinov. That was a cruel thing to do and it makes him a clever, calculating crime lord. Not a killer."

Bel's father, a crime lord? How could Mikhandor not be worried about that?

"You will not call him this." The hostility in Bel's voice was unmistakable. "My father is a respected businessman. Not the criminal you make him out to be."

Mikhandor held his hands up in an apologetic gesture. "By Ingravian standards that is, of course, true. But you'll have to agree with me that it was a cunning move that prevented him from having to kill the man."

What, by Zinnir's beard, was going on? What had this Leks done to deserve such a cruel fate? *Through no fault of his own*, Bel had said, and yet whatever it was, was punishable by death according to Ingravian law?

"Think about it." Mikhandor seemed not the least bit ruffled. "What were his options? His peers wanted to see blood. So he maimed and exiled the man who had been his best friend and most trusted advisor, claiming that was a fate worse than death."

"You clearly have no idea what you're talking about. Leks was a strong, healthy man. It would have been much kinder to just kill him. They took everything from him. His wealth, his family, his strong physique. His honour. Everything that made him a valuable member of our society. They reduced him to nothing. A Reject. Then he was forced to leave our country, with barely enough resources to survive the next sevenday." Bel took a deep breath. "You don't know what it is like to be exiled."

"True. But the fact remains. Your father does not kill."

Bel snorted. "If that makes you believe he's not dangerous, you are a fool."

"Young lady..." Mikhandor leaned forward and peered into Bel's eyes, "I never said, or indeed even assumed, he was not dangerous. Of course he is. And so are you."

"Me?" Bel sounded so innocent, Niels had no way of telling whether she was being honest, or if she was trying to mislead Mikhandor. "A fragile cripple in a wheelchair? How could I possibly pose a threat to anyone?"

Mikhandor chuckled. "Do you see how well she's playing the game, your Holiness?"

Niels nodded, though in all honesty he had no idea what was going on between those two.

"Gentlemen. You wound me." Bel stroked her upper legs gently. "These legs are as good as useless, as you both know, and here you are accusing me of taking advantage of my disability. How can you two be so cruel?" She blinked, as if trying to ward off tears.

Niels felt awkward. Was this just a game for her, or was she really distraught? He went into the kitchen and busied himself with the tea.

"Very good," he heard Mikhandor say. "You are a natural."

"Fine. Suppose I really am dangerous. Then why are you here? And even more curious, why have you offered to instruct me in the combative arts? Isn't that a little foolhardy?"

Niels came back into the living area, balancing three cups of scalding hot tea. He arranged them carefully on the table before he sat down on the sofa. He would like to know Mikhandor's answer too. What had been his motives for this audacious move?

"It's quite simple," Mikhandor said. "Someone desperately wants his Holiness dead, and has both the power and the resources to send a veritable horde of assassins after him. Thus, we need friends. And the more dangerous they are, the better."

"I see." Bel nodded. "But what makes you think I won't turn against you?"

"Intuition."

"You'd better pray to your god, whichever one it is, that your intuition hasn't deceived you then. Better yet, pray to all seven gods. And their parents." She turned her chair towards the door. "I'll join you gentlemen at the gym tonight."

"But, Bel..." Niels was perplexed. "Your tea." She hadn't even touched it.

"I'm good, Niels, but I really have to go. No need to see me out." And just like that, she left.

"Feisty woman, that," Mikhandor said. "We need her on our side. Her, and her family."

"I don't like this, Mikhandor." Niels paced the room. "To tell you the truth, I think this is all highly disturbing. Don't you think we have enough trouble as is?"

Mikhandor shrugged. "She's going to be extremely useful to us. She and her family. Just wait and see."

"Useful? Is that who we are now? Are we reduced to thinking of people as if they were mere commodities? That is despicable."

Again, Mikhandor shrugged. "Look, it is your skin that's on the line. Not mine. Do you want to live, or not?"

"What do you know about Beldenka and her relatives?" Niels sat down again, but his unease made him bounce his legs up and down in a relentless rhythm.

Mikhandor didn't answer immediately. He pressed his fingertips against each other and sat like that for a moment, staring into the distance.

"Ingravian culture," he said finally, "is very different from anything you have ever known. Part of that may have to do with its geographical location, the harsh climate, and the unique flora and fauna of the country.

"The Ingravian people are a tough, proud people. We tend to think of them as criminals and barbarians, but that's not at all how they think of themselves. I'm sure you noticed Miss Nadinov's reaction when I made the mistake of calling her father a crime lord."

Niels nodded.

"That wasn't just because I was talking about her father. Had I referred to one of her family's rivals as a crime lord, she would have reprimanded me just as sharply.

"Ingravians define crime differently. We may think of the way Mr Nadinovik and the other lords conduct their businesses as corrupt. We would call their behaviour dishonest and aggressive. They don't.

"Men like Mr Nadinovik are held in the highest esteem. Though he is currently still a minor lord, he is *this* close to becoming a grand lord." He gestured with his thumb and index finger.

"Wait, wait, wait!" Niels held up his hands and shook his head in bewilderment. "What is it with all those titles? I thought there were high lords and minor lords, but now you are talking about grand lords and... Great gods! Just slow down a bit, will you? Also, corrupt, dishonest, and aggressive? Explain."

"Yes, that's an aspect of your education that we may have glossed over a bit." Mikhandor scratched the nape of his neck. "We didn't think you needed to know all that much about Ingravia. In retrospect, I think we must concede that we were remiss there."

He picked up his cup of tea, brought it halfway up to his mouth, then put it back on the table again. "To start with their business model... uh, they won't hesitate to swindle people out of their money, or even torture or kill if that's what it takes to make their enterprise grow.

"Now, for the Ingravian nobility. It's fairly complicated. Titles are either merited or inherited. Anyone, literally anyone, can become a lord, based on his or her achievements. The higher the achievement, the higher the title.

"Also note that there are only lords. No ladies. Women can, however, become lords and are held to the exact same standards as men.

"The aristocratic system is merit-based, and anyone can advance from a lowly vagabond to grand lord almost overnight. That's how Mr Nadinovik's grandmother became a grand lord. She'd have become a king too, if she hadn't been murdered by one of her rivals on the eve of her coronation. This man, Lord Volzkan Kovkatim, became king in her stead, since he had now earned that right."

"But that's atrocious!" Niels felt the blood drain from his face.

"Not by Ingravian standards. Or haven't you heard what your cute little cantor said about Mr Bogrovik? That it would have been kinder to kill him? Death, to an Ingravian, is preferred over humiliation."

Niels suppressed a shiver. "And you still think this was a good idea? Me coming to the Barlows, when you already knew my cantor might not hesitate to kill?"

"Yes. And for exactly that reason. She is a minor lord, by the way."

A minor lord? Things were becoming ever weirder. "Beldenka? How? I mean, she was, uh... exiled when she became disabled. She is a Reject, whatever that is. How can she possibly be a lord?"

"That is the beauty of the Ingravian system. As I said, titles are not only granted on merit, but the title of minor lord is also heritable. And irrevocable. Once you are or become a lord in Ingravia — minor, high, or grand makes no difference — all your children are automatically granted the title of Minor Lord."

"Erl's balls!"

Mikhandor coughed and looked at him. "Really, Your Holiness!"

"Sorry. I forgot how you feel about that. It's just... it blows my mind. And it unsettles me. Besides, I still don't follow your logic. I fail to see why I should need another killer in my life."

"That's easy." Mikhandor leaned back and crossed his legs. He locked his hands behind his neck. "There is a dangerous and deranged killer on the prowl, determined to bring you down. We cannot run from him forever, and to be honest, I don't want to. I am tired of playing this cat and mouse game.

"So, what we need, are allies. Not well-meaning friends and relatives, but strong and unyielding fighters. Formidable men and women, who won't hesitate to do what is necessary. That is why we need Miss Nadinov and her tribe."

"I still don't like this."

"You don't have to. But you will do everything you can to make this work. Understood, Your Holiness?"

"Yes, you merciless son of an Erl, and stop calling me Your Holiness, or I shall have to ask my dangerous cantor to chop off your testicles."

Mikhandor grinned. "I'm glad I've got your attention."

They sat in silence as they drank their tea. Mikhandor leaned back, his posture relaxed, but Niels felt only dread. Part of him could see that his friend was right, but then there was that other part of him; the scared little boy that only wanted to hide in a dark, solitary place. Forever.

Why? He sent his thoughts to the Lady, *why did you choose me? Why not someone else? Someone bold and strong?* But the Goddess didn't answer. He hadn't expected her to. That was not the way things worked.

"What more can you tell me about Beldenka?"

"Loads." Mikhandor put his empty cup back on the table. "But I won't. Not immediately. And some things not ever, because they are not mine to tell."

"Fair enough." Secrets and uncertainties. Niels hated them, but he knew Mikhandor well enough. No use trying to pry those hidden truths out of him. "Then just tell me what I need to know."

"Mirtalya Grigonov."

"The violinist. What has she got to do with anything?"

"She is your cantor's mother, and a high lord. And I have been able to verify that she killed at least two of her competitors. With her own bare hands."

"Stones! You can't be serious!" That woman looked every bit as delicate as her daughter, and her music was so divine, it moved grown men to tears. The thought of her killing people, with her bare hands, no less, made his insides churn.

"That's what made her a high lord." Mikhandor sounded awed, but not the least bit shaken. "Then we have the brother and sisters. One of them older, the other three younger than your cantor. All four of them perfect Ingravian lords. Cunning, ruthless and extremely dangerous."

Four siblings, and all of them potential killers? He didn't need that kind of excitement in his life. What was Mikhandor thinking? Did he not care about the danger?

Not even a sevenday ago he'd been happy to be here, in the Barlows. This place where nothing ever happened, but now... He suppressed a shiver. Dug his nails into his palms. Tried to keep his breathing under control.

"And the best part is, even though our Miss Nadinov is a Reject and has been unofficially exiled, her parents and siblings have never stopped loving and supporting her." Mikhandor's grin spread from ear to ear. "They come and stay with her regularly, and of course your cantor attends her mother's concerts as often as she can. In fact, she was at one of these concerts when you had your welcome reception here."

"Holy gods!" Niels jumped up from the sofa. He didn't want to hear another word. It was too much. There was dangerous, and then there was dangerous. "You should go. I need to be alone."

He nearly tripped over his own feet as he bolted from the living room and fled into his bedroom.

CHAPTER SIX

Locked in

early
despair relived
unsettles holy man
wheels turn to wrestle hidden truths
open

He sat down on the floor, curled up in a ball, and started rocking back and forth gently, humming to himself in a low voice. He had experienced these, what he called panic attacks, for as long as he could remember. Only, back when he was a child, they had most often looked more like temper tantrums.

They weren't. They were neither tantrums nor panic attacks. He knew this with absolute certainty, though he didn't know what else to call them. Nobody seemed to know. Not even Papa, who was a paediatrician. He once said some children simply were like that. They were easily overwhelmed and would either break down or shut down when they could no longer cope. They could learn how to handle their overwhelm better, but as far as Papa knew, they never outgrew it.

Papa had been right, of course. Even now, aged thirty-two, he still hadn't outgrown them. And he hated himself for it.

◆○◆

Visitors. Again. Tante Berline and Oom Rijkhardt with Duive, Swanilde and Hilvert. They didn't like Niels, and knew how to make him feel like he was some kind of weird freak. But that wasn't even the worst of it. They stank. All five of them. And they were loud.

These past couple of sevendays — ever since Machteld was born — far too many visitors had already invaded the sanctity of their home, and the mere thought of having to spend even one heartbeat with his uncle, aunt and cousins was more than Niels could bear.

He kicked the wall and started crying, and pulling his own hair. He threw himself to the floor, still kicking and screaming. Tears were streaming down his cheeks. His nose was stuffed up, and his clothes felt so scratchy he wanted to take them all off. But his hands had taken on a life of their own and refused to do his bidding.

"Niels!" Mama's face, too close, almost touched his, and he could feel her hot, damp breath. The smell of the kaw brew she'd just been drinking made him gag. "Stop this nonsense immediately!" She picked him up from the floor, held him in a painful grip and dragged him into the kitchen.

"No!" he wailed. "No, no, no, nooo!" He knew what was coming, and it was dreadful. By the time they reached the sink, he was screaming at the top of his lungs, and his arms were flailing wildly.

Mama paid no heed to his distress. She turned on the tap and wrestled his head underneath the strong flow of icy cold water. He fought. He spluttered. He couldn't breathe.

Then it stopped, and he heard Papa's voice. "Aleid, what are you doing?"

"Gijs, I... it's hopeless! These tantrums of his... I can't..."

Mama released him, and he felt Papa's arms around him. Safe and secure.

"Ah, look at him. Those aren't tantrums, love. He is completely overwhelmed, our poor lad." They were back in the hallway, and Papa sat down with him. Started rocking him gently. "Does this happen often, Aleid?"

"It seems..." Mama sniffled. "Seems like they're happening all the time lately. So much worse than when he was little, and I... I just don't know what to do any more."

"You should have told me. I might have some helpful ideas. We can talk about that later. Why don't you take everyone out for a walk in the park, and a nice drink at De Soete Pimpernel? It will do you good to be out of the house for a while. I'll take care of Niels." He still held Niels in a comforting embrace, and hadn't stopped rocking him.

Back and forth, back and forth. Ever so softly. He started humming a monotonous tune in a low voice.

Mama left with her obnoxious relatives, and finally there was peace and quiet in the house. The weird stench still lingered but was less overpowering now that the stinkers were gone. Little by little, Niels began to feel more like himself again.

He began to notice other things. Good things. The way Papa smelled. Not his aftershave, which was a good scent too, but the very essence of his skin. Strong and musky with just a hint of vanilla. The regular ticking of the clock in the living room. The faded colours of the light that fell through the stained glass front door window. The way the wind moved the leaves of the large oak in front of the house, and the shadows this created on the living room carpet. The soft, woolly texture of the rug on which they sat.

Niels wanted to experience it all. And so he stuck the tip of his tongue out — slowly, and carefully — to taste the skin of Papa's hand. It had a smooth feel and slightly salty flavour.

"Do I taste good, lad?" Niels could hear the smile in Papa's voice. He nodded and grunted happily. He ran his fingertips over the rug. Wriggled his fingers in the coloured light and enjoyed the patterns they made.

Still unable to speak properly, he pointed at the door. He bobbed up and down.

"Do you want to go outside, son?"

Niels loved how well Papa understood him, even when he had no words. He nodded vigorously. *Yes.*

Papa looked at him. "Don't you want me to clean you up a little first?"

Niels shook his head. *No, no, no! Outside first.* Outside was more important than clean. He needed to catch the wind, before it was gone. Clean could wait, but he needed to feel the warm glow of the sun on his skin. He bounced up and down again, and felt like he could go on forever. He pointed at the door once more.

"No time for a cleanup? Well, let's go outside then. Can you walk?"

Niels climbed out of his father's lap, grabbed his hand, and started towards the door. He still felt the dried snot on his face, and the salty lines where the tears had run down his cheeks, but that didn't matter. Not any more.

He went outside with Papa, who loved him. He felt the warmth of the late afternoon sun on his face. The wind played with his hair and made him giggle. He started running in circles, arms wide, and squealed in delight. At last, all was well.

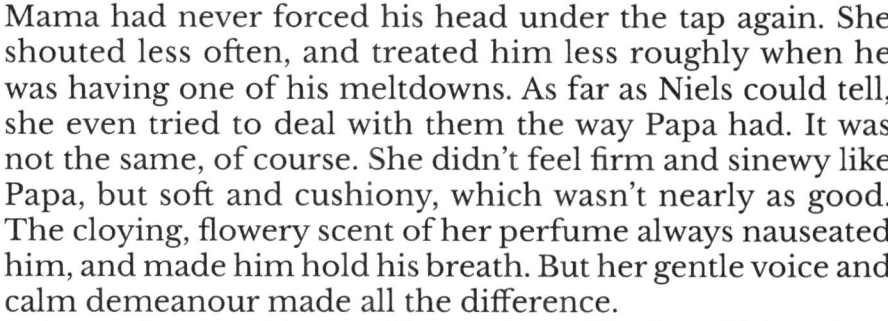

Mama had never forced his head under the tap again. She shouted less often, and treated him less roughly when he was having one of his meltdowns. As far as Niels could tell, she even tried to deal with them the way Papa had. It was not the same, of course. She didn't feel firm and sinewy like Papa, but soft and cushiony, which wasn't nearly as good. The cloying, flowery scent of her perfume always nauseated him, and made him hold his breath. But her gentle voice and calm demeanour made all the difference.

Funny, how rocking and humming still calmed him when things got too much for him to handle. Was it because that was what Papa used to do when he was little, or had Papa somehow intuitively picked up on what he needed?

His soul ached thinking of his father. It had been such a long time. He would be sixty-four turnings now, and Mama sixty-two. Rem, Kas and Machteld, like him, had been children when he left for Ebaru. They were adults now, probably with families of their own. They would have partners and children that he didn't even know about and might never meet.

But they were safe. He had to hold on to that. As long as they believed him dead, they, at least, could live their lives without fearing the king and his assassins. For their sakes,

Niels would keep away from them for as long as Hanassan of Ebaru lived.

He got up from the floor. Time for a long, relaxing soak in the tub. Clean clothes. A light, but nourishing meal. He should not train on an empty stomach.

When Niels arrived at Yeleksim's Gym, Bel and Mikhandor were both already there. They were seated at the bar, talking with the man Niels assumed to be Yeleksim Bogrovik. He didn't have much choice but to join them.

"Niels," Bel said, "this is my friend Leks. He'll be joining us tonight." She turned towards Leks. "Leks, this is our new priest, Niels Bosch."

"Pleased to meet you, sir," Niels said. In truth, he wasn't happy at all, but the niceties had to be observed. His parents had taught him so when he was still a wee lad. "Manners, Niels," they would say. "Mind your manners."

"And you, young man." Leks's toothless grin looked genuine enough. "Please, call me Leks." He pointed at the long-handled copper kaw maker. "A brew before we hit the mat?"

"This man here," Mikhandor gestured at Niels, "thinks he can fight." He nodded at Bel and Leks. "You two are going to prove him wrong. Not today, and probably not within the next couple of moons, but you will. Eventually."

Niels had no reason to doubt his friend, though how he was going to achieve that goal was beyond him. A tiny woman in a wheelchair and an old man with a prosthetic leg and three missing fingers. It seemed like no match for him.

"How?" Bel asked.

"Simple. You two have been thinking of yourselves as disabled. As of today, you will reframe your minds, and ditch the 'dis'. It is of no use to you. You, young lady, have a formidable weapon under your butt. I'll bet you never thought of it that way."

Bel looked momentarily surprised. Then a mischievous grin appeared on her face. "You're right," she said. "This is rather a nice chunk of metal. Perfect for breaking human bones. I like your approach, Mig."

"I knew you would." The smile on Mikhandor's face broadened. "And you, my old friend, have this very nice leg that you can take off at will. I can already see so many possibilities there. Can't you?"

Leks chuckled. "Never thought of it that way, Sensei, but yes, sure can. Shoulda thought of that meself."

The way Bel so casually mentioned her chair's usefulness for breaking human bones was chilling. So was Leks's glee at the thought of taking off his prosthetic leg and weaponising it. How could they enjoy the prospect of hurting people — even if those people were their enemies?

"Let us have a closer look at that chair of yours, Miss Nadinov," Mikhandor said. "It seems fine to me, but looks can be deceiving. It appears to fit you quite well."

"Ha!" The satisfaction in Bel's voice was unmistakable. "It should. It is brand new. I had it fitted less than half a turning ago."

"Good. Now get out of it." Without warning, he pushed Bel out of her chair.

She scrambled upright, her face contorted with anger. "Dragon's breath! What do you think you're doing, you big brute?" She seized his ankles and yanked him off his feet.

"Well, what did I say?" Mikhandor sounded almost too happy. "You've got what it takes, my lovely. Now grab that chair and lift it."

"What?"

"I said, grab your chair and lift it. Go on, do it."

Face grim, Bel stood and took two unstable steps towards her chair, then gripped the backrest with one hand and the frame with her other. Her legs were trembling with effort as she raised the chair maybe a handspan above the mat. She let go of it, and flopped to the floor.

"Not like that." Mikhandor shook his head. "Pick it up from your seated position."

"You maniac!" Bel grabbed her chair, and heaved. Nothing happened. She changed her position, and the way she took hold of the chair. Again and again Mikhandor made her do the exercise. She failed about as many times as she succeeded.

"Good. I have seen enough. That chair is too heavy. You need one that weighs about half as much."

"You've got to be joking! These things are as expensive as a small karr. And the lighter they are, the more expensive. Do you know how much a cantor earns?"

Niels had no idea, but it couldn't be more than what he himself earned, and although it was quite a sufficient wage, it would not sustain unlimited spending.

"That won't be your problem, young lady," Mikhandor said. "I shall be funding it. I'll send someone over to fit you a new chair as soon as possible. And Leks, I understand you've got a wheelchair on standby too?"

Leks nodded. "It's an oldie, though. Weighs at least three times as much as young Bel's chair. Thing is more like a wheelbarrow. No good for daily intensive use." He shrugged slightly. "Hardly ever need it anyway, so it's good enough for me."

"Not any more, my old friend. I'll have my guy fit you out with a new, ultra-lightweight chair as well. You may not need it often in your everyday life right now, but you never know what fate has in store for you, and I want you to be able to use your chair as a weapon."

"Sounds good to me."

"Now let's see what we can do with that leg of yours. Would you mind taking it off?"

Almost immediately it became clear that using the leg as a weapon was not nearly as easy as it had sounded only moments ago. Although it came off readily enough, without the prosthetic Leks could barely keep his balance, especially when he started swinging the thing around.

Mikhandor's posture became increasingly rigid, and his sentences ever shorter as he came up with one wild idea after another, but none of his suggestions worked. Leks could brandish his leg just fine when he sat or lay on the mat, but no matter how hard he tried, he could not remain standing without it.

"Well, that's annoying," Mikhandor said at the end of their training, "but this is just not working. I'll have my technician look at that leg of yours, and see if he can come up with some clever ideas. We are going to need every advantage we can get."

"So, what's going on, exactly, if I might ask, Sensei?"

"Oh, you may certainly ask, but I'm afraid I cannot answer your question. Not here. Not now. We can't risk being overheard."

"Sounds dramatic." Leks pulled a face.

"That's because it is dramatic. And even more so than you could imagine. Trust me on that."

"So... I provide you with a spy-proof room, and I get to hear the whole story. Deal?"

Leks led them into his office, closed the blinds, locked the door, and put out the lights. In the pitch dark he activated a secret door, which led them into a low, narrow passage. So narrow, Bel couldn't even enter with her chair, so Niels was forced to carry her on his back, because Leks was too old and disabled, and Mikhandor too big.

After several turns and more secret doors than he could count on the fingers of one hand, they entered a small room with four blind walls, a desk, a bench and two simple wooden chairs. The space was lit by one bare, unornamented lightsphere.

"Absolutely safe." Leks sounded pleased with himself. "No technology in here. No windows, almost impossible to find, and no hiding places. It don't get much better than this, my friends."

Mikhandor nodded. "This is perfect. You're already proving to be a very useful fellow, Leks. Very useful indeed."

"The story. I gave you my room, so now I get to hear the story. That was the deal."

In an instant, all eyes were locked onto Niels, and he hated it. Being in this cramped room with four smelly people, on this uncomfortable bench with Mikhandor's shoulder touching his, only exacerbated his discomfort.

Niels rubbed his clammy palms on his pantaloons. He closed his eyes, only to open them again immediately. His heart was beating wildly in his chest. The stench of human sweat made him wrinkle his nose. The heat radiating from Mikhandor's body made his skin crawl.

"What do you need to know?" It came out more peevish than he intended. If only he could make this stop. He didn't want to talk.

"Everything." Leks leaned back in his chair, took off his leg, and laid it pontifically on the table. It was a gesture that spoke louder than words. "You could start by telling us who's so eager to kill you. And why."

Niels shook his head. "It wouldn't make any sense to you."

"Tell us anyway. Who and why."

Erl's balls! That man was annoying. Niels bit his tongue in an attempt to prevent himself from growling like an enraged manewolf. Involuntarily, his hands balled into stiff fists.

"King Hanassan of Ebaru. Because the man is insane." It was true, though his madness was only part of the reason why he wanted Niels out of the way.

"What?" Bel's voice sounded about an octave higher than usual. "The king of Ebaru? But that's absurd! I don't understand this."

Niels let out an annoyed breath. "That's what I said."

"But Niels, how? How does he even know you? As far as I know, you're just an ordinary priest. Or...?" She bent forward and glared at him. "And you said you grew up in Darsrijck."

"See? I told you. You cannot make sense of this unless you know everything. From the very beginning. It's a long and complicated story." Niels stared at his fingertips. His stomach cramped. "And I hate talking about it."

"More than getting yourself killed?" Leks toyed with the long braid of his beard. He stared at Niels from behind his sardonyx-rimmed spectacles.

Niels breathed heavily. He kept silent for a few heartbeats longer. Then, still looking at his hands, he began telling his story.

"I was born on the twelfth day of First Moon 9720, in the capital city of Ebaru. Not the part you know from the vidisphere and magazines, where the people wear silken robes, the streets are paved with gold, and the sun radiates brilliantly from the white marble palace walls and their golden-roofed towers. That was not the Ebaru my mother knew."

CHAPTER SEVEN

FATED

daughter
of agony
heritage of heartbreak
ancestral perspective observes
the pledge

The Ebaru my mother knew was a forgotten place, where crime and narc abuse ran rampant. A place where people lived in ramshackle huts that hardly provided any shelter from the suffocating heat by day or the predators that roamed the nights.

My mother died within hours after giving birth to me. As far as the young lady who was my primary carer before my adoption could tell, my mother had no living relatives left. She did, however, wear a priest's medallion, which indicated that she was a priestly daughter. The moment I was born, I inherited that medallion. Though useless to my mother, it saved my life; something for which I have not always been appropriately grateful.

Shortly after my first birthday my new parents, Gijsbregt and Aleid Bosch, took me home with them, to a cold Dorhedde, where the snow lay ankle-deep on the streets. It can't have been easy for them, those first turnings with me. Not only was my health still delicate, but soon it became apparent that I was different from other children my age. Quieter, and more serious. Easily overwhelmed. It didn't seem to matter to them. They simply tried to find ways to accommodate my needs.

For as long back as I can remember, I was plagued by dreams and visions so vivid it felt as if I were physically drawn into them. Most often they featured a delicately built young woman with long black hair, bronze skin, and eyes as azure as the ocean. Her lips were curved just like mine. Though I did not know her name, I knew who she was. She wore my medallion.

As far as I could tell, she lived alone in an old building with a leaky roof and walls that had partly collapsed. The place was dirty, pest infested, and littered with empty liquor bottles, used syringes, and other objects I couldn't even identify.

Sometimes, the visions would show her parading down a run-down, dimly lit street at night, talking to slick gentlemen dressed in perfectly tailored suits or flowing, colourful robes. Occasionally, one of these men might take her to his home, but more often, she would go with them to a small, dilapidated pavilion in the nearby park, or maybe join them in their vehicles. It always ended the same. Her coming out alone, and crying. Though too young to realise what was going on, I could easily see that whatever it was, broke her heart — and I was convinced I felt her pain as acutely as if it were my own.

The visions I dreaded most, however, were those where she entered this abandoned temple. She looked different. Bald patches showed on her scalp. What little hair she still had, fell in lustreless strands alongside her hollow cheeks. Her stained, tattered dress pulled taut around her swollen abdomen, and she stumbled several times before she collapsed on the cold stone floor of the building. There, in that holy place, at the foot of a statue weathered with age and neglect, I was born. A young woman dressed in a simple orange kaftan took care of both her and me, but despite this lady's best efforts, my mother died that day.

I never spoke about these visions. They were a private thing that I didn't wish to share with anyone, not even with my parents. But they put a heavy drain on my already limited energy levels, and it was not uncommon for me to end up sick and feverish afterwards.

Mama, who had been a paediatric nurse before I was adopted, and Papa, who was a paediatrician, thought my delicate health was simply a consequence of my mother's addiction. I, though too young to really understand, knew by intuition that there was more to it than that.

On my seventh birthday I first went to school. Eager to learn, I had been looking forward to it and had not wanted to wait even a day longer, but school turned out to be one big disappointment. I did not find the intellectual stimulation I'd been hoping for, and was only taught things I already knew; and if that alone weren't bad enough, there were all these noisy, smelly, wriggly children who for some obscure reason seemed to take great pleasure in bullying me. More often than not, when I came home from school, I would hide in my room and just sit there, rocking back and forth in a gentle, steady rhythm until the chaos in my head dissolved.

School wasn't all bad, though, and not all other children were bullies. Shortly after my first day in school, I met the twins Anur and Rasu Amari, who soon became my friends. Through them, I also got to know their father, Shadu, who was a priest.

Because my parents were not religious, I had never seen a priest before and was intrigued by the man. All other men I knew wore shirts and pantaloons, usually paired with a waistcoat and cravat, but the priest wore long blue robes. He was a quiet man, who observed rather than engaged. Most of the time, I would find him seated at their plain wooden dining table, reading from an impressive looking leather-bound book.

I wanted to ask him why he was so different from others. Why did he wear these strange garments, and what was this book he was reading? Was it always the same book, or did he have several of these hefty tomes, and did they all just look the same?

But I could hardly just go over to the holy man and bother him with my childish questions, so I kept my distance, until one day the priest asked me to come along with him to The House of Prayer.

Up until that day, I'd never been inside a House of Prayer, so I had no idea of what to expect. I was so nervous, I could barely breathe. The moment we entered the building, I was overcome with awe. Just off the far wall, facing the entrance, stood the white marble statue of the Goddess, twice the size of a man. A little to its right was the altar with the Sacred Candles that filled the space with their sweet, warming scent. The Fountain of Renewal stood to the left. Its tinkling waters sounded like a hidden waterfall in a primal forest. If I closed my eyes, I could almost smell the trees and the rich, humid earth. It was like nothing I had ever experienced before. Yet, at the same time, it all felt strangely familiar, and deep down I knew: This was where I belonged.

The priest went to the altar, and I listened carefully as he recited the ancient blessings over the Candles. Close by his side, I watched in wonder as he chanted the blessing over the Holy Water, dipped in a finger and brought it to his lips. Finally, he stood in front of the statue, hands raised. He didn't speak, but his words, a prayer for guidance and understanding, resounded clearly in my mind.

"My young brother," the priest said when at last we sat down on one of the wooden benches that stood in rows facing the altar, "I wanted to show you a special item. A holy object."

He pulled something out from under his robes. A golden pendant, that looked like an exact copy of mine. Only, his was attached to a crude black leather string, whereas mine hung from a precious golden chain.

I stared at it for what felt like an eternity, unable to utter a word. Barely able to believe my eyes, I blinked. Was it my imagination, or was his medallion really tugging at my mind?

"You recognise it, don't you, Niels?"

Always vaguely aware of my own pendant's comfortable weight against my chest, I nodded, and fumbled under my shirt. Folded my fingers around the ornament. Warm. It was warm, and an almost imperceptible pulse emanated from it.

"But do you know what it is? What it really is?"

"It was my mother's." My hands went up, down, and sideways in sudden excitement. There was something special about this pendant, but I had no idea what kind of special.

Mama and Papa just insisted that I should always wear it, and never take it off. That was what my carer had told them, back in Ebaru.

I didn't think they knew any more than that, but I had long been sure that this was no ordinary piece of jewellery. Although my parents probably thought that wearing the medallion would strengthen my sense of identity, or something like that, I knew in my heart there was more to it.

"What do you know of your birth parents, my young brother? Do you know their names?"

"No sir, I don't. I was with the ladies of some religious order before Mama and Papa adopted me. They didn't know my mother's name. Only that she was on narcs, and nobody knows who fathered me, but..." I hesitated. I wanted to tell him about my visions, but wasn't sure if I should.

"You've been having dreams and visions, haven't you, lad?" His voice sounded calm and convinced. That troubled me. It was irrational to assume that he knew, and yet I was certain he wasn't guessing. How on all seven worlds was that possible?

"I... I saw her, you know," I blurted out. "My Mama. She was in this really old building, with a statue just like the one in here, and then there was this lady, but she said she was not the Goddess, and..."

A sudden insight made me bob up and down like a bouncing ball. "It was the medallion that saved my life, was it not, sir? And it's the medallion that's been giving me all these weird dreams and things too, right?"

"Yes to both questions, my young brother. The most important thing for you to know about it right now is that this is a priestly medallion. It has certain characteristics that no ordinary jewellery has, and that is why it's so important for you to wear it at all times."

He looked me straight in the eye when he added, "You did know that, eh? That you should never, under any circumstance, take it off?"

I looked down. "Yes, sir. Mama and Papa told me so when I was little. But I don't think they know why. Or if they do, they never told me."

"It is quite complicated and I cannot be more detailed at this moment. I don't want to flood your young mind with more information than you can process at once. But rest assured that I'll tell you more once you're a bit older." He patted me on the shoulder and despite my best efforts to remain calm, I flinched with discomfort.

"You'd better run back to Anur and Rasu now. You came to play with them. Not to be abducted by their boring old father." He winked, and smiled, and I wondered what he thought was so funny. I didn't stay around to find out, however. My friends were waiting for me.

In the sevendays that followed, I kept replaying that conversation in my head. I had been excited about it at first, but the more I thought about it, the more confused I became.

Why had the priest thought it necessary to show me his medallion? There had to have been a purpose to it. And why in the House of Prayer and not just at his home? What was the difference? Why had he wanted to know about my biological parents? How was that important?

Then again, maybe he hadn't really wanted to know at all. Maybe it had just been his way of trying to make me aware of something I hadn't uncovered yet. People could be so hard to gauge.

I hoped he would talk to me again soon, and tell me more. He did not. When I was at his place to play with the twins, he would look at me, a small smile playing around the corners of his mouth, but he never spoke to me. Not about those things anyway. Just practical little things, like at what time I had to be home again.

Meanwhile I was drawn irresistibly to The House of Prayer, and I invariably slipped in there for just a few stolen moments on my way back home. I would remain standing near the entrance, looking at the statue of the Goddess, but never daring to come closer.

Sevendays turned into moons, and the moons became a turning, and still the priest had not talked to me again. Then, on a cold, blustery winter's day, he paid us a visit. I was surprised to see him. He had never come to our home before.

He talked to Mama and Papa for a heartbeat or two before he approached me.

"Niels, my young brother, I noticed you always spend some time at the House of Prayer on your way back home when you've been playing with my boys. If you would like, I could teach you the Holy Tongue, which is still spoken in Ebaru, and a little more about our faith."

I stared at him in disbelief. Was he joking? Of course I wanted to learn more about his faith. I wanted to know all about it. I wanted to be like him. I looked at Papa. Would Mama and Papa approve?

"I already talked to your parents," the priest said, as if he had read my mind. "They think it might do you good to learn more about your religious heritage."

"Oh, thank you, thank you!" I jumped up and down, unable to contain my excitement. "Can we start right now? Please? Will you tell me how to do those rituals with the candles and the fountain? And will you tell me more about the medallion? Please, please, please?"

"Not so fast, young brother. Not so fast." I thought I heard a smile in his voice. "I shall teach you everything I can, but all in good time. Let us start at the beginning: the Creation of the Worlds."

We sat down on the sofa in the living room. My brothers were nowhere to be seen, but I could hear them playing some loud game upstairs, in their room. I heard Mama doing the dishes in the kitchen, and Papa was just leaving to see a patient whose parents had no money to pay for a hospital visit. Papa said they needed medical care too, so he would see them for free in his own spare time.

"Are you ready for your first lesson, lad?" the priest asked.

I watched Papa walk past the bay window, the wind tugging at his blond hair. I looked at my little sister who sat playing with her blocks on the floor in a corner of the room, babbling to herself in her sweet, soft voice. I nodded. I was ready.

"Before the Worlds and their times were created, the Goddess Eylah and Her Divine Siblings dwelled in the boundless vastness of The All, and for an immeasurable era they were happy. But one day, the youngest of the Seven, the Goddess Doruya said: 'My spirit is aching and disconsolate. There is nothing new to do for us here, and every day is the same. We stare at each other's noses and pick silly fights. Why don't we create worlds, to entertain our thoughts and keep us from going to war with one another?'

"The other Siblings approved of their younger Sister's idea, but the God N'kell, the deepest thinker of the Seven, said: 'If we are to create ourselves worlds, we will need to lay down some rules beforehand. Our worlds cannot be mere toys. That would be unfair and cruel to the living beings we would create to inhabit them.'

"And so it was agreed that they would each create one world, to love and take care of. They would give their peoples free will, and the intelligence they would need to provide for themselves. And the Goddess Eylah created the most beautiful of the Seven Worlds: the Human World. Our world. Sor."

It was shortly after my fourteenth birthday, and I was at the priest's residence for my weekly hour of religious instruction.

"Niels, my young brother," the priest said, "the time has come for me to tell you about your medallion. Shall we go to the House of Prayer?"

I was stupefied. It had been seven long turnings, and now he finally thought the day had come to tell me? After all this time, did I still want to know? And what exactly could he tell me today that I hadn't found out on my own yet?

Because I had discovered quite a few remarkable things about my medallion. I already knew, of course, that it saved my life when I was a newborn baby. I also knew it gave me my visions. But I had found other uses as well.

If I concentrated really hard, I could influence moods. Not my own, unfortunately, but those of my parents, brothers and sister. I could listen in on private conversations nearby, which I thought was rather neat. I could store memories in it. I had no idea how, but I could pull them out at will, so I was absolutely certain they were in there.

I followed the priest to the House of Prayer all the same. He was my mentor, after all, and it was not my place to tell him to bugger off and leave me alone, which was what I really wanted right that moment.

After we said the blessings, we sat down on one of the benches.

"The medallion. It is exceedingly special indeed, Niels. It links your past, and the pasts of your ancestors, with your future and that of your offspring. The important memories of all of its previous owners; your fathers, and sometimes your mothers, are preserved in it. As are your own, which I'm sure you have already figured out by now.

"Like me, you are from a generation of priests. I am sure of that, my young brother, but you will need to have your DNA tested in order to have that confirmed. This can only be done in Ebaru, where you were born and where all priests originally came from."

"Why would I want to do that?"

"Have you not been listening, lad? You are from a generation of priests, which means you are destined to become a priest yourself. However, you can only be admitted to the Seminary when you can provide a record that confirms your ancestry.

"Usually, that's as easy as giving the head of admissions a copy of your birth certificate. In your case, that wouldn't suffice, but a specialised DNA test will tell us exactly who your ancestors were."

"Hmm." I nodded. A priest? I could become a priest? That was something I never seriously considered before.

"Now, about your medallion... In Ebaru nobody in their right mind would ever want to even touch one of these medallions unless they were from a family of priests. It would bring them nothing but grief."

"But..." I thought of my precarious health. The bullying. My sense of not belonging.

"I know, Niels. Your life hasn't been altogether easy. You've had more than your share of pain, but that was not the medallion's doing. It saved your life when you were a baby. You already know this. It also helped you to be strong, and become the wonderful young man you are today.

"Apart from that..."

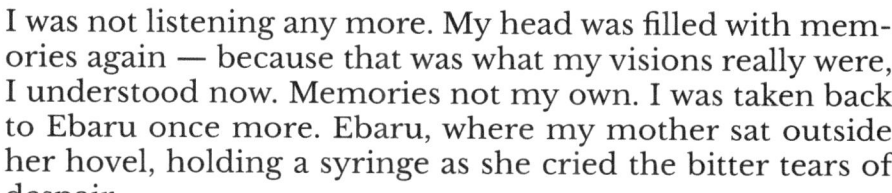

I was not listening any more. My head was filled with memories again — because that was what my visions really were, I understood now. Memories not my own. I was taken back to Ebaru once more. Ebaru, where my mother sat outside her hovel, holding a syringe as she cried the bitter tears of despair.

I was eerily close to her. So close, it felt like I could almost reach out and touch her. She was just a girl. Barely older than me. More than anything, I wanted to take her in my arms and comfort her. I longed to take her pain away and make her happy. It was utterly frustrating to realise that, no matter how real it all felt, there was nothing I could do.

She stuck the needle in the hollow of her elbow and injected a cloudy liquid. The vile stuff looked even more repugnant than I had always imagined. I shivered as I felt the needle pierce my skin and the liquid travel up my arm. As she got up and staggered to her kitchen, I noticed she was with child.

In a vain effort to force my mother's memories back into the medallion, I closed my eyes and buried my face in my hands, but the vision merely shifted and now it made me witness her entering the ancient temple. It wasn't hard to guess what was coming next. I had seen it countless times before.

That day, however, the vision was different. More detailed than before. I saw her totter inside, and crawl over to the statue of the Lady. She clutched her abdomen. Tears were streaming down her cheeks, and her face was contorted in pain.

For a long while she just lay there, on the cold stone floor, moaning softly as one contraction after another made her body double up and cut off her breath.

A young woman clad in a simple orange kaftan and brown leather sandals appeared and held my mother, wiped her sweaty face with a clean cloth and offered her a drink of water.

I shut my eyes even tighter, and started rocking back and forth, trying with all my might to block the vision. I didn't want to see it. It terrified me. It broke my heart. I couldn't bear it.

Then she lay in a bed, washed clean. She now wore a spotless white nightgown. A too small baby slept fitfully in a basket, his breathing irregular and belaboured. The woman in orange sat on a straight-backed wooden chair beside the bed.

"No!" she cried out as my mother took her last gurgling breath. "Don't you die on me. Don't die!"

CHAPTER EIGHT

Gloom's grip

<pre>
            substance
        smothered by doubts
       heir questions integrity
    understanding shared in silence
             restores
</pre>

Strong arms were holding me. I heard the purling sound of water and smelled the delicate, waxy aroma of burning candles mingled with the musky, slightly sweetish scent of human skin.

"Are you alright now, lad?"

I opened my eyes and looked up at the priest. "Why did the medallion not save her?"

He had not been inside the vision — not like me — but he had witnessed everything. I didn't understand how that was possible, but I was sure of it, so there was no need for more words.

"She was the keeper, my young brother. You are the heir, born to be a priest. The moment you took your first breath, her destiny was fulfilled, and she was allowed to go into her rest."

I was broken. Born to be a priest. Who cared?

Who was I anyway? A nobody. An occupational accident and an orphan. A freak who didn't even know how to behave like a normal person. A weirdo with no real family. Born an addict. Son of an addict who prostituted herself so she could get her daily fix. None of that sounded very priestly to me.

I wondered about the man who fathered me. Which one of the many had it been? How had he treated my mother? Had he been gentle with her, or had he hurt her? Had he been a beast, or a so-called gentleman? Even more importantly, would I grow up to be like him? A guy who used women just because he had silvers to spare?

A priest? Me? Not in a million turnings. Not with my background. It could never be. I shouldn't even have been born in the first place. My entire life was one big, cruel joke.

Ever deeper I spiralled into my depression. I hardly left my room. I avoided my parents, brothers and sister as much as possible and spoke even less than usual. I didn't touch, or even look at, my beloved books any more. Though at first I still went to school out of some misplaced sense of duty, I finally stopped doing that too.

Most of the time, I lay on my bed, staring at the ceiling. The vision kept assaulting me, both by day and by night. The vision of my mother birthing me. And dying. Dying, I assumed, from a combination of narc abuse, malnourishment and exhaustion. She was just a girl, and far too young to die. What had life done to her? Why had it treated her so badly? What happened to her parents, my grandparents? Who were they? Where were they? Dead, like her?

In desperation, I attempted, again and again, to unlock their memories, but because I didn't even know what I was looking for, I got nothing. It frustrated me. I needed access to these memories, yet the only ones available to me were my mother's. I didn't want those, but already got them inescapably anyway, so in the end I gave up.

The priest, my mentor, came to see me several times a sevenday, but I refused to talk to him. I couldn't even be bothered to get up from my bed. Had I asked for his pity? Had I asked for anything at all, from anybody? All I wanted was to be left alone. Still more than that, I wanted my misery to end. Forever.

Yet my moody silence failed to put the priest off. Even more stubborn than me, he kept coming. Kept trying to reach me. He would sit his holy arse on my desk chair, beside my bed, and read to me from the Holy Book of Eylah, and I wouldn't even listen.

I knew I hurt him with my behaviour. What was worse, I hurt my parents, my brothers and sister too. They worried about me. I was well aware of that. They wanted to see me happy, but I would not allow them past the invisible wall I had built around myself. No matter how much they all longed to help me, there was nothing they could do.

In the end I didn't even bother to get dressed in the morning. I stopped eating. I didn't bathe, comb my hair, or brush my teeth, and didn't give a pigeon's arse about the smell that soon permeated my room. What was the point? Nothing mattered any more, and I would have welcomed death.

Finally, late one night, I made my decision. I took my medallion off, looked at it one last time, and locked it away in the wooden box I kept in my desk. The priest could take it. I would not be needing it any longer.

"Dragon's breath! You addle-brained sheepskull! You torching tried to off yourself? Were you completely off your stones?" Bel looked as if she was about to spit fire, and her dragonet screeched and flapped its wings.

Niels stared at her. His mouth fell open. What was she so upset about? "I was fourteen, Bel. I had no idea what I was doing, and besides, it obviously failed to work."

"Gods, Niels!" She sounded even more exasperated now. "How can you be so obtuse? This is not about your age, or that you didn't succeed. This is about... Oh, Dragonmother! You stupid, idiot bark eater! You cave cork! I would gladly strangle you with my own bare hands!"

Holy gods, but that woman could swear. And to think she had called him sweary.

"Humans!" Mikhandor's voice sounded commanding. "Peace."

Niels knew better than to argue with Mikhandor when he used the word humans. Bel did not seem impressed, though.

"And who," she said in a voice that could freeze burning oil, "are you really, Mister Muscle, to call us humans and assume that you can boss us around?"

To Niels' utter surprise, Mikhandor started laughing. "You, young Miss Nadinov, are quite adorable when you are angry. And to answer your question, I am your priest's guardian. Appointed by the Supreme Council. It is my holy duty to protect his life with my own. I have to admit, I was rather cross with myself when I found out he had tried to commit suicide."

"This is not the answer to my question, Mig." The emphasis on his name spoke volumes. "And you know it."

"I am sorry, miss, but this is the only answer I can give you right now. Do you want to hear the rest of his story, or shall we call it a night?"

It was late, and Niels was tired. He would give anything to be allowed to go home now. But Bel looked at Leks, and the old man grinned. "I love me a good story and sure won't mind losing some sleep over it. Lemme just go get us a nice big pot of kaw."

I wrote a little note and put it under my pillow.

"I love you. Eternally."

On silent feet I slunk down the stairs, to the bathroom. I knew Mama had been to the pharmacy. She'd had that faint smell of medicine mingled with perfume around her when she entered my room to bring me a cup of tea that afternoon. A smell that lingered in my room long after she had left. There should be plenty of what I needed in the bathroom cabinet.

It was almost too easy. I took all those pills, leaving none in their containers, swallowed the deathly cocktail with half a glass of water, and went back to bed again. There, I lay listening to the darkness for a moment, half fearing Mama or Papa would come upstairs, but nobody seemed to have heard me, and all remained silent.

Soon, my eyelids became heavy. I fell asleep, content and at peace.

I woke up in a strange environment. The bright white light hurt my eyes and I closed them again immediately.

"Niels, Niels!" A sweet, gentle voice called from what seemed like another world. Something warm and soft brushed my cheek. A delicate, feathery touch.

I shivered. Not with cold, but something else. Something I could not define. My brain was foggy, and slow.

"Niels, please, wake up." The little voice sounded so desperate, I had to open my eyes again. Despite the hurt and the blinding light.

A small face hovered over mine. Sad blue eyes stared down at me.

"Machteld?" It was no more than a whisper, but it was the best I could do.

"Niels, please don't die. I love you so much." She started to cry and I tried to reach out to my sister, but my hands were too heavy, and I couldn't move them.

"I love you too, Machteld. Please don't cry," I whispered. Exhausted by the effort, I closed my eyes.

Later, it could have been days, or just hours, I woke up again. It was night and the room was dimly lit. The silence was only broken by the low humming of the machines that stood by my bed.

My mouth was dry. I wanted a glass of water but was too weak to be able to sit up in the hospital bed, let alone get out of it to get myself a drink. And even if I had the strength, how would I do that, with all those drips, lines, and whatnots dangling from just about every part of my body?

"You should never have taken it off, Niels." The priest handed me my medallion. "And leaving it in your desk like that was extremely careless of you. What if your sister had picked it up?"

His voice was calm. Too calm. I knew he was angry, and that scared me. I had never seen him angry before.

Earlier that morning, I had been transferred to the Dr Lubinn Institution, and now I sat on the floor in the hall of the ward, doing nothing. Until my visitor arrived.

"I apologise." I couldn't bring myself to look at him.

"Were you completely out of your mind? What were you thinking, boy? You had no right to do that." The words came out in a low growl. "What of your parents? Rembrant and Kasper? Machteld? Your friends? All the people who love you?"

One of the other patients, a giant of a man with a mob of unruly, almost white hair, looked at us in a funny way before he grabbed the newspaper and left the hall, and for a moment I wished I could have gone with him.

"You didn't care about the pain you would cause all of us, did you? You never thought of anyone but poor, poor Niels. Wallowing in self-pity! That doesn't become you."

"I apologise." I kept staring at the floor. "Honest, I do. It's just that... I... it all felt so pointless. And I hurt so much inside." I still did.

"That, my young brother," he said as he sat down on the floor beside me, "is why you should have talked to us. We were there for you. Your father and mother. I. Your brothers. Your friends. Even your little sister in her own way. We all wanted to help you carry that burden, but you wouldn't let us."

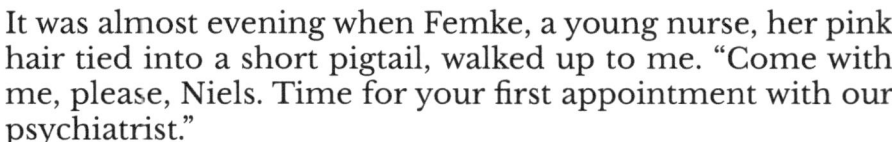

It was almost evening when Femke, a young nurse, her pink hair tied into a short pigtail, walked up to me. "Come with me, please, Niels. Time for your first appointment with our psychiatrist."

An illusory fist clenched around my stomach. I held my breath as I pushed myself to my feet.

"Nervous?" Femke's voice sounded too cheery. "There's no need to worry, Niels. Sebben is a sweet, gentle man. You'll see."

I watched her heels as I followed her through a long, drab corridor that led into an equally gloomy square hall with several doors facing it from all four walls. She knocked on one of them, and within a heartbeat a thin, weaselly man opened the door.

"Niels Bosch?" he asked in a voice so silky it sent shivers of disgust down my spine. I looked at Femke, hoping she'd take me back to the ward again, but she only smiled at me, and nodded before she retreated and left me alone with him.

"Come in, young man. Take a seat, and let's get to know each other."

The next moment, I was alone with him. He closed the door and sat down in the chair across from me. "My name is Sebben Dansinger," he said — and I struggled not to let it show just how much that velvety voice of his upset my senses. "Do you know why you are here?"

Unwilling to answer, I crossed my arms in front of my chest.

"Niels?"

"Because those daft pills failed to do their job," I muttered through clenched teeth.

"Is that how you see it?" Rat-face sounded amused. Or at least, I thought he did. "What should they have done?"

Did he really want me to spell it out for him? I snorted. "What do you think?"

"It doesn't matter what I think, Niels. This is about you. What do *you* think they should have done?"

"I think I'm done talking to you."

"As you wish. I'll take you back to your ward." He sounded so calm and in control, I wanted to tell him to get his arse humped by a Northern Bear.

"You what?" Bel's voice cracked. "Niels!"

"I didn't say it out loud." He shrugged.

"But... that's so rude! Even just thinking it. This man was only trying to help you."

"I..." he broke off. She was right. She usually was. "I was just a boy, Bel. Confused, angry, and scared."

He shrugged again, spread his hands, and looked up at her for the shortest of moments. He cleared his throat before continuing his story.

I had been in hospitals before. They were all the same. The Dr Lubinn Institution, however, was unlike any of them, and that scared the blazes out of me. Those first few days at the Lubinn, I mostly sat on the floor, watching my surroundings in an effort to make sense of it all. I studied the comings and goings of the ward. Took careful measure of both staff members and other patients. Who was safe? Who was not?

Though at first I felt small, scared and intimidated, I soon discovered that things weren't quite as awful as they appeared. Insanity wasn't as crazy as it seemed, and life at the hospital wasn't nearly as horrible as I had expected. In a strange sense, it was better than life outside.

With all the madness going on inside, the hospital was a safe haven from the hostile sanity of the world outside. The visions would come and go like they had always done, but at least now they didn't upend my life as much as they used to. I never had to pretend to be strong when all I wanted was to curl up in an out of the way corner and wait for the world to come to an end. No need to keep up appearances. Nobody in the madhouse did.

The mornings were for therapy, and we usually had the afternoons to ourselves. Mama and Papa visited me on El-day, with Machteld and Kas. Rem showed up at least twice a sevenday, right after school, and Anur and Rasu weren't afraid to come visit me either.

Priest Amari usually came to visit me in the mornings. The Priest's Privilege, he called it. We would talk about the medallion, the visions, and my deceased mother. Oft-times, I felt like he really understood my pain. But more than that, he helped me by just being there for me. Even when I didn't want to talk, he was still there. He knew how to respect my silence and listen to the words I did not say.

The first of my fellow patients to approach me was a stout woman with long red hair. Jolijn was her name.

I sat on the floor, quietly minding my own business when she stood before me, running the tip of her tongue slowly across her lips. She let her gaze wander down my body, until it came to rest on my crotch. I suppressed a shiver. What did she want from me?

"Got rum?" She bent over and breathed into my face. Pulled her chemise down her shoulders and waggled her ample bosom. When I tried to look away, she got down on her knees and leaned in even closer. She grabbed my hands and made me touch her.

I shuddered. This couldn't be happening. Where were the nurses when you needed them?

"I know who you are, matey," she crooned. She pulled up her skirt and crept closer still. Before I fully understood what was happening, she had already climbed onto my lap, and was riding up against my thigh. My head swam, and my heartbeat pounded in my ears. I wanted to get up and run away, but found myself paralysed with terror. Forgot to breathe.

"That delicious caramel skin of yours..." She licked my cheek. "Those delightful golden eyes. You are a prince. And you're mine. Kiss me, my prince. Kiss me."

I closed my eyes and pressed my mouth tightly shut, but to no avail. She planted her lips firmly on mine and pried her way in with her tongue. I gagged, and my pulse raced, but despite my repulsion, my body reacted to her unwelcome advances.

Betrayed by my own body. My initial shock turned into a rage so fierce, I lost myself in it. With a strength I didn't know I possessed, I shoved her from me. She smashed into a chair, which clattered to the floor. Jolijn fell on top of it, and started screaming. Almost immediately, several nurses came running.

Shaking, I sank down to the floor, folded in on myself and started rocking back and forth, humming Papa's song. From far away, Jolijn's ludicrous cries of "he's my promised one, the noble Ishvat's secret son," drifted into my ears. I kept rocking.

"She's mine!" a male voice roared. It shocked me right back into reality. Mig, the white-haired giant, burst into view. "I am King Erlirond of Farlandia, and I've come to claim my bride." He dropped his breeches and sprang forward, completely naked. "Her father, King Vexx of the Rough Seas promised her to me when we were both little. She's mine."

He made a wild grab for her, but Femke stepped in front of him, and said, "Not now, Mig. I need you to come with me first." Mig growled at her, but she stood firm. He puffed up his chest, and growled some more. Another nurse, a big bloke, stood beside Femke and stared Mig down.

Jolijn hissed and shook her fist. She turned around, pulled up her skirt all the way to her waist and bent over, showing her bare bottom. "You can kiss my arse, Mig. I'll marry the little prince."

"The dogs tell me he's no prince at all, Lijntje." A balding guy with a large mole on his nose joined into the mess of a conversation. "He's just a harlot's son, like that impotent husband of yours."

"Oh, bugger off and get your pickle sucked by your precious dogs, Ilias. You pathetic little killjoy."

"Enough now, people," the big nurse said. "I'm giving you a choice. Either you back down, or you'll spend the rest of the day in seclusion. What's it gonna be?"

Ilias was the first to leave the scene. Then Jolijn strutted away, hips swaying as she went. Finally, Mig picked up his breeches and put them on again. He walked past me, and retrieved his shirt before he flopped down on the couch. For just a moment, he caught my eyes with his, and winked. Then, he grabbed an old newspaper from the table, and started reading. Weirdos, all three of them.

I got up too, and went in search of Sofieke.

Sofieke, with her sixteen long auburn braids, olive skin, emerald eyes, and exotic dresses. Sweet and shy, she kept herself apart from the others. As far as I knew, she never spoke. She just sat on the floor, in an out of the way spot, and stared wide-eyed at something only she could see. Listened, or so it seemed, to something only she could hear.

Quiet, gentle Sofieke. I wanted to take her in my arms and hold her. I wanted to protect her from the monsters that inhabited her private little world — but deep down I knew I would only scare her if I would even try to touch her. So I just sat down beside her.

Not knowing what to say, I asked the standard question most people seemed to like so much. "Are you alright, Sofieke?"

She didn't react. Not at first, anyway, but after several heartbeats the unexpected answer came. "Same as always, Niels. But how are you?"

Her voice was softer and higher than I had imagined, and its beguiling beauty made my entire body tingle. For the second time that afternoon, my pantaloons felt too tight. My face hot with embarrassment, I pulled my knees up to my chin and wrapped my arms tightly around my legs.

"I..." I closed my eyes. Swallowed. "I don't really know."

Another long silence. Then a whispered, "I saw what she did to you. Makes you feel dirty, eh?"

My breath stuck in my throat. How did she know?

"It's not your fault, Niels. Sebben told me so. It wasn't my fault."

What was she trying to say? It felt important, but I didn't understand.

"Sofieke?"

I looked at her, wanted to ask more, but she'd already shut off again. She was trembling, her head buried in her hands, and I knew her private demons were torturing her once more.

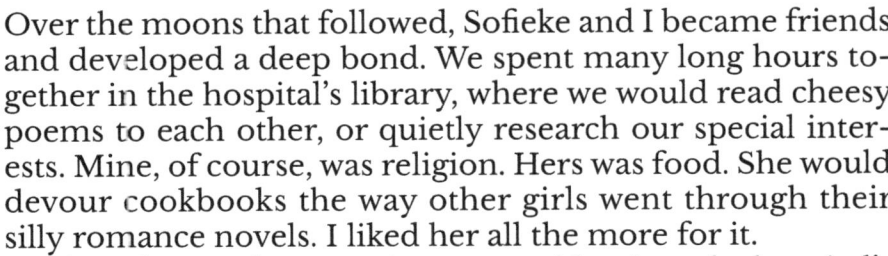

Over the moons that followed, Sofieke and I became friends and developed a deep bond. We spent many long hours together in the hospital's library, where we would read cheesy poems to each other, or quietly research our special interests. Mine, of course, was religion. Hers was food. She would devour cookbooks the way other girls went through their silly romance novels. I liked her all the more for it.

When the weather was nice, we would go into the hospital's enclosed garden, where we sat in the shade of the trees, or walked around idly. We needed no long conversations to understand each other. Our shared silences brought us closer than words ever could.

By the end of that summer, I was sure we were meant for each other. Then, one grey autumnal morning, she failed to show up for therapy.

CHAPTER NINE

Crisis

brutal
charges of guilt
spark violent thoughts of death
imprisonment brings rare comfort
from grief

At first glance, I didn't see her, but when I opened the door further to step into her room, something heavy thudded against it. I turned and saw the most horrible thing I had ever seen.

My breath caught in my throat. I gasped. "No! Sofieke, no." Though I was screaming inside, the words came out a choked whisper.

I grabbed her around the legs. Warm. They were warm. And soft. Not dead then, I told myself. She's not dead. With all the strength I could muster, I tried to take her down, but she was too heavy. I renewed my efforts. She was not dead. She couldn't be. Not my Sofieke. Not the girl I loved.

"Sofieke, wake up. Please, say something!" I shook her. Nothing happened. "Sofieke, please!"

"Your fault," a voice in the back of my mind accused me. "You should have cured her with that fancy trinket of yours."

"Niels, come with me." It was Femke. What was she doing here? Had she come to take me away from my Sofieke? I wasn't going to let that happen.

"Too late, you loser," the voice taunted me. "She's dead now. Dead-dead-deeaaad, ha-ha! Ha, ha-ha! Serves you right, you piss parsnip!"

"Niels." Femke again. Why didn't she just shut up? Could she not see that I needed to save Sofieke? Even if she were dead, I could bring her back. I was sure of it. I only needed to pull my medallion out and —

"You need to come with me, Niels. There is nothing you can do here." Femke's voice sounded even more urgent now, but I was determined to stay.

"Sofieke," I whispered. Tears stung behind my eyes. "My sweet Sofieke." I brought one hand underneath my shirt, and closed it around the medallion. I could do this.

Femke grabbed my wrist and tried to pull me away from Sofieke. I resisted, but she intensified her grip, apparently determined to thwart my plan. Did she not care? Something inside me snapped. I jerked myself free, and struck her side, punched her in the face. I hit, I kicked. I growled, I snarled. I roared.

Exhausted from the fight, I sank down on the floor. I was shaking over my entire body. My throat was sore from screaming. My heart was racing. My clothes were damp with sweat. Angry tears ran down my cheeks. Femke, Sebben and two bulky blokes stood looking at me, all four of them panting. As I looked at them, I felt like a caged animal, waiting for its chance to escape.

"I shall give you something to help calm your nerves a little, Niels." Sebben sounded a bit shaken, but not angry, and for the first time in all these moons I wondered if I might have misjudged him. He almost sounded as if he meant well. Maybe, just maybe, I could trust him.

"Femke, Tempaz, 5 standard units, IM."

Femke nodded and left the room. Within moments, she was back with a syringe, containing some suspicious-looking liquid.

I started fighting again. How could I have thought for even a moment that Sebben might not be all that bad? My mother died of that stuff. Were they trying to kill me? Was this so-called hospital secretly in league with a body farm?

I lay on a bare mattress, wearing nothing but my smallclothes. There were no sheets, and no pillow, and the rough blanket felt scratchy against my skin. The walls and floors were of a rubbery green material that had a distinct and unpleasant odour. In the corner of the room stood a lidded bucket. A few rags lay on the floor beside it. The high window, protected by a metal grate, was so tiny not even a cat would have been able to escape through it.

"Niels, how are you now?" Sebben hunkered down beside my mattress. His voice sounded deeper than usual, and almost reassuring, but he couldn't fool me this time. Injecting me with that nasty stuff. I couldn't trust him, that much was abundantly clear. Shifty bugger.

I shrugged. Did he really think I was going to talk to him? After what he'd done to me yesterday? If it even was yesterday. I might as well have been out for a sevenday or longer. "Tired, and I have a headache."

"That may have been brought on by the Tempaz I've had to give you yesterday. It's quite a common side effect."

In the silence that followed, he kept looking at me, as if trying to read my mind. Slippery snakefish. "But apart from the headache and fatigue, Niels? Do you think we could safely let you out again?"

Even though he didn't specifically mention it, I knew he was referring to the fighting. Odd, how he didn't even sound angry. It made me all the more suspicious.

"I guess so." I stared at my fingernails. "I... I never fought before."

"We can talk about that later today. In the meantime, don't beat yourself up over it, young man." He stood up and took two steps towards the door.

"I'll ask Femke to let you out now, so you can wash and get dressed."

Before I could say another word, he left, and locked the door behind him. The sounds of the ward indicated that it was probably somewhere around the second hour of morning, and I was nowhere near ready to face the day and the horrors it would bring.

The next day, Sofieke was buried, but I was not allowed to attend her funeral. My moods fluctuated wildly, and because of that I was supervised by one of the nurses at all times. I was never alone, anywhere. They even stood watch in front of the door when I had to use the facilities, and if I took too long, they would unlock the door and embarrass me by coming in and asking if I was alright.

Every night, I was locked up in seclusion. It didn't matter. Unlike Jolijn, who would scream her throat sore to be let out every time she was placed in seclusion, I would just lie down on my hard, bare mattress, cover myself with that itchy blanket and close my eyes. I had no tears, and no words to express my grief. I was numb.

Oddly enough, there was something calming, almost comforting, about the bare cell that had become my temporary bedroom. Ever more frequently, when the everyday hustle and bustle of the ward overwhelmed me, and I felt yet another breakdown coming on, I would ask one of the nurses to lock me up in there. Then, I would curl up in a corner and rock as hard or as gently as I needed, until my head cleared.

Like before, I withdrew into myself. Even though I couldn't physically get away from the people around me, nothing could stop me from locking up inside. I would spend most of my days sitting cross-legged on the floor, blocking the world out. The voices of the others became a distant mumble. A noise in the background.

My memories, bittersweet reminders of the time I spent with Sofieke, were always on my mind. They were all that

I had left, and even if I'd wanted to blot them out, I could not. They haunted me by day, and filled my dreams at night. Over the past few moons she had been my reason to live, and now that she had died, my life seemed empty and meaningless again.

Like before, I wanted to die, but this time there was no escape. Besides, I didn't even have the energy to come up with an actual plan. Exhausted with sorrow, all I wanted was to sleep both day and night. Sleep, and never have to wake up.

The staff, however, were relentless. They dragged me out of bed every morning. Made me wash and dress myself. They threatened to tube-feed me, should I refuse to eat my three meals a day. Took me to therapy, and to my stupid talks with Sebben. All of it so incredibly futile. Nothing could ever make life worth living again.

The hospital, once my refuge, could no longer shelter me from the cruel reality that made my life ever more unbearable. Now, it was just another place where Mirk's demons could torture me and delight in my despair. If only I could leave, and hide somewhere truly safe.

Autumn turned into winter, and life dragged on. Day by dreary day until, impossibly, one morning during a group therapy session, Sebben and the nurses were called away on an emergency. Without thinking, I dashed out of the room. I had no plan, just the need to escape. This was my chance. I would not pass it up.

The first few corridors were empty, and soon I was safely in the oldest part of the building. That gloomy section where the constant stench of urine and old people made my stomach queasy. It was the home of Drivelling Diede, and Pieneke Pee-stain. Running here would get me noticed, so I kept my head down and shuffled along like all other patients in this depressing place. Meanwhile, my heart beat so loudly in my chest, I feared everyone could hear it. Every time I saw a small group of nurses approach, my heart skipped a beat, but no one took a second look at me, and nothing happened. Finally I reached the old servant's entrance and slipped outside, unnoticed.

I walked away, still careful not to attract any undue attention, but when I turned a corner I heard a man yell my name. Fast footsteps came closer and, without even a glance back, I started running. In blind panic I raced as fast as I could, as far as I could, until my side hurt so badly I collapsed on the pavement.

My heart thumped wildly in my chest. My breath came in short, ragged bursts. I heard the blood pumping in my ears. My feet ached. The soft drizzle that fell down from the sky and had already soaked my clothes didn't let up. As I looked over my shoulder, searching for my pursuer, I shivered. To my relief, the street seemed deserted. I rubbed my arms in a feeble attempt to drive out the clammy cold that seeped into my bones.

The sound of a small twig breaking, and fallen leaves being disturbed, made my heart skip a beat. Who was that, in the bushes? Was that mysterious guy still after me? Unnerved, I got up and walked a few paces, but my side still hurt, and my feet were killing me. A large stray dog burst forth from the thicket and jumped at me. Its wet tongue lolled out of its mouth and dripped saliva on my shirt.

"Sorry, dog," I said as I patted the beast's head. With its soft brown eyes it looked up at me, and I wished I could take it with me. I could do with a friend. "I have nothing for you. And I cannot stay to play with you either." I stroked its matted fur once more, then forced myself to move on. I could not afford to remain in one place. The city guards were probably already informed of my escape, and would be on the lookout for me. I was, after all, a dangerous lunatic.

How I ended up at the cemetery I didn't know, but I was not surprised. Was this not the place where I needed to be? Soon, I found the spot where Sofieke lay buried. Overcome with grief, I fell down on her grave and started clawing at the cold, black, humid earth. All I wanted was to dig her up and bring her back to life.

"Sofieke!" My voice was thick with unshed tears. "Come back to me! Please, Sofieke, please!"

"Niels."

I looked up, my mind deluded into thinking I would see my love again, but it was the priest, Shadu Amari.

"Niels, my young brother, what's this? You shouldn't be here, lad." He stood beside me, and held both hands out to me. I grabbed them, and allowed him to pull me up. Gently, he led me away from Sofieke's grave.

He took me to his bungalow, where he told me to sit down on the couch.

"I think we need to talk, Niels," he said. "But first I should let the hospital know you are safe here, with me. I won't be long."

While he was on the *portadire*, his wife Saryda brought me a cup of tea. It smelled funny, and I wrinkled my nose at it, but she smiled and said: "It's a special herbal tea, Niels. Just drink it. It will make you feel better."

Suspicious, I took a small sip. It didn't taste bad. As I drank it, a nice, soothing warmth spread through my body and made me feel better than I had in a lifetime.

The priest sat down beside me. "Tell me, Niels. What is this all about?"

"Sofieke." I fidgeted with my fingers. "She's still there, you know. At the hospital, I mean. I can hear her. See her, feel her, smell her. It's driving me crazy. I start to talk to her, only to realise she's not really there. I..." I shuddered. The memory was almost too much. "I see her hanging there again."

He said nothing as I struggled to hold back the tears.

"Please, don't make me go back."

"Don't worry, lad. I won't." His voice sounded reassuring. "But, in all honesty, this is going to be a bit of a problem. You're still so troubled, and so many issues in your life need to be addressed. It's not just about Sofieke. There is so much more at stake.

"We had hoped the hospital would be a safe place for you, where you could find firm footing, but..." He sighed. "I'll ask your parents to come over, and then the four of us will figure out what to do."

Mama and Papa came, and they talked for what must have been hours. I simply listened most of the time, and only spoke when I really had to. My head was too full of thoughts that flitted around in random order. It all went so fast. This morning, I woke up in my cell in the hospital, and now I was here. Free, apparently. I still couldn't believe it.

"The medallion Niels has been wearing since his birth," the priest said, "what do you know about it?" He looked at Mama first, and at Papa next.

Papa took a sip of his tea. "Not very much," he said after a short silence. "His carer said it was a family heirloom, and he should never take it off. Not even when bathing."

"Yes." Mama made a funny face. "It was special and would protect him, his nursemaid said. But we should try not to touch it, because it might bring us bad luck, or some such gibberish."

The priest got up and walked over to his bookshelf.

"That's the, uh... abridged version, and I can see how that doesn't make much sense to you." He took a small booklet from the shelf and sat down again. "What if I told you I wear a medallion that is an almost perfect copy of his? And, moreover, that all priests have one?"

"How so?" Papa looked at the booklet in Priest Amari's hands.

"It is, in fact, a priestly medallion. Doesn't the boy ever tell anyone anything?"

Mama laughed and shook her head. "You've been mentoring him for what? Seven turnings? Eight? Surely, you must have noticed he's not exactly talkative."

Not exactly talkative. Not exactly talkative. I mimicked Mama's words silently inside my head. What was it with people always wanting me to sarding talk — even when I had nothing to say?

"That's one way of putting it." Something in the priest's voice caught my attention. For a mere moment, I looked at him in an effort to read his face. Was he annoyed? Amused? I couldn't tell.

"Anyway," he continued, "like I said, it's a priestly medallion, and that means your son comes from a family of priests, and is himself destined to become a priest."

"A priest? You can't be serious!" Mama's voice had this telltale metallic ring to it, as if she were angry, or upset.

"I'm sorry to spring all this information on you like this, but these are things you need to know. I should have told you before, but I mistakenly believed Niels would tell you himself." My mentor heaved a sigh.

"These medallions, all of them, contain a trace element of the Divine, which grants them certain unique characteristics. Regrettably, I'm not at liberty to discuss these with you. But if you wish, I can lend you this booklet. It deals with the history and uses of the medallion, and was written for the non-clergy." He held the booklet out to my parents and, eventually, Papa took it from him.

"Unfortunately," the priest said, "I have so far been unsuccessful in teaching Niels how to control his medallion. He needs someone more competent than me, and the sooner the better."

Papa shook his head. "I will read your book, Shadu. But a medallion with divine properties, however minute… well, that is stretching my imagination."

"I understand that, Gijs. But his lack of control is a major contributor to his current condition. Believe me on this."

"What do you propose?" Papa might not understand, but he would do as my mentor suggested, provided it was not too outrageous.

The priest remained silent for a moment. He looked from Papa to Mama, and from Mama to Papa. He stroked his beard.

"This is asking much, and you won't like it," he finally said. "My good friend Akdi Erumin is not only a kind and caring man, but also an extremely gifted and capable priest. He is the current High Priest, and I'm sure he would be more than willing to guide Niels through this difficult patch."

"The current High Priest." Papa sounded doubtful. "Does that perchance mean he lives in Ebaru?"

Shadu held out his hands in what looked like an apologetic gesture. "That was the part you were not going to like. It is, however, his best chance to heal. Completely — unless I'm very much mistaken."

Papa looked at Mama, who didn't seem too happy either, but she shrugged, and then nodded. Papa sighed. "If that's what it takes, then so be it."

Nobody thought to enquire after my opinion. This was my sarding life, and here they were making all kinds of perfectly horrible decisions. Conspiring to send me off to the very last place I wanted to be. Trying to get rid of me, as if I meant nothing to them.

"Sod that!" I banged my fist on the table. "I don't want to go to Ebaru. I don't pissing want to go anywhere!"

"Niels." The priest just looked at me and said nothing else, but I could hear his thoughts inside my mind. Unspoken words that said I knew he was right, and I would go to Ebaru, even though my entire being rebelled against it. My shoulders sagged under the crushing weight of his message. I covered my ears with my hands — as if that could help at all — and started rocking back and forth.

Then Papa's arms were around me, just like when I was little. Safe. I was safe with Papa, who still loved me. I rocked harder, and Papa with me. Nobody spoke, and the silence felt like a small present from the gods.

CHAPTER TEN

Flight

<pre>
          draken
       wings sail into
     endless days of summer
and futures unknown where pasts wilt
            away
</pre>

The next two sevendays went by in a blur of activity. So many things needed to be done. I needed identification papers. Inoculations against several tropical diseases. Mama insisted on buying me a new wardrobe, and a travel bag. I had to choose which books to take with me, and which I should leave behind. It was a hard choice. I wanted to take them all, but that was not possible. Papa joked that their combined weight would crash our draken, but I didn't think that was funny at all.

On the day of my departure, the sixteenth day of Second Moon 9735, I woke up long before sunrise. I checked my bag. Took a piddle. Checked my bag again. Went downstairs to see if Mama was up yet, but the kitchen was empty. I grabbed a roll of bread, then decided I wasn't even hungry, so I put it back in the bread bin. An iron fist clenched around my stomach as I looked around the kitchen. How long would it be before I'd be back? I trudged up the stairs. Checked my travel bag a third time. Fell down on my bed and lay staring at the ceiling until I heard Mama call my name.

We had breakfast as a family. For the last time. I couldn't eat. Machteld couldn't eat either and climbed on my lap. She rested her head against my chest and her little hands inched their way towards my medallion again. She never really touched it. Not directly anyway, and as it always grew just a little bit warmer at her almost-touch, I saw no reason to discourage her.

"I don't want you to go, Niels," she said.

"I know, and I don't like it either, but we don't have a choice, little one." I stroked her soft blond hair. Gods! I was going to miss her. Rem and Kas too, of course. And Papa and Mama. But her most. My sweet little sister. I blinked a few tears away. No use being a baby.

Shortly after breakfast Priest Amari came, and Papa called for a *karrosse*. Too soon, a sleek black karr stopped in front of our house, and the driver, a woman in a fancy maroon uniform, rang our doorbell. Hasty goodbyes were said and before I knew it, I sank down in the luxurious black leather back seat. Dazed. My mentor took his place beside me, the driver closed the doors, and we were on our way.

Just before noon we arrived at Valkenbergh International Drakenport, the largest drakenport on the entire Briscan Continent. I'd looked it up on Papa's Logatome several hundred times in the last few days, and memorised its entire layout. I knew where all the shops were. The restaurants and lunch rooms. The facilities. The Pass-and-Enter. It didn't help me any. The knot in my stomach would not uncoil.

We sat down on a hard, cold metal bench in the central terminal area, the priest and I. He retrieved a lunch box from the smaller of his two bags and offered me a roll. I declined. Even though I hadn't eaten at all yet, I was still not hungry. I hugged myself tightly, and hummed a silly little tune as I rocked back and forth. Back and forth.

When people kept staring at me and I realised what I was doing, I scolded myself for being such a turnip, and forced myself to stop rocking. Instead, I wriggled my toes inside my shoes. That, at least, didn't attract any unwanted attention. I scanned my surroundings. Tried to get my bearings. I pulled at the priest's sleeve.

"Please, can we go and watch the runways?"

He looked at me for a moment before he nodded. "Sure, lad."

We took our bags and walked the few yards to the glass wall that looked out on the runways. Several drakens, some larger than others, stood waiting for their next flights. Their wings lay flat against their carbotanium bodies, and their eyes were closed. Mechanics scrambled around, checking the aircraft for any possible defects. Flight personnel entered a middle-sized purple draken and not long after, the machine opened its eyes, unfolded its wings and taxied off to one of the runways.

After what felt like an eternity we boarded our draken. Our seats were near a window, and as the draken lifted off into the air, flapping its wings, I settled back into my comfortable chair and closed my eyes. I didn't need to see the land that I used to call home disappear from view, and figured I might as well try and get some sleep.

It didn't work. My curiosity got the best of me, and I watched in a mixture of dread and wonder as the coastline slowly disappeared from view until at last there was only water below us. Miles and miles of deep, dark, cold water. As far as the eye reached.

A steward served us a drink, and asked if all was according to our wishes. I wanted to tell him to bugger off and mind his own business, but of course, this was his business, so I bit my tongue and kept my mouth shut.

Not even an hour later, the same steward served us a meal. Again those questions. Were we comfortable? Did we enjoy our meal? How did we like the flight so far? Was there anything else he could do for us?

No, I was not comfortable at all. And how did he expect me to enjoy any sort of food, when my stomach was tied into a big knot of despair? How, indeed, did he imagine I could even begin to appreciate the flight? I hated it. All of it. But it would be rude to speak my mind aloud, so once more, I bit my tongue and kept silent.

After our meal, the priest took his travel copy of the Holy Book out of his bag. I watched him read for a while, then decided I should follow his example. We were stuck in this gods-accursed draken for the next eleven hours or so, and since I couldn't sleep anyway, this would at least give me something to occupy my mind.

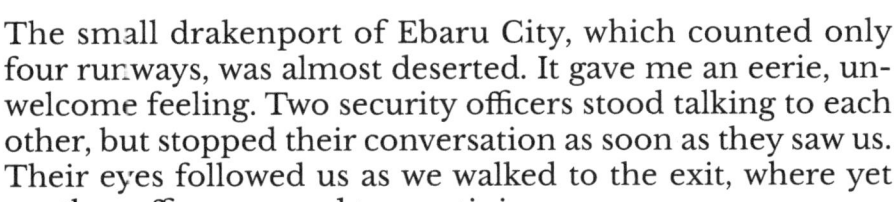

The small drakenport of Ebaru City, which counted only four runways, was almost deserted. It gave me an eerie, unwelcome feeling. Two security officers stood talking to each other, but stopped their conversation as soon as they saw us. Their eyes followed us as we walked to the exit, where yet another officer seemed to scrutinise our every move.

As we stepped outside, the bright sunlight hurt my eyes. Already, I felt homesick. Never had the cold dark gloom of a wintry Darsrijck seemed more attractive. I longed to see thick white snowflakes dance in the air. To feel the icy frost bite my nose and ears. But here in Ebaru it was high summer. A perpetual summer.

"Shadu, my friend." A tall, angular man in black ceremonial attire embraced my mentor.

"Akdi. Look at you. Not a day older than last time we met."

"Is that your boy?" The High Priest threw one hurried look at me, and didn't bother with pleasantries. "We'd better get home as quickly as we can. It is not prudent to hang around here for any longer than we need to."

"What's going on, Ak? And why the black robes?"

"Haven't you heard the news?"

"What news? I've been up in the air for some time, my friend."

"Of course. Well, it's nothing short of disastrous. The royal family was assassinated last night. All of them, with the notable exception of Prince Hanassan, who will be our new king."

"No! You can't be serious!" I saw the blood drain from my mentor's face.

"It's been all over the news ever since we woke up this morning. See for yourself." He gestured at the vidisphere. Then he turned and looked down at me. "Young man. Niels, is it? I hear you've been adopted. Do you know who your biological parents are?"

I shrugged, and pretended I didn't care. I was tired and hungry, and my too-hot clothes clung uncomfortably to my sweaty skin. "I saw my mother in my dreams and visions. She left me the medallion."

"And your biological father?"

Why was the high priest more interested in that horny goat than in my natural mother? Wasn't my mother's line the most important one? She had been the daughter of a priest. He was just some licentious beast.

"I don't want to talk about him. He's just an animal. A loser, who took advantage of my mother. I don't even want to know which one of them it was. Nor do I ever want to see him. That lecher is not my father. My father is Gijsbregt Bosch." I turned to watch the news broadcast on the vidi.

A young lady stood in front of the Royal Palace, talking about the tragedy that took place last night. She talked to passers-by and tried to interview a liveried servant as he exited the gates, but the man shook his head and hurried on his way.

Back at the studio, portraits of the late king, his queen, the princes and princesses, their partners and children were shown. Twenty of them in total. All killed. Preliminary findings suggested they were poisoned, the medical examiner stated.

Then Prince Hanassan was interviewed. As soon as I saw his face, I knew. I had seen him in my visions, but never realised how much my features resembled his. And, seven hells! Even his voice sounded like a fully adult version of mine.

CHAPTER ELEVEN

Manifest

> hidden
> key opens door
> to darkness quelling aches
> protector's skills cannot handle
> lightly

Niels took a deep breath and closed his eyes. "My worst nightmare had just come true."

"You mean..." Bel sounded befuddled. "You mean King Hanassan of Ebaru is... he's your..."

"The man ejaculated his semen into my mother and impregnated her. Yes." He needed to go home. Now.

"Ona's tits! Imagine that. What are the chances? You're a —"

"Shut up!"

He could take it no more. The onslaught of his memories. Too vivid. The unwanted attention of Yeleksim and Beldenka. The ever increasing sweaty smell that hung in this sepulchral room. The oscillating light of that single sphere. It was too much. He stood brusquely and fled, driven by just one thought: home.

"What was that?" Bel stared at Niels' empty seat in exasperation. "And how do I get out of this room now?"

"To answer your last question first, Miss Nadinov, I shall have to carry you." Mig's face betrayed no emotion. "It's going to be uncomfortable for both of us, but I see no other option. And to answer your first question, I'm assuming Niels got a little overwhelmed and felt he needed some time alone. He will be fine."

Bel had her doubts. He was a sensitive guy, that much was quite clear by now. She would have to check in on him. Tonight, no matter how late the hour. She couldn't afford to lose another priest. Three of them in as many turnings was more than enough.

"So he's a prince?"

"Yes and no." Mig scratched behind his ear. "He is His Majesty Hanassan's illegitimate son, and since the man has no legitimate children... it's a bit complicated. The real problem, however, is that the king doesn't seem to like competition, whether it be real or imagined."

So that was why Niels was on King Hanassan's hit list. Poor bastard. And if Niels was a prince, even if only unofficially, then Mig was no ordinary Transient.

"You are an Erl." She had already spoken the words before she realised her mistake.

"We prefer to be called Sylphans, but yes." To Bel's relief, he didn't sound angry. "How did you figure that out?"

"Easy enough. I read all of my father's best books when I had just lost the use of my legs." She gave him her sweetest smile. Sylphan. She had to remember to never call him an Erl again. Not when he could hear it, anyway. They could be a bit touchy about that. "Besides, you really are tall. Taller than any man I ever met before."

"Unfortunately, there isn't much I can do about that. It's a good thing most people aren't as observant as you."

"So can we finally know your real name now?"

"If you insist. It is Mikhandor, but please, just keep calling me Mig. It makes me stand out less. I'm sure you understand the importance of that."

She nodded. "Mig it is, then. But it's good to know who's behind this name. I guess I don't get to ask how old you really are?"

"You just did, but I'm not answering that question. Maybe try again in some two hundred turnings or so." He stood and stretched. "Time to go. Ready, Miss Nadinov? And you, Leks?"

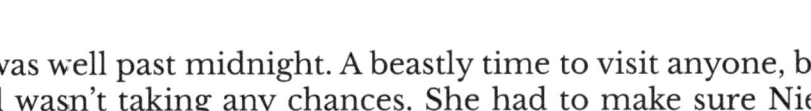

It was well past midnight. A beastly time to visit anyone, but Bel wasn't taking any chances. She had to make sure Niels was alright. She knocked on his front door, but no answer came. The cottage was shrouded in complete darkness, so he might be asleep already. Could she risk waking him up?

Could she risk not waking him? If, indeed, he were sleeping?

She knocked again, louder now, and more insistent. Still nothing happened. Bel felt a knot form in her stomach. She wasn't going to lose this one. He was young and strong. And, dragon's breath, she liked him.

There was no helping it. Good thing she still had that key. She fished it out of one of her hidden pockets, unlocked the door and, as she entered, lit a lightsphere. She would not sneak around and take him by surprise.

"Niels," she called. "Niels, are you awake?"

No answer.

She entered the living room and lit another sphere. "Niels?" She didn't see him. Not on the sofa, not at his desk, and neither in the kitchen. She was about to knock on his bedroom door when she heard an almost indiscernible noise. She had no idea what it was, but it was definitely there.

Her eyes searched the living room again, and there he was. Huddled up in a dark corner. Motionless. Head on his knees, arms wrapped tightly around his legs. She rolled over to him, lowered herself out of her chair and sat down beside him on the floor. What was she to do? Should she say something? Touch him?

Tentatively, she reached out and laid a hand on his arm. A sharp intake of breath indicated that this was probably not the best thing to do. Oh, fangs! Now what? She couldn't allow him to withdraw into himself like that. Not after everything he'd just told them. No suicides here. She wouldn't put up with that kind of stupidity. One way or another, she had to get through to him.

"Niels?"

"Go. Away."

Two one-word sentences? What in the Dragonmother's name was that about? And if he thought she would just leave him, he was wrong.

On her bum, she slid closer to him and, wordlessly praying this was the right thing to do, she wrapped her arms around his torso and held him in a tight embrace.

He groaned. His muscles stiffened, but she didn't let go. Instead, she began humming a tune her mother used to sing to her and Lin, when they were little. She rocked him to the rhythm of the song, as if he were a mere baby. It was the weirdest thing she'd ever done, but surprisingly, he seemed to relax. Slowly. Little by little.

For how long they sat like that, she didn't know. It didn't matter. She needed Niels to be his ordinary self again. Her clever, sexy and sweary priest. Not this pitiful wretch, who was clearly unable to engage in even the most basic of human interactions.

"Thank you," he finally said. He sounded exhausted.

"Are you well now?"

"I will be." His expression was completely blank. Bel didn't like it at all, and was far from convinced.

"Do you need anything? A drink?"

He shook his head. "Just sleep. And... holy gods! But you should be home, Bel, sleeping. Why are you even here?"

"I was worried, you sheepskull. Go get some sleep. I'll go home now and sleep too. We talk tomorrow."

She rolled out of the room, turned her head and looked at him one last time. "Are you sure you'll be alright?"

He nodded. "Positive. Now go." He sounded almost like himself again.

"What happened last night, Niels?"

They sat in his living room again, two cups of fresh nettle tea on that ugly crate he used as a table. What was it with men and their complete lack of interest in interior design?

He didn't answer immediately. Instead, he started toying with his tassels, a distant look in his eyes.

"I, uh..." he paused. Looked down at his fingernails. "There was too much going on."

"Too much going on?" That didn't make sense. It had just been the four of them, in a bare, soundproof room. And, apart from him telling his story, there had hardly been any talking at all. Granted, his story was a grim one, and what he'd gone through would have been enough to mess anyone up, but still. His reaction seemed extreme.

"The memories, Bel." He put a hand on his chest. "I can't expect you to understand. You're not a priest. It is the medallion. It..." He bowed his head and rested it in both hands.

Bel resisted the urge to scratch her head. She just couldn't comprehend what had caused yesterday's breakdown, or whatever it was. Grown men didn't hide in dark corners. Grown men didn't speak in one-word sentences. He'd seemed so miserable. And now, looking at him, she saw that same agony again, only this time without the peculiar behaviour. It broke her heart.

"Niels?" She wanted to lay a hand on his arm, but last night's events had taught her he might react adverse to that. There was so much she didn't understand about this man. He was unlike anyone she'd ever met before, including his predecessors. Reticent to the extreme, yet sensitive and empathetic. Probably more intelligent than anyone she knew, but at the same time he seemed completely oblivious when it came to human interactions. She just couldn't figure him out. "What did you think you were you doing, hiding in that corner, curled up like a little boy?"

He lifted his head and produced something that almost looked like a smile. "Maybe you could just forget about that. It's humiliating, but I couldn't... couldn't... It's like, uh... I guess you could call it sensory overload or something."

He hugged himself tightly. "This wasn't the first time, and neither will it be the last." His voice faltered, and he hung his head. "If I'm lucky, I can find a place where I can hole up until the storm inside has run its course, and nobody will witness it."

"Was that why you ran away? So you could break down in private?"

"Yes. My father... did I tell you he's a paediatrician? He, uh... he said some children just were like that. Seemed to react to things differently. As if they felt everything more acutely than others. At times, they might explode into a rage, or shut down completely." Again, he started fiddling with his tassels. Always fidgeting.

"He... he also said he'd never seen any of these children grow out of it. The best he could do, was teach them how to cope with their overwhelm and avoid injury."

"So this is what was happening last night?" She shook her head. What was that boarbrain thinking? Locking himself up in his cottage and hiding in the dark, so nobody would know about his inner turmoil. Why would anyone do such a thing?

"That's what Papa taught me. Go to your safe place." He managed a half-baked chuckle. "It grieves me that you had to find me like that. You honestly should not have come."

If she still had the full use of her legs, she'd have stamped her feet. This was infuriating. What was wrong with him? Moreover, what was wrong with her? She never had any trouble reading people. Zilla, sensing her anger, screeched. Bel reached up and stroked the soft fur of her chest.

Easy, girl. He's just being stupid. Not dangerous. I'm not angry with him. I just hate that I can't understand him. We both need to calm down now.

Niels didn't need Zilla's bad behaviour. Or hers. Not now, when he was already so vulnerable.

"Don't be ridiculous," she said. "I was glad I came. I'm glad I could be with you, so you didn't have to go through this alone. You don't have to do this to yourself. And you should not."

"It served me well enough all those turnings."

Stubborn harehead of a man.

He got up from the sofa.

"Sit. Back. Down. We're not done yet, Niels."

What in all seven hells was he thinking? Running away from a much-needed conversation.

"Bel?"

Those eyes of his! All innocent and confused. The uncertainty in his posture. Poor dear. Again, she had to fight off the urge to hug him.

"I'm sorry. I didn't mean to sound harsh, but we need to talk, Niels. We really do."

With a sigh, he sat down again. "What more is there to talk about?"

Where to begin? She bit her lip. Tapped her fingers on her thighs. This was going to be so awkward.

"I've been thinking... all these things that happened when you were hospitalised. And the way you recoil from physical contact... I mean, you really hate it when I touch you. Almost like it scares you."

He shook his head. "I'm not afraid of you, Bel. In fact, I like you. Really, I do. But I just... I don't know. People touching me... it just makes my skin crawl."

"But this is not entirely true, Niels. Because you told us how your dad's embrace made you feel safe, and loved. How this Priest Amari's embrace comforted you. And how you wanted to hold this girl, Sofieke."

Sofieke. Why did she resent that girl so much? It was just a girl Niels had a crush on many turnings ago. A dead girl, for the sake of all the gods. She should know better than to feel intimidated by a ghost.

Niels scratched his head. "But that was different."

"Obviously. And that's what made me think... this thing that this woman did to you... Joline, was it?"

"Jolijn." His voice was devoid of emotion, and his face looked like a lifeless mask. It was all the confirmation she needed. It still haunted him. "I don't want to talk about that."

"Did you ever talk about it?"

He shrugged, and shook his head. "No need."

"Yes, I can totally see that." She scowled.

"Good. We are in agreement then. We should go to the House of Prayer and get some work done."

Bel stared at him with raised eyebrows. How had he not heard the sarcasm in her voice? How had he not seen her annoyed expression? What *was* wrong with that man?

By the time she had collected herself, he had already opened the door.

"Are you coming, Bel?"

CHAPTER TWELVE

Candid

anger
battles pity
as trouble roams the night
the tender opposes the strong
in love

Over the next few moons Niels slowly got accustomed to life in the Barlows. Bel was with him often. Perhaps a little too often to his liking. Not only did they work together, but she seemed to think she needed to mother him. Likely, she had done the same to his predecessors. But he was not them. He needed his time alone to unwind and recharge.

One day, she had come in carrying some impressive tools in a small trailer behind her chair. Niels had been stumped. All his belongings had been unpacked, his furniture assembled, and the cottage didn't show any obvious defects, so why those tools? But she had pointed at his table and said, "That just won't do. I'll make you a real table. Unless you're awfully attached to that ugly thing there."

"No." He'd shaken his head. "It's convenient. I keep some paraphernalia in it, but I can take those out."

So he had taken his things out. The stylo and pocket clock Papa had given him just before he left for Ebaru. The little portrait book that had been Mama's present to him. Rembrandt's handcrafted map of Sor, rolled up and kept safe in its leather casing. Kasper's own compass. And sweet little Machteld's hairbrush and her favourite set of ribbons. "So you'll always have a piece of me with you," she had said.

Remarkably, impossibly, underneath the smoky stench of the fire, they still carried his sister's scent. Or was that just his too vivid imagination?

Bel had quickly taken the crate apart, and transformed it into a real table. It even had a bottom shelf where he could put his current reading material, a scratch pad and some stylos. He loved it. It looked so much better than the crate.

Combat training, three nights a sevenday, had become very much a social affair, with Bel and Leks always there too. Though Niels would have preferred training with Mikhandor alone, this certainly had its benefits. Despite his disability, Leks was strong, agile and resilient, and his turnings of combat experience showed. When sparring with him, Niels had to keep his wits together, or the old man would best him. Bel, although she'd never had any training before, was born to be a fighter. She was incredibly fierce, as she had already shown on that first night, and certainly made good on her unspoken promise that she would be a worthy opponent.

Things got even more exciting when the new wheelchairs and Leks's special prosthetic arrived. Those things were true masterpieces of technology. The chairs were so light, even Bel could lift them one-handedly, from a seated position. And not only that, but she could throw her chair wherever Mikhandor told her to, and did so with obvious delight. Then, she would lunge into a forward roll towards the chair, grab it and launch it again. The thing easily cut through wooden planks, and could withstand all the abuse Bel put it through, without sustaining any real damage. The same held true for Leks's chair.

Leks's new leg was a veritable piece of art. Custom made according to Mikhandor's specifications, it was as strong and lightweight as the chairs, and had several unique extras. A detachable dagger was integrated into it, as well as a smaller throwing knife, and a modest baton. All of them practically weightless, yet effective and durable, Mikhandor and his technician asserted. Made from the strongest, yet lightest material in the All.

Leks would, of course, have to adapt his clothing for easy access to his new weapons, but the old man ensured the others that would not be a problem. He had been a private investigator, back in Ingravia, he said, and still knew all the tricks of the trade. It made Niels wonder, was the man perhaps still a secret agent? After all, why would an ordinary gym owner need a secret, soundproof room? And was it not just a little too coincidental that both he and Bel had ended up here, in the sleepiest part of Briscona? What made the Barlows so attractive to Lord Natoniev Nadinovik?

Apart from combat training and Bel's constant fussing over Niels, nothing much happened. There were, of course, the daily Prayers and Offerings, Niels' visits to the sick and elderly, and his weekly hour of religious instruction to a mere handful of children. Finally, Niels had landed his dream job, and he would have given anything for this to last forever. But deep down he knew he would be lucky if he could remain hidden here for any longer than just a couple of turnings. Sooner or later, King Hanassan's spies would find him, and then it would be a matter of days before the assassins came for him again.

Often, he would lie awake at night, agonising about what would happen then. He worried, and not only about himself. More than that, he feared for Bel. Sweet, enchanting Bel, with her dark hair, delicate face and flawless, ivory skin. As annoying as she could be, with her apparently deeply felt need to baby-sit him, he liked her.

She was easily the most wonderful woman he'd ever met. Intelligent, musically gifted, and confident. But even more than that, she understood people. She seemed to instinctively know how to deal with his awkwardness and peculiarities. With her, he didn't feel like he had to play pretend. He didn't want to lose her.

What if the assassins targeted her first? What if they tortured, mutilated and finally, once they got tired of their grisly games, killed her? The thought alone was enough to make his stomach somersault.

Those were the nights when he had to put in conscious effort to block the visions that connected him to his biological father. The visions in which, Niels knew, the poor mad king was out in the streets of Ebaru, looking for his son, his firstborn. Looking for him, and howling in despair when, once again, he could not find him. Despite the anger he still felt towards the king, Niels couldn't help but pity him. In his heart, he knew he really only wanted to heal him. And maybe he could, if only the risks would not be so disproportionate.

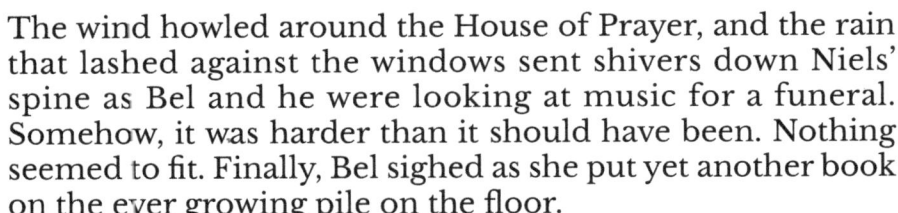

The wind howled around the House of Prayer, and the rain that lashed against the windows sent shivers down Niels' spine as Bel and he were looking at music for a funeral. Somehow, it was harder than it should have been. Nothing seemed to fit. Finally, Bel sighed as she put yet another book on the ever growing pile on the floor.

"Niels," she said, "My mother will be performing in Freyborough several nights next sevenday. I'd like to take these days off, so I can go to the concerts."

"By all means, do," Niels said. "It won't be a problem. I am sure I can manage without you for a couple of days." That was a lie. He'd come to depend on her expertise and guidance more than he liked to admit.

"After the last concert, my parents will be coming home with me. They'll probably be staying for a couple of sevendays. It's been a while, and we have a lot of catching up to do. There is even this very slight chance that one of my sisters will be able to join us."

Niels nodded, and tried not to let his confusion show. Why did she tell him all of this? Her private life was none of his business.

"I think you should meet them. You and your friend Mig both."

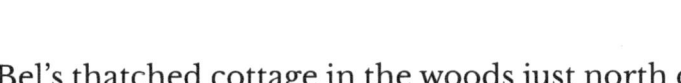

Bel's thatched cottage in the woods just north of Upper Barlow was as charming as the woman herself, but Niels hardly noticed its quaint beauty. His hands were clammy, and his heart beat furiously in his chest. He dared barely breathe as he trudged down the path towards the bright red front door.

Mikhandor had, of course, agreed with Bel that they should meet her parents. In fact, he'd been downright eager to meet the pair. Eager! Sarding Erl.

Niels wasn't happy about it at all. Mirtalya Grigonov was a cold-blooded killer and Natoniev Nadinovik a ruthless criminal. He had absolutely no desire to meet them. These were the people who hadn't even given their own daughter a wheelchair when she needed one, but instead sent her away to a foreign country and told her to never come back home. It stood in shrill contrast to how devastated his own parents had been, when they had been forced to let him go to Ebaru.

He'd tried to get out of it, of course, but both Bel and Mikhandor had insisted that he should come. Hells, even old Leks had taken their side, so here he was. With dragging feet and a pounding head, but he'd been given no choice. He lifted the elegant dragon-shaped door knocker and struck it twice against its copper plate.

"Come in, Niels." Bel's short curls danced around her face, and her smile seemed even brighter than usual. She was dressed in a long maroon gown. Quite a change from the breeches she normally wore.

"Bel, you look absolutely enchanting."

"Thank you, Niels. You don't look half bad yourself either." The smile she bestowed on him made his heart skip a beat, and he felt the colour rise to his cheeks, but she didn't allow him any time to dwell on his self-consciousness. "Everyone else is already here. Follow me."

She rode swiftly to the living room, and Niels marvelled at how easily she manoeuvred her chair and managed to keep her dress from getting entangled in the wheels.

The first thing he noticed upon entering the living room was the large portrait of Bel and a handsome young man presenting a wedding orb. Bel looked no older now than she did in the portrait. But where was the husband? What was his name? His occupation? And why did she never talk about him, or about her marriage? Come to think of it, had she not told him once that she lived alone?

Leks and Mikhandor sat on one of an identical pair of red velvet sofas. The other sofa was occupied by Bel's parents.

Natoniev wasn't anything like the shifty, hook-nosed ruffian Niels had imagined. He was a slim, elegantly dressed man with a friendly, open face. His dark chestnut hair with the one silvery grey lock at the forehead suggested he was in his early fifties. Nothing about him said *dangerous criminal*.

Bel's mother was even more breathtakingly beautiful than her performances on the vidisphere suggested. Her long ginger hair, diamond shaped face, and porcelain skin gave her a dainty, almost ethereal look. Yet something about Mirtalya made Niels uncomfortable. This was not a woman to trifle with.

Like her daughter, the violinist had a dragonet perched upon her shoulder, and the little thing appeared to be as possessive about her as Zilla was about Bel. It also seemed quite interested in Bel's pet.

"Papi, Mumi, this is Niels Bosch, my new priest." The couple rose from the sofa. "Niels, meet my father, Natoniev Nadinovik," the man inclined his head, and Niels did likewise, "and my mother, Mirtalya Grigonov." The famous musician curtsied almost imperceptibly, and Niels bowed ever so slightly.

"Elderberry wine?" Bel poured the deep red liquid from a crystal decanter into a silver goblet, which she handed to Niels.

"Niels, you are the interesting young man," Natoniev said in a thick Ingravian accent. "I hear you are on list of King Hanassan's assassins. And yet you not fight it. You run and hide, although this already proved ineffective. Why?"

The Ingravian lord certainly didn't waste time on pleasantries. Though the subject made him uneasy, Niels found it refreshing to not have to talk about inane futilities like the weather.

"I am a priest, milord." Just because he could fight, didn't mean he had to. It was a priest's duty to protect lives. Not to destroy them.

"First, you cannot forever hide behind the priesthood. Unless, of course, you like being prey, and because of you see friends and family die. If this is really your choice, then why deny you such pleasure?" His warm bass sounded almost amused, "and second, stop milord nonsense. Toni, the friends call me."

"I'm just a…" Niels stopped mid-sentence. How could he say Lord Nadinovik was not his friend without offending the man? "I am honoured that you would consider me your friend, mi... uh, Toni."

Natoniev smiled. "Friends of my little dragon, my friends."

Little dragon? Was that his nickname for Bel? That was an entertaining thought. It was fitting. Not only was she always accompanied by her dragonet, but she had rather the temper too. He could easily picture her sprouting wings and breathing fire.

"I..." Niels searched for the right words, but there were none. "I don't know what to say. Beldenka is... she's an extraordinary person. She is precious."

"That her." Natoniev beamed. "We proud of her. If only other lords could understand! They so near-sighted."

Mirtalya nodded vigorously. "But we can, of course, use their superficiality to our advantage. If we did not, we would be fools and unworthy of our titles." The woman's graceful accent and suave inflection made her sound almost harmless. She took a sip of her wine, then let her gaze rest on Niels. "And you, young man? How serious do you take your duties?"

"Very seriously, mi..., mi..." Gods! He couldn't possibly say milord, but she would certainly not appreciate being called milady. Why was Ingravian culture so weird? So contrary?

"Call me Mir, Niels." Her smile looked just like Bel's. "You say you take your responsibilities very serious. And yet you allow your father's killers to destroy those who are dear to you. I am afraid I'm not a very smart woman, because I do not quite understand this. How I see it, this seems irrational."

Niels stared at his wine as he swirled it around in its goblet. What could he say? The way she presented it, his behaviour did appear at least a little foolish. But was it? He couldn't make his mind up.

"One more question, if I may." Mirtalya's gaze lingered on him and made him squirm. "How are you going to protect my daughter?"

"Mumi!" The vehemence in Bel's voice surprised Niels. "I can protect myself. If anything, Niels needs *my* protection. He is too tender-hearted by far. And for what it's worth, I don't think he is even capable of being irrational. Just because we don't understand his reasoning, this doesn't necessarily mean his conclusions are invalid."

"Allow me to enlighten you." Mikhandor sounded so sure of himself, Niels could almost kick him. "There were indeed several compelling reasons for His Holiness not to fight. Some of these still apply. One of these reasons was that we did not have the right people to help us. We are dealing with an extremely dangerous man here, who has this world's best assassins at his bidding."

Natoniev leaned forward, his smile even wider than before, and Mir sat up just a little bit straighter. The dratted woman almost purred as she said, "Sounds good, does it not, my kitten?"

"My treasure," Toni rumbled in his deep bass, "I'm playing game if you are. But first let us ask the guy. I think he should have say, right?" He poured himself another drink and topped up his spouse's goblet without asking. He held up the carafe and nodded at Niels. "More?"

Niels didn't even get the chance to object.

"So, what will you think, boy? Solving your little problem, you want our help?"

"I uh," he stared at his fingernails. "That is a very kind offer, but why would you do that? You don't even know me."

If he were completely honest, he had his doubts. Did he really want these people's help? They were Ingravians. What if their help entailed killing King Hanassan? He had no desire to bring about the king's demise. The man was his biological father, after all, and it was not really his fault that he had such a disturbed mind. Maybe Bel was right, and he really was too soft, but all he truly wanted was for the king to get well.

And was that not exactly what the prophecies hinted at, that the Chosen One would be able to lift the curse by curing the king of his illness? The prophecies certainly didn't say he would bring about destruction.

"Young man, how many reasons you need? As said, Bel's friends, our friends. That alone would be enough, yes? Friends help each other. But that not all. With you I will speak frank. Only about our own interests we care. About protecting our daughter. About challenge. Also about honour of us; but you will not understand. You are not Ingravian. Of honour, you have the different view."

"Yes," Mir chimed in. "That is just like Toni says. We do this only for our own benefit. Young man, you are doing us a favour by letting us help you. So what will you say?"

Niels couldn't suppress a sigh. He fiddled with his fingers. "I, uh, I guess, if you put it like that... it would be uncouth of me to refuse, but to be honest, I am a little bit worried. This may seem strange to you, but I don't want the king getting killed."

"Why not in all seven worlds?" Mirtalya's voice went up by maybe half an octave, but Natoniev nodded slowly, as if he truly understood.

"The father of you he is. I understand why you not want kill him. We will find the way to keep him alive by eliminating this danger. I am sure we can think of something. I have the reputation for being creative. Of this reputation I am proud."

"I've seen some of your handiwork." Niels looked at Leks, and shuddered.

"Yes," Toni admitted. "Unfortunate that, but in that situation, no other way out I could see."

It almost sounded like he really regretted what he had done to his old friend, but Leks didn't seem to care. He even chuckled.

"Compensated me well enough, chief. All been worth it."

"Even so..." Toni spread his hands.

"Enough talk for now," Bel said, "I am famished. Leks, would you help me serve supper?"

CHAPTER THIRTEEN

Pursuit

hidden
behind false names
they keep their secrets close
to their hearts as they fight against
whispers

Bel was strict about it. No business talk during supper. That included talk about their expedition to Ebaru, so they were reduced to small talk, in which Niels had no interest whatsoever. His mind wandered to Bel's mysterious husband.

"Bel," he said finally, "what's your husband's name? And how come I have never met him yet?"

Bel dropped her knife and fork. She stared at her plate. Her parents looked from him to Bel and back again. Leks drummed two fingers on the table. Nobody spoke a word.

Had he said something wrong?

"His..." Bel's voice faltered, but she took a deep breath and resumed, "his name was Lastor. He died."

Niels felt like a fool now. Bel must think him a heartless barbarian. "I apologise. You have my sympathy." What else could he say?

"It's alright," Bel said, but her voice sounded choked, and her eyes were brimming with tears. "I should have told you, but..." she shrugged and fell silent.

Niels didn't ask any further questions, and everyone else remained silent for a while as well. Eventually, the idle chatter picked up again, but neither Niels nor Bel engaged in it. Bel looked devastated, and guilt gnawed its way into Niels' gut. What had he done? What should he do now? What could he do?

He wanted to reach out over the table and hold Bel's hand, but that would be inappropriate.

"Bel?" He kept his voice low, and wasn't sure if she'd even heard him, but after a few heartbeats she looked up at him. "I didn't mean to hurt you, Bel. I'm such an utter turnip. Forgive me, please."

"There is nothing to forgive, Niels. You didn't know. The fault is entirely mine." She sounded uncharacteristically vulnerable.

"Still..." He ran his hand through his hair, "I wish I could do something — anything — to make you feel better."

"You're already doing this. You're showing me you care.- That means a lot to me."

When the meal was finally over, and the table cleared, Bel rolled a large map of Sor out on the dining table. "We need to draw up the plan."

Her movements were certain, and her voice as confident as ever. As if nothing had happened. How did she do that?

"We are here." She put her index finger on an unmarked part of Briscona. "Our destination is over there." She placed her other index finger on Ebaru City. "How do we get there, and what's our story?"

"I sure have business in city of Ebaru." Toni chuckled. He seemed eager. Too eager. "Or at least, I will. Soon."

"And I," Mirtalya joined in, "will need an invitation to perform at the Royal Concert Hall. We will need to plan well so that our schedules coincide."

"I say we want Niko to join us. He take my cargo to Ebaru, and you four go with him and his team. Mir and I take the draken. For us, I would not travel by sea. This would arouse suspicion in both kings and commoners."

"Who is Niko?"

"My little brother, Nikomir, who recently got married." Bel sounded excited. She turned her face towards her father. "So I finally get to meet his wife?"

"Yes, little dragon. She never leaves him."

"Good. She'd better make sure he doesn't mess up. He's done enough of that for his lifetime, I should say."

"The girl has a good, solid head on her shoulders." Mir nodded, as if to emphasise her words. "You will like her. But back to business. How does the Niels get inside the palace without dying?"

"First we see how to get this guy to city of Ebaru without losing our heads, right?" Toni certainly had a way of putting things into perspective. "We take care of rest later. Young man, how good do you fight?"

Niels shrugged. "Well enough, I guess. I've been training three times a sevenday with Mikhandor for almost twenty turnings now."

"Starting tomorrow, you train combat at least two hours every day. Those killers of your father's, they are just training every day of their lives, from childhood. You are very lucky if you survive fighting only one of them; and it will happen. This we cannot avoid."

Niels' heart sank. He knew Natoniev was right, but he didn't want to fight. He enjoyed sparring with his friends, but fighting, real fighting — that was something else entirely. And fighting to kill? He didn't even want to think about it.

"I know, boy," Toni said in a fatherly tone. "I too hate the fighting. I know you otherlanders call us crime bosses and think we are the unscrupulous criminals. In truth, we are human beings like everyone. We share same emotions, but we deal with them in the different way. This does not make our task easier, but responsibilities we must fulfil. And you too. Put yourself together and deal with it."

He studied the map again, mumbling what Niels thought might be names and numbers, in his native tongue. Niels was fascinated. What was the man doing?

"Four sevendays." Toni stood back and stretched. "I need four sevendays. Maybe five. It will work for you, Mir?"

Mirtalya closed her eyes. She put her fingertips to her temples. "Let us do five," she said after a short silence. "Just in case. By that time, I will also have arranged something."

"In meantime, you four train as if the life depends on it. For, make no mistake, it is." Toni looked at each of them, one by one, and held their gazes just long enough to make Niels squirm. "You take whatever steps necessary to board Niko's ship after three sevendays. Leks will provide you with identity documents and travel documents you need. It is clear?"

"Clear as the finest *brozka*, chief," Leks said. "Leave it to me."

"I trust you, *korli*. Do not disappoint." It sounded almost like a threat. Warm and friendly though he was, Natoniev Nadinovik was indeed a dangerous man.

They were in Leks's secret room again, discussing their next moves. Niels didn't like it one bit, but he had no choice in the matter. Deep down he had known for many turnings that it would eventually come to this. He had to come face to face with his father, the king. If only that meeting could be postponed by a few more turnings.

"We have three options, and they all have this one thing in common. They suck like leeches." Bel held up a finger. "One: We meet up with Niko in Midhaven. Two: We board his ship in Freyborough. Three: We go all the way down to Tiria, in Tirona. Obviously, my personal preference would be Midhaven, but this might not be our best choice."

"Tiria," Leks and Mikhandor said in unison.

"You two sound awfully convinced," Niels said. "From where I stand, Tiria seems like the absolute worst option. What in all seven worlds makes you think we should go to that gods-forsaken place?"

"Simple," Leks said. "Midhaven and Freyborough are too densely populated. Too easy for spies and assassins to blend in with the crowds. Tirona's about as isolated as it gets. Natives there aren't exactly known for their love of foreigners. Especially foreigners of your colouring. Ideal."

Niels wanted to pull all his hair out, and tucked both hands out of harm's way, under his buttocks. "These things you mention — they are exactly the reason why I think it's a perfectly horrible idea. Those barbarians will want to feed me to the prowlfoxes the moment they see my skin." With difficulty, he managed not to growl. Why couldn't they just use a portal and avoid all of those unnecessary risks altogether? "I say we go to Swartemeer Portal and from there straight to Ebaru."

"I don't think so," Mikhandor said. "And Leks is right. These Tironians may not very much like seeing you around, but as long as you are in our company and refrain from behaving suspiciously, they'll most likely leave you alone. Hanassan's hirelings don't have that advantage. They have every reason to stay well out of Tirona."

Probably. But then again, maybe not. Niels got up and started pacing the cramped room. "I still don't like it. You know how they feel about priests, and Bel will be in constant danger there too."

Mikhandor shrugged one shoulder. "Bel will be Leks's property. That should keep her safe enough. And you are going to be Mistress Beldenka's attendant. Nobody will know you really are a priest."

Property? How utterly demeaning. What was that Erl thinking? Bel belonged to no-one but herself. And if Mikhandor really thought Mirk's priests wouldn't find out who he really was, he was delusional.

"One of their own priests will sniff me out."

"That is a risk we shall have to take." Mikhandor sounded as if it didn't bother him at all. "You will be far better off having to fight their priests than the king's assassins."

"Lucky me." Niels balled his hands into stiff fists behind his back. With some difficulty, he resisted the urge to punch his old friend on the nose. He kicked the unyielding stone wall, and suppressed a yelp of pain. "How absolutely delightful. And what makes you think we could treat Bel as property, or a helpless wretch in need of an attendant? Does she look like she's incompetent?"

Bel laughed. Niels gaped at her and shook his head in bewilderment. What was so funny? And why was that annoying little dragonet of hers cackling along with her? Stupid beast!

"Oh, Niels." Bel wiped her face and took a deep breath, only to start giggling again. "You really don't get it, do you?"

Niels sat down. He buried his head in his hands and sighed. Women! And Erls. He didn't know which of these were more impossible.

"Papi said it the other night, Niels. Leks would give us new identities. Fake identities, my dear, dumb priest." She looked at Leks then. "So what have you come up with, and how does Mig know more than I do?"

"Yes, well..." Leks stared at the three fingers of his right hand. "Migs and I've been brainstorming together. Man's not just a bunch of muscles, you know. He's actually got two or three working braincells as well."

"I'll have you know that it's five," Mikhandor said. His lips curled into a barely visible smile. Bel laughed.

"You, my sweet Bel," Leks continued, "are an Ingravian merchant who got crippled when she was attacked by a gang of brigands. I've been your guard ever since you started your business, and got injured defending you and your wares. That's why you got yourself a second guard now, Migs here. And you've a personal attendant, because you've decided that coming across as a needy invalid could actually be advantageous in your business negotiations."

Bel smiled, and nodded. "Brilliant! Do you have a leash? For when we're in Tirona?"

"A leash?" Niels couldn't believe his ears. "What in Zinnir's name is wrong with you people?"

"Nothing is wrong with us, Niels, but everything's wrong with these Tironians and their creepy religion. Women are not just property there. They are playthings. Being owned by Leks will protect me from being used as a toy by them. The leash is just a symbol that says, hands off of this woman."

"That's... that's..." he didn't have words to describe his shock and disgust, and in the end he shook his head in defeat.

Strangely, Bel didn't seem bothered at all, and continued her interrogation of Leks and Mikhandor. "What are our names? Or have you not decided on them yet?"

"Leks will only need to change his last name, which will be Igrovik, whereas I won't have to change my name at all." Mikhandor sounded rather too pleased with himself.

"We thought the two of you would like to choose your own names. Miss Nadinov?"

"Beldenka is a common enough name in Ingravia, so I'll keep that. As for my last name, uh... Nisandrov would be fine. Mistress Lord Beldenka Nisandrov."

"Sounds good to me," Leks agreed.

Mikhandor just nodded. "And you, Niels? Who will you be?"

"Moradin Salendi."

"Moradin? Do you really think that would be a good idea?" Mikhandor frowned. He sounded sceptical.

"Yes." Niels looked at the toes of his shoes. If he absolutely had to change his name again, he would at least have the name his mother gave him. "Every other boy in Ebaru is called Moradin, so it is no more dangerous for me to be called Moradin than to be called Rasmi, Fatrim, or Nasu."

"As you wish. But..." Mikhandor paused and only continued speaking when Niels looked up at him, "remember this: The king knows his son's name is Moradin."

"Wait, your real name is Moradin? Is that the name your mother gave you?" Bel's voice sounded shrill. "And you never saw fit to tell me? Even though I asked several times?" She hissed at him. Hissed like that pesky little dragonet of hers.

"My real name is Niels. That is the name my real parents, Gijsbregt and Aleid Bosch, gave to me. And you are one to talk! You never told me about your husband, remember?" The moment those words left his mouth, he wanted to take them back. This was low. He didn't want to hurt Bel. Yet, he was sick of her hypocrisy. Always accusing him of being secretive when she was every bit as enigmatic herself.

"Humans!" Mikhandor got up and loomed over them. "Stop your bickering. That is an order." He paused for a moment and looked from Niels to Bel and back again. "We have plans to make, and no time for your silly little quarrels. How do we get to Tiria? How fast can we travel, and how soon should we leave? Remember we want to avoid populated areas as much as possible."

"Fastest way to get from here to Tiria," Leks said, "is to take a multikarr to Midhaven first, then board a draken to Freyborough, and from there hop on an international tunnelrider to Tiria. Would take about one day. But we're not doing that."

He crackled a laugh, and Niels wondered why Leks would think that was so amusing. "Instead, we take my battered old karr and travel the mountain trails. Going to be lots of fun, and will take a sevenday. If we're lucky." He chuckled again.

"Is your karr safe?" Mikhandor asked.

Leks shrugged slightly. "Safe enough. Dirty. Has some dents and scratches, but it's structurally sound. Just looks beat-up, which is exactly what we want. Eight-seater. Large enough to carry our luggage, including the two chairs."

Niels' heart sank. "A sevenday if we are lucky, you said. And if not? Ten days? Two sevendays? Longer still? How will we eat? And where will we sleep?"

"Good questions, chum." Leks sounded far too happy. "You're catching on already. We have to leave, uh... overmorrow, I'd say. I'll bring enough dried food, small cask of brozka, and some mead beer. We sleep in my karr. Or under the stars, if you prefer."

"Overmorrow already? That's almost three sevendays! Surely, it shouldn't take that long."

Too soon. He wasn't ready. Not nearly.

"Is that really necessary?"

"Yes. Overmorrow." Leks sounded determined. "My gut tells me we won't be lucky. Sod's law, young man. Sod's law. Besides, we'll still be training two hours a day. Every day. That gobbles up a bit of time, too.

"You three go to your own homes and get packed now. I'll have our documents ready by tomorrow evening. Only pack what you really need. Leave your portadires behind. We don't need to make it too easy for our adversaries to track us. Oh, and no priestly robes, Niels. Sorry."

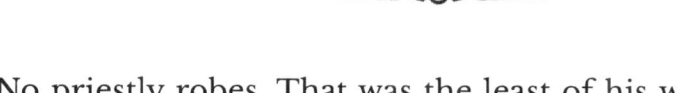

No priestly robes. That was the least of his worries. Those things were dirt cheap in Ebaru. But what about his books? The presents from his parents and siblings? Who was going to look after the chickens? Who would tend his garden? Who would minister to the needs of the people of the Barlows during his absence? His poor little congregation, without a priest yet again — for the gods only knew how long. And if that weren't bad enough, now they would have to do without their cantor as well.

Niels looked at his clothes. How much did he really need to take with him? Two pairs of pantaloons would probably be enough. Two shirts too. Two pairs of smallclothes, and two pairs of socks. Wash one, wear the other. It would have to suffice. He needed to take the Holy Book, and his treasured keepsakes.

No more than one travel bag each. That was what Leks had said. Otherwise, there wouldn't be enough room for the wheelchairs and the food they needed to bring. Even so, it was going to be cramped in the karr. The thought alone was enough to make Niels want to hide in a dark corner, curl up into a ball and close his eyes. Forever. Or at least until his friends had left without him.

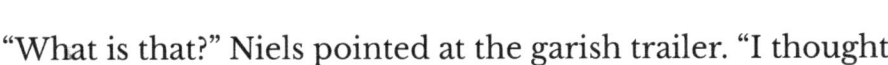

"What is that?" Niels pointed at the garish trailer. "I thought you said we didn't have room for much luggage."

"That, young man, is no luggage." Leks puffed out his chest. "Them's our wares."

"Our wares? What do you mean, wares?" He could not keep the annoyance out of his voice.

"Yes chum, wares." The old man certainly knew how to sound condescending. He lifted the flap of the monstrous thing. "Travelling merchants, remember? Our Mistress Beldenka is hoping to trade these exquisite Ingravian rugs, fine Antorian linens, superb Risian weaponry, and beautiful Briscan leathers in Ebaru. She also plans to pick up some Tirone bone art, which is currently quite in demand in Ebaru."

Niels' mouth fell open. Everyone could see that the contents of the trailer was worth a small fortune. How could Leks even afford that? Or was this Mikhandor's doing? He looked at his guardian, but the Erl shrugged and shook his head.

"I had nothing to do with that, your Holiness. I'm just as surprised as you are."

"Efficient communication goes a long way." Bel lifted her chin. A smile played around the corners of her mouth. Holy gods! But she looked breathtaking in that beguiling dress that accentuated every curve of her body. Niels swallowed. He wiped his suddenly clammy palms on his pantaloons as he tried not to stare at her bosom. "Papi approved of our plan and promised to make sure we had some convincing merchandise."

"But how?" Niels still could hardly believe his eyes. Collecting these goods from Ingravia, Antoria and Risium should have taken close to two moons already, and sending them over to Briscona another couple of sevendays. Yet, it hadn't even been two full days.

"He's got his contacts." Bel sounded unimpressed. "Are we about ready yet? The sooner we're out of here, the better."

CHAPTER FOURTEEN

Fare

> cautious
> night time travel
> shelters the innocent
> where dragons' kin pursues her prey
> and kills

Leks drove like a maniac, and now that they were on this narrow mountain road, Niels was even more worried than before. He couldn't understand how the man managed to keep his karr and the trailer from plummeting into a ravine, but so far no accidents had happened. Yet.

What was worse, the man was singing. Loudly, and very much out of tune. It hurt Niels' ears, and he was sure Bel couldn't enjoy it either. She was a professional musician, after all.

To exacerbate things even further, bush fires had destroyed all vegetation in this part of the mountains two turnings ago, and though some of it had grown back, nothing provided any shade. There wasn't a single tall tree. Just some small shrubbery and the occasional sapling. As the summer sun neared its zenith, the heat became unbearable. The sour smell of four sweaty people and a filthy dragonet did nothing to improve Niels' mood. How on all seven worlds he was going to survive this journey and preserve his sanity, he couldn't fathom.

"Are you alright, Niels?" Bel asked in a whisper.

"Just tired." She meant well, he was sure, but he didn't want to talk. Not now, when he was already overwhelmed.

"Zilla tells me you are lying."

"Holy gods!" That little pest. "Your dragonet doesn't know anything. It's just a pet, Bel. Besides, dragonets can't even speak, so I would say you are the one who's lying." He sounded more aggravated than he intended.

Bel shook her head. "You are wrong. Zilla is much more than a pet. Dragonets have telepathic abilities, Niels, and believe it or not but Zilla has taken a liking to you. Right now she's worried." She was silent for a while, then ordered Leks to pull over at the next pass-and-rest area. "I've got a headache and need some fresh air."

"Sure thing," Leks said. "Wouldn't mind stretching these old legs either. And resting me eye for a bit."

"You know what?" Mikhandor patted Leks on the shoulder. "I could do the driving. I've got two good legs and eyes, and I actually enjoy it."

Niels knew the latter was a lie, but managed to keep his mouth shut. Mikhandor was a good driver. If Leks thought he was doing Mikhandor a favour by allowing him to drive, that would be much better. For all of them.

Bel asked Mig to get her chair out, and the Erl hastened to do her bidding. Everyone seemed eager to get out of the karr for a while.

"Walk with me please, Niels," she said. She needed to get him away from the others. The poor man looked perfectly miserable, and she wanted to know why. Such a pity Zilla couldn't read his thoughts.

"Do you need my help? Should I push your chair?"

"No, you silly." She laughed. He could be so adorable. So innocent and childlike. It made her want to hug him, and ruffle his hair. "This is no harder than a cobbled road, and I navigated plenty of these back in the Barlows."

"Oh." He said nothing else, but just walked quietly alongside her chair.

It was funny how, unlike most people, he didn't appear to feel that need to fill silences. In fact, he seemed to enjoy them. But they didn't have time for his reticence now.

"I need you to tell me what's going on. You are obviously not feeling well, and I need to know why — and how I can help to keep you from going to pieces while we're on the road. It's going to be a long trek, you know."

"I said, it is nothing." His voice sounded flat, and his face was an expressionless mask. "I told you, I am just tired."

That stubborn git! It drove her crazy. "And Zilla already told me you are most definitely not feeling well, so out with it."

"Bel, I..." His movements became jerky, and his voice sounded panicked. "Nothing. Leave. Me. Alone."

What was it he'd said again, that night, when she had found him huddled up in the darkest corner of his living room, hiding like a terrified child? Something about sensory overload. Was that what was happening now?

"You're getting overwhelmed, aren't you?"

He nodded.

"What can I do to help you cope?"

"Leks. Not him. Do not let him drive. It is the only thing. Only thing that can be changed. You cannot banish the heat. Or the sweaty stench. Or the noise or... All these other things. Let Mikhandor drive. Please. He makes me feel safe. Safer."

"Leks is a disastrous driver, eh? I think this might be because he's only got one eye. That okular of his, no matter how good it is; it won't make up for the loss of his real eye completely." She shook her head. As far as she knew, he'd given up his eye willingly, but still... What had Papi been thinking? "I figure you don't like his singing either, do you?"

He nodded again. "It is sarding awful. He probably enjoys it a lot, but it makes my ears want to fall off."

"I know." The old man was a real sweetheart, but she could very well do without his dreadful singing. "I can't stand it either, but what's a good girl to do? I love this man. He is like a grandfather to me."

They walked on in silence again, and Bel wondered what else she could do. Niels was definitely not going to last the entire journey if things didn't change fast. He was clearly on the verge of a breakdown already.

"Let us go back and join the others. I think I might know how to mitigate your problems at least a little bit." She really hadn't the foggiest, but something would come to her. Or so she hoped.

Mig and Leks sat in what little shade the trailer provided. They were eating, and chatting amicably. Bel was glad to see the two of them getting on so well.

"We thought we might as well have lunch." Mig gestured at the large wooden bowl filled with a fresh, colourful salad, and the insulated flask with cold water. "Please, join us." He stood up and made room for Bel, so she could enjoy the relative cool of a place in the shadows. Leks scooted several feet, so he was still partially protected from the scorching sun, as Niels took his place in the shade.

"Thank you." Bel's heart swelled with gratitude. They were good men, both of them. She grabbed a bowl and filled it generously with the salad, then handed it to Niels before she got her own meal. He picked at the food with his fork, but didn't seem very interested in it. Her own appetite was voracious. She felt like she could eat an entire manewolf all by herself. She tapped into Zilla's awareness. *Are you hungry, dear? Go hunt. Find some nice rabbits, eh?*

"I've been thinking," she said as the solution presented itself to her. "We have to step into our roles now. We want to get comfortable in them before we emerge in society again. Also, even though it's unlikely for us to meet other people here in the wilds, this is by no means impossible."

She looked at her newly established guards, and they both nodded. For now, she tried to ignore Niels, who sat staring off into the distance, a blank expression on his face. He probably didn't hear a word she said. "As I'm sure you guys have noticed, I'm already wearing my merchant's attire. You two are going to need uniforms, whereas Niels... I mean, Moradin, will need a carer's suit. I see you are wearing black breeches, Mig. This is perfect. Do you have black breeches with you, Leks?"

Leks nodded. "Guy's nothing without black britches, dearie."

"And this is another thing." She bit her lip. "You cannot be informal with me any more. I am your boss now, and... well, I'm sorry." She truly was. But her role required that her employees should address her respectfully and formally at all times. "From now on, it is Mistress Beldenka. Always."

"Dragon's dung! That's harsh."

"I know. I hate it too, but this is how it has to be until all of this is over." And she could only hope they would all make it through alive. The odds were not in their favour.

"But I'm glad the two of you already have black breeches. How about a basic white shirt?" She looked at the men, and they both nodded. "Good. This means we'll only need to get you guys a goatskin waistcoat of the kind mercenaries might wear. Because this is what you are now. Mercenaries."

"I quite like that." Mig grinned.

"I figured you would. Unfortunately, we'll need to use two — or even three — of our beautiful skins, because you're such a big fellow. I hope you can sew, as I'm not doing it for you.

"Now, we've got a little problem on our hands." She couldn't keep herself from looking at Niels, but reverted her gaze back to Leks and Mig almost immediately, in hopes they hadn't noticed. "The current heat and lack of shade are doing none of us any favours. I've got a giant headache, and Niels is even worse. This means we have to change our schedule. We, or rather, you two, are going to make camp now, and we'll do our travelling by night until we reach the woods."

That was one problem solved.

"One more thing. I saw some tracks just now, when Niels and I were having our little chat. *Mountain Misks*, if I were to guess. We don't need them to take us by surprise. So, Leks, you will guard us and our belongings when the three of us are asleep. You can do your sleeping in the karr, while Mig is driving."

Leks didn't look too happy, but that couldn't be helped. At least this way, she had most of Niels' problems with the current situation under control.

"Gentlemen?"

"Yes, Mistress Beldenka. We'll set to work immediately." Mig stood up, and collected the bowls. "I shall do the washing up first. Meanwhile, Leks, if you could detach the trailer and set it at a straight angle with the karr? Then, if we can find something that could act as a shade cloth, we could roof the area between our vehicles with that."

"Plenty of cloth in that trailer." Leks sounded a little happier already as he undid the flap of the trailer and started rummaging inside.

With both Leks and Mikhandor busy, Bel turned her attention to Niels again. She gasped. Was he rocking? She watched closer. Yes, although almost imperceptible, he was definitely rocking. Dragon's breath! That was the last thing they needed.

She rolled over to him, slipped out of her chair, wrapped her arms around his shoulders, and went along with his own movement. She started singing that old Ingravian lullaby again, ever so softly. And gods be praised, the rocking slowly subsided and his breathing became deeper. Calmer.

"Feeling any better now?" she asked when he looked up at her.

"A bit. I apologise." He ran his fingers through his hair and scratched at the nape of his neck. Fumbled with the buttons of his shirt. "That should not have happened."

"I have arranged for us to travel by night, and Leks will be sleeping during most of our travelling hours." She thought Niels would be happy to hear that, but his expression remained blank. It was a weird thing. Sometimes his facial expressions were so vivid, they seemed almost theatrical. Rehearsed. Then, at times like these, his face showed absolutely nothing. "Oh, and Mig will do all of the driving."

"Thank you," he said. His voice too, was completely devoid of emotion. Maybe he was truly just exhausted?

"I told the others we need to assume our roles now, so we'll be completely at ease in them when we resurface in society. From this moment on, I'm Mistress Beldenka, and you are my carer Moradin. This dress — I'm sure you've noticed it — is the typical Ingravian merchant's dress. With the exception that I tailored mine to have a straight skirt, which makes it easier for me to ride my chair."

Like earlier that morning, Niels stared at her dress, or rather how it showed off her boobs and, again, his cheeks turned just a shade darker. Bel suppressed a satisfied smile.

By the forgotten gods, it felt good to have a man notice her. Especially a good-looking specimen like him.

"You, my dear Moradin, are going to need an attendant's suit. Your black pantaloons look fine at first glance, and so does your shirt. You don't happen to have a waistcoat and tailcoat, do you?"

He shook his head. "I never needed them."

"No cravat either, I'm sure. So we shall have to provide you with this. Can you sew?"

"I can sew on a button." He actually managed to sound proud of that.

"That is hardly enough. And I can't have you messing up. These linens are our merchandise, and torching expensive, too. So I shall have to take your measurements and sew your new clothes." She tried to keep the frustration out of her voice. She hated sewing.

The dragonet, which Niels hadn't liked very much at first, turned out to be quite useful. She would go hunting at night, and on return she would bring pigeons, quail and pheasants, or sometimes an *ikorn* or rabbit, so they had fresh meat with their dinner each day. That was far better than the dried meat Leks had said they'd be eating during their journey to Tiria.

Zilla also did, indeed, seem to pick up on his moods, and somehow cued Bel in. This allowed Bel to talk to him about what was going on before things went out of hand. They were rather the pair, Bel and her dragonet. Niels wondered about that. Was it just a telepathic connection they shared, or was there more to it? As he pondered that question, he rolled the silk of his blood-red cravat between thumb and middle finger.

True to her word, Bel had made Niels an attendant's suit. It was the most sophisticated attire he had ever owned. A costume fit for a lord, not a servant. Yet he was required to wear it. Day by sodding day. It felt odd, and wrong. He was not a man to wear classy suits. He always wore practical, informal clothes when he wasn't on duty and wearing his robes.

He needed his clothes to be comfortable. This outfit consisted of the most uncomfortable pieces of clothing he'd ever laid eyes on. Each and every piece fit too snugly. The seams irritated his skin. The stiff fabric made him itchy. And, worst of all, Bel even took in his pantaloons, which now stretched so tightly around his hips, they left nothing to the imagination, and made him feel like an exhibitionist. The only thing he liked was the soft, smooth cravat. It was a piece of clothing he could fiddle with when the panic hit, and that somehow helped. A little. At least he'd had no more breakdowns. That was a small blessing.

It took them several nights to get to the part of the mountains where the woods were still intact. With Leks keeping watch during the day, and sleeping at night while they were travelling, life had become much more bearable. No loud, godsawful singing battering Niels' eardrums. Just Leks's monotonous snores. It still wasn't perfect, but certainly better. Much better.

Although the trees provided shade, so they could now travel by day, Bel had decided against it.

"We're used to travelling at night, and I think it would be wise to continue to do so. This way, we'll be less likely to meet other travellers. Also, don't forget, we'll be crossing the border into Tirona in a couple of days. The fewer people we encounter there, the better."

Niels agreed. He worried about Tirona. Most of the locals there were members of the Church of Mirk. Their priests were said to be real fanatics, who were always on the lookout for the clergy of other religions in their country, so they could sacrifice them to their Dark Lord. According to Niels' information, Mirk had gifted his servants with a magic that helped them to literally sniff other priests out.

"Moradin," Bel said as they made camp in the woods, "Zilla tells me she spotted a nice stream down there. I need you to come with me, so I can bathe. I smell like a mountain goat in heat."

"Yes, Mistress Beldenka. At your service." That was the easy part, answering his "mistress" when she requested his help. He had memorised the words, and they came to him easily now. The hard part was actually helping her in such a way she wouldn't get annoyed with him, for she hated that part of her role. The needy invalid.

Silently cursing the vines and brambles that kept latching onto the wheels, he pushed her chair through largely undisturbed undergrowth until they reached the rivulet. The water looked inviting, and if Bel hadn't been there, he would have taken off his clothes and jumped in without hesitation. He was well aware of how horribly he stank.

"Strip to your smallclothes and help me undress, Moradin."

CHAPTER FIFTEEN

Alight

> the flames
> of hatred die
> where sunshine brightens gloom
> evil dies and nightmares are laid
> to rest

Niels stared at her, his eyes wide with disbelief. "*What?*"

"You forget yourself, Moradin. Help me undress."

This wasn't happening. He could not do that. He was a priest.

"Bel, I cannot! It wouldn't be proper."

"It is *Mistress* Beldenka." Her gaze lingered on him in a way that made him squirm even harder. "And yes, you can. You are my carer. This is your job."

"I'm still a priest." This was madness. Bel knew it was prohibited. "I am not allowed to look on a woman's nakedness, unless she is my wife."

"Then don't look. Just do it." She sounded indignant, and the dragonet responded to her anger by hissing at Niels.

"Bel, I beg of you, do not make me do this." He wasn't only a priest. He was also a warm-blooded man, and she a gorgeous woman.

"My dear Morad," her voice sounded almost tender now, which made things only worse, "I know this is hard for you, but I know the Scriptures too. And you are, in fact, allowed to do this if it is needed to protect the woman's life."

"But you are not in any direct danger, Bel." He could already see where this was going, and he didn't like it.

"Not right now, no. Yet there is danger and we — all of us — may well lose our lives." She looked him in the eye and, flustered, he bowed his head. "We're playing these roles to save our lives so there is, in fact, a direct need."

"Bel..." he began, but she placed a gentle finger on his lips and he, utter turnip that he was, kissed it.

"Hush now," she said. "Don't think about it any more. Just do it."

Niels sighed, and began to take off his suit, as Bel had instructed him to do. The sarding woman was watching him unashamedly. He laid his clothes, folded into a neat bundle, on a smooth rock so they wouldn't get dirty, and turned towards Bel.

He looked at her once more, pleading with his eyes, but she refused to budge. With trembling fingers he undid the buttons on the back of her dress. All twenty-one of them. He wiped his clammy palms on his smalls. He helped her wriggle out of that impossible dress, and carried her to the stream, trying his hardest not to look at her perfect breasts. Gently, he lowered her onto the mossy bank.

"Strip," she commanded as she took off her drawers. "Or would you rather sleep in wet smallclothes?"

If only circumstances were different, this would have been a dream come true. Now it was more of a nightmare. Here he was, with the most beautiful woman he knew, and both of them naked; yet he was not allowed to touch her. Not like lovers do. To make things even worse, he was required to carry her into the stream and stay by her side. It was pure torture.

As he lifted her in his arms, she wrapped hers around his neck and rested her head against his chest.

"You smell even worse than I do." She giggled like a schoolgirl.

"Why are you doing this to me, Bel?" He wanted to kiss her so badly. Gods knew he wanted so much more than just that. Cautiously, he stepped into the stream. The burbling water came to just above his knees. Bel didn't loosen her grip on him, so he decided to sit down.

"Make me your wife." She held on even tighter. The way her breasts pressed against his torso drove him mad with desire.

"Bel?" He must have misheard. "What did you just say?"

She pressed a kiss on his lips before she answered. "I said, make me your wife."

"Beldenka, I..." What was he to do? What could he say? If only things were that easy!

She kissed him again, caressing his lips with the tip of her tongue. "I know you want to. Don't even think to deny this. I've seen the way you look at me. And I want you just as badly, so what are we waiting for?"

"Oh, Bel, I... I cannot," he heard himself say. He wiped the sweat out of his eyes. It took him all his self-control not to answer her kiss. "It wouldn't be fair. You don't want the life I would offer you. You deserve better."

"You stupid git!" Sudden tears rolled down her cheeks, and she pommelled his chest with her fists. He'd probably develop some nasty bruises there. Bel clearly didn't recognise her own strength. "I do. I want to spend the rest of my life with you."

"Bel, look at me." He held her wrists to stop her from hurting him. What could he say to make her understand? "You would be marrying a priest, and end up being married to a king. Is that truly what you want?"

"I don't torching care." She sniffled. "I'll be your cantor for as long as you're a priest, and when you become king, I shall be your queen."

Niels sighed. "Still. I cannot just marry you. I need the approval of no-one less than Yumænor, High King of the Erls."

"What?" Bel's voice sounded shrill. "High King Yumænor? I thought he was just a legend. And... and what's he got to do with you?"

"Yes, I used to think that too, when I was a boy. That he wasn't real. Then I met him. Several times, even." He closed his eyes as the memories threatened to overpower him. "I guess I'm going to need to tell you the rest of my story. We'd better get dressed again."

He carried Bel out of the water and sat her down on the bank. Then he realised he'd forgotten to bring a towel, so he handed her his cravat. The silk probably wouldn't absorb the moisture very well, but it was the best he could do.

Leks was tending a small fire. The rich, meaty smells that came from the bubbling cauldron made his mouth water.

"What's that delicious smell?"

"Zilla brought us a nice, fat rabbit today, and Migs dug up some fresh roots, and found us some tasty leaves and fungi. You enjoyed your bath, chummy?" His cackle suggested the man had indecent thoughts. Niels set his jaw. Nothing had happened, no thanks to Bel.

"He was here to help me, Leks. Not to enjoy himself," Bel said in what had to be her most frigid voice. "Now, do you have tea for us?"

"Sure, Mistress Bel. Made that before I got started on our meal." He poured them all a cup of blackberry leaf tea, and winked at Niels as he handed him his cup.

"The rest of your story, Morad," Bel demanded. "We are dying to know."

"Yes. Well." He tried to order his thoughts. Where had he left off, and where should he start now? "Uh... so... when I saw him on the vidisphere, and heard him speak, I knew this Prince Hanassan was the man who had sired me."

I had seen him in my visions, of course, but never made the connection, and now I wondered how I could have missed it. He featured so prominently in my visions, and I looked so much like him. Especially that younger version of him, the Naz that lived in my mother's memories. I had his skin, his eyes, his build, and even his voice.

More disturbingly, he was not the animal I always thought the man who impregnated my mother would have been. I'd only ever seen him treat her gently, and with kindness. As far as I could tell, she had actually liked him and, much to my chagrin, I could almost understand why.

My entire being rebelled against the notion of my biological father being a good person. I wanted to hate him. He got my mother with child, yet was not there for her — or for me — when I was born. He had left her to die, and made me an orphan. But it was hard to hate a man who had, in a weirdly twisted way, been good to her.

Naz, she had called him, and he called her Lali. Spring flower. A nickname, for sure. Had he even known her real name? She'd been inside his house. His palace, I realised now. For all I knew, he had been one of her regulars. They had eaten together. Played games, joked. It certainly hadn't been about his carnal desires only, though obviously she'd been required to satisfy those too.

"Niels, young brother," the high priest said, "as you have just seen for yourself, you look an awful lot like Prince Hanassan. We need to know for sure if you are, indeed, related to him. Is there anything you can tell us?"

"I saw him in my visions. My mother and him. I... I think they may have spent a lot of time together."

Both priests nodded.

"We'll have your DNA tested as soon as possible," the high priest said. "I shall send for my sister, who has access to the Royal Laboratory. Meanwhile, we need to talk. Your life may be in danger."

My life in danger? Certainly, things couldn't be that bad? My confusion must have shown on my face, for Priest Amari said, "There have been rumours about Prince Hanassan these last few turnings, and now that the Royal Family has been assassinated, there will certainly be even more. Rumours that may well be true, alas."

I didn't understand. "What kind of rumours?"

"Lad, don't you think it strange that of the entire Royal Family, only one man survived? A man who, by all accounts, is not the most emotionally stable person?"

My heart sank. Was he implying that Prince Hanassan was responsible for the deaths of his father and mother, his brothers and sisters, and their spouses and children? And what other rumours? Just because I wanted to hate the man, that didn't mean I wanted him to be a murderer.

"No," I said. "No, that cannot be true. He did not..." I couldn't say it. "He can't possibly be that evil. He just can't."

"Evil?" The high priest arched his brow. "I would not call him evil. That would be too easy, young man, and wrong too. Let us go up to my study. My wife and children should be home again soon, and we'll not want to bore them with our political talk."

The study, an octagonal room spanning the entire top floor of the house's tower, was so far away from all other rooms, and so well insulated, nobody would be able to overhear our conversation. That, I assumed, was the real reason why we were here.

"There are some things you need to know about Prince Hanassan."

"I know enough already." I didn't want to talk about him. Didn't want to hear any more. The man whose genes I carried, was a murderer. What more did I need to know? I turned to look out of the window.

"No, you do not. You don't know nearly enough, young man." The high priest's voice sounded grim. "Turn around and listen to me. We are not talking about the weather here. Your life may well depend on how well you can listen."

"Good. Fine. I'm listening." Reluctantly, I stepped away from the window and turned to face him. "Happy now?"

"People talk, and unfortunately I've had to listen to many more of their tales than I would have ever wanted to hear. It's one of the downsides of being a priest. These last few turnings, I have heard of children, even known some of them, who bore a striking resemblance to our only remaining prince. All of them golden-eyed, like you."

He seemed lost in thought for a moment before he continued, "All of these children, boys and girls alike... they died."

"No!" I covered my ears with my hands. "I don't want to hear it."

The high priest glowered at me, and I wanted to scream, but found myself unable to. Nor could I extricate myself from his unwavering gaze. Only when I removed my hands from my ears, did he continue his story. "Some of them fell mysteriously ill, others had suspicious accidents. Not one of them is alive today. Their deaths were never investigated, but it's not hard to guess the truth."

"No. You're lying!" I covered my ears with my hands again, hunched down on the floor, and started rocking back and forth in distress. My medallion burned against my chest, so I tore it off and threw it from me. I tried to take off my suddenly itchy clothes too, but my hands decided to do some wild flailing instead, and refused to do as I wanted.

I heard voices in the distance, but could not decipher what they were saying or to whom they were talking. Other noises assaulted my senses too, and strange smells. The sunlight that poured into the room through the window hurt my eyes. Then, a warm, sweaty hand pressed down on my shoulder, and I writhed away from it in agony.

When I came to my senses again, I lay curled up on the floor, hot and drenched in sweat. I was completely exhausted. To my utter dismay, my shirt was torn in several places. That had never happened before.

"Feeling a bit better now, lad?" Priest Amari was still there, and handed me my medallion. "You lost this," he said simply.

Back downstairs I met the high priest's wife Navida, their son Tasim, who was my age, and their young daughter Tulia. I also learned I would be sharing a room with Tasim. I had mixed feelings about that. He seemed like a nice enough boy, but I didn't know him, and that made me uncomfortable. That, and I had never shared a room with anyone before. I had no idea what to expect. What if he snored?

As we were having our tea, I heard the front door open and close again, followed by light footsteps in the vestibule. A woman clad in a simple orange tunic entered the room. She looked at me and, as I looked at her, I realised I knew her.

"Moradin!" She dropped her bag, a hideous bright yellow thing, rushed towards me, and tried to take me in her arms. In a reflex, I shrank back.

I know you, I wanted to say, but the words would not come.

"My Moradin," she whispered. She retrieved her bag and sat down beside me. "I never expected to see you back, after all these turnings. Look at you. Such a handsome young man you have become."

My hands began to take on a life of their own again. I had to say something. Anything. Fast. Before I had another breakdown. One was more than enough.

"You were with my mother when I was born." It was the first thing that came to my mind.

"You were so tiny, my sweet Morad, and so sick. So weak." Her voice sounded funny. I hoped she wasn't going to cry. "But deep down I knew you would survive. You were special. I could sense that the moment I first held you."

Before I could stop her, she took me in a tight embrace, and immediately the memories flooded me. My own memories, my first ones, preserved by the medallion.

She sat by my mother's bedside, talking to her. "I gave him the medallion. It will give him the strength he needs. Was it your father's?"

"My naa's," my mother said. "His wife and sons died long before I was born. My mam was his only remaining child."

"I see. I'm sorry. What is your son's name, dear?"

"Moradin."

So that was why this lady called me Moradin. It was the name my mother gave me. I said it out loud. "Moradin." And again, "Moradin."

"Yes, Moradin," the woman said. "That was your name, before these nice people from Darsrijck adopted you. Did they never tell you?"

I shook my head. "Moradin," I said again. "I like it. It's a good name."

"It certainly is." She beamed at me. "So, my brother tells me you need your DNA tested, and we can't really go through the official channels."

"I am sure you can see why, Farrah," The high priest said.

She rummaged in her bag. "That is rather too obvious, I'm afraid. We really need to do something about that. If only I had known, I'd have... ah, here it is."

She held up a white cotton bag, opened it and placed its contents on the table. Just some swabs and two small glass vials. "This is a DNA-kit, Moradin. Now, don't you worry, this won't hurt one bit. I only need to take some saliva from the insides of your cheeks. Open your mouth, please."

When she was done, she put each swab into a separate vial. "I'm going to the Royal Laboratory of Sciences now, and will run all necessary tests. That shouldn't take overly long. I expect to be back tonight with the results."

She did not return that night, however, and I was worried. Had something happened to her? And what if someone else had gotten hold of my DNA?

The next day the Royal Family was buried. I, of course, could not attend the funeral. I was just a nobody after all. Instead, I watched the sad ceremony on the vidisphere, with Navida, Tasim and Tulia.

Priest Amari and the high priest, however, were required to attend the Royal funeral, and I felt lost without my mentor by my side. I didn't know what to think or feel. Was it sadness? Anger? Both? Something else?

Those people were my relatives. My grandparents, my uncles, my aunts, my cousins. Not my adoptive relatives, many of whom thought me a weird freak, but blood relatives, and I couldn't help but wonder. Would they have understood me? Loved me, even?

Twenty white coffins, sparkling in the tropical sunlight. Twenty freshly dug graves. Twenty innocent people killed in just one night. My cousins had all been younger than me, and two of them still mere babies. One of my aunts had been expecting. Her baby died in her womb. Nobody would ever know this child's name.

It was unreal. Brutal. And here I was, watching it all on the vidi, unable to fully comprehend what had happened, and why. The Naz from my visions would never have done such a thing, I was sure of that. What had happened between then and now, to turn him into a murderer?

I still could scarcely believe it. The man I saw on the screen didn't look like a cold-blooded killer. He looked like a man in shock. A man who truly grieved for the sudden loss of his loved ones. But what did I know? Maybe he was just a good actor. Or maybe I simply saw what I wanted to see.

"Yo, Niels, wassup, *b'radar*?" Tasim sat down on the couch beside me with a cup of kaw. "You look like you're about to go to pieces."

I blinked. Drummed my fingers on my legs. "You would never understand, Tasim."

He put his cup down, grabbed me by the shoulders, and looked me square in the eye. "Try me." It almost sounded like a challenge.

"Those people... they..." I looked away.

"That is quite enough, Tasim." Mrs Erumin clipped her words. "Go to your room right now and leave Niels alone. The boy is here to recover from his recent illness."

Tasim got up, muttered some choice words, and stamped up the stairs. Our bedroom door slammed shut.

"I'm sorry for my son's behaviour, Niels. He should know better than to pry into other people's business."

"I..." I didn't really know what to say, "I'm sure he means well, Mrs Erumin."

"Please, not so formal. Call me Navida." She smiled at me, but her smile turned into a frown almost immediately.

"Are you alright, my dear boy? You do look rather unsettled."

I frowned, and tried to rub the wrinkles off my forehead. Clearly, she didn't want me to talk about my kinship to the Royal Family, or she wouldn't have sent Tasim upstairs like that when I was about to open up to him. What did she want me to say?

"Just tired," I said at last. That, at least, was not a complete lie. The ten-hour time difference between Darsrijck and Ebaru truly was taking its toll on me.

CHAPTER SIXTEEN

Rise

steadfast
against illness
and death the righteous stands
who from darkness brings forth child of
promise

"Thank the seven gods, there you are!" The high priest rushed towards his sister and held her tight against his chest. "Where were you, Farrah? What happened?"

"Nothing to worry about, brother dearest." She patted his shoulder and smiled at him. "There were others at the lab yesterday, and I could well do without curious eyes watching my every move. So I decided to wait till today, when most of my colleagues were attending the funeral. Thank the gods, I wasn't invited, and had the entire lab to myself.

"I ran the tests this morning. The papers are here." She laid two sealed envelopes on the table. "The authentic ones, and the amended set — the set Moradin will need to show to the Council when he applies for admission to the Seminary."

"Can... can I see them, please?" My voice sounded unsteady and I was trembling with a mixture of fear and excitement. Did I really want to know?

"Not yet, my dear Morad," Farrah said. "I think our friend Shadu here needs to tell you something first."

She turned to face my mentor. "I discovered something, Shadu, and it made me wonder..." She scrutinised his face. "Why don't you open that first envelope and have a look at the test results? Then tell me, did you know?"

The priest picked the envelope up and read the document, a small smile playing around the corners of his mouth. He nodded as he carefully folded the papers and placed them back in the envelope.

"I wasn't entirely sure, but I definitely had my suspicions. I dared not believe it, though. I didn't think..." He did not finish his sentence. "Niels, lad. Let's go to the study. There is indeed something I should tell you. Something personal."

My mind raced as I followed Priest Amari through the kitchen into the gloomy corridor that led to the black wooden spiral staircase. What was going on? What personal thing could possibly be so important that it couldn't wait until after I'd finally read those papers myself? It didn't seem fair, that everyone got to see them before me. Why did they have to keep me in the dark like this?

To distract myself from my anger, I started counting the steps. "One, two, three... twenty-seven, twenty-eight... thirty-six. Thirty-six steps. Plus those five or six before I started counting.

The door to the study opened with a creak, and as we entered the room, the heat cut off my breath. Silvery speckles of dust danced in the golden ray of sunlight that fell through the window. My heart skipped a beat, and I swallowed the bile that rose in my throat.

My mentor sat down behind the high priest's desk. "Let me start by telling you a little about my own life." With a small gesture, invited me to take a seat, too.

"Forty-five turnings ago, I was born to Anur and Ravanna Amari as the youngest of eleven children. I had nine sisters and one brother. Although he was only twenty-three turnings old, my brother was already a priest, and the youngest professor ever at the Seminary. He was married to the love of his life, Shulmi, who had given birth to their third daughter, Yasira, only a few sevendays before I was born. Their other daughters, Shirra and Adira were four and two turnings old.

"My brother and his wife had two more children. Two boys, Ghanil and Shaldik."

"Wait, what?" My surprise made me speak before I realised I shouldn't interrupt my mentor. "Five children when he was just twenty-three?"

"No, lad." Priest Amari chuckled. "The boys were born later."

He fell silent then, and breathed deeply several times before he continued his story. "Sadly, Shulmi and four of my brother's five children died during the global outbreak of the Swivian Reptichitis. My brother was heartbroken and Shirra, his only remaining child, also became depressed. They were by no means the only ones in Ebaru who had suffered heavy losses. There was hardly anyone out there who hadn't lost loved ones to the Ophidian Death. Seven of my sisters had died too."

He blew out a long breath and shook his head slowly. Somehow, he suddenly looked older.

"Shortly after this tragedy my parents decided to leave the country. They said they couldn't live here any longer, in this place where they were haunted by the memories of the horrors they had not only witnessed, but also gone through themselves.

"My brother, however, insisted that he couldn't leave his people and stayed behind with his daughter. He gave up his job as a professor at the Seminary and became Priest of the Poor."

"Why are you telling me this?" I scratched my head. "I mean... I don't want to be rude, but why would I need to know these things?"

"Just listen, lad. You'll understand. I promise." He sat staring at me for a long moment, stroking his beard.

"When I came back to Ebaru to start my studies at the Seminary, Shirra's husband, a man named Ardu, had recently gone missing, and she was now a single mother with three young children, Shansi, Asra and Siana. Shansi was a beautiful girl, and far too clever for her five turnings, Asra a mischievous toddler, and Siana still a baby."

So many names! Shirra, Shansi, Asra, Siana... and then all those others. Was I really supposed to remember them all?

"I would visit my niece and help her out with the children as often as I could during the six turnings I was a student at the Seminary, and grew fond of her and her little ones.

"Meanwhile, time had not been gentle on my brother. He had become a broken, bitter man, whose morose moods made even the air around him feel oppressive. His sunken eyes were darker than I remembered, and he had lost so much weight, his skin hung from his bones like a heavy, formless shroud. Three turnings after my arrival in Ebaru he died in my arms. He was only forty-four turnings old."

My mentor was silent for a moment, and seemed lost in his own sad memories.

"When I had finished my studies and was about to become a priest in Dorhedde, I tried to convince my niece to come with me, but she wouldn't leave Ebaru. The last time I saw her was on the night before my departure. One last time I pleaded with her to come with me, but she was just as headstrong as her father had been all those turnings ago.

"When I came back to attend a conference and visit my friend Akdi several turnings later, the Poor told me that she and the two youngest children had died from the Ikorn Pestilence. Only Shansi had survived, but nobody would tell me where I could find her. All I ever got when I enquired about her whereabouts were evasive answers and embarrassed looks.

"Though I searched for her everywhere, I never found her, and didn't know what had become of her until that day, eight turnings ago, when you walked into my life."

"When I walked into your life?" I stared at him in bewilderment. What was he on about?

"Through my own medallion, I felt a deep bond with you. A kinship that went beyond what your priestly ancestry alone could account for. Still, I would not allow myself to believe.

"Then, just after your fourteenth birthday, I was drawn into one of your visions, and immediately recognized Shansi. Sweet, innocent Shansi, who had become someone she was never meant to be. I think I'm not exaggerating when I say that I hurt almost as much as I knew you did."

He got up and went over to the window. There he stood staring at the world outside, probably thinking of all the people he had lost. He didn't move or speak.

"So we are related," I finally managed to say, still hardly able to grasp this new truth. "You are my... my... great-granduncle, or something?"

"That's right, lad." He looked at me and smiled that special smile of his. The one that had made me wonder so many times. Now I understood.

"Are you surprised?"

"Yes. No. I mean... I don't know. It does explain a lot. Things that never seemed to make sense before. Like the way you sometimes look at me, and why you are going through all this trouble for me. It seemed strange that you would do that for just one of your students, but now..."

"You were never just one of my students, Niels. You reminded me of... of so many things. My country. A past that was taken from me. The people I loved and lost. You have always held a special place in my heart. And you always will."

"So... what do I call you now?" I could not continue calling him sir. That felt wrong. He was family.

"Shansi called me uncle. Ammu Shadu. I would like for you to call me that."

We were in the living room again. The others enjoyed a hot kaw, but I hardly touched mine. Still unable to comprehend it all, I read the documents again. 'Son of His Royal Highness, Prince Hanassan Dolanthi of Ebaru', they read, and 'direct descendant of Priest Moradin Amari, of hallowed memory, in the female line.'

"She named me after her grandfather, the priest," I finally said. "And she birthed me in a temple, at the feet of the Goddess's statue." It seemed significant.

"Yes," Ammu Shadu said. "I remember well how fond she was of him. And he of her. I still don't know how she did it, but young as she was, she was the only one who could, temporarily, pull him out of his misery. My little princess, he used to call her. They spent many hours studying the Scriptures together. That was one of the few joys left in my brother's life."

Little princess. And then, ironically, she got pregnant by a prince. His Royal Highness Prince Hanassan Dolanthi of Ebaru. It was quite the mouthful, and an uncomfortable truth. What consequences would this have for me, presumably his only living child?

"Will he try to kill me?" I blurted out. "Hanassan, I mean. Once he finds out about me? Would he really do that?"

"What do you think, boy?" The high priest arched his eyebrows. "What did we all witness this morning? If that does not answer your question, then what will?"

"But don't worry, Moradin dear," Farrah said in her soft voice. "I brought some things that should help conceal you from him." She patted the monstrous yellow bag in which she had carried my documents. "I think we need to have supper first, though, as this will take a while, and I am hungry."

After our meal she took me upstairs, to the bathroom, where she got a bottle filled with a greenish gel out of her bag and told me to strip to my smallclothes. She put on rubber gloves, and spread the gel evenly over my face and body.

"This will darken your skin overnight. Don't bathe, or even wash your hands or face until tomorrow morning, or it will wash off and not work properly. We need to reapply this gel once every moon."

Next, she took what looked like a wig out of her bag. "These are hair extensions," she said. "I'll braid them into your own hair. Like the gel, this will hold for about one moon, so you might want to grow your own hair out."

The braiding took forever, but when Farrah was done and I looked in the mirror, I barely recognised myself.

"Just one more thing left to do, Morad, but unfortunately this is rather uncomfortable, and it needs to be repeated every evening." She got a small vial out of her bag and held it up for me to see.

"Your gorgeous golden eyes are quite rare and make you stand out. These eye drops will darken the irises, and turn them a deep brown. I'll ask Shadu to help you with this, until you're able to do it yourself. It will take some practice, and a lot of determination. It will sting for a couple of heartbeats upon application, but it's probably the most important part of your disguise."

I nodded. I would do anything to keep from being targeted by a homicidal king — which struck me as illogical, since only a couple of sevendays ago I would have welcomed death, and frankly, my life had only got worse since.

We went downstairs, where Farrah instructed the others on what needed doing and when. "Also," she said, "I think it would be a good idea to call him Moradin from now on. Niels is the name in his travel documents, copies of which will soon be in Hanassan's possession, along with portraits taken of Moradin at the drakenport."

"But Niels is also the name on these papers you just brought."

Farrah just shrugged. "So I'll make yet another set. Easy enough."

I also needed a new surname. I, of course, chose Amari. That was, after all, the name of my great-grandfather. It would explain why I was with Shadu. We were related by blood, and since I was an orphan, he raised me. That was going to be our story.

Hanassan's coronation was on my third day in Ebaru. I watched the ceremony on the vidisphere. Both priests were required to be there.

In fact, High Priest Erumin played quite an important part in this preposterous affair. As far as I was concerned, the entire thing was highly offensive. As if our good Goddess would ever approve of this blasphemous performance, let alone give that terrorist her blessings.

But of course, the high priest had no choice but to cooperate. If he refused to perform the necessary services, he would no doubt lose his head. And so he took my father's vows to be a good king, and faithful servant to his people for as long as the good Goddess gave him to reign. Hollow words, coming from the mouth of the man who killed his entire family, as well as dozens of children that might possibly have been his.

As my biological father sat knelt down on a thick red velvet cushion, the high priest placed the crown — a simple golden circlet, inset with rubies — on Hanassan's head, and invoked the Lady's blessing. "May our good Goddess bless your reign and our country with prosperity. May the Lady's wisdom guide your decisions, and may she bless our gracious king with life eternal and good health."

He then raised King Hanassan up and cried in a loud voice, "Long live the King!" All the guests echoed his cry. "Long live the King!" A loud applause went up, and in a reflex I covered my ears. Even though the noise couldn't have been nearly as loud on the vidi as it would have been in the Hall of the Kings, the din still hurt my head.

"Well, that's it, then," Tasim said. "I can't believe that man is our new king. As if things weren't bad enough already under Ignoble Ishvat's reign, now we're going to be ruled by a total psycho. A booze belly and a whore hopper."

He snorted. "The man obviously thinks he's a god. He'll want all of us to worship him, and he probably thinks he really has eternal life too. Just wait till someone poisons him. That should serve him right."

I didn't say anything. I just sat there, still staring at the screen. King Hanassan stood on the dais, a blank expression on his face, as if he hardly registered what was going on. Again, the disbelief crept up on me. How could this man possibly be a murderer? He looked lost, rather than dangerous. I shook my head. He probably just faked it. And why should I even care anyway?

An impossibly tall man with a round face, spindly legs and a huge torso walked up to him, took his elbow and guided him into the mass of people. A small orchestra started playing and the festivities began.

"Who is that bizarre man?" I asked.

"Baldy Balloon, you mean?" Tasim guffawed. "He's Hanassan's Chief Eunuch. Weird chap, with his singsong voice and funny mannerisms."

"Chief Eunuch?" I echoed. "He's got eunuchs? That's insane!"

"I know, right? But he doesn't think so. He thinks he's so special, he needs unmanned servants to keep an eye on his ever-changing harem of whores."

His use of the word unmanned should have cued me in, but it didn't. "Harem?"

Tasim laughed. "Yes, b'radar. Harem. What else did you think he needs eunuchs for? Their great cooking skills? Their unparalleled musical talents and exceptional singing voices?" He squeezed his crotch, yowled like a cat in heat, and doubled over with laughter again.

I gave him a blank stare. "Are they really great cooks then, and talented singers?"

"Gods, Moradin! Don't you know anything?" He wiped his eyes, but immediately burst out laughing again. Annoying rapscallion. "They are no more talented than anyone else, except at keeping it in their breeches."

"Keeping it..." Then it finally dawned on me. I felt the blood drain from my face. "Oh," I said. "Oh. Holy gods! I never... I'm such a turnip."

The truth was, before that conversation I never really understood what eunuchs were. They were exotic fairytale figures, and slaves to kings. That was as far as my knowledge went. The word castrate held no meaning to me. Not until that day.

CHAPTER SEVENTEEN

Hold

*words fail
when dread provoked
by sovereign grasp induce
nightmarish visions of torture
and grief*

His three companions were howling with laughter.

"Oh, Morad," Bel said, "this is so cute. So innocent. And to think you were... what? Fourteen? Fifteen?"

"Fifteen." Niels felt the blood rush to his cheeks. "I just..." He hung his head. What could he say?

"But really. All these coincidences. Priest Amari your great-granduncle. And then the high priest's sister, who happened to be your carer when you were a baby. And your father a king. You'd think that stuff only happens in stories."

"I do not believe in coincidence, Bel. I think it was providence. If I interpret the Prophecies correctly, and I think I do, then this was all meant to be."

"I'll have to agree on that," Mikhandor said. "The priests made sure he studied your own human prophecies rigorously, and I guided him in his studies of the Sylphan Prophecies myself."

"Can I get on with my story now?" He wanted to kick something. Instead, he grabbed some twigs, threw them on the fire and watched the sparks fly. He hated this, and would be just as happy to go to sleep now and not have to talk about the past ever again.

I lay on my bed, staring at the ceiling. Though it was far too early to go to sleep yet, my bed was the only place where I could be alone with my thoughts. That night, however, my medallion had other ideas.

"Moradin still needs to learn a lot." I heard Farrah's voice as clearly as if she were in the same room with me. "Elementary things even. Why has Shadu not taught him how to use the medallion yet? The boy has absolutely no control."

"That medallion of his... there is something about it. Something that makes it more special than any other I have ever seen. It has an exceptionally strong aura. Surely you have noticed that, my dear?"

A short silence followed, and I could almost see Farrah nod in agreement. "It's funny, though. I cannot remember it being that strong when he was a baby. It felt no different from yours or Padr's. Well, maybe a little, but... Then again, he was just a baby, of course."

I sat up in an effort to pay better attention to their words.

"Babies don't really have a sense of self yet. That may explain why you didn't recognise its potential back then. It seems perfectly reasonable to assume it would have developed and grown stronger as he grew up." In the short silence that followed his words, I caught myself biting my nails.

"Shadu tells me that pendant has got a mind of its own, and I'm inclined to believe he is right. I can feel it, too. The problem is, whenever Shadu wants to teach Moradin how to use it, the medallion decides to treat the young man to yet another vision, and Shadu gets pulled in as well."

"He *what?*"

"That's right. Whenever he is within, let's say, five hundred yards of the boy, he shares in all of his visions. Their familial bond creates a remarkably strong connection between the two of them and their medallions. More, in fact, than I would have expected.

"Obviously, Shadu cannot teach young Moradin how to use it when he has to deal with these visions himself at the same time. They are quite triggering for him too. He cared for the youth's mother as if she were his own daughter. I assume that's the real reason why he asked me to do this."

"I see. Did he know about Morad's royal descent?"

"He had no idea. But my heart jumped into my throat when I picked them up at the drakenport and saw the boy. Those golden eyes of his! The place was positively swarming with guards. They must have noticed the resemblance, and I'm telling you: The king will know about Moradin's arrival before this sevenday is over."

"That is why he needs the disguise. It's a good thing he turned out to be related to Shadu as well. It lends credibility to our cover, and his recent illness helps too. People won't think about his fluctuating moods twice when they know he suffers from a mental affliction."

I heard a door open and close, and a familiar voice said, "You two should watch your words. I could follow your entire conversation from the moment I entered the street. Where is my nephew?"

"Zinnir's beard!" The High Priest's voice rang so loud, I could have heard him even without the aid of my medallion. "So now that sparkler of his is even listening in on our private conversations? The nerve of that thing!"

"Ak, will you shut up and tell me where Moradin is? I need to see him. Now!"

I couldn't believe my ears. My mentor, shouting at the High Priest. In all these turnings I had seen him angry only once before. That was on the day when he first visited me after I had unsuccessfully tried to end my life.

"How in the name of all the gods would I know?" the high priest yelled back. "Try upstairs in his room. That impossible youngster sequesters himself in there all the time. How on all seven worlds does he think we're going to be able to help him if he keeps doing that?"

In an instant, the medallion went mute. As if someone had somehow slammed it shut. I heard footsteps on the stairs. A knock on my door. I didn't bother to answer. He would come in anyway. I closed my eyes. Why could they not just leave me alone? I never asked for any of this, so why did that sarding high priest have to get mad at me? Was it my fault? Was I to blame for all the horrors that were going on in this rotten world of his?

"Morad, are you alright?"

He sat on the edge of my bed. I could smell the evening breeze on his clothes, the kaw on his breath, and the sweat on his skin.

"What do you think? That sarding high priest hates me, and my biological father is a madman and a murderer." I slammed a fist into the wall, and looked in bewilderment at the crater it left behind. What were these walls made of? Paper? "I want to go home."

"That won't be possible, lad. You know this as well as I do. I cannot teach you how to control your medallion. It is too strong, and I am not a particularly gifted priest. Akdi is. He is the only one I know who will be able to teach you how to use your medallion."

"There must be others, and kinder than him."

He shook his head. "There are none. He was chosen to be our High Priest for a reason. You need him." He tried to look me in the eye, but I looked away, at the tiny bookshelf with only six measly books. "Morad, I'm truly sorry you don't like him. He may be a bit abrupt, but I can assure you he doesn't hate you. Even so, I can find you another place to live, so you won't have to be around him all day, every day."

"Do you think I could stay with the Maidens of Eylah, perhaps? I like Farrah. Even though she just said that I'm a lunatic." I looked down. "That was blunt, but she is right."

"No Morad. That was not what she meant, and you should never think of yourself like that. You've been suffering from a nasty depression, but that doesn't make you crazy. You are a sensitive, intelligent young man, who's simply had too much on his plate. You are not crazy, do you hear me? Not crazy."

He grew reflective then. "Unless I am very much mistaken, you're going to be an extremely strong and gifted priest. I can feel it. Stronger even, and more gifted, than my brother was. And I think there might be more. The Prophecies..." He stood up and, doorknob already in his hand, he said, "you will need to repair that hole in the wall. I'll bring you the supplies you need." He closed the door behind him, opened it again and, almost as an afterthought, added, "will you be alright, lad?"

Then he was gone. He didn't even wait for me to answer. I wondered what had him so excited all of a sudden. We had been studying the Prophecies together for several turnings now, and although they were certainly interesting, I didn't think they warranted that kind of excitement.

Over the next couple of days Ammu Shadu was so absorbed in his studies of the Prophecies, he hardly paid attention to anything else, and I wondered if he had forgotten about his promise to find me another place to live.

It was the fourth hour after sunrise and both Tasim and Tulia were in school. The priests had decided that school would be too risky for me, so I was being home educated. It was the best thing ever. No more noisy, smelly classrooms. No more bullying. No waiting for the slower minds to finally understand what the teachers had been explaining a hundred times already.

I had taken a copy of the Holy Book out of the bookcase and sat on the couch, reading the prophecies, trying to understand what could be so incredibly special about them. Ammu Shadu sat beside me with his own copy of the Holy Book and High Priest Erumin was about to join us in our studies when a loud knock on the front door startled me out of my skin. A woman's voice called, "Open the door for your king!"

As the high priest went to allow our uninvited guests entry, I jumped off the couch in terror and ran towards the back entrance. Before I was even halfway there, however, Ammu Shadu blocked my way and held me in a too-tight embrace.

"Calm down, Moradin," he whispered in my ear. "I am here to protect you, my boy. No harm will come to you. You are safe."

"Your Majesty." The high priest's voice sounded almost too deferential. "What brings you to my humble abode?"

"I am looking for this young man, revered servant of our good Goddess," the king said in his rich, deep baritone. I heard a soft, rustling sound. As if he pulled a piece of paper out of his pocket. A portrait of me, I assumed, taken at the drakenport just after my arrival in Ebaru. "His name is Niels Bosch, and my vizier has informed me that the boy should be staying with you."

"He did indeed, your Majesty, but I'm afraid he is not here now."

"Where is the boy, good priest?"

The king's voice sounded sharper now, and I feared I would wet myself if he stayed around for much longer.

"Unfortunately, I cannot give you the information you need, your Majesty, sir. The youth went away one night and did not come back. He never said where he was going, sir."

What on all seven worlds? The high priest was deceiving the king, but at the same time he wasn't quite lying. Not really. How did he do that? It scared the blazes out of me and I clung to Ammu Shadu with all my might.

"Who is the young man over there?" My father's voice thundered through the room. I shuddered. He would surely recognise me, and then... Unwelcome visions of death by torture assaulted me. He would take me with him to his palace and throw me in a dark, damp dungeon with a spiked ceiling that moved ever downwards, at a snail's pace. Or maybe he would feed me to his piranhas. Poison me with some slow-acting venom that would paralyse my muscles one by one. I moaned softly.

"That is my colleague's nephew Moradin. The poor boy isn't well in the head, your Majesty." Again, no lies.

A surprisingly gentle hand grasped my shoulder, and made me turn round. A forceful surge of something indefinable, something I'd never experienced before, went through my body, and frightened me even more. "Show me your face, young man."

His tone was perfectly agreeable now — almost affectionate. Yet, when he looked me in the eye, I lost it completely. I howled in agony and flailed my arms like the nutcase I was. My stomach cramped, and my gut churned inside of me.

"Hush now, Moradin." Ammu Shadu held me securely once more, his arms wrapped around me so tightly, I could barely breathe. "There's no need to panic, lad. Our good king only wanted to see your face."

"No, no, no," I whimpered, grappling for words, and failing. "Hurt. No!"

"My apologies, your Majesty," Ammu Shadu said. "As High Priest Erumin already mentioned, my nephew is not well. He lives in his own world and scares easily."

"There is no need to apologise, good priest." The king's voice sounded soft and gentle, with even a hint of sorrow. "I understand. One of my nephews was like that. A beautiful, sweet little boy — but he never spoke, and no one ever knew what was going on inside his mind. He would..." He didn't finish his sentence.

I felt his hand on my shoulder again, and winced as I recoiled from his touch. "Don't be afraid, young man." His voice was so genteel, it tugged at my heart. "I would never hurt you. Never."

Finally he took his hand off my shoulder. He stroked my cheek with one finger, and all my muscles pulled taut. Then, I heard him walk away from me. Relieved that he seemed to have lost interest in me, I let go of the tension a little. I shook like a leaf.

"If you find the youth back, good priests, I urge you to escort him to my palace immediately. It is absolutely imperative that I meet him as soon as possible."

"Of course, your Majesty," High Priest Erumin said. "It is our honour to serve you. We shall do all within our power to find Niels and bring him before your throne."

That night I had a strange, disturbing dream.

I was in what I assumed was my father's palace, and looked at him as he stood talking to nobody, or so it seemed.

"You worry too much, sweetheart," he said in the same warm voice in which he had spoken to me that afternoon. "He will be fine, I promise you."

From out of nowhere, Princess Shadira appeared and stood facing my father, her shoulders slumped and the corners of her mouth turned down. "You know he won't, Naz. It's this horrid curse. My poor little boy... and what of my baby? I don't think I could bear it, if she too..." her voice broke and she started to cry.

To my utter surprise, my father took her in his arms and held her in a comforting embrace. Unable to believe what I saw, I crept closer as she continued to cry, and he stroked her back tenderly.

"Dira...." Gently, he wiped the tears from her eyes and kissed her cheek. "I will cure him, trust me."

"Hanassan, don't be such a lizardbrain. You know you cannot," a voice that sounded almost the same as my father's said. "None of us can lift this curse. Only the Chosen One can do that. And last time I looked, there was no sign of him yet."

Immediately, my father let go of Princess Shadira and turned round. He growled and hissed like a feral cat, ready to pounce. I ducked and covered my head with my hands, afraid of what would happen if he saw me, but I needn't have feared. He looked right through me and started shouting at his brother, Prince Asandor, who stood just a few feet away from where I sat huddled on the floor.

"Chosen one, my pickle and onions! Don't give me that donkey dung again, Sandor. We do not need him for that. This only requires plain, old logic, b'radar." He snorted. "You are just jealous because I have worked out how to achieve this, when you barely even remember the history of our fathers." Hanassan lashed out at his older brother and tried to punch him in the face, but Prince Asandor calmly stepped aside, so my father lost his balance and fell.

The vision blurred, but I could still vaguely see the eunuch's round face hovering over my father's. I could still hear his muffled words.

"I should better escort him to his rooms and give him his medicine. I am worried about him, ma'am, sir. His condition looks to be deteriorating."

"Moradin!"

I woke up with a scream as I felt a hand on my shoulder.

"Yo, Morad, wassup b'radar?" It was Tasim, who stood beside my bed. He looked down on me, his brow furrowed into a frown. "You were thrashing about in your sleep b'radar, talking gibberish."

"I... I was?" That was embarrassing.

"Having a nightmare, eh?"

I nodded. "Sort of. He... he was here this morning, you know." I almost choked on my words, "The man came looking for me."

"Who? King Psycho? What happened?" Tasim sat down on my bed. He shook his head in apparent disbelief. "How did he know?"

"The guards at the drakenport, most likely. He showed your father a portrait of me, and demanded to know where I was. He even knew my name." A shiver ran down my spine. "Of course your father pretended he didn't know, but then the king saw me, and wanted to know who I was."

"No way! He didn't! Oummi's nipples, but that man is such a creep!"

"Hmm... Well, anyway, I was scared out of my smalls and acted like a manewolf on Oracle. The only good thing is, he didn't recognise me, so I am probably safe. For now, anyway."

"So now he came haunting you in your sleep, eh?"

"Yes, sort of." I didn't know what to make of that dream. This was not just an ordinary dream, that much I knew. It felt similar to the visions I'd been having of my mother for all these turnings — just not quite the same.

"We had better go back to sleep, Tasim. It was just a dream. No use making a big stink over it."

"Yo, sure." Tasim gave me one of his I-don't-believe-you looks — he was quite good at those — but went back to his own bed anyway. "Just remember you can talk to me any time, b'radar."

CHAPTER EIGHTEEN

Ruin

lessons
in history
redouble sense of doom
crippling ancestral curse governs
ill minds

"I'm scared. I don't want to end up like King Hanassan, but it's already in my genes, isn't it? His madness, I mean."

It was the first thing that went through my mind when I woke up that morning, and I had been unable to think of anything else since. I could still hear my sire's ludicrous boasting, and could almost feel his pain as he lay convulsing on the floor of his palace.

Now that Tasim and Tulia had left for school, Akdi was out on an errand and Navida tending her garden, I could finally speak freely with Ammu Shadu. From last night's dream, or whatever else it had been, it was quite clear to me that King Hanassan was suffering from a mental condition which, according to his eunuch, was worsening. On top of that came the seizures.

I carried his genes. I had run away from the mental hospital not even one moon ago. I was going to be like him. Probably even worse.

Ammu Shadu shook his head. "Morad, lad, things are a bit more complicated than that. Have you ever heard of the Curse of the Erlen King?"

"Of course. But that's just a dumb old legend." It was a silly folk tale, made up by superstitious people, hundreds of turnings ago. How could that have anything to do with me? Or my father, the king?

"The cautionary tale the people of the Briscan Commonwealth have been telling their children for generations, yes. That is, indeed, a legend. An embellished version of what really happened. I guess I'd better tell you the true story. You will need to know all of this sooner or later anyway."

I leaned forward, eager to learn more of the history of my ancestors.

In the spring of Turning 9265 King Haniman, Ruler and Overlord of the Dalanthian Continent, was faced with a dilemma.

His only son, Prince Aleyshan had fallen in love with the Sylphan Princess Shælam, daughter of Yumænor, High King of the Sylphans, and wished to marry her. Aleyshan however, had already been promised to Imperial Princess Dalenka of Morynthia.

Although King Haniman wished his son nothing but happiness, the proposed union between Aleyshan and Dalenka would be politically beneficial to both the Dalanthian and the Morynthian realms, and neither King Haniman nor Emperor Fedromir of Morynthia were eager to break their promises to each other.

A few sevendays before the Royal Wedding was to take place, High King Yumænor appeared to King Haniman in a dream. "Haniman, King of Dalanthia, hear me," he spoke. "I'm warning you as a friend: listen to your son's pleas, and do not marry him to the Imperial Princess Dalenka.

"If you proceed with this wedding as planned, the consequences will be disastrous. It will bring down a terrible curse on both your families and all of their descendants, and cause much personal suffering in each generation of both ruling families until, ultimately, it will result in the downfall of both the Dalanthian Realm and the Morynthian Empire."

The next day, King Haniman consulted with the High Priest who, after studying the prophecies in the Holy Book of Eylah, urged him to listen to High King Yumænor's words and allow his son to marry Princess Shælam instead of Princess Dalenka.

This was not the advice the king had been hoping for, and he sought the guidance of the twelve members of his Royal Council, who disagreed with the High Priest and insisted that the king should marry his son to the Imperial Princess.

Much to his chagrin, Prince Aleyshan was forced to marry a woman he did not love. But love, he knew, had never been a prerequisite for a royal marriage. Duty always came first, and if you were lucky, you grew to love your spouse.

Aleyshan was not one of those lucky few. Though the young couple eventually learned to appreciate and respect each other, the marriage between Aleyshan and Dalenka never became a happy one.

Soon after Dalenka had given birth to their first child, Siman, she started behaving strangely, claiming she saw Eyades and Kradim stalking her and trying to steal the baby. The child was just one moon old, when Aleyshan found him dead in his bassinet.

Dalenka sat on the floor a few feet away from the crib. With hollow eyes, she stared at the pillow she cradled in her arm, as she repeated the same words over and over again: "The Eyades made me do it. It was their will."

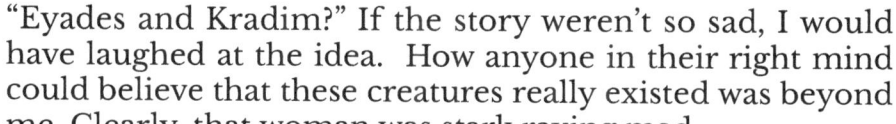

"Eyades and Kradim?" If the story weren't so sad, I would have laughed at the idea. How anyone in their right mind could believe that these creatures really existed was beyond me. Clearly, that woman was stark raving mad.

"Yes, my boy. Eyades and Kradim. It's not quite as bizarre as you might think. Keep in mind, this was five hundred turnings ago. Science was still in its infancy, and many people believed in those folk tales back then. It was their way of making sense of the world."

I nodded. Then another thought struck me. "What if one day science evolves to the point where we stop believing in the gods and their gifts to mankind?"

"What if the moon falls from the sky?" Ammu Shadu raised one eyebrow, and the corner of his mouth went up with it.

"But that's impossible," I said. "The laws of nature make sure that won't ever happen. And what's that got to do with anything anyway?"

"What I mean to say, Morad, is that you shouldn't worry about it. It probably won't happen, but even if it did... that might not necessarily be a bad thing. Progress always comes at a cost, but it's a price we're willing to pay."

My chest tightened, and my head started to throb. "I'm not sure I would." I rubbed my temples.

"Honestly, lad," Ammu Shadu repeated, "don't worry about it." After a moment's silence he said, "Shall I continue with the story now?"

"I guess so." I didn't really want to hear more, but this was the history of my ancestors, and I needed to know it.

Dalenka bore Aleyshan two more children, a son and a daughter, but to prevent a tragedy like the one with little Prince Siman from ever happening again, poor Princess Dalenka was locked away in the most isolated wing of the Royal Palace and was only allowed to see her children once a sevenday under the strict supervision of their bodyguards.

By the time Prince Aleyshan became king, he had turned into a sad, bitter man, who drowned his misery in absinthe and left the rule of Dalanthia to his vizier Sayif, who abused his position and made sure he became one of the wealthiest men on the entire Dalanthian continent.

Aleyshan's reign lasted only six turnings. He drank himself to death and left his son Haref a badly ruled kingdom with exploited and unhappy citizens, who were starting to rebel.

Haref worked hard to make up for the mistakes of his father and succeeded in gaining the trust of his people, but the Dalanthian realm never became as prosperous as it used to be in the days of Haniman.

Unfortunately, Haref was not interested in women and refused to get married. When he died, his sister's son Shaldin became the new king of Dalanthia.

Like his grandfather, Shaldin suffered from severe depressions, but contrary to the late King Aleyshan he managed to stay away from the bottle. However, he committed suicide at age thirty-six. His rule had lasted only one turning.

Because Shaldin's son was too young to become king yet, the late king's brother Arkash became the Child-King's regent until at age fifteen King Hashandor was ready to assume the throne.

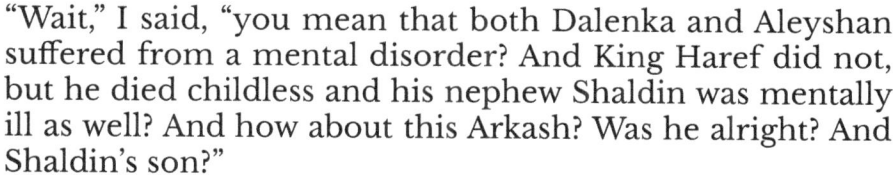

"Wait," I said, "you mean that both Dalenka and Aleyshan suffered from a mental disorder? And King Haref did not, but he died childless and his nephew Shaldin was mentally ill as well? And how about this Arkash? Was he alright? And Shaldin's son?"

"I was getting there, Moradin, I was getting there. Hashandor seemed to be a good enough king at first, but then he had his first psychotic episode, and claimed that the gods told him he should be the sole ruler of the Morynthian Empire. So he went to war with Emperor Radukan IV of Morynthia. A war he lost. From there, things only got worse.

"In each generation at least one of the children of the royal family suffered from some kind of mental disorder. Some were not affected too badly, but others were... well, I don't mean to be disrespectful, but..." He spread his hands and heaved a sigh.

For a moment Ammu Shadu seemed lost in thought, then he continued, "Some of them were so sick, they had to be locked away like poor Princess Dalenka, lest they should harm themselves or their loved ones, but even so, accidents still happened."

I closed my eyes. It was too much, and instead of being glad to actually know at least some of my family's history, I was even more scared now. Did this whole story not confirm my worst fears? That I was doomed to become a mentally disturbed criminal like King Hanassan?

"I don't understand. You say I will not become like him. Like... well, the king, and yet you tell me about this Curse of the Erlen King and how it affected the entire royal family of Dalanthia, and all of King Haniman's descendants."

I frowned. "I also don't comprehend how High King Yumænor could be so cruel as to evoke this terrible curse upon our family. Couldn't he just marry his daughter to someone else and forget about it? It seems so petty."

"Please! One thing at a time, Moradin. Let us get one thing straight first. Your father suffers from a psychotic disorder, whereas you were diagnosed with a major depression. These are two completely different conditions.

"Regarding the Erlen Curse... High King Yumænor did not curse your family. He warned King Haniman. He knew the prophecies and wanted to prevent all of this from happening. It was Haniman, not Yumænor, who called this curse down upon himself and his descendants."

He walked over to the bookshelf and took the Holy Book, then sat down beside me on the couch again. "Now, there are some prophecies that, if I am not mistaken, are nearing their fulfilment. The signs are there. If this is indeed true, then the Curse of the Erlen King is about to be lifted."

"Will you show me these prophecies, please? Can we study them together? Will my father be healed?" I was surprised by my last question. Why should I care about a man who had just killed his entire family? A man who murdered his own children?

Ammu Shadu smiled. "That was indeed my intention. To study the prophecies with you. That, at least, is something I can do. Your medallion does not usually interfere with that." He opened the book. "About your father... I wish I knew. I certainly hope he will. Nobody deserves to suffer like that poor man does."

I stared at my fingernails. Part of me resented the king, but another part of me knew that I should not blame him for things that were truly beyond his control. If it weren't for that sarding curse, he might have made a fine king. If only Haniman would have listened to the Erlen King. Now I hated King Haniman and his asinine thirst for power.

"Such a grim story," Bel said. Niels thought he heard a small tremor in her voice. And was it just his imagination, or did she really look smaller and more fragile than usual? "I could do with another tea. And is supper ready by now?" She manoeuvred closer to Niels and slumped against his side.

Instinctively, he wrapped his arm around her shoulders, then realised what he had done and silently cursed his stupidity. He was only making things harder for himself, but Bel seemed so vulnerable right now, he didn't dare withdraw his arm for fear of hurting her feelings.

For a moment, he considered using his medallion to lift her spirits, then decided against it. This close to Tirona, it held too many risks.

"Are you alright, Bel?" he asked in a low voice, so only she would hear it.

She looked up at him. "The Erlen Curse," she said just as softly. "We have our own version of the legend in Ingravia. I always thought it was just a story the elder generations had made up to explain and enhance historical events.

"My matrilineal ancestors, they are direct descendants of Emperor Fedromir. Your story made my blood run cold. Us Ingravians, Niels, we're not an easily intimidated people. But this scares the Northern Lights out of me."

"Erl's balls! You are... oh Gods! This cannot be happening. How well do you know the Prophecies?"

"Not nearly as well as you, I'm sure."

"There is this passage that reads, *'And by the same way that ruin fell upon the Great Houses, so shall it be reversed.'* I never knew what to make of it. It seemed so obscure, but now..." he looked away from Bel.

"You proposed to me," he said in a barely audible voice, "and you are a direct descendant of Fedromir. And I a direct descendant of Haniman."

"Dragon's breath! I... I was born in Moringarad, which used to be the capital of the Morynthian Empire. I'm liking this even less now. I thought you were the Chosen One. I have absolutely no desire to be chosen as well. I am just a cripple and a Reject. I made my peace with this."

"Would you say you are an outcast, and despised by many?"

Bel bit her lip. "I'm a torching Reject, Morad. And I have been living amongst strange people in a strange land, ever since I was eight turnings old. Do you really think..." She didn't finish her sentence.

"I don't know. I shall have to study the prophecies anew. Some of them seem to fit you, others definitely not, but I'm wondering now: Could it be that not all of them are about the same person, as we always assumed?" Niels scratched his head. "I have no answers. Just more questions."

He woke up with Bel cuddled up in his arms. She certainly hadn't been there when he fell asleep. This was worrisome. He didn't want to overstep his boundaries, but it almost seemed as if she was determined to make him do just that. He wasn't going to last much longer if she kept behaving like this. He quickly got up and went in search of Mikhandor.

The Erl liked to go for a late afternoon stroll before taking his seat behind the steering wheel. Niels found him by the stream, filling his flask with fresh water.

"Mikhandor, I need to see the high king. Urgently."

Mikhandor looked up. "That is an unusual request. Especially coming from you. What is this about?"

"Bel." The memory of how he had carried her into the stream made the heat rise to his cheeks.

Mikhandor burst out laughing. Sarding Erl!

"I see," he said when he finally had his laughter under control. "Unless I am very much mistaken, there is a portal in these mountains, not too far from here. I should be able to locate it easily. I've been feeling its presence growing stronger with each mile we've travelled since we entered the woods."

"How long do you think, before we get there?"

"Not long. Somewhere tonight, I would say." He screwed the lid on his flask, and started walking back to their camp.

Bel was awake, and sat by their small fire with Leks. When they came closer, Niels overheard Leks's words. "... need to stop this, Bel."

"Lady and gentleman." Mikhandor stood even taller than usual. "We are going to make a little detour. It should not delay us by much, but something has come up that needs to be dealt with as soon as possible."

"What do you mean, a detour?" Bel glared at him. "There is nothing here."

Mikhandor glared back at her. "Yes, there is. You'll find out soon enough. I suggest we break camp now and get moving. The sooner we get this over with, the better."

CHAPTER NINETEEN

Charge

exiled
and rejected
dragon defeats hunter
but surrenders to innocent
dreamer

Leks had lectured her about her behaviour towards Niels. She hadn't liked it, but he was right. He usually was. It wasn't as easy as it sounded, though. Looking back, it had been there right from the start, but she had suppressed her feelings immediately.

She'd been afraid to love again. Loving Lastor was the biggest mistake of her life. Zilla had hated him. Leks had warned her off. So had Papi and Mumi. They had seen what she, in her foolish infatuation with him, had refused to accept. The man was a scoundrel. A predator.

A gallant and charming one, but a hunter even so. She found out too late that he had only been using her for his own sinister purposes. People got hurt. Because she'd been such a blind *mouldywarp*. She'd had no choice but to act. With Zilla's help she had dealt with the problem. It had been a gruesome mess, and the memory still haunted her, but she'd seen no other way.

Because of her so-called courageous act of honour, Papi and Mumi had somehow been able to convince the House of Kings to elevate her to the status of Grand Lord — a title she never even wanted — despite the fact that she was still a Reject and an exile. That had never been done before. Not that it mattered much. Her new status was a carefully kept secret.

Then Niels walked into her life. She'd been stunned to find out that not only was their new priest a young man, but a good-looking one too. Those gorgeous golden eyes. That childlike air of innocence. His pure honesty.

She had fought her feelings until, on that first day of their journey, she could no longer deny them. Now the lid was off, and she had no desire to put it back on again. She wanted him. She wanted to love and feel loved. But she would have to tell Niels about Lastor. He needed to know what kind of woman she was before they got married — if he still wanted her, once he knew.

She turned her head and looked at him as he sat studying the Prophecies, a small hand-held crystal lighting the pages of the Holy Book. How could he do that, read in the karr? Whenever she'd tried to do the same, it had given her motion sickness.

Mikhandor reduced speed and drove the karr off the road, into the woods. He deactivated the power-magnets and said, "This is as far as I can take the karr. We'll need to cover her up and go the rest of the way by foot."

Leks woke up. He yawned. "Morning already?"

"No," Niels said, "but this is as far as we can drive tonight. Can you help cover up our vehicles?"

"Sure thing. These old bones could do with some exercise."

They got Bel's chair out first, made her sit in it, and would not allow her to help. She felt useless. Worse than useless. She'd be unable to ride her chair through these dense woods, so they would have to carry her and her chair. She would be a burden.

Her mind quested out to Zilla, who had caught a nice fat forest mouse and was gorging on it now. She waited till the dragonet had finished her meal, then asked her to return. Zilla's presence, at least, brought some comfort.

"Mistress Beldenka." The slight tremor in his voice indicated that Niels was even more uncomfortable than usual. "We're going to have to make our way through these woods here, and your chair will not be of much use to you, I fear. Mig has kindly offered to carry you, while I take your chair with me."

"Thank you, Moradin." She wanted to scream. She hated this. What was going on? What was so important in this dragon-cursed forest here? There was definitely something, and it pulsed. She could feel it. Zilla felt it too, but neither of them could make out what it was.

They carried just two crystals with them. Not nearly enough to light their way in these pitch dark woods, but that didn't seem to bother Mikhandor. Niels and Leks had more trouble keeping their footing. Neither of them complained, but both of them were panting. Leks even worse than Niels.

"Here it is." Mikhandor lowered her onto a tree stump. "Before we go any further, I need to sit down and rest for a little while."

Bel looked around, but saw nothing out of the ordinary. Not by the light of their two crystals, and she doubted she would be able to see much more by daylight. It didn't seem like daylight would make much of a difference here. However, the low throbbing sound that seemed to come from the trees themselves, was so intense now, she could feel it in her bones.

She closed her eyes and concentrated. Whatever the source of this rhythmic thumping was, it was right in front of her. Almost afraid to look, she peered through half-closed eyelids and there it was, almost luminescent in its majesty: A giant tree, probably thousands of turnings old, and as wide as a house.

"What are you?" she asked inside her mind, and its song beckoned her to come in. She got out of her chair and took a few wobbly steps in its direction. Then Niels blocked her way and caught her in his arms as her legs gave in.

"Bel, don't!" He sounded panicked.

"Torch you, Niels!" Angry tears streamed down her cheeks, and she beat his chest with both fists as he carried her back to her chair, but he acted as if he didn't even feel it.

Gently, he put her back in the chair and laid a hand on her shoulder. It seemed innocuous enough, but Bel knew he would restrain her if she'd even try to get back up again.

"But he invited me in!" She glared at him, then realised he would be unable to see her angry expression in this darkness. It made her scowl. At herself, and the world in general.

"I know, Bel." Niels' voice, so warm and gentle now, awakened the beetles in her belly. "And we are going in, but Mig needs to catch his breath first. He needs to guide us. We wouldn't want to lose our way, or get separated."

"What you two talking about?" Despite the thick murk, she knew Leks was staring at them. He probably thought they had both been bitten by a red fire beetle.

"There's a portal here." Niels sounded as if he thought it was the most normal thing in the world. But of course, he would have travelled portals dozens of times before with his Erlen guardian. "Mig felt it the moment we entered the woods. I've been feeling it for a while too now, and it turns out our Mistress Beldenka can also feel it."

"I have no idea what you're on about, chum. Can feel absolutely nothing out of the ordinary."

Bel gaped at Leks. How on all seven worlds could he not feel that? She couldn't ignore it even if she tried. It was so pervasive.

"That is because you have no magic." Again, Niels' voice sounded as placid as ever. "It does not matter much. You don't need magic to travel a portal. Not when you have a guide."

Leks snorted. "Magic, eh? Us Ingravians, we don't believe in that kind of whale dung."

It was the same thing that went through Bel's mind. Magic? What in the name of the Dragonmother was Niels thinking? Had he completely lost his faculties?

"I know," Niels said in the same stoic manner. "I will explain later."

"Right." Leks sounded as if he had just swallowed a turd. "Where are we going, if I may ask?"

"I apologise, but it's better if I don't tell you. Not here."

"Enough of that," Mikhandor cut in. "Let's go."

The portal was unlike anything she could ever have imagined. Not like in the storybooks she read as a child. To start with, it was completely invisible. Leks could have walked past it and never have known it was there. And, though she was convinced there was no so-called magic involved, she could hear Mikhandor communicate with the portal. In his own unintelligible Erlen language.

Niels took off his cravat and used it to tie Bel to her chair — though he said it just the other way round — and Mikhandor told them to hold hands. All of them. She held hands with Mikhandor and Niels. Niels took Leks's hand in his free hand. Next, Mikhandor had laid his free hand on the trunk of the ancient tree and asked for permission to enter. Not out loud, but Bel had heard it all the same.

The tree did not open, like she would have expected, but instead it simply swallowed them, and then they were inside. Only, inside was actually a young and neatly cultivated wooded area with seven smooth paths of hardened sand that diverged in seven different directions. Mikhandor warned them once more to keep holding hands, looked around and chose a meandering path, shaded by broad-leaved trees.

They walked the path for an indeterminate amount of time, until they arrived at a clearing from which, again, seven paths branched out. Mikhandor thanked the tree and bade it farewell, and immediately they were on a grassy slope that was sprinkled with the most fragrant pink and white flowers.

"Home," Mikhandor said, as he let go of her hand. He looked happier and more relaxed than Bel had ever seen him before. Niels sighed with obvious relief as he retrieved his cravat. A serene smile graced his face as he sat down in the grass.

"This Erlenland?" Leks asked as he looked around. Bel heard the excitement in his voice, and saw the wonder in his one real eye.

Mikhandor laughed a merry laugh. "I guess you could call it that," he said. "This is my home world, Thorf. Relax, my friends. We are safe here." He laid himself down on the soft turf and promptly fell asleep.

"What's all this talk of magic about?" Bel couldn't contain her curiosity any longer.

"You mean you didn't know?" Niels looked incredulous. "For how long have you had Zilla?"

"My entire life, of course." Such a silly question. Didn't everyone know the bond between a dragonet and their human was for life? "And I don't have her. I told you before, she is no pet. She's my companion. We are equals."

"You said she has telepathic abilities. Tell me more about that."

"Don't order me around." That came out fiercer than she intended.

"I would not do that, Bel." Niels sounded perplexed. Maybe even a bit hurt. "That is not my style. You ought to know that by now. I just need more details."

"I'm sorry. It's just... your suggestion of me having some sort of magic really upsets me." It was more than simply not believing in the Obscure Arts. In Ingravia, magic was punishable by death. Her grandfather got killed because some superstitious zealots thought he was a wielder of magic. "Anyway, there isn't much to tell. Zilla just knows my thoughts and feelings, and I hers. She, of course, communicates with other dragonets. That's how I keep in touch with my mother and brother. And we can also connect with dragons." They didn't usually bother, of course. Dragons tended to be a haughty lot.

"You said she could sense my moods."

Bel shrugged. It was just a minor thing. "Yes, but she doesn't even have access to your thoughts, so it's not really all that useful."

"And you both sensed the Song of the Portal." Niels held her eyes with his for a short moment, then looked away again. "That is something only those who are gifted with magic can."

He played with his cravat, as he often did when he seemed ill at ease. "Most of what you've told me so far is not necessarily indicative of magic, and could be attributed to strong telepathic abilities. But your sensitivity to the Portal has nothing to do with telepathy. That is magic, so there has to be more. What are you not telling me?"

Bel struggled. The only other thing she could think of, was that unfortunate business with Lastor, but she wasn't ready to talk about that yet.

"It's... I'll tell you later. I can't. Not right now."

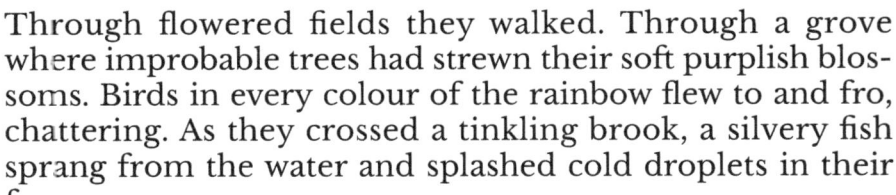

Through flowered fields they walked. Through a grove where improbable trees had strewn their soft purplish blossoms. Birds in every colour of the rainbow flew to and fro, chattering. As they crossed a tinkling brook, a silvery fish sprang from the water and splashed cold droplets in their faces.

Bel laughed, and almost squealed with delight. She felt like a child in a giant playground. Nature was so beautiful here. More beautiful than anything she had ever seen on Sor. But the best thing was, she could ride her chair anywhere she wanted.

A narrow, winding path? No problem. It widened and straightened enough so she could navigate it with ease. Boulders rolled aside to let her through. Flat wooden bridges rose up from streams where she needed to cross them. Yet, when she looked back, everything had gone back to its original state again.

She wasn't quite sure where or when they entered the Royal Palace. Strangely, it didn't look like a palace at all. It didn't look like any building she'd ever seen in her entire life, but rather like a structure that had grown there over hundreds or maybe thousands of turnings. As if built by nature itself.

They halted by a wide archway from which warm red and bright yellow flowers cascaded down in rich clusters. A young man dressed in all white made a florid bow before he addressed them.

"The Father is expecting you." He said in a high, boyish voice. "I shall announce your arrival."

The youngster stepped through the archway and as Niels followed him, exuding a confidence she had never noticed in him before, so did Bel. Mikhandor and Leks followed.

"His Royal Highness Prince Moradin of Ebaru, Grand Lord Beldenka Nadinov of Ingravia, and her protector Lord Yeleksim Bogrovik of Ingravia."

"Come, sit with me." The man at the far end of the room bore an uncanny resemblance to the Erlen king Yumænor from the storybooks Papi used to read to her when she was a little girl. Bel gasped. Her eyes nearly popped out of their sockets. Could it really be?

High King Yumænor got up and embraced Niels. "Moradin, my dear friend, I am delighted to see your face again."

"Thank you, your Majesty. It's always an honour, and a great pleasure to see you." Strangely, Niels didn't even sound impressed. In fact, nothing showed of his customary awkwardness. What was up with that? How well did he actually know the Erlen king?

"Lord Nadinov." The king nodded at Bel. "I am beyond pleased to finally meet you." Funny, how his eyes looked too old for his face. But then again, he had to be hundreds of turnings old. Bel felt so nervous, she nearly wet her drawers, but it wouldn't do to show even a hint of weakness. She would not bring shame upon her parents or her Ingravian heritage.

"Your Majesty." She inclined her head. "The pleasure is all mine." She was lying through her teeth. There was nothing pleasant about meeting a legendary king who should have been dead for aeons already. It was scary as all seven hells.

"And Lord Bogrovik." King Yumænor smiled at her old friend. "A man after my heart."

"Thank you, your Majesty." Leks made an awkward bow. His keen eye studied the high king with interest. "You honour me."

"My dear son." The old king's bright blue eyes sparkled as he drew Mikhandor in a tight embrace.

"Father." To Bel's utter surprise, the giant's voice sounded smothered, and he held onto the frail looking man as if he would never let go. It was one thing to address your king as 'Father', but this... Surely, the ancient king couldn't really be Mikhandor's father? That would make him a prince. A legendary prince, no less. Colour rose to her cheeks as she thought of all the rude things she'd said to him. She really should have guarded that rash tongue of hers.

"Let us eat. I had a feast prepared for you as soon as I learned that you were coming."

"I thought you were a Minor Lord, Bel" Niels said, and it almost sounded like an accusation. "That's what Mikhandor told me."

They were alone — or as alone as they could hope to be here — in a secluded part of the Royal Gardens. A young Erl, ostensibly Bel's personal assistant, stood watching them discreetly, just far enough away so she couldn't overhear their conversation. Or so Bel hoped.

"This is what people are supposed to believe. The House of Kings has been keeping my promotion to Grand Lord under wraps. It embarrasses them. They've never had to elevate a Reject to even High Lord status, let alone Grand Lord, but my parents can be rather persuasive." She bit the nail of her thumb, then caught herself in the act and tucked both thumbs safely away in tightly closed fists. "I did not want this promotion. If it were up to me, I wouldn't even be a lord at all. It is all dragon's droppings to me."

"What brought the kings around?" Niels' gaze rested on the spot between her eyes, and with a shock of surprise she realised that was what he always did. He never made real eye contact if he could avoid it. Had life hurt him that much?

"I will tell you. Everything. But you're not going to like this." Bel stared at her fingernails. She took a deep breath. "You wanted to know about my magic, as you call it. You wanted to know about my husband. And you need to know these things. They may well change your mind about me."

She closed her eyes in a vain attempt to banish the image of her husband as he lay bleeding, his eyes wide with pain and disbelief. The memory still hurt. Undeserving though he was, she had truly loved him.

"Lastor... He was everything I thought a man should be. Charming, courteous, good-looking, elegant, intelligent, musically gifted. Everyone liked him. And he, this incredible man, saw me. Not the poor cripple in her wheelchair, but the woman Beldenka Nadinov. And he never passed up an opportunity to let me know just how much he adored me.

"He said I was too precious to be wasting my life away hiding in the Barlows, so he took me on dates to Midhaven and Freyborough. We went to concerts and plays. We dined at the fanciest establishments. He showed me off to the world. He would introduce me to his friends and colleagues. 'Meet my beautiful and talented betrothed, Beldenka Nadinov,' he would say with obvious pride in his voice. He was the man of my dreams, and I couldn't believe my luck when he asked me to marry him."

Annoyed with herself, she wiped her eyes. She shouldn't be crying over that creep. He wasn't worth her tears.

"I was willing to quit my job in the Barlows and was already looking for a position in one of the cities. I even had a few job offers. Ridiculous, demeaning offers, where I would be paid less than half of the wages I got in the Barlows. The message was clear. *We do not want a crippled cantor.*

"But Lastor... he believed in me. He said the perfect job offer would come. It made me love him even more. He raised my spirits when I was down. He made me believe in myself."

She sighed. If only he had really been the wonderful person she had believed him to be.

"Papi and Mumi did not approve of him. Leks didn't like him. Zilla hated him as passionately as I loved him. They warned me time and again, and they all said the same thing. He was not the man he pretended to be, and could not be trusted. He was too smooth, too refined. I should have listened to them."

Niels' posture became alert. "What did he do to you?"

"Nothing. He was always the perfect gentleman towards me. It was what he did to others. He was a hunter, and little boys his prey." Bel shuddered. To this day she didn't know how he had managed to keep his sordid escapades a secret, or how he made all of his little victims disappear so completely, but she had her suspicions. "I found out too late that he did not love me for who I was. He loved that he could make a good show of being the perfect husband to his poor, disabled wife. I was only ever his cover."

"That's horrible." Anger burned in Niels' eyes. "Absolutely despicable."

Bel nodded. She bit her lip. Already, she felt so miserable she could barely control her voice, and the worst was yet to come.

"When we found out, Zilla and I, we knew we had to stop him." She paused to swallow the lump in her throat. "I still don't know how it happened, but the two of us sort of merged and became an enormous Ingravian Broadwing Dragon, while our natural bodies remained behind where they were. We... we..."

A wave of emotion crashed into her and made her sob uncontrollably, and Niels, that sweet man, held her and patted her back in his own clumsy way. "There," he said. "There now, there."

"It still haunts me day and night. I'm a murderer, Niels. You cannot marry me." Her chest tightened and pressed her throat shut. As she sat gasping for breath, a flood of snot, drool, and tears rushed out through her eyes, nose and mouth. She knew she looked a horrid mess, but there was nothing she could do to stop the tide.

CHAPTER TWENTY

Foresight

*Erlen
king shares visions
of futures that might be
and cautions holy man to choose
wisely*

As he continued to try and comfort Bel, Niels' mind was reeling. He couldn't believe it. Bel, his cantor, had killed a man. And not just any man, but her own husband. Granted, what the wretch had done would have earned him a death sentence in Ingravia and most other countries around the world, but still.

Tiny, disabled Bel, a killer. He'd known she was dangerous, and had even accepted that fact. Reluctantly. But dangerous was a broad concept. Her father was dangerous too, but had always found other ways to dispense of his adversaries or deal with problematic situations. Or at least, so Niels thought.

It had never occurred to him that Bel would be capable of taking a life. Not really. He had assumed she was more like her father. And he'd been wrong.

To be fair, she had not quite been herself. It had been her magic, the Dragon Magic, in which she was clearly untrained, that had taken possession of her, but the fact remained. She had tasted blood. Quite literally. She might well kill again, her remorse notwithstanding.

Undeniably, he loved Bel, and he'd been ready to ask for High King Yumænor's permission to marry her. Now, he feared the answer — no matter what it might be.

"Milord, might I borrow Prince Moradin from you for a little while?" Niels hadn't heard the High King's approach, but that was nothing new. The Erlen king had perfected the art of stealth, and without even trying, Niels was sure.

Bel looked up as she wiped the last tears from her eyes. "Always, your Majesty." Her voice sounded only a little unsteady.

Yumænor looked at her. "I have asked Janæla to prepare you a nice hot bath, so you can relax a little. The two of us shall talk later."

Bel nodded. "Thank you, your Majesty. This is very kind of you."

The young Erl that had been watching them came closer, and Niels rose and walked with the high king.

"If I were to guess," Yumænor said after a short while, "your cantor just told you about that unfortunate business with her late husband."

Niels nodded glumly.

"I can imagine how shocked you must be. You see a delicate woman in a wheelchair. A kind and deeply compassionate person. A woman who hates iniquity. You have come to love her for exactly those qualities, and then you learn she has killed her husband. That's a scary idea, isn't it, my friend?"

Again, Niels nodded.

"She hates herself for it," the ancient king continued. "Even though what she did was right. If she hadn't killed him, someone else would have done so. Several people, from several worlds, were after his blood. People who might not have hesitated to kill her along with him, and that would have been a huge problem. She has her destiny to fulfil, just as you have yours."

They walked in silence as Niels pondered Yumænor's words. "I was going to ask for your permission to marry her," he finally said, "but this troubles me. I'm a priest."

He fell silent again. Fumbled with his medallion. Stared at his feet as they wandered on through the high grass. "Can I marry a woman who has killed, and yet remain true to my calling?"

"I understand your dilemma. Let me share with you some of the possible futures I saw. And keep in mind that my precognition is not infallible, no matter what some people may think. The ultimate choice will have to be yours."

He stroked his long white beard with his gnarled hands and, not for the first time, Niels wondered just how old the Erlen king really was.

"In the first scenario, you break with Beldenka completely. She is so upset, she decides to go back home as soon as you enter into your own world again. She doesn't want you to travel back to the Barlows with her. So, while you and Mikhandor wish to continue your journey, she and Lord Bogrovik take their belongings and go back.

"You now have no merchandise, and no means of transportation, so you have to travel along by foot. With Beldenka, you lost all your other future companions too, because her entire family has withdrawn. You are also out of a job, but Mikhandor gets you a new job in another isolated part of your world. The Royal Assassins of Ebaru never find you, and you live your life out in peace. You never get married, and die childless. Your destiny remains unfulfilled."

"To be completely honest, a peaceful life is a rather attractive option. Never getting married seems but a small price to pay."

"That is exactly the thing I expected you to say, and this life might be within your reach. However, here is the second scenario. Again, you break up with Beldenka, but she decides she still wants to accompany you on your quest and help you fulfil your destiny.

"So you go back to your own world, and proceed as planned, but because both Beldenka and you are in a hurry to get this mission over with, you make some costly mistakes. As a result, your whole party gets captured and killed by members of the cult of Mirk, in Tirona. Again, your destiny remains unfulfilled."

The cult of Mirk. Niels shuddered. "That is a grim future, and certainly not one I fancy."

"Nobody in their right mind would, my friend, but personally, I think this is the more likely scenario of these two. Beldenka is a woman of her word. I don't think it very likely that she would abandon you just because she is hurt. Do you?"

Niels shook his head. Bel was, indeed, a woman of her word. High King Yumænor was right. She would want to finish this task she had taken upon herself, no matter what.

"Now, if you were to marry Lord Nadinov, your future would be vastly different. You would get to Ebaru safely, though your journey would, or course, not be without problems. You would, to a certain degree, be able to restore your father's health. You would become king, and fulfil your destiny." He stopped to smell a flower, and Niels watched him with interest.

"Things are a fair bit more complicated than that, of course, but I gave you the short versions of these three possible scenarios. I cannot and will not reveal details to you."

"So, I can only fulfil my destiny if I marry Beldenka?"

"As far as I can see, yes. There might be other scenarios, but if so, I have no knowledge of them."

They sat down in the grass by a small pond and watched the fish play in the water.

"Your Majesty..." Niels cast a sideways glance at Yumænor. "What about Bel's magic? As far as I can tell, she didn't even know that what she and her dragonet share is a magic connection, and she has no control over it. Nor does she have any training."

"That is indeed a problem that needs to be addressed. The sooner the better."

"But how? My magic is too different. I can't think of anything I could possibly do." He fidgeted with his cravat.

The old king smiled, and shook his head. "Don't sell yourself short, my friend. The basics are the same for all kinds of magic. I imagine you could teach her those. This may not sound like much to you, but she has to start somewhere."

Strangely, it were not any priest's words that came to his mind first, but Mikhandor's.

"Control your breathing, and you control your mind."

Bel was a singer. Controlling her breathing should already be second nature to her.

"Now, my young friend, when you leave Thorf, I suggest you go to Senkerland first. Up in the Senkeberghe lives an old man, who fled Ingravia long ago, when all magic, and even the belief in it, was outlawed. His companions are a Green Firecrest Dragon and two dragonets. He is known as Guren Fonvernum, and is well versed in the Dragon Magic.

"This Guren is a hermit and nurtures a profound mistrust of strangers. Unless you get help, finding him is going to be nigh impossible, but Beldenka needs him. The magic runs extremely strong in her, and will certainly kill her if she doesn't learn how to control it."

Bel felt a lot better after her bath. Janæla had provided her with new clothes that fit her perfectly. She now wore a pair of the most comfortable breeches, made for sitting, and a soft white shirt, tight-fitting at the waist, but with plenty of room around the shoulders. Just the way she liked it. Her silken stockings were seamless, and her shoes of thin, pliable leather.

She sat in the shade of a blossoming tree with her chaperone, because that was what Janæla really was, of course. Here to make sure she wouldn't seduce Niels. As if the man would ever allow himself to be seduced. He could be so stuffy!

He surely wouldn't want to marry her now, and how could she blame him? She wouldn't be too thrilled to marry a man who had killed his first wife, now, would she? Nobody in their right mind would want to take that kind of risk.

This was going to make everything so much harder. She couldn't just abandon him. They had to deal with King Hanassan and his assassins once and for all, so Niels could finally... well, could do what exactly? Become king? Choose someone else to become king, so he could live out his life as a simple priest, which seemed to be what he really wanted?

"Your king," she said, just to break the silence, "is he really the fabled High King Yumænor from the legends?"

"Of course he is. We age a lot slower than you humans do, and we live much longer. That said, The Father is, of course, the oldest Sylphan alive. He is an Intemporal, created by our goddess Doruya herself, when our world was young."

Bel toyed with a lock of her hair. "So... you look like you are younger than me. Maybe not even twenty turnings old yet, but in reality you're a fair bit older than that, am I right?"

Janæla laughed. "You really are obsessed with age, aren't you, young lady? Would you believe me when I told you I am older than your grandfather?"

"Older than my grandfather?" Bel's mouth fell open. "But he is eighty-four turnings old! And you're older than that? That is..." she shook her head. This was beyond her comprehension. It shed a whole different light on Mikhandor's *ask again in about two-hundred turnings* when she had inquired after his age. The man might well be two-hundred-and-something already.

"Don't worry about it," Janæla said, "it doesn't matter all that much. The really important thing is that we have finally met, and I won't have to hide from you any more. That is going to make my life a lot easier. And yours too."

"Finally met? What do you mean, finally met?"

What was it again, that Niels had said about Mikhandor? That it was his job to keep Niels safe. But Niels was a prince. She was no royalty.

Ingravia's royalty ceased to exist back in 9587, when Emperor Bartomir III was deposed. Murdered in a most gruesome way — and the rebels hadn't stopped there. They had captured all other members of the Imperial family, and made the men watch them violate their wives and daughters. Then, they had forced the women to watch as they emasculated the males, even the youngest boys, and left them to bleed out. Finally, they decapitated the women and girls. All of them.

Or so they thought.

As if by some miracle, Bartomir's pregnant granddaughter Lillenka had managed to escape to the mountains where she hid amongst the dragons and gave birth to her son Nazradim.

When Nazradim was in his twenties, he fathered the twin boys Dragomir and Viktomir. Bel was a direct descendant of Dragomir, but these days that meant absolutely nothing. They were just ordinary people. Lords by accomplishment.

"Didn't you know?" Janæla's voice brought her back to the present. "We have been watching over every kind of royalty ever since the worlds were created. This is our sacred duty, which we take very seriously."

"But I'm no royalty, Janæla. I am just a descendant of a deposed emperor."

"And Prince Moradin is the unlawful son of King Hanassan. What's the difference, child?"

"Easy," Bel said, "his father is a ruling king. My mother is just a lord. One of many. And the Empire is no more. Our kings earn the right to be king. Birthright means nothing in Ingravia."

The woman awarded her an almost condescending smile, and shook her head. "The prophecies, both yours and ours, appear to indicate that changes are coming. Soon."

"Suppose you are right..." Bel's mind called out to Zilla. She needed her companion. "... why should you guard me? My mother should be first in line, followed by my sister Belinska. She is the older one." Only by several heartbeats, but it still counted. Besides, Lin was no Reject. "Or even Nikomir." Younger than her, but a man, and back in imperial times, gender mattered.

Janæla watched as Zilla descended on Bel's shoulder. "You have the Dragon Magic."

Bel wanted to stamp her feet. Funny, how after all these turnings that urge still kicked in when she got angry. "What are you people on about, with your torching Dragon Magic? There is no such thing. I am no priest. I have no supernatural powers. Besides, my mother talks to her dragonet too. And my brother to his."

"And we guard them too, Milord, but the prophecies indicate that you..."

"Will you cut this Milord nonsense? It is Bel. Just Bel. I don't do these fancy titles." A hot, stinging sensation welled up in the pit of her stomach, rushed upwards past her vocal folds and, as her breath escaped in a high whistle, a tiny flame erupted from her mouth.

"What on all seven worlds was that?" Somehow, she managed to fight down the sudden panic. The flame had died almost instantly, but what if she had ignited that beautiful tree? And worse than that: How was she breathing fire now?

Janæla's lips curled into a barely visible smile, and her eyes twinkled. "That, Mi... uh, Bel, was your magic."

"I don't..." She felt the fire burn inside her belly, then rise in her throat, and before she knew it, she belched yet another flame. Mortified, she looked down. She held her breath as she tried to calm herself but that, of course, wasn't working. "Alright, you win. So, I have this thing you all keep calling Dragon Magic. Now what? I never even heard of it before today."

She rolled away from her spot under the tree. Not as fast as she usually went — she wanted Janæla to be able to keep up with her — but being so close to anything flammable seemed too dangerous right now.

"You learn, of course."

"How? When there is no-one to teach me?" Mumi and Niko, Bel was sure, didn't know any more than she did. Maybe even less. Magic had been dismissed as a myth in Ingravia around the same time Emperor Bartomir had been deposed, and since people kept believing in magic, it had been made illegal and punishable by death around the time Papi was born.

"The basics are the same for everyone." Her chaperone sounded almost indifferent. "You learn to control your breathing."

As a singer, she knew pretty much all about that. Only, she had never applied this knowledge outside of a professional context. "That easy?"

"That easy." Janæla picked some incredibly pink berries from a shrub. "Here, try these. They are sweeter than any berries you will find on Sor."

CHAPTER TWENTY-ONE

Alliance

> dragon
> shall rule again
> as love brings unity
> remnants of glory shall prosper
> anew

Bel looked more beautiful than ever. Her green silken shirt and slightly darker breeches accentuated the sparkle in her gorgeous verdigris eyes. She wore padded fingerless gloves in the same shade of green as her breeches, and a string of delicate white flowers was woven into her hair. A precious jadeite, a wedding gift from High King Yumænor, hung from a fine silver chain around her neck.

Niels himself wore a simple but comfortable seamless silken robe in a rich, deep brown. He felt good in it, and hoped he'd never again have to wear that uncomfortable suit Bel had made him.

They'd been on Thorf for nearly a sevenday now, and much had happened. The day after their arrival, he'd gone to visit Akdi, who sat in a comfortable rocking chair by the window, and seemed in better shape than he'd ever been since the fires.

"Back again, boy?" He looked at Niels, his expression as serious as ever. "No bad news, I hope?"

"I'm not sure, sir. It's..." Niels looked at the floor, wondering where to start. "It's complicated. I, uh... I met a woman."

"A special woman, I gather?"

"More special than you could imagine. I..." Why was this so difficult? "I wanted to marry her, but..." His breath caught in his throat. He started pacing the room.

"I feel your turmoil. What is it, boy?" Akdi sure didn't waste any time on meaningless talk. Some things never changed.

"She killed a man," Niels blurted out. "Her previous husband."

For a moment, they both were silent, then Akdi said, "That's no small thing. No small thing at all." He motioned at the other chair. "Sit down and tell me."

"She only told me yesterday, and I'm sure she left out lots of details, but the gist of it is, he turned out to be a thoroughly depraved man. When she found out he abused and murdered young boys, she... well, her magic took possession of her and made her kill him."

"Magic?" Akdi lifted an eyebrow.

"She has the Dragon Magic. As it turns out, not all of Emperor Fedromir's offspring were killed. Beldenka is one of his descendants."

For a moment, Akdi remained silent. Then he chuckled, and his chuckle turned into full-blown laughter. Niels stared at him, mouth agape. What had got into that man? He hardly ever even smiled, and now he was actually laughing?

"Sir?"

"Sorry, young man, but this is just too coincidental. You know the prophecies. *'And by the same way that ruin fell upon the Great Houses, so shall it be reversed, and the reign of the dragon shall be restored.'* Who would have guessed that these words were to be taken so literally, hmm?"

"So you think I should still marry her? Despite what she did to her first husband?"

"What else should she have done, Moradin? Allow him to continue his sordid practices? How many more innocent boys should he have raped and killed?" He shook his head.

"She did the right thing, this Beldenka of yours. I want to meet her."

Niels nodded slowly. "It scares me, you know. All of this."

"Of course it does. It's a tremendous burden that the prophecies are placing upon your shoulders. But it would be a shared burden. You'd have a strong woman by your side. What does High King Yumænor say?"

"He doesn't exactly make things any easier. He tells me I can choose whether or not I wish to fulfil my destiny."

"Your destiny. The word you've always been so allergic to. How's your allergy now, young man?" Akdi sounded amused.

"I still don't like it. I don't think that will ever change, but I also know I can't live with myself unless I do everything that's within my power to reverse this curse. I owe that to my friends, my family, and my country. Above all, I owe it to those who died for me, so their deaths won't have been in vain." Niels sighed.

Both men stared silently out of the window as their shared grief hung heavily in the air around them.

Finally, Akdi nodded. "You marry that woman, Moradin. Marry her and mend our world."

"Prince Moradin Dolanthi of Ebaru," High King Yumænor said, and it felt strange and wrong to be called so, "are you ready to take as your wife, the imperial princess, Beldenka Nadinov of Ingravia? Do you vow to love, honour and support her, now and forever?"

Niels swallowed the sudden lump in his throat. "I, Moradin Dolanthi of Ebaru, am willing and ready to take as my wife, the imperial princess, Beldenka Nadinov of Ingravia, Beloved of the Dragons. I vow to love, honour and support her with my entire being, now and forever."

He looked at Beldenka. His Beldenka, his beloved. He still couldn't understand what he had done to deserve her love.

"Princess Beldenka Nadinov of Ingravia," the Erlen king addressed Bel, "are you ready to take as your husband, Prince

Moradin Dolanthi of Ebaru? Do you vow to love, honour and support him, now and forever?"

Bel's eyes were shining and her voice was clear and melodious as she spoke. "I, Beldenka Nadinov of Ingravia, am willing and ready to take as my husband, Prince Moradin Dolanthi of Ebaru, Priest and Chosen One of the Goddess Eylah. I vow to love, honour and support him with my entire being, now and forever."

Yumænor laid one hand on Bel's head, and his other hand on Niels'. "I hereby proclaim you husband and wife. May our Gods bless you and your union, and grant you to fulfil your destinies." He then handed them their wedding orb.

After the ancient king had taken a step back, Niels pulled his priestly medallion from under his robes, placed it carefully in Bel's right hand and positioned his own right hand on top of it. He closed his eyes, concentrated on his breathing and marvelled as through the medallion his mind made direct contact with Bel's wonderful and incredibly complex mind.

They stole away from their wedding feast early, to a secluded part of the Royal Gardens and, for once, it was just the two of them. No chaperones, no protectors. Even Zilla was somewhere else.

"Now, my sweet Bel," Niels said as he fumbled with the buttons of her shirt, "I finally get to enjoy not just that brilliant mind of yours, but also that perfectly divine body."

Bel's laughter sounded like music. "So you did look, back at the stream."

Niels laughed, too. "How could I not? And why does this shirt have so many buttons?"

"That, my love, was by design. Too tiny and delicate for such big clumsy hands like yours, they build up your desire like nothing else, as you desperately attempt to undo them."

"You are making that up, aren't you?" He honestly couldn't tell whether or not she was joking.

Bel kissed him even more ardently than the other day in the stream. "I am. But it does work that way even so, right?"

"Gods! Yes, it does." In fact, it had already built up to the point where he would gladly rip the clothes from her body.

"If it's any comfort," Bel whispered in his ear, "it is doing the same thing to me."

"I know," he said. "I can feel it. And I'm sure you can feel my, uh... passion. It is the medallion."

"Dragon's breath! Is that what's happening to me? And here I thought Zilla had somehow found herself a mate here. The poor thing must be going crazy with our excitement." She bit her lower lip. "I had better mask from her."

"Bel," Niels asked as the storm in his body continued to rage, "would you mind very much if your shirt got accidentally..."

She wrapped her tiny hands around his wrists and made him tear the shirt apart. "There. That's better," she murmured, and Niels agreed.

INTERLUDE

INTERLUDE 1

Marauder

*hardened
man of rough seas
in search of the dragon
pained by resonance of magic
succumbs*

Two sevendays. The Aurora has been anchored in Tiria harbour for a good two sevendays, but still nothing. Nikomir Nadinovik was becoming worried. His dragonet Gizzim had tried to find Zilla — several times even — but not a trace. As if his sister had fallen from the crust of Sor.

"Still nothing?" Lorinka came up from behind and placed a hand on his shoulder.

Niko turned and shook his head. "It drives me crazy. I am starting to fear that something could have happened to Bel and her group, and with the crew becoming more unmanageable every day, I feel like I'm losing my mind."

"Don't get me started on the crew." His wife's eyes flashed with sudden fury. "We may have to keelhaul some of them if this goes on for much longer. And I'm inclined to remove that pizzle Rinn's left eye for the way he keeps staring at my butt."

"That might be a good idea." Niko nodded. Rinn's misplaced infatuation with Lori had not escaped him — or the crew. It could very well be one of the reasons why they had become belligerent. He should have done something about that sailor's behaviour much sooner.

His gaze roamed the unnaturally clean harbour, and his eyes narrowed at the sight of the barely clad, leashed women scrubbing the cobblestones. He hated Tiria. Hated all of Tirona and that creepy religion of theirs. Their despicable views on women. If he were a man, he'd... but he couldn't risk the lives of his crew.

"Do you think I should contact my mother? She should be in Ebaru now, getting ready for the concert. I wouldn't upset her, but you know what she is like."

"What does Gizzim think?"

"Gizzim wants to mate and cannot think coherently right now." Niko took Lori in his arms. "You are so beautiful," he whispered in her ear as he undid the top two buttons on the back of her bodice.

She pushed him away gently. "Not here, captain. Not if you want your crew to respect you."

"You're right, but Dragonmother! Why do you have to be so gorgeous?" And why did Gizzim's arousal always have this effect on him? This was not the time for that. Confound that prurient little dragonet. He almost got drunk with desire just looking at Lori as she fastened those buttons again. "Anyway, I think I know what to do. Pack one or two sets of clothing, and also one set for me, please. I will go and tell Felnar that he is in charge of the ship, and then I'll find some of our best people to accompany us."

"Accompany us?" She looked up at him. Her bright blue eyes held a million questions. "What are you up to?"

"The only thing I can do. I will search for Bel and find her. Or find out what happened to her. No more waiting. Time to act."

He felt better now that he knew what to do. Let Felnar handle his unruly crew. Let him keelhaul a couple of those louts. And take Rinn's eye. That should put things in order. Then he could set those lazy sailors to work on repairs and other boring but necessary jobs. He wanted the ship to look like new when he returned from this mission.

He would, of course, ask Flar to join their search party, but who else? Maybe Eshtolya Galniev. Lori spoke highly of her, and he trusted the common sense of his wife. And this new boy, Pashovny Karstunvik. He seemed like a good guy. Strong and reliable, as far as Niko could tell, so that would also be a smart choice. Lori would definitely approve. He counted on his fingers. That made five. He needed another crew member just in case. Zeralize Kalnabris. Maternal type, and an excellent cook, who knew everything about herbs and their healing properties. He nodded to himself and hummed a sea shanty as he went in search of his special team.

It was well past noon when they finally set out. He'd had to find a vehicle, and that had turned out to be much harder than he thought. He had been to all seven rental companies in Tiria, but none of them would rent him a karr, and in the end he felt that he had no choice but to borrow without consent.

So he had walked around for a bit, looking for suitable vehicles, taking inventory in his mind which ones he saw, and where. The moment he returned to the Aurora, he had gathered his Elite Force and told them to act as if they were looking for what the Tironians called an eatery. Then he'd ordered Felnar to set sail to Keshire Bay.

"Flar," he said as he handed his friend two leather leashes, "you protect Zeralize and Eshtolya. Defend them with your life if anyone tries to take them."

Impatient as ever, Lori had already fastened the third leash around her own neck and handed Niko the loop. "You'd better make sure nobody tries to run off with me, Captain. I won't be having any other guy touching me."

"As if any of those savages would stand a chance against me and Gizzim. I swear, we would roast them alive." He meant every word he said. "Now let's go."

They found the karr of his choice easily enough, and while Flar and Pashovny distracted the handful of passers-by with a heated mock-argument about Flar's women, Lori pried the lock of one of the doors open with a hairpin. She got in quickly, opened the other doors to let their team in, and activated the power-magnets. It all took less than a few heartbeats, and as far as Niko could tell, none of the people in the street took any note of their illegal borrowing.

Still, they'd wasted no time leaving the city, and now they were speeding towards the Briscan border. It was best to avoid unnecessary risks. Most people did not approve of having their belongings borrowed without consent. They called it stealing. The Tironians, unfortunately, were even worse than others — and Niko didn't fancy getting his nuts offered to their demon-god Mirk.

"This is madness, Niko, and you know it." Though Lori scolded him, her eyes were twinkling, and Niko heard the excitement in her voice. She loved the thrill of adventure. Perhaps even more than he did.

"Yes." He chuckled. "And I haven't had so much fun in a long time."

"You may call it fun." Without looking at him, Niko knew Flar's expression matched the grim tone of his voice, "but ultimately I will be the one who has to save your sorry arses when the Tironians get their hands on you. They are not a forgiving people, and you know it."

"So we just make sure they don't catch us." His grin broadened, and he accelerated into an even higher gear. It was a good, sturdy karr. He knew about the risk, so he had made sure to select only the best karrs he saw. So far, this one had not disappointed him.

They crossed the bridge over Lannstriken River into Briscona as the sun began to set, and the landscape changed almost immediately. Though the mountain ridge was less jagged, the roads had probably not seen any repairs in the past ten turnings. It made for a bumpy ride, but Niko didn't mind. As long as no one followed them, that was all that mattered.

His stomach rumbled. It had been a long time since lunch. They drove through a small village. If one could even call it that. Only a few farms, and useless to them. They needed a city. One with an inn and a rental company.

"Could you check the map for us, Lori? We are looking for a medium-sized town."

"Sure." She held out her hand, and one of the others handed her a small scroll. She rolled it out on her lap and studied it.

"Right. Make a U-turn and take the mountain road we passed about a mile back. Go west where it forks. From there it should only be three more miles. Small town called Hedbury Vale. It's the only town this far south."

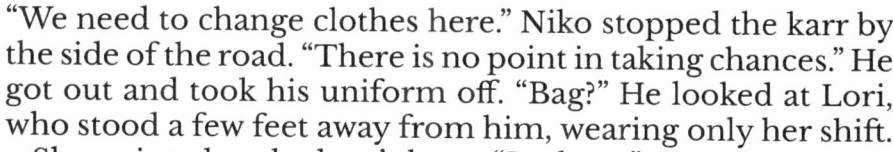

"We need to change clothes here." Niko stopped the karr by the side of the road. "There is no point in taking chances." He got out and took his uniform off. "Bag?" He looked at Lori, who stood a few feet away from him, wearing only her shift.

She pointed to the karr's boot. "In there."

He nodded and grabbed the only bag that was still in the boot. In it he found a loose-fitting shirt and a pair of breeches. Ordinary worker's clothes. He smiled and nodded his approval. Where would he be without Lori?

As soon as all of them had changed clothes, Niko drove the karr to the edge of the cliff and jumped out just before it plummeted into the deep dark depths of the ravine. It was a real shame, but he saw no other way. They couldn't risk anyone finding that vehicle any time soon. His right foot landed on a stone and his ankle twisted. He lost his balance, but managed to grab onto Flar's outstretched hand, which saved him from plunging to his death in that ravine.

Before long, he could feel his ankle swell up in his boot. It throbbed worse with every limping step he took, and by the time they got to the town, tears of pain were burning behind his eyes.

"About time we found our inn, eh, captain?" The concern in Zeralize's voice was unmistakable. "I need to take a look at that ankle of yours."

"That would be good." Niko nodded. "That, and I wouldn't mind a hot drink."

"And food, please." Pashovny rubbed his stomach with both hands. He was a large man, with a corresponding appetite.

"I think we're in luck," Lori said. Her voice sounded eager. "Look over there. I'll eat my late grandfather's smallclothes if that's not an inn. Hear that singing? Sounds like they've got a bard."

The humid heat inside took his breath away, Lori's bard turned out to be a drunk who sang terribly out of tune, and the stink of stale ale and human sweat was nauseating, but Niko was glad he could sit down and rest his aching leg. Zeralize dropped to her knees almost immediately, removed his boot and sock, and examined the throbbing ankle.

"You got a good swelling there, boss. No wonder you were limping. It is already crimson. But, as far as I can tell, it's not broken." She rummaged in the leather pouch she always carried on a rope around her waist, held up a small porcelain container, removed the stopper, and sniffed its contents.

"That should work." She spread the ointment on his sore ankle and massaged it in. It had a cooling effect.

"Now," she said as she pulled a piece of cloth out of her bag and began to tear it into long, thin strips, "I'm going to bandage your ankle, to help reduce the swelling. Ideally, you shouldn't walk on it for at least two sevendays."

Niko barked a short laugh. "Not going to happen."

"I know, boss." The worry in her silvery grey eyes made his stomach cramp. He didn't have time for this. "I'll find you a walking stick in a moment."

"No," he said, "Pav can do that." He looked at the young man. "Won't you, boy?"

"Immediately, sir." He was out of the door before either of them could say another word.

Flar and Lori came back from the bar with large mugs of dark ale. "This was the best we could get." Lori made a face. "It tastes like horse pee. However, that's still better than their rancid smelling wine with the little bluish flakes floating on top."

"Dung!" Niko made a face. "And here I was hoping for a good hot drink." He took a draft of his ale and nearly spat it out. Horse pee probably tasted better.

"To make matters worse, this is the only inn in town." Flar wrinkled his nose. "But the good news is, they've got rooms for us... though I dread to find out what those might look like."

After the worst night's sleep Niko could imagine, he decided to skip breakfast and went looking for a karr rental. As he walked the streets of Hedbury Vale, he saw dirt and grime everywhere and his heart sank. He was about to give up, when he spotted the sign. "Rent-A-Karr".

When he entered the tiny office, he was greeted by a girl who couldn't be a day older than thirteen. "How can I help you, Sir?" she piped.

"I need a karr accommodating six for a couple of sevendays."

"Aw, that's a real pity, good Sir. I've only got an eight-seater. The best you will find in town, I might add."

He didn't doubt it. Though everything in this gods-forsaken town seemed old and broken, nothing was broken in this building — not as far as he could see, anyway — and while not flawless, it was as clean as a karr rental could be.

"I'll look at it." He leaned heavily on the thick branch that served as a walking cane as he followed the girl. He would have to ask Flar to drive.

To his surprise, everything looked good. Not as great as the karr he'd left in the ravine, but still good.

"How much does it cost?"

"For such a fine gentleman as yourself, I should say only 100 Commonwealth Silvers a day, to be paid in advance for two sevendays, and a deposit of 500 Silvers. Or, if you wish to pay in Dragon Golds, the charges would be 55 Golds a day, and a deposit of 275 Golds."

That was outrageous, but what choice did he have? No matter how small the child was, she was cunning. She could have been an Ingravian Lord in a previous life — if such a thing existed.

"I'll tell you what, young miss." He couldn't help but smile. "I like you. You are smarter than many adults. I will do it, even if you really should give me two karrs for this price." He counted out 1900 Commonwealth Silvers, thanking the gods that he had prudently taken a bag of 100-Silvers with him, and filled out the paperwork, stating his name as Lord Artoman Rustovik of Tolyinsk.

After several days of driving in the scorching heat, eating roadside kills, drinking lukewarm water and sleeping under the stars, they saw the landscape change again. The forest was denser, with more, and lusher greenery. The air felt different. These were the legendary Briswoods, with their majestic trees, some of which were said to be older than the world itself. Complete nonsense, of course. People also claimed there was magic in this forest. Magic, his pickle and onions. No such thing existed.

Unfortunately, there was still no sign of Bel and her friends, and Niko grew more worried with each mile. Lori, the other women, and Pav chatted, but Flar seemed tense and distracted.

"What's wrong, Flar?" Niko asked his friend.

"I am not entirely sure yet, but I have a feeling we may find out soon what happened to your sister."

Niko didn't ask any more questions. Flar sometimes had these strange premonitions and, more often than not, he was right.

Just before sunset, Flar steered the karr off the road and into the woods. "We should make camp here," he said, "and explore tomorrow."

When he was about to get out of the karr, his mother's dragonet Izhioa contacted Gizzim.

"Where are you?" Mumi's thoughts sounded urgent. The concert would have been last night, and she would have no excuse to stay in Ebaru much longer. Not unless Papi could somehow drag out his business negotiations.

He'd better tell her that Bel had not shown up and they were looking for her. She would rip off his skin, if he didn't come clean now. She would already be furious that he hadn't contacted her sooner. If he didn't tell her everything he knew, her anger would only be worse.

"We're looking for Bel in the mountains of Briscona." In the ominous silence that followed, Niko became aware of a strange pulsing sound that seemed to come from the forest itself.

"Looking for Bel." Mumi's thoughts went silent, then returned with a force that hit him so hard, he nearly fell off the moss covered rock on which he was sitting. "Looking for Bel. And you never thought to let me know?"

"I'm sorry, Mumi. We did not want to upset you needlessly. Not just before the concert."

"You didn't want to upset me. Am I a child?" The frosty edge to her thoughts made him shiver. "Is there any sign of her yet?"

He shook his head, although he knew his mother couldn't see him. The strange throbbing gave him a headache and deprived him of his ability to think coherently. "No, I don't know. I have a headache. It is these dragon-cursed woods. I will contact you tomorrow."

He retreated and, although he hated himself for shutting his mother out in this way, shielded. He stood up and was about to find the source of the thumping when Flar stepped in front of him and stopped him.

"Not tonight," he said. "That is not safe for you. We shall investigate tomorrow."

"Dragon's dung, man! I am going to find it now and stop it."

"No, you will not." Flar's fist hit his temple and everything went black.

Early sunlight filtered through the foliage and bathed the clearing in a soft greenish glow. Niko's head still hurt. He had barely slept that night, and now Flar had the gall to shake him awake and pretend like nothing had happened.

"What in the Dragon's name did you do that for?" It took him all his self-restraint to resist the urge to remodel Flar's face with his walking stick. He fingered his temple gingerly.

"You were endangering our entire mission, and I didn't think I would be able to talk you out of it. I have known you for too long." Flar gave him a wary look. "Stay away from it, and help us uncover that thing over there."

It took them most of the morning to remove all the hardened mud, leaves and twigs, but long before they had removed the last remnants of the covering, Niko's suspicions were already confirmed. He knew this dented karr. It belonged to his father's old friend Yeleksim Bogrovik. They didn't have to remove the flap of the trailer for him to know what was in it. These were Papi's wares.

He sank down on a tree stump and held his head. "It's theirs," he said in a barely audible voice. Panic and grief warred inside his head. What happened to Bel? And what was he going to tell his parents?

Lori knelt down beside him and took his hand. She didn't speak. The strange throbbing in his head still wouldn't stop.

"What happened to my sister?" His voice sounded hoarse.

"I cannot say for sure." Flar furrowed his brow, "but I can guess. There is something in these woods, pretty close by, and it is extremely dangerous to those who don't know what they are dealing with. I think they went to investigate, and something went awry."

"You mean..." he couldn't say the words. He didn't even want to think about it. Bel had to be well.

"They may yet turn up. If, and only if, they had someone with them who knew what he was doing. For now, there is nothing we can do. I am sorry."

Niko stood up. He felt awful. "Zera, can you drive?"

"Yes captain."

"Good." With effort, he straightened up. "Take Lord Bogrovik's karr and follow us. Pav can ride with you."

"Yes captain," Zeralize said again, and Pashovny — silent as always — nodded respectfully.

"I need a moment," he said, "and then we'll head back. Not to Tiria, mind you, but to the Keshire Bay. Once we are there, Felnar will send a dinghy to take us to the Aurora."

He withdrew a short distance from his team and told Gizzim to establish contact with Izhioa.

SENKERLAND

CHAPTER TWENTY-TWO

Recovery

>   dragon
> master shelters
> daughter of lost empire
> rekindles flame of life inside
> her soul

They were inside the portal again, with Mikhandor leading the way. He chose a different path from the one by which they had come. Despite Bel's misgivings, they were not going back to Briscona, but rather to the Portal of Senk, as Mikhandor called it.

Just before entering the portal, they'd had a heated discussion about that, because neither Bel nor Leks had liked the idea of leaving their merchandise in the Briswood Heights unguarded.

"What about my karr? And the trailer?" Leks had objected. "We cannot just leave our vehicles out there for only the gods know how long. Our wares are worth a fortune, and Toni will have all my other fingers if that stuff gets stolen."

"He will not." Bel shook her head so vigorously her curls danced around her face. "It wouldn't be your fault, so he can't possibly blame you."

Leks scowled. "Didn't stop him last time."

"I rather think he would have Mikhandor's fingers this time, but you are absolutely right that Papi's not going to like this. And he's already going to be angry with me for getting married without inviting him to the wedding. I'm going to have a torching hard time explaining all of this to him."

She looked at Niels. "You may thank all the gods that he really likes you. Because if it weren't for that, he might just decide to have your big toes."

"I'm sure he will understand. From what I have seen, he is a reasonable man. I'm honestly more worried about your mother's reaction. She does not seem to like me all that much."

"Are you joking?" Bel sounded genuinely surprised. "She absolutely adores you! Which is a good thing, as we're going to need her help trying to assuage my father's anger. He really is going to be furious.

"Also, Niko will surely hate having to turn his ship around and pick us up in the north of Senkerland. The harbours there are the stuff of nightmares, he says, and I've no reason to doubt his judgement. It's not just all those cliffs. The sea is permanently frozen up there, and navigating through all those ice floes is hard and dangerous, or so I've been told."

"Look, I'm sorry for them," Niels said, "but I don't see that we really have all that much choice in the matter. Either we go to Senkerland, or we die in Tirona. Besides, Bel, you really need to learn how to work your magic. This Guren is your only hope."

Bel sighed. "I know. But that still doesn't mean I have to like it."

They stepped out of the most majestic spruce tree Bel had ever seen — and growing up in Ingravia and Senkerland, she'd seen quite a few of them. *Thank you. You are so beautiful.* She could swear she actually felt the tree's love.

"What do we do now?" As she looked around, she saw nothing but trees. Despite her warm clothes, she shivered.

"Now we sleep," Mikhandor and Janæla said in unison, and immediately they curled up on the needle-strewn forest floor and fell asleep.

"What's up with that?" Bel asked, as she remembered how Mikhandor had fallen asleep the moment they entered Thorf as well.

Niels shrugged. "Portal travel wears them out."

"Stuck here for the next couple of hours, eh?" Leks scratched his armpit. "Should build us a small fire. I'm freezing me old balls off here."

"To sum up..." Bel looked at her companions as they sat around the fire with a cup of fir tea, "we're somewhere in the Senkeberghe, without transport, and my chair is useless to me here. We also have no clue as to where this Guren might be hiding out. Did I forget anything?"

"Yes," Niels said. "You need to contact your parents and brother, and inform them of our changed plans."

"Ona's leaky nipples! Why did you have to remind me?"

"But you asked."

Typically Niels. Always so torching serious.

"Dragonmother! I'm really not looking forward to that. But I guess I might as well get it over with right away." She let her mind become one with Zilla's and went in search of Izhioa, her mother's dragonet.

"My little Sparkle," Mumi's concerned thoughts soon came to her, "are you well?"

"Never better, Mumi," she sent back, "I've..."

"Where in the name of gods and dragons have you been? We've been worried sick." The intensity of her mother's thoughts took Bel by surprise. They'd only been gone for a sevenday, and unless something disastrous had happened, Mumi wouldn't even have tried to contact her during that time.

"Has something happened, Mumi?"

"Has something happened? Has something happened? Beldenka! You've been missing for over three moons! We — and by that I mean Niko's search party — found your karr and trailer in these dragon-cursed Briswoods, and not a sign of any of you. We thought..." Mumi was crying, and even though she knew it wasn't her fault, Bel felt guilty.

"Over three moons? I don't understand. We can't possibly have been gone for that long. I wish I could be with you to explain what happened. I know this is going to sound insane, but it's true nonetheless. Please, dry your tears Mumi." Her mother's restrained crying tore at her heart. "I have happy news for you."

She waited for her mother to regain her composure.

"Did Niko by any chance feel anything strange in those woods? Did he mention anything at all?"

"Apart from the fact that this forest gave him a pounding headache? No. Nothing."

Bel reflected on her mother's words for a moment. As far as she knew, Niko never had headaches, so it had probably been the Song of the Portal that had caused it. She was going to have to interrogate her little brother about that.

"That may or may not be important. You know about Transients, don't you?"

"Beldenka!" She felt indignation from her mother. "I'm not stupid. Of course I know about Transients. In fact... wait! This big, muscular man. With the platinum hair. What was his name again? Mik? He...?"

"Yes, Mumi. He's an Erl, and there's a portal in those woods, and Mig took us through to Thorf, because... oh, Mumi, you're not going to believe this! I got married. By the legendary Erlen king Yumænor himself."

"Bel?"

"No, not to Mig, Mumi. Most certainly not! To Niels, of course."

"Well, well. So you've finally admitted it to yourself. Congratulations. May dragons bless and guard you."

Their thoughts went silent for a while, but they were still in each other's presence.

"Your father sends his love to both of you, and promises he won't hurt Leks . Tell me, where are you now, and why have you been gone for such a long time?"

"I honestly don't know how we managed to be away for so long. We were only on Thorf for a sevenday. But give all my love to Papi too, Mumi. We are in the Senkeberghe now. Just exited the Portal of Senk, and we need to find some hot-tempered misanthrope who goes by the name of Guren Fonvernum. He... Mumi, what's so funny?"

"Oh, little Sparkle, I know him. This man Guren is a grumpy old git who sends Iorthen, his dragon, to scare strangers away. You will love him. In fact... but no! I won't spoil your surprise."

Bel grimaced. She was fed up with all the surprises she'd had to deal with lately.

"If you want, I can contact him for you. Tell him you're looking for him."

"You..." Suddenly she understood. "So that's why you sent me to Senkerland? So this Guren could secretly keep an eye on me?"

Her mother laughed. And then cried again. "You were a little girl with a great talent for the Magic. What else were we to do? You weren't safe in Ingravia. Not if our secret got out. That's the real reason we sent you away and forbade you to come back."

Bel gasped. Why had Mumi never told her?

"You torching knew about my magic, and never thought to inform me? Not even after I graduated and moved to Briscona? What else did you keep from me?"

"Of all the people who got the virus, you were the only one who survived. Leks looked into it for us and discovered that you were the only one who had a connection with dragonkind. He gave us copies of all patient files and destroyed the original ones. There were thousands of them. None of these others had a dragonet."

Leks... had Papi tortured and exiled him because of her? Surely, he couldn't have been that callous. Irrationally, she covered her ears with her hands, as if that could shut Mumi's thoughts out.

"I've got to go, Mumi. We can talk again later." She retreated from Zilla's mind, and buried her head in Niels' chest.

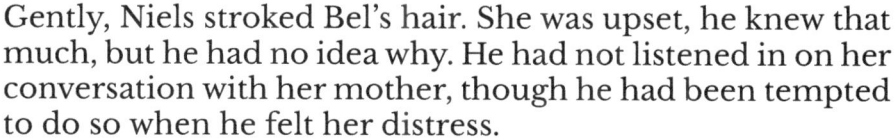

Gently, Niels stroked Bel's hair. She was upset, he knew that much, but he had no idea why. He had not listened in on her conversation with her mother, though he had been tempted to do so when he felt her distress.

He did not speak. Did not ask any questions. He hated when people intruded into his private space when he felt unsettled, so he would never do that to others. Especially not his own wife. She would tell him when she was ready.

"She said we'd been gone for over three moons, Moradin," Bel said at last. "I don't understand."

Though her voice was steady, Niels felt the turmoil inside her head, so he kept holding her. "Time is not a linear thing," he said, "and the gods experience time in a different way. So a sevenday here might be just one day on any other world, or several moons, or even turnings. The portals are supposed to synchronise our time with the times of the other worlds, but they aren't perfect. That is why a party travelling through a Portal needs one or two guides, who sort of pull our times together and keep everyone in the group in the same time."

"Is this also why we needed to hold hands the entire time we were travelling the Portal?"

Niels nodded. "Judging by how exhausted those two over there are," he briefly glanced at where Mikhandor and Janæla lay sleeping, "our times might have been aeons apart. They would have had it easier, had we gone back to that portal in the Briswoods, and we might even have gotten back there just a couple of heartbeats after we left those woods; but unfortunately that was not an option. Not really."

He felt surprise from Bel, and confusion, but again, she didn't show it.

"My parents and brother," she said, "and probably my entire family, have been beside themselves with worry. Niko even sent out a search party and found Leks's karr and the trailer deserted. And no sign of us, obviously."

"Glad they found our belongings," Leks muttered, "but not looking forward to my next meeting with Toni. He's going to have my hide for this."

"No, he is not," Bel's voice sounded triumphant. "Mumi said he promised he wouldn't hurt you this time, so you are safe. But I need to know, Leks. What was the reason he had... he made you a Reject?"

"Sweetheart, that was so long ago. Just a dumb mistake, really."

"Torch you!" A flame erupted from Bel's mouth, and her eyes went wide. Her emotions were so intense, Niels shielded himself from them. He needed to keep his head level.

Bel stood up, limped a few steps in the old man's direction, fell and cursed again. "What happened, Leks? Tell me!"

Leks tugged at his braided beard. "Did some research for your parents. About your illness. The Mortiferous Hedgehog Heat, doctors called it, because it was spread by hedgehogs and its high fevers literally burned the patients' brains to dust. Except yours, though many of your neural pathways were damaged. But you were young, and your body eventually repaired most of the damage by regrowing connections. Only, your sensory and motor pathways..." He did not finish his sentence.

"Everyone thought you would die, just like all other patients. But you had one thing all of these others lacked. Your dragonet. If any of my colleagues found out about that and made the connection, you would have been dead. You, your mother, and your brother. All three of you. Couldn't take that risk, so I wiped the storage drives, drenched all other evidence in pentane, and burned the entire faculty building down.

"Unfortunately, someone must have seen me, as my name appeared on the suspect list, and with only one other name on it, your father had no choice but to deal with me. Told him to just kill me — would have been my greatest honour to die for you — but he wouldn't hear of it. Sentimental fool man."

Leks added a handful of twigs to the fire. "He needed me, he said, and bought me the Gym in Ambleville. Had some minor stuff going on there, but I think his real intention had always been to provide you with a safe place to live there, once you were out of school. Suited me well enough. Really liked my gym." He stared into the flames. "You do realise we're probably never going back, eh?"

Bel nodded. "I liked it there too. Life was good in the Barlows. Uncomplicated."

Niels had been listening to Leks's story with growing surprise. There was so much he didn't know. Mortiferous Hedgehog Heat? He had never heard of that before. Even Bel had never told him the name of the virus. Could it be she hadn't known either? And Leks doing research for Mir and Toni. It was hard to imagine the unassuming old man being a scientist, but from what he just told them, Niels' best guess was that he had been a medically trained neuro specialist.

"*Lyts* Beldenka Nadinov!"

The three of them looked in the direction of this new voice that intruded into their privacy, and there, hidden between the trees, stood a broomstick of a man. His too-wide hooded cloak gave him an even more skeletal appearance.

"Master Gerrolf?" Bel sounded as if she couldn't believe her eyes.

"What are these people doing in mine own fine forest, young miss? And making a fire, nay less! For shame! You should know better than to endanger mine own trees." He took a step forward, threw one irate look at the fire, and the flames died. Niels had never seen anything like it before. Or heard anyone speak like this man did.

"Your mother has sent me," he grumbled. "So here I am."

"My mother?" Bel asked, "You are... Guren?"

"Of course I am. Anon, are you coming or what?" The man did not sound all that friendly to Niels, but strangely, Bel acted as if she were happy to see him.

"I would love to, but how? My chair is useless here in these woods."

"Dragon's tail, Beldenka!" Guren gestured at their little group. "You have brought an unholy amount of people with you, and you would have me believe not equal one of these folk is stout enough to carry you? You are testing my patience."

Niels did not think that was funny at all, but Bel laughed. "Nothing new there. Or did you really think I had changed all this much, old man?"

"One could desire. Anon, wake those two sleepers, or I shall leave those folk behind."

"What do you know of the Dragon Charm?"

Bel was alone with the man she had known as Gerrolf Drachlieb — her brain still had trouble thinking of him as Guren Fonvernum now — and this was his first question.

"As good as nothing, I'm afraid. I didn't even know it existed until a sevenday ago, when Moradin told me so."

Guren snorted. "Fie! Such negligence! I shall have to speak to your mother about that. The lady ought to have... Anon, what have you been able to do with your charm so far? As far as you know."

"I killed my first husband." She bit her lip.

"Typical." Guren chuckled, looked at Bel, chuckled some more and then broke out into gales of laughter, until tears were streaming down his cheeks. "You always had a talent for the grandiose." He shook his head and hiccoughed some more. "Of course your first magical act had to be something dramatic."

"I don't find that the least bit amusing, old grave dodger." She suppressed a shiver as she remembered Lastor's bloodied face. His skin torn away, flesh and bones exposed by the dragon's sharp talons. Her talons. Saw, again, the light of life fade from Lastor's broken eyes. Eyes that stared at her in a combination of anguished sadness and absolute terror. Heard again his helpless whimpers of pain. His last belaboured breaths.

Guren's keen violet eyes stared into hers. Finally, he nodded approvingly. "Good," he said. "Good. Killing people is a horrible thing. We should never take pleasure in it. Anon, what more can you do with your charm?"

Bel fiddled with her necklace. "I sometimes breathe fire. But only when I get angry."

"Hmph!"

The silence that followed hung in the room for what seemed like an eternity.

"What else?"

"Nothing," Bel admitted. She felt small and stupid. She was twenty-seven turnings, apparently gifted with extremely strong magic, and unable to use it in any significant way.

"Nothing?" Guren whispered. He pounded his staff on the floor in a slow but steady rhythm. "Nothing?" he thundered. "What in the name of the Archdragon was your mother thinking? The lady belike did not teach your brother aught either. She should have allowed me to teach you when you were young. Shame on her!"

Clearly agitated, he paced the small room. "Well, it cannot be helped," he said after another too long silence. "We had better begin."

He stood before her, uncomfortably close. "Breathe in but soft, the way you do when you are singing, all the way down to your belly. Allow your midriff to expand. And breathe out but soft. You know how this works. You are a singer."

That was too easy, and Bel had already done the same thing with Niels at least a thousand times these last few days, but she did as Guren said anyway. She breathed in and out slowly, until both her body and mind felt relaxed.

"That's it," Guren said. "Empty your mind and just be. Anon, picture a tiny blue flame in your mind's eye."

It was harder than she expected. Either the size or colour was wrong, or, when she did manage to get it right at first, it almost immediately morphed into a big bonfire. At last she lost her temper. "Torch it!" she muttered, and a huge, mostly white flame erupted from her mouth.

Guren snuffed it out promptly. "Not quite what I had in mind," he said in a calm voice. "Try again."

It took all afternoon, but finally she was able to not only picture a minuscule blue flame in her head, but also produce it. Not erupting from her mouth, but dancing on the palm of her outstretched hand. It wasn't much, but it was a beginning of control.

CHAPTER TWENTY-THREE

Shaded

danger
prowls in darkness
ready to pounce and slay
heralds of dawn and favoured of
the gods

Their rooms at the Stark Elster Guest House were cramped and none too clean, but the fire was warm and the mulled wine wasn't nearly as bad as Niels had feared. Though he could not wear the robes he had been given on Thorf, his new pantaloons, shirt and doublet were far more comfortable than that horribly tight attendant's suit. Now that he was not the merchant's carer any longer, but her spouse, he was expected to wear proper merchant's attire. Only the best was good enough for Master Moradin Salendi, and so he wore soft, rich clothes with flat, invisible seams that didn't irritate his too-sensitive skin.

"I never took you for a scholar, Leks," he said. "I thought you said you used to be a private investigator."

Leks took a draw on his white ceramic long stem pipe, a habit he had picked up — or perhaps rekindled — during their stay on Thorf, before answering. "Trained as a neurosurgeon. Thought I could heal people. Didn't work out. Lost several patients to Yat S'ber on the operating table. Realised I made the wrong choice. Decided to become a researcher instead. Only had to cut up skulls of people that were already dead. Far better choice.

"Would work as a forensic pathologist on occasion, and that's how I met Mir and Toni. Zigmandas Grigonovim, Mir's father, ended up on my slab. The man had died under suspicious circumstances. Discovered he'd been poisoned, but that wasn't my most disturbing find." Leks paused and blew blueish-grey ringlets of smoke in the air. Niels inhaled the spicy-sweet tobacco scent as he watched the hazy vapours drift towards the ceiling.

"Zigman's brain showed some interesting anomalies in the limbic system, which was far more complex than one would expect to find. It was also a bit larger, but not significantly so. The connections in and from the limbic system, however... these were the really interesting ones. They told me why the man had been killed: he possessed the Dragon Magic.

"To protect Mir and any children she might bear — she had only just got married to Toni — I kept my discovery under wraps, and offered my services to the young couple. That's how I became their private investigator. To avoid suspicion, I kept my job as a scientific researcher." He looked at his pipe, which had gone out, but did not relight it.

"We never talked about the magic, and — like any good Ingravian — pretended it did not exist. I now question the wisdom of that decision. In trying to protect them, we may have inadvertently hurt Bel and her brother Niko. Retrospect is a wonderful thing that only shows up when it's too late."

"Yes." Niels stared into the dwindling flames of the hearth. "I know all about that." Reluctantly, he rose from his chair and added some wood to the fire. "I wonder how Bel is doing with Guren. He doesn't seem like a very kind person to me."

"Gruff behaviour of his is just an act. He's a very old man, pretending to be tough; but he's a softy at heart. Can see it in the way he treats Bel. Their banter. Game of two people who are comfortable in each other's presence."

Niels thought about that, but no matter how hard he tried, he failed to understand what Leks meant. He had seen two people arguing all the way to Valtstrom-Nehr, which thankfully wasn't too far from the portal.

When they arrived at the inn, Guren had told them bluntly that he would take Bel with him and did not want any of the others near his home, ever, or he would send his dragon to deal with them. He said he would return Bel to the inn after her lessons.

"So," Leks said, "when do you think Migs will resume our training? I miss it."

"So do I, and I wish I knew. We should ask him when he wakes up. He's taking really long this time."

"This time?" Leks raised an eyebrow. "You mean you two have done this kind of thing before?"

"Several times. The first time Mikhandor took me to Thorf, however, he had no time to find a portal, so he created a vortex. I threw up when we exited that thing. That's how bad it was for me, but strangely, Mikhandor wasn't tired at all, and went right back. At the time, I didn't know the first thing about world-hopping, and I really wasn't paying too much attention either. I was still thinking of the inferno we had only barely escaped."

"What happened?"

"The assassins found out where I lived and set the place on fire while we were sleeping. Cowards. Mikhandor dove right back into his vortex, and was able to save my cousins, but not Tasim, who had become my best friend. What made things even worse... he was not the only one who died that night. I went mad with guilt and grief over the murders of my friends."

He studied his wine as he made it swirl in its goblet. It had been ten turnings, but in moments like these, he felt the pain as acutely as on that catastrophic night.

Silent as always, Bel entered their room. "Leks, I need to speak to Moradin. Alone."

"Sure thing, Mistress Beldenka." Leks slipped neatly into his role. "Was going to find my own room anyway. I am but an old man, and need my afternoon nap before supper."

He got up and left the room. Niels put his goblet down on the table. He wasn't going to drink any more of that wine anyway. Not when his spirits were this low.

"This is a bit awkward, Nie... uh, Moradin, but I need to know. Are you doing anything to prevent me from conceiving?"

"To *what?*" He didn't understand. Why would she accuse him of doing such a despicable thing? And why now, when he already felt so miserable? "Of course not. What makes you think I would do that to you?"

She bit her lip and shook her head. "That is not what I meant. Let me rephrase. Is there anything you can do to make sure I won't get pregnant?"

Niels felt the blood drain from his face. Why did she have to do this to him? He had assumed they would have children, like any married couple. What was more, as a priest, he had a moral obligation to procreate. "You..." He swallowed. "You don't want children?"

"Oh, Morad!" She smiled as she shook her head again, slowly. Smiled. Did she not understand how much she hurt him? "Of course I do. But not right now. We're on a quest, my sweet, silly husband. I don't even want to think of how much harder everything would be if we had a baby to look after. Or the risks we would be taking with our child."

"Ah." He let out a long, relieved breath. "Of course. I hadn't thought of that yet. But can we not just go to a pharmacy and buy us a few packets of rubber barriers? Or better yet, pills?"

"Not here in Senkerland. The population has declined to the point where the government has decided to outlaw all forms of contraception for at least two generations. You can only buy contraceptive devices from dodgy back alley shops, and I most definitely don't want to take that risk."

"Neither would I."

"So..." She kept her distance, which was probably a good thing. "Can you? Do something to make sure I won't conceive?"

"In theory, yes. I should be able to... uh, plug things up, so to say." He looked down at his hands. "But I have never needed to do that, so I can't guarantee it will really work as intended."

"Guren will teach me how to control my reproductive system, as he called it so delicately, but this is going to take a while, and I," she rolled up to him, "want you now."

"Whoa, give me a moment, Bel." Niels took a step back and blocked her chair with his foot. "We don't want me to mess this up, do we?"

Bel laughed her glorious laugh, but rolled back a few paces to give Niels the space he needed.

As he got the medallion out from under his shirt, he tried to remember the high priest's lessons on the subject. Lessons that were never taught at the seminary. He cursed his younger self for not having paid better attention back then, but he had only been sixteen turnings, and every bit as belligerent as boys that age could be.

He took the medallion in his right hand, placed his left hand on top of it, closed his eyes and breathed in and out deeply, slowly. He visualised his anatomy, focused on his reproductive organs and how they functioned. It wasn't nearly as hard as he remembered.

Then he stopped. Blocking the passage would be counter-productive. It would stay the release his body needed at that point, and leave him in a heightened state of arousal. That could not be healthy. He had to do something else. Maybe he could neutralise the flow, somehow.

He delved deeper. This was going to be tricky. If he messed up, he could end up dead. Bel would not like that.

The effort it took was enormous. Sweat squeezed its way through his pores and formed tiny beads on his forehead as he worked his magic. The sound of his own heartbeat hammered on his eardrums. His breathing quickened.

"Done." He opened his eyes again. His hands were trembling as he tucked the medallion back under his shirt. Tiny black-and-green flecks floated in front of his eyes. "Let's hope it works the way it should. I am not fond of surprises."

"Neither am I," Bel said. "Not of that kind, anyway."

She rolled back up to him, got out of her chair and Niels had no choice but to catch her as her legs gave in. He was pretty sure that was exactly what she intended. But he was exhausted and couldn't support her weight, insubstantial though it was. He staggered backwards and they both fell, Bel on top of him.

"Niels, what..."

He woke up in a strange environment. Though the room was tiny, and sparsely lit, the air smelled clean, and it was neither too hot, nor too cold. He heard birdsong, and muffled voices. This was not the inn, so where was he? And what had happened? He tried to sit up, but the sudden, nauseating vertigo made him abandon that effort.

As he lay quietly, eyes shut, concentrating on his breathing, he remembered. He had been a bumbling fool again, experimenting with his magic. Doing something he was sure nobody in his right mind had ever done before. He would have to check if all his body parts were still in place. Find out if he hadn't accidentally moved internal organs that should have stayed in place. Later. He drifted off to sleep again.

When he awoke again, Bel sat beside his bed. She held his hand, but seemed to not even notice he had opened his eyes. She looked unhappy. Though he wanted to connect to her mind, he knew now was not the time. He had to regain his strength first.

"Bel." It came out a whisper.

She looked at him. "You stupid unthinking pizzle! You manewolf's arse!" She dragged her free hand over her eyes. "You could've been dead, you brain bereft piece of boar plop!"

"Well anon, Beldenka," came an old man's voice from outside the room, "that's nay language for a lady."

"Oh sard off, you old grumbler. I'm a lord, not a lady, and shall torching well use even fouler language if this piss parsnip here doesn't behave."

A gaunt old man with long silvery white hair and a milky complexion appeared in the doorway. "You have nay valid colours for cursing like a fell sailor."

He turned his head to face Niels. "You gave us all rather a fright, young sir. Been working your charm a tad too hard, eh?"

"Yes." He felt sheepish now. "And not for the first time either, I fear."

"So the big bloke told us. That is not a healthy habit. You ought to be more careful, young sir. I hear you have a destiny to fulfil. You and lyts Beldenka both."

Niels sighed. This wasn't the first time someone told him to be more careful, and he doubted it would be the last. "For how long have I been out?"

"Three days and four nights."

"Holy gods!" Never before had he been unconscious for that long. No wonder Bel was so upset with him. She must have feared for his life. Maybe he really should learn to be more careful.

"Yes," the old man — Guren, Niels assumed — said in a voice that sounded too grave, and too deep for his slight frame. "I have never seen a man wake up from Magical Slumber after such a long timespan. The gods might not but very much favour you."

"Any developments during that time?"

Bel looked at him, and Niels feared she would spew fire again, but instead, she said, "Master Guren found us a cabin in the woods. Leks and Mig have been working their arses off cleaning the cobwebs and doing repairs, so we can move into it as soon as you're doing a bit better."

"Does that mean we'll be staying here for a while?" He tried to sit up, but it was too soon and, light-headed, he fell back into the pillows again.

"Yes. I need my training, and you need time to recover. The healer said you would need several sevendays. At the very least."

"Healer? What healer?" He hoped they'd been prudent enough not to bring in some quack with just enough knowledge to treat a common cold.

"Miss Felling, of course. Mig's sister." Bel gave him an exasperated look, as if she knew what he had been thinking. "Mig came running just moments after you lost consciousness, and contacted her immediately. It was weird. How could he have known?"

"It is a strange thing indeed," Niels said, "and I don't claim to know how this works, but the moment something goes wrong with me, he just knows and shows up. Instantly. Even if we are worlds apart."

He had fallen asleep again, and woke up to the sound of footsteps approaching. A light tread, a woman. Most likely Rasælna, here to check up on him. She would be doing that religiously for at least the next couple of days, Niels knew from experience.

"Good afternoon, your Highness. I'm glad to see you finally decided to wake up." Her slightly too large charcoal eyes scanned his face. "You know the drill."

He did. She would examine him first, and berate him after. He tried to pull the blankets off, but lacked the strength.

"Still a bit weakened, I see." Rasælna pulled the covers off and placed her cool hands on his bare chest. She closed her eyes and moved her hands over his body.

"Well, you've really done it this time, young man." She covered him up again. "Will you ever learn?"

"I wish I could promise to never do anything stupid again, but we both know I would probably break that promise. And likely sooner, rather than later." The gods really had their hands full, keeping him alive.

"I don't know what you were trying to achieve, but whatever it was, I would urge you to never do it again. I put all of your bits back in their proper places for you and restored their functionality." Did she really sound amused? Or was that just his head messing with him?

"What? Just now?"

"Moradin, how well do you know me?" She rolled her eyes. "I don't take risks. And least of all with you. Do you honestly think you would have survived if I had waited that long? Tell me, what was it again you were trying to do?"

"I was..." How could he explain? "Bel and I... we cannot afford to have children yet, so I wanted to make sure..." he shrugged. He felt utterly deflated.

"Oh, Moradin." She shook her head slowly. A barely noticeable smile played around her lips. "There are much safer and easier methods to achieve that. We've got a herb growing on Thorf, the blackdrop thistle. It causes temporary infertility in men. I shall bring it once you've got your strength back."

That was a relief. Of sorts. He felt like an idiot. To think he had gone through all that trouble, and apparently nearly got himself killed, trying to do something completely unnecessary.

"How long do you reckon, before I can get out of bed again?" The way he felt, it might be several turnings.

"You have always surprised me with your resilience, so..." She paused for a moment, closed her eyes and moved her lips, as if she were doing the maths inside her head. "Normally I would say a sevenday, but with you... a couple of days. Maybe even tomorrow."

"That doesn't sound too bad."

"It's just a guess, Moradin. And don't think for even a moment that being out of bed means you will be back to your ordinary self soon. That is most definitely going to take a couple of sevendays. At the very least." Rasælna gave him another stern look. "Even with your luck. Two or three moons seems far more realistic."

Niels groaned. That was not what he wanted to hear. He needed to get back on his feet. They had already lost three moons travelling the portals. He should be in Ebaru now, finally dealing with these attempts on his life.

CHAPTER TWENTY-FOUR

Emergence

*anger
rouses dragon
and reason dissipates
in scintillating clouds of hot
passion*

A sevenday went by, and Niels was finally able to spend most of the day out of bed, but that was about all. Even something as simple as doing the dishes after their meals wore him out. He wanted to move into their cabin in the woods, if only to be away from Guren, who got on his nerves with his grouchy behaviour.

Bel seemed to be getting on with Guren well enough, though, which was a good thing. He was her mentor, after all. As far as Niels could tell, their magic was a dangerous, destructive thing, and he had no idea how Bel would ever be able to use it for good. Yet, both Bel and Guren insisted it was a beautiful thing if practised wisely. He could only hope they were right.

"Look what I learned today, Moradin," Bel said as they sat by the hearth, enjoying a kaw brew. She looked at the fire intently and it died. She kept staring at it, and a moment later it sprang back to life. "Neat, eh?"

Niels smiled. Putting out fires with seemingly just a thought... now that could certainly be useful. "So your magic... it is all about fire?"

"Yes," Guren answered. "Our element, the Element of the Dragon we name it, is fire. Fire, like all other elements, has two sides. Life and death. If we were to set mine own home on fire, it would leave nothing but ashes. But at which hour we contain the fire to the hearth, it warms the house and allows us to cook our food.

"Your element, the Element of the Divine, is similar in that it can bring both life and death. You know this better than anyone else, I would bethink. You've experienced both sides of this power, have you not, young sir?"

He nodded. When the old mage was teaching, Niels genuinely liked him. He was a good teacher, who invited his students to think for themselves.

"Wind, ordinary people would say. Us priests, we call it the Breath of Life. Make it flow, and life flourishes. Take it away, and we die. That is what happens when I overestimate what I can do with my gift. If I use up too much of the Breath of Life, I deprive my brain of oxygen and my internal organs will start to fail. It is a delicate balance."

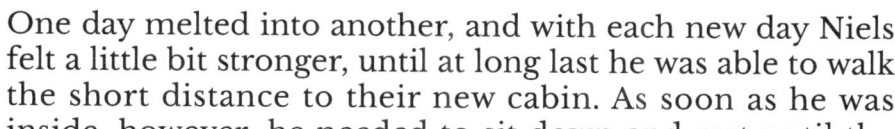

One day melted into another, and with each new day Niels felt a little bit stronger, until at long last he was able to walk the short distance to their new cabin. As soon as he was inside, however, he needed to sit down and rest until the vertigo had passed.

"So this is to be our home for the next couple of moons, I suppose," he said to no-one in particular. "It looks nice. Cosy."

"Just wait till you see our bedroom." Suppressed laughter coloured Bel's voice, and her eyes were twinkling. "Leks and Mig really outdid themselves on that one. You'll want to spend all your time in bed. With me, of course."

"Sleeping, you mean, my sweet." He hated to disappoint her, but he was nowhere near recovered from his mishap. "I still feel as if I inhabit the body of a two-hundred turnings old corpse."

Bel's face paled. "That bad?"

Niels nodded.

"I had no idea. I just thought... you have such a perfect body, it's hard to imagine..."

"I know," Niels said. "That might well be why I do these stupid things. Because my mind tricks me into thinking I'm invincible. I should have learnt by now that I am not."

"I could ask Zilla to scorch your eyebrows a bit, the next time you're about to pull some dumb stunt," Bel said, and Niels wondered whether she was serious or not.

"Rather not." A chill ran down his spine. "I am not all that fond of fire, to be honest." Again, the memories of the fire that killed Tasim assailed him, and he closed his eyes in a vain effort to banish them from his mind.

"Oh, I never got around to telling you..." Bel changed the subject, apparently picking up on his anguish, "Niko is coming this way, and he's bringing all the stuff we left behind in the Briswoods. How's that?"

"That makes me happy." He would have the presents from his parents, brothers, and sister back. The little mementos they had given him the night before he went to Ebaru. The only physical reminders of his life with them.

"They should be here soon now. Zilla tells me they are close."

"They?" For a moment he had thought Niko would be coming alone, and he was fine with that. But he didn't want a whole bunch of people around. He could not deal with that. Especially not now, when he was still so weak.

"Niko, his wife and his Elite Force, as he calls them."

"Elite Force? What's that supposed to mean? Has your brother brought an army or something?"

"No you silly. Just a few of his best people." Bel kissed his forehead. "You worry too much."

"I... Bel, I just..." A muffled sound from outside made him stop and listen more carefully.

"Well, this is even faster than I thought." Bel turned to face the door. "Here they are!"

A gust of wind ruffled his hair, and the sudden cold made his skin pucker. Niels buried his head in his hands and closed his eyes. A knot formed in his stomach. He couldn't deal with that many people.

"Beldenka," a deep bass almost sang, "marrying without even warning us, eh?"

"And this from the man who didn't bother to invite his favourite sister to his wedding, and still has to introduce me to his wife," Bel countered.

The sounds of laughter, too many pairs of feet stomping around on the wooden floorboards, people hugging, kissing, and clasping hands, assailed Niels' ears. The stench of sweat, and humid clothes that had been worn for too long mingled with the smells coming from the kitchen — broiling meat, and vegetables simmering in spiced wine.

Instinctively, Niels folded in on himself, tucked his head between his knees and tried with all his might to keep himself from rocking back and forth. He felt the tension build up in his muscles. He needed to get out of here, but his body refused to cooperate.

"... Lorinka..." he heard, and "... over here... little accident..."

"... get you to bed, Morad..." Bel's voice was almost in his ear. "... Mig... help..."

Then he was in his bed, and lay humming to himself softly, his hands covering his ears as he tried to shut the horrid din of all these people in the living room out.

Several times that night he'd woken up from weird, vivid dreams about his sister, all grown up. Dreams of her dancing and drinking beers with a bunch of rowdy people. Dreams of her buying food at a market in a far-away, exotic country. And dreams of her sitting alone in an opulent study, in a plush chair so large she almost drowned in it, and looking at an old, yellowed portrait, tears streaming down her cheeks.

It was early morning now, and he could still feel her, so real had his dreams been. So strong. Quietly, so he would not wake Bel, he got up and went looking for the kitchen. He only had to follow his nose, as somebody was already up, and making flatbread. It was the smell of home.

A slender young woman, her long blond hair gathered in a loose bun, stood by the stove. She turned her head as he entered, and her eyes went wide.

Niels' heart skipped a beat. "Machteld?" he whispered. Could it be true?

"Niels!" She flung herself at him, and buried her face in his chest. "You were dead," she said between sobs. "They said you were dead. All those turnings…" Then she righted herself, wiped the tears from her eyes and slapped him across the face.

"You miserable piece of dragon's dung! You let us believe you were dead! I hate you! You…" Her tears kept coming.

Awkward, Niels took her in his arms and tried to comfort her. "There," he said. "There now, there." He kissed her crown, her brow. With his thumbs, he carefully wiped the tears from her cheeks, before he pressed a gentle kiss on the tip of her nose.

"What are you doing with my wife," a deep voice thundered, and a fist collided with his temple.

"Curse you, Niko!" both Bel and Lorinka yelled at the same time.

"Now look what you've done!" It took Bel every ounce of control to not torch her stupid brother's face. She lowered herself out of her chair.

Lorinka sat cradling Niels' head in her lap, crying like an overgrown baby, and Mikhandor looked as if he could strangle Niko.

"Your husband kissed my wife, Bel! Kissed her!" Niko looked as if he was about to spew fire, too, and Bel could only hope it wouldn't come to that. And yet…

"He kissed her?" She couldn't believe it. Had she, once more, fallen for a scoundrel?

"He's my brother." Lorinka sniffled. "My brother, and we thought he was dead." She brought her head even closer to his, and said in a smothered voice, *"Niels, word wakker. Niet doodgaan. Ik kan niet…"* The girl started sobbing again.

Though Bel didn't understand a word of the young lady's anguished mumblings, it was all the confirmation she needed.

"Your brother?" Niko was still fuming, "Who do you think you are fooling?"

"No, Niko, I believe her. It's true." It all made perfect sense now. "His real name is Niels — I can't believe Papi and Mumi didn't tell you! — and he was adopted by a Darsian family. And you," Bel addressed Lorinka, "were born in Darsrijck and your name used to be Magtold, right?"

"Machteld Bosch."

"Oh, dragon's dung!" Niko turned on his heels, and stamped out of the kitchen.

"We lost him three times, Bel," Lori said. "First when he tried to kill himself. Then when he went to Ebaru; and finally when these people came to tell us he had died in a house fire. I cannot lose him again now. I just can't."

Bel sat beside Niels and Lorinka, and took the younger woman's hand in hers. "His healer is already on her way, I'm sure." She looked up at Mikhandor, who nodded. "And your brother is strong. He will live. He has to. I'll personally kick his holy arse back to life if he dares die on me."

Niels' eyes fluttered open. "Machteld," he croaked, and then, "Bel," and his eyes fell shut again. His breathing came in short, ragged bursts, and sweat stood on his brow.

That idiot brother of hers. He knew Niels was still weak from his unfortunate magic accident, and despite that he hadn't bothered to control that foul temper of his. It was always the same with him. Act first, think later.

"You, young lady, out!" The healer, Selna, she called herself, stood in the doorway and greeted Lorinka with a critical stare.

"Mig," she ordered her brother, "carry Prince Moradin to his bed. Lord Nadinov can come with us."

Together, Mig and Selna took off Niels' shirt and pantaloons. Then the healer placed her hands on Niels' chest, closed her eyes and moved her hands slowly and systematically up and down his body. It was the weirdest thing. Bel had never seen a healer work like that and yet, somehow, she appeared to be quite effective. Already, Niels' breathing seemed less belaboured, and some colour had returned to his face. Still, this would only extend his already too-long recovery period. If things went on like this, they'd never make it to Ebaru.

"What happened this time?" The woman sounded vexed.

"My idiot brother knocked him out." Bel snorted. She didn't want to talk. She wanted to go after Niko and whack all the stupidity out of that sheepskull's pea-sized brain.

"You will tell your brother he can either behave, or find other lodgings. I do not want anything happening to your husband. We've been extremely lucky that he survived his latest magic injury and I will not risk losing him at your brother's hand. Am I making myself clear? Or do I need to take Prince Moradin with me to Thorf?"

"Understood. And for what it is worth, I couldn't agree more." She felt the anger inside of her coming to a boil. She would go tell that boarbrain Niko what she thought of him and his irresponsible behaviour.

"Your husband is not to be allowed out of bed today. I am sure he won't like that, so you may have to tie him up — it's happened before — but we cannot take any chances. Make sure he drinks enough. I will be back tomorrow."

The healer left, and Bel went outside, in search of Niko. She didn't have to go far. He stood, back towards the cabin, muttering curses as he was carving one of his dumb stick men. So predictable.

"What in the name of the Dragonmother did you think you were doing, you stupid piss parsnip?" She rode up to him fast, and had to force herself not to smash her chair into his shins and break his legs. "You could have killed my husband. You knew he wasn't well."

"This worthless, sick son of a streetwalker was kissing my wife! He had no shagging right —"

"He was comforting his sister," Bel cut him off. "What's so terribly wrong with that?"

"His sister, my pickle and onions!" A flame sprang from his mouth.

Incensed, Bel produced a larger flame that ate his. "You don't get to do that here."

"Says who?" He breathed another flame. Another tiny thing, hardly worth its name, and Bel quenched it with just a thought. Her lessons with Guren were paying off.

"I should kill that degenerate. You have a remarkably bad taste for men, Bel." Niko's words made her want to knock that deprecating scowl off his face.

"You should not have said that." Bel was pushed out of her chair by what could only be fledging wings on her back. She sat on hands and knees, and glared at her brother as her body continued to change. Her smock tore open and revealed a layer of vibrant, wine-red fur. She felt scales growing on her back, and small horns forming just above her ears. Her face elongated, and a strong tail grew from her tail bone. As she turned her neck to look at it, she noticed it had a beautiful heart-shaped tip.

Back and forth she swung her tail in agitated excitement. She flapped her wings and was up in the air, hissing and growling. A flame, bigger than any she had ever produced before, erupted from her mouth and scorched her brother's hair.

Niko stood staring at her, a look of awed delight on his face. Was he even aware that she had just burnt him? Surely, he should have felt something! She heard his thoughts directly inside her mind. "You great dragon, you."

Her anger melted away. He was just her little brother.

She danced in the air, a grand Ingravian Broadwing Dragon, and felt more alive than ever before. She was complete. Though her legs were as weak as always, and thinner than any dragon's legs ought to be, she could move them graciously, as they had no weight to carry. Her short arms, ending in sharp talons, were strong and muscular, and not particularly suited to dancing, but her feathered wings and long tail more than made up for that.

Zilla danced beside her, and with a shock she realised they hadn't merged, like the previous time. Zilla was still just Zilla. Not Bel and Zilla. And Bel's natural body was neither in her chair, nor on the ground. She hadn't left it behind. Only her torn clothes lay on the forest floor. She wasn't Bel any longer. She was her dragon. A dragon named Vindicia Feroxi.

"Join me," she sent to Nikomir, but he shook his head.

"I do not know how," he sent back, and Bel could feel the regret in his thoughts.

"Play time is over." Iorthen Priscii, a slight Green Firecrest Dragon, the fur on his chest greying with age, flew towards her. Despite his advanced age, Guren in dragon-form still looked impressive. "Come down," he gnarled. "We have work to do."

She landed on all fours, and promptly rolled over as her legs gave in. As she lay on the soft moss beside her chair, waiting for the transformation to complete, Iorthen landed beside her and in an instant changed back into Guren. Guren, as naked as the day he was born.

"Vindicia Feroxi." Guren, now wrapped in Niko's cloak, looked at Bel, as she sat in her chair, covered by the blanket Niko had hastily fetched from the cabin. "A worthy name for a truly majestic dragon. What has made her come out? Anger?"

Bel bit her lip. She wasn't proud of herself. "Yes."

"I am not surprised. I'll teach you how to control her." He turned to greet Niko. "If yond isn't our friend Lord Nikomir Nadinovik. You took your time, young sir."

Niko nodded politely at the old mage, but his eyes were dark with anger. "I came as soon as I could, Master Guren. My mother sends her regards."

"Regards have nay meaning to me," he grumbled. "She should have taught you two about your heritage. Follow me."

"Master Guren, please..." Bel couldn't leave. Not yet. "I need to get dressed. And check on my husband before I go. He had another unfortunate setback earlier this morning."

As she made her way into the cabin, she wondered. Who was he really, this man she had known as Gerrolf Drachlieb first, and who now called himself Guren Fonvernum? His dragon had felt familiar. And how did Mumi know him? Were they by any chance related?

CHAPTER TWENTY-FIVE

Uncharted

> bereft
> of kin and home
> lost to their names they sail
> into new beginnings and find
> more grief

He lay in his bed, eyes still closed, trying his hardest not to feel like he had been mauled by a wild animal. It didn't work, of course. Though not by a savage beast, he had been assaulted. By his brother in law.

In all fairness, he couldn't really blame the man. He might well have done the same if he had seen another man hold Bel, and kiss her so tenderly.

Someone was with him, but it wasn't Bel. She — it definitely was a woman — felt different. Smelled different. And yet, there was this deep sense of closeness. Of kinship. That meant this could only be one person.

"Machteld?" He still kept his eyes closed. He feared opening them. The dim light in the room might hurt his head.

"Niels, are you... are you..." She sounded anxious.

"I will be alright. Don't worry." It came out a whisper. He wanted so badly to sound strong. To sit upright. To get out of bed, even. But he couldn't, and it scared his baby sister. If only he could reassure her.

"The healer said you should stay in bed today. And drink enough. Shall I get you some water?"

That sweet voice! Only now did he fully realise how much he had missed her. How much he still missed Mama and Papa, Rembrant and Kasper. He had wanted them to be safe, but now that Machteld was here, none of them were safe any longer, and he wanted to let them know he was still alive. Wanted to see them.

He tried to nod, but his head was so heavy, he could barely move it. "Yes, please," he whispered.

"Don't try to get out of bed, or I shall have to tie you up. Doctor's orders." She sounded just like Mama. He wanted to laugh, but that too, was too great an effort. She had no need to worry about him getting up. Even if he were so inclined, he still would not be able to actually do it.

Machteld supported his head as she helped him drink a few sips of water. Even that was exhausting.

"Sleep, big brother. I'll stay here with you, and be right by your side when next you wake. Unless Bel is back by then. I wouldn't want to take her place." She placed two butterfly kisses on his eyelids — one on each — and soon he fell asleep again.

He slept till well after dark, and when he opened his eyes, Bel was with him. He didn't feel much better than before.

"You're awake."

"Yes." His voice sounded scratchy, but that was because of the thirst, rather than lack of strength. "Water, please?"

"Can you sit, or do you need help?" Bel asked.

He tried to sit up but only managed to lift his head a little before he sank back in his pillow again. Then Bel's hand was under his head, and supported him as he drank.

"Thank you. How is your brother?"

Bel snorted. "That idiot still refuses to believe you really are Lori's brother, and nothing we can say will convince him otherwise. The stubborn fool. He is determined to hate you for the rest of his life."

"I have something that might help him see. It is in my luggage," Niels said. "They did bring my luggage, didn't they?"

"Sure. It's still in the karr, though. We were..." her voice faltered, "we were too busy arguing to think of that, I have to admit."

"Oh, Bel." He couldn't help himself. He smiled. Bel and her brother, they obviously both possessed what Niels had come to think of as the dragon temper. So volatile.

"I might have scorched his hair a bit," she said in an even smaller voice.

"Scorched his hair a bit?" That didn't sound good. No wonder the man refused to believe them. He had every reason to balk at whatever Bel might tell him. "Tell me, how would you feel if he had scorched your hair a bit?"

"That sheepskull insulted you, and he wouldn't stop. And when he said he should have killed you, I just snapped. I honestly didn't mean to, but..." She shrugged. "Anyway, now he's feeling sorry for himself because his good looks have been ruined. And Lorinka... Magtold... is angry with him because he won't listen to reason, and... Dragonmother, we made such a mess of it!"

"I am so sorry, Bel. And all of this would have been unnecessary if I'd only had enough common sense not to experiment with my medallion. We would have just fought it out, your brother and I, and then after that I would have been able to explain it all to him, and prove that Machteld really is my sister."

"But how? How can you possibly prove that?"

"Portraits, Bel. I have old portraits, from when we were little. I took them with me. I always do. They're in my luggage." He closed his eyes and felt his mind drift off to sleep.

Niels sat in the living room, in a comfortable chair by the hearth. He had been in bed for three full days, and was happy he had finally regained enough strength to be able to at least spend some time with his friends and family. They had tea, and hot buns with myrtleberry jam and clotted cream, and Niels felt like he could eat a week's worth of all of the delicacies that were set out on the table.

Nikomir was still moody, but that had probably more to do with his burnt hair than with Niels' behaviour. The portrait book had convinced Niko that he was, indeed, Machteld's brother. His hair would grow back, of course, but for now his bare, reddened scalp was a sad sight to behold. Niels felt sorry for the man.

"Machteld," Niels said, "tell me about your life after I went to Ebaru. And about Mama and Papa. And Rem and Kas."

"I may not be able to tell you all that you want to know, Nie... uh Moradin. Sorry, I still can't get used to it. Such an exotic name."

Niels nodded. Even after all these turnings in Ebaru, it still felt unreal to him too, to be called Moradin. He didn't feel like a Moradin. He was not Moradin Salendi, his current alias. Neither was he Moradin Amari, the name he had when he lived in Ebaru. He wasn't even Moradin Dolanthi of Ebaru, as the Erlen king called him. He was just Niels. Niels Bosch.

"So... Moradin." She looked at him, and repeated the name. "Moradin... I was such a little girl still, when you left. Not even seven turnings old, and there's a lot I don't know. I could see Mama and Papa weren't happy about your departure. None of us were. I hated it, and couldn't understand why. I just wanted my big brother back.

"I wanted you to read to me from your Holy Book, like you used to do before you got ill, and tell me about your goddess Eylah. I wanted to visit the House of Prayer with you, and watch you light those candles and play with that fountain."

She moved her chair closer to Niels and took his hands in hers. "I wanted to snuggle up in your lap and rest my head against your chest, so I could feel the warm vibrations of your medallion. That beautiful, glimmery pendant I wasn't allowed to even come near." She placed a hand on his chest, over the priestly medallion, and though separated by several layers of clothing, Niels felt the ornament warm at her affectionate touch.

It was only a few days after you had left, that Papa told us we were going on a trip. Mama had packed some travelling bags, and a picnic basket, and we drove all day. There was no picnic, as I had expected, but instead, we just ate in the karr. When Rem asked where we were going, Papa said it was a surprise, and he wouldn't tell us anything else.

It grew dark, and late, and, though I tried my hardest to stay awake, somewhere along the way I fell asleep. I woke up in Papa's arms as he was carrying me through the cold, moonless night. The air smelled salty, and I heard what I thought were pebbles, crunching under Papa's feet.

When he noticed I was awake, Papa put me down on the rocky beach and looked me in the eye, a finger pressed to his lips to indicate we shouldn't speak. Then he took my hand in his and we walked towards the shore where, by the light of the stars, I could just make out the shape of a dinghy. It all felt like a marvellous adventure to me.

The dinghy took us to a large vessel and we were taken aboard and led to our cabins. When I awoke the next morning, there was nothing but water all around. We were the only passengers on the ship. The captain, an elderly man with a short white beard, had a wooden crate carried into our already cramped quarters.

"Your genealogy," he said as he handed Papa a leather briefcase. Then, he pointed at the crate. "Your family heirlooms. Use your time on my ship wisely, Doctor Kakriovik. Make sure you and your children know your history and our customs."

"What was that all about?" Rem demanded. His hands were clenched into fists, and he sounded both confused and angry.

Papa closed the door before he answered. "Something happened in Ebaru that has put all of us in danger. We have been given a new life, with new names, in a new country, far from where we used to live. We cannot ever talk about our lives in Dorhedde, nor can we ever talk about Niels. For our safety and his, we shall have to pretend he never existed."

"But I want him back! And he wants to be with me, I can feel it." Tears sprang to my eyes, and I stamped my feet as I wiped those babyish tears from my face. "I can feel him, in here." I pounded my fist on my chest. "He's telling me he wants to come home. He doesn't like Ebaru."

"Sweetheart," Mama said, "I know. We all want him here with us, but that isn't possible. Not right now."

"As of today, I am Doctor Yanush Kakriovik," Papa said. His voice sounded more solemn than ever before. "I don't know where I'll be working yet, but we shall find out soon enough, I trust." He looked at Mama. "You are Olriya Bartalov. The messengers said nothing about your new job, so... I don't know. Maybe there's something in these papers here. Rem and Kas, your names shall be Winslav and Ilyakim Kakriovik." He turned towards me and touched the tip of his finger to my nose. "You, little gem, will be Lorinka Kakriov. That shouldn't be too hard to remember, eh?"

He sat down and started reading the papers. Mama sat down close beside him to get acquainted with our new family history too. Since there was little else to do, Rem, Kas and I went out on the deck and annoyed the crew with our attempts to help them.

We spent several days at sea until, on another cold, blustery night, the dinghy took us ashore. Our new family heirlooms were divided over our travelling bags, and Papa carried the briefcase with the papers. One of the crew members, a young man whose name I have forgotten, accompanied us on our journey inland, until we arrived at a tiny hamlet. He led us straight to an old farmstead, knocked three times on the door, and when an old woman opened, he said, "Your family has arrived," and left.

The woman led us into the kitchen, where she served us a light meal, and fussed over me as if I were a baby. After the meal, she showed us our rooms — I was given a small but cosy room in the attic — and we all went to sleep.

For the next several moons we stayed with her on the farm in Saryevsk, and I learned how to milk her cow, and feed the hens. She was supposed to be our grandmother, Bep Nilya, and she told us stories about her life, her deceased husband, and her daughter Olriya, who met that dapper young doctor Yanush when they were both working abroad, and married him.

She gave us many valuable lessons on the Ingravian way of life, and by the time Papa got his new job as an orthopaedic surgeon in Batazny, near Moringarad, we had adapted pretty well to our new lives.

For the next couple of turnings we lived as quiet a life as any ordinary Ingravian family possibly could. Papa had his job, Mama had hers, and Win, Ilya and I went to school. We made friends and did just about everything everyone else did.

When he was eighteen, Win went to Paliava, in Antoria, to study fashion and design, and found himself a cute boyfriend, Arteus, whom he later married.

Just a couple of days after my fourteenth birthday, we had a visit from two strangers — tall men both, whose eyes looked older than their other features suggested. They were messengers, they said when all four of us were gathered in the library, and had grave news for us. The illegitimate son of King Hanassan of Ebaru, Moradin Amari, had been killed in a house fire. They gave us a copy of the *Ebaru Patriot Reporter*, with an article describing the inferno and a picture of the unofficial prince of Ebaru, as he was dubbed in the news item.

Again, we were reminded that we should never talk about him, and if the news ever came up in our conversations with others, we were to act as if we had never known him and the news meant nothing to us.

That was the worst day of my life. All these turnings I had clung to the hope that one day I would see you again, Niels, but now that hope had been brutally crushed and we weren't even allowed to grieve. Not openly, anyway.

A few days later, I cut that picture out of the paper, and stuck it in my diary, where I still keep it. Old, and yellowed, but it was all I had left of the brother I had loved so dearly. Often, I would sit in my favourite chair in the library, with my diary and take that portrait out. I would look at it and think of the brother I had lost, and I would feel his warm presence, so near, and so real. Then I would cry, because I knew I was only deluding myself.

"And now you are here, and I'm still put out with you for making us believe you were dead."

Niels squeezed his sister's hand gently. "I really was in that fire, and would certainly have died if Mikhandor had not saved me. We thought it would be best if the world believed I was dead. Safer for me, and for the people I loved. That absolutely includes you. You have no idea how much I missed you, Little One. How many times I wished I could just be with you, and tell you I was fine. But then I realised the danger you would be in if you knew I was still alive, and... well, all I can say is, I am sorry. Truly, deeply sorry. For everything you have been through on my behalf."

He shook his head, and swallowed the lump in his throat. "And it has all been in vain too, for now you all are in danger, and I won't even be able to visit Mama and Papa any time soon. Or Rem, or Kas. And even though they still think that I am dead, that will not keep them safe any longer."

He looked at Bel. "Is there any way we can at least let them know I live?"

"Simple enough," Niko answered. He seemed to have abandoned at least some of his bitterness. "Your parents are my father- and mother-in-law, and they live in the same area as my parents. I can contact my mother, and she will tell your parents. What will you say to that?"

Niels nodded. "I would appreciate that."

"Your turn," Machteld said. "The fire. What exactly happened?"

"It is a long story, and I am too tired to tell you now, but I will soon. I promise." He put his empty mug on the table. "Mikhandor, please help me to my bedroom. I need to rest."

CHAPTER TWENTY-SIX

Dedication

<blockquote align="center">
when breath
of life wavers
friendship is forged in stone
to safeguard mankind's destiny
from doom
</blockquote>

It was happening again. King Hanassan of Ebaru was prowling the dark streets of the city, his eunuch following him like a devoted puppy. His hair was greying at the temples, and there were lines on his face that Niels had never seen before. The streets, however, had barely changed. They were dirty and littered, with holes in the pavement and broken light spheres. Scantily clad women strutted up to the men that drove by in their karrs, windows rolled up, appraising them as if they were sale objects.

Yet, Hanassan walked, as he had always done. His gait was uncertain, his posture too rigid. In his hands he held a piece of paper.

"Woman!" He grabbed a young lady's upper arm and made her turn towards him. "Have you seen my son?" He shoved the piece of paper under her nose. "He's a bit older now, but he won't have changed much. Have you seen him?"

"No sir, haven't seen him around, but you look pretty good yourself. How about we spend some time together, eh? Just the two of us?" She licked her fingertip and trailed it down his cheek. She then winked, and blew him a kiss, but he wasn't having it.

"I'm not here for that. I need my son, woman. Now stop playing games and tell me where he is. You're hiding him, aren't you?" His voice rose, and his eyes narrowed to slits. "Tell me!"

The woman leapt back. "I'm sorry, sir." She shuddered. "I haven't seen him, I swear."

"I don't believe you." He moved in on her, and she recoiled once more. "You..." Spittle flew from his mouth. "You have..." The eunuch held him back as he was about to advance on her again.

"Nassan, you're scaring her."

"I need..."

"You need to leave her alone." His too-high voice sounded strangely commanding.

"No! She has my son!" He tried to pull himself free from the eunuch's grip, but the grotesque looking man was stronger.

"Come with me, Nassan."

"No!" The king's lips curled into a snarl. He threw his full weight at his servant, and kicked the man's shins. Still the eunuch didn't budge. "I need..." He started hyperventilating. His eyes rolled upwards, and not a moment later he lay on the cracked pavement, convulsing violently, and frothing at the mouth.

Immediately, the eunuch dropped down beside him, and cradled Hanassan's head in his lap, the way Niels had seen him do so many times before.

Niels woke up, gasping for breath. With one hand, he wiped the sweat from his brow. Beside him, Bel stirred. Her eyes fluttered open, and in a drowsy voice she asked, "you alright, my love?"

Too shaken to answer, he remained silent. He hadn't had any of these dreams over the past few turnings. Why now?

"Morad?" Already, she sounded fully conscious. She reached out, placed a gentle hand on his arm. "Bad dream?"

Still unable to speak, he nodded. He lay down again. This was no time to be awake. Bel snuggled up to him, and he wrapped his arms around her tightly. Her sweet, comforting scent made him feel better. Calmer. He kissed her hair, her neck, her bare shoulder. With a sigh of contentment he closed his eyes. Tomorrow the world would look brighter. It already did.

It took a little less than a sevenday before Niels was well enough to be out of bed all day and help out with light tasks in and around their cabin. Every night, as he watched the others enjoying their daily combat training with Mikhandor, he felt envious. He wanted to join them, but could not, and he had no idea when he would have regained enough strength and stamina to resume his own training. How was he ever going to be able to fight off these assassins of his father's if he couldn't even practice some basic defensive moves?

During the days, when Bel and Niko were off to their magic training with Guren, Niels spent many hours studying the prophecies anew, looking for clues he might have missed earlier. With his father's memories intruding into his dreams again, he felt like he was running out of time.

After yet another dream-filled night, Bel urged him to talk to Leks.

"He knows just about everything there is to know about the human brain, love. If there's anyone who can help you figure out what to do, it's him."

"He won't know how to stop those dreams from entering my sleeping mind, Bel. I do. I'm just not strong enough at the moment, but once I'm back to my old self, I'll be able to block them."

"But we don't know when you will be fully recovered, do we?" She sounded tense. Or maybe not so much tense, but rather stern.

Niels sighed. "I really don't see how talking to Leks could help at all, but if you insist…"

"I insist."

Stern. Definitely stern. She'd probably never grow out of that apparent need to mother him. He would talk to Leks. Not to help him stop those dreams, but to help him understand. Once he knew how his father's brain worked, he might be able to use that knowledge when the time came to cure him. If he didn't get killed first. And if curing the king from his madness were even possible.

Breakfast took too long, and the meaningless chatter was more annoying than ever, but finally it was over. The dishes were done, and everyone had left the cabin. Everyone but Niels himself and Leks.

"Leks, what do you know about the psychotic brain?" he asked as he sat down in his favourite chair by the fire.

"A lot." The old man took off his spectacles and started cleaning them with the hem of his shirt. "And there's even more that I don't know."

"Tell me."

Leks grumbled. "This really would work best with illustrations. If only I had my portadire with me, I could show you."

Niels shrugged. Leks had been the one to tell them *no portadires*, and now he was complaining? That made no sense. "What's wrong with stylo and paper?"

"My drawing skills, chum. My drawing skills."

Niels handed him his own stylo. The one Papa had given him the night prior to his departure for Ebaru. "Do it anyway."

"You're a persistent fellow." Leks scowled as he reached for a piece of paper. "But don't tell me that I didn't warn you." He stroked his long braid, made another face, and started scribbling.

"This here is supposed to look like the human brain. Don't laugh. I told you." He glared at Niels, and Niels tried his hardest not to show his amusement. Leks's drawing looked more like a malformed egg than anything else.

"I've seen better representations of the human brain, but that doesn't matter. I appreciate your effort. Now tell me what's going on in the psychotic brain."

When Leks started talking, Niels almost wished he hadn't asked, but he needed this information. However, all these intimidating-sounding words, like *tuberoinfundibular and nigrostriatal pathway, nucleus accumbens*, and many, many others, made his head spin. Was he really supposed to remember or even understand those words?

Leks's drawings, inaccurate though they were, helped a little, but not nearly enough. He feared he'd have to spend many more mornings listening to Leks's incomprehensible lectures about the brain before he'd be able to, hopefully, cure his father from his horrible illness.

"So basically," Niels said as he tried to order his thoughts, "it is as if the psychotic brain is on fire, and this fire destroys this *substantia gri*... wait, that's what normal people call grey matter, correct?"

"Yes, grey matter. And yes, that would be the short version. The very short and simplified version. As far as we currently know, I'd like to add to that."

"You mean...?" As far as we currently know. What was up with that?

"Nothing is ever permanent in science, chum. Nothing. We have no certainties. What we think is true today, might be proven wrong tomorrow. That's how science works. It's not about the answers. It's about the questions we ask and the process of procuring our answers."

"So... scientific truths have a habit of changing?" Niels shook his head. This was too bizarre for words.

"Yes, chum." Leks grinned. "Happens all the time."

"Then I'm glad I'm not a scientist. I don't like changes."

"I'd never have guessed."

They were gathered around the hearth after combat training, enjoying a hot kaw and freshly baked gingerbread cakes. Niels was so comfortable, he was about to doze off, when Machteld said, "You still haven't told me your story, Morad."

"Yes, love," Bel joined in, "tell us... did your great-granduncle find you another place to live?"

"Oh yes, and it was even better than I could have hoped for. But then I managed to almost kill myself when I tried to be a hero."

As the days passed and turned into sevendays, and the sevendays into moons, I settled into a new routine studying the Holy Scriptures with both priests in the mornings, and spending my afternoons at the house my great-granduncle had bought us. It was a quaint old house near the Abandoned Temple that needed a lot of work to make it habitable again. I loved to work with Ammu Shadu on the renovations. If nothing else, it distracted me from my worries and the recurring dreams of my father, the king.

Often, Tasim would come and join us when he got home from school, and sometimes Tulia came with him as well. It was on one of those afternoons, during our tea break, that Tulia fell out of the tall tree in our backyard. All three of us, Ammu Shadu, Tasim and I saw it happen, and for a moment we sat frozen on our improvised seats: a tree stump and two wooden crates. Time stood still, and she just lay there, motionless, her skin ashen.

The moment I recovered from my initial shock, I sprang up and ran towards her. She was dying, and I could not let that happen. She was just a little girl; no older than my sister. Not even realising what I was doing, or how, I got my medallion out from under my shirt, lifted Tulia's tunic a little, and pressed the medallion to her bare chest.

I closed my eyes and channelled some of my own strength through to her. She didn't move, and had stopped breathing. I gave her more of my strength. It still was not enough, so I gave her even more, until finally she opened her eyes, coughed up some blood, and sat up. As I tried to put my medallion back on, I passed out.

When I came to, I was lying on a mattress in a dimly lit room. My own room, in our new home, I realised as my mind cleared. Although I wore nothing but my smallclothes,

I was drenched in sweat. Yet, it wasn't really all that hot in the room.

On the floor beside my bed sat Ammu Shadu, reading the Holy Book.

"You gave us quite a fright, lad," he said as I sat up. "Don't you ever do that again."

"How is Tulia? Is she alright?" I tried to get up from the bed, but Ammu Shadu pushed me gently back into the pillows.

"Tulia is fine, and behaving as if nothing ever happened. But you nearly got yourself killed, Moradin." His voice sounded soft, but firm, "You shouldn't have done that. For now, you are going to stay in your bed, young man."

I looked at him as his words sank in. I nearly got myself killed? Had he really said that? Surely it could not have been that bad?

"Killed?" I could barely hear my own voice.

"Yes lad." He shook his head. "You never actively used the medallion before, and there you went and did something most priests would never be able to do. Not even with all their training and turnings of experience. It zapped all the energy right out of you, and left you with barely enough strength to just continue breathing."

He caught my eyes with his. A deep frown creased his forehead. "You cannot just go around and do things like that. Not without proper training and preparation, my boy."

I felt stupid now. "I... I apologise. I didn't know. But I couldn't just let her die, could I? She's just a little girl, and reminds me so much of Machteld."

"Well, it's a good thing our new neighbour and his sister saw all of it happen, and came running. As it turns out, she's some sort of doctor, and she was able to save your life. But you are going to have to stay in bed for at least a couple of days; and a full recovery may take up to a moon or so."

"That long?" Surely, it couldn't be that bad. "And, what neighbour?" As far as I knew, the semi-detached house next to ours was in far worse condition than our new home, and uninhabited. At least, I had never seen anyone around there in all those sevendays we'd been working on the house.

"Yes, a friendly young gentleman, I would say. Big guy. He just bought the house and was busy renovating. Said he wanted to move in in about a sevenday — though how he's going to be able to make his house even remotely habitable in such a short amount of time is beyond me."

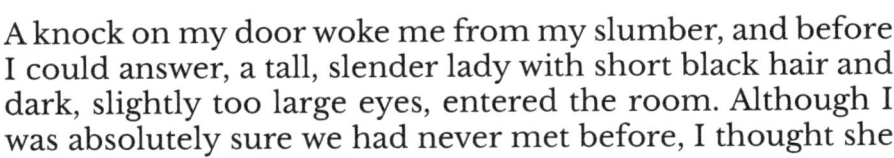

A knock on my door woke me from my slumber, and before I could answer, a tall, slender lady with short black hair and dark, slightly too large eyes, entered the room. Although I was absolutely sure we had never met before, I thought she looked strangely familiar.

"Good morning, Moradin," she said, "I am Rasælna Faylinn, your healer. You gave us all quite a start yesterday, young man. What you did was brave, but rather foolish and unnecessary. I saw the little lass fall out of that tree and would have tended to her injuries if you had not stepped in. I am pretty sure I would have been able to save her life. You, on the other hand... well, let us just say you were lucky that I was here when you lost consciousness."

She shook her head slowly. She stared at me, but didn't say a word until finally I looked up at her. I felt as if an invisible fist squeezed my stomach. I closed my eyes and moaned softly. Too embarrassed to face this doctor any longer, I hid my face in my hands.

"Moradin." The healer's voice was almost in my ear, and I felt her hand firmly on my shoulder. "Look at me. It is not my intention to hurt or upset you, but you need to understand that you have to be very careful about the things you do. We cannot afford to lose you, do you understand?"

Weird woman. Who was I to her, that she should care so much? "Not really, doctor Faylinn, but I promise I will try to be more careful."

"That is good enough for me." She seemed relieved, and for the first time she smiled at me. "And please, it's Rasælna. I am not a doctor. I'm a healer, which is something else entirely. I do not work the way traditional doctors do. I wouldn't even know how."

She then asked me to take off my nightshirt, so she could examine me. Reluctantly, I did as she said. What was all this fuss about? I had passed out. I might have asked a little too much of myself, but right now there was nothing wrong with me. Nothing a good night's sleep would not cure.

This lady was, indeed, unlike any doctor I had ever seen before, and her methods were unconventional, to say the least. Unlike ordinary doctors, she used no medical instruments at all. She simply placed her cool hands on my bare chest and closed her eyes in concentration as she moved them slowly over my body. I shivered with cold and discomfort.

"And done already," she said. "You can put your shirt back on, young man. Was it really that bad?"

"I... my apologies." I suppressed another shiver. "It's just that... I hate it when people touch me. Always have. It makes my skin crawl."

"I see," she said. After a short silence, she continued, "you're quite a bit better than yesterday. As far as I'm concerned, you may spend a few hours out of bed today. But don't overexert yourself. I shall be back to check up on you again tomorrow."

I slept most of that day, and the next couple of days were pretty much the same. The hours I spent out of bed wore me out, but I tried to stay up for a little longer every day regardless. I felt like an old man, and hated it. I wanted to be able to help Ammu Shadu with the house, or even to play one of these stupid ball games with Tasim.

It was about a sevenday later, when I first met our new neighbour. Still not allowed to do anything more strenuous than combing my hair, I sat in the garden, watching Ammu Shadu and Tasim prune that enormous tree, and here he was. A giant of a man with intense eyes, grey as charcoal. His long silvery white hair, which he wore in a ponytail, contrasted nicely with his suntanned skin and dark clothes. His tight, black leather trousers left little to the imagination, and a short, black leather waistcoat barely covered the most muscular torso I had ever seen. I could not help but wonder: How much time would that man spend working out?

He walked up to me and inclined his head slightly. "Moradin, right?"

Unable to tear my eyes from his beautiful face with its elegant, almost feminine features, I just nodded. There was something about this man, something incredibly familiar, but I could not figure out what exactly. Had I met him before? And if so, where?

"Mikhandor Faylinn," he said, "your new neighbour. Pleased to make your acquaintance."

"And you too," I mumbled, staring at my feet.

"I brought you a little something, to break the ice, as your people say." He pressed a small, smooth stone into my palm. "It is a gem from my homeland, called Turquoise Stardust Quarlite, and it symbolises friendship. You are supposed to wear it on a necklace, or even a leather string, around your neck."

I looked at it. It was beautiful. "Thank you," I said. I attached it to the same necklace on which I wore my priestly pendant. "I'm afraid I have nothing to give to you, though."

"But you already did, my young friend."

I looked up at him, confused.

"You live. That is more important to me than you can possibly know. Let us go inside the house, and I'll explain."

We went into the living room, which was fully furnished by now, and I sank down in a comfortable armchair, whereas Mikhandor sat on the sofa.

"I trust you know that Erls, as you humans call us, are not just fairytale figures," he began. His choice of words, *you humans*, sent a chill down my spine. I did not like what I thought that implied.

"And you are," I swallowed the sudden lump in my throat, "an Erl? And if so, why are you telling me this?"

"I am indeed an Erl, although we prefer to be called Sylphans, and there is something you need to know about us. For now, I shall just give you the short version."

He looked at me and waited, though I had no idea what he was waiting for. Strange man.

"Since the beginning of our histories, we have been watching every kind of royalty on all worlds. Guarding them. This is our sacred duty, which we take very seriously. I have been appointed by the Supreme Council to guard you, Prince Moradin, and I have done so since before you were born."

My mouth fell open. "Prince? Before I was born?" That sounded ludicrous. How could they even have known that I was sired by a prince?

"Yes, your Highness. You are a prince, and if I am not mistaken, a rather important one. We knew that the moment we found out that your mother was pregnant with young Prince Hanassan's child. There are certain prophecies about a king who is also a priest. We can look into that more in-depth later."

Prophecies. Again. What was up with these prophecies? And, more importantly, did I really want to know?

"It was I who, without your mother ever realising it, coaxed her into going to the Abandoned Temple to give birth to you. It was I, who sent Farrah to be with her and make sure you survived. I also made sure you were adopted by a couple with a solid medical background. And I cursed myself when you were in the hospital after your suicide attempt. I should have seen it coming and prevented it."

"Oh holy gods!" I gasped for air, closed my eyes and shook my head, hands pressed against my stomach. "You were Mig! Back at the Dr Lubinn Institution."

"Yes. I needed to be as close to you as I possibly could, and that was the easiest way. Then you ran away. Really, young prince, you know how to get on a guardian's nerves. I followed you to the cemetery, and was quite relieved when I saw Shadu take you home with him. I knew he would not let you out of his sight."

"And now you became our next-door neighbour so you can keep spying on me. Am I supposed to thank you for that?"

He chuckled. "The thought has crossed my mind."

I scowled at him. "What if I don't like it, and want you to just sard off?"

He shrugged one shoulder. "That would be too bad for you. It would not make the slightest difference. I'm afraid you will just have to deal with it. What you want, does not factor in here. Like it or not, you have a destiny to fulfil."

Prophecies, destiny... what other hogwash did life have in store for me?

"Listen, young prince. I cannot change the facts for you, but I may be able to make them more bearable. If you will let me. I came to offer you my friendship, because I think friends are better than bodyguards. I can be a rather useful guy, you know."

I sighed. "Bodyguard, friend, useful... What does it matter? I just want a normal life, like any other boy my age. School. Friends. Girls. And what do I get? A destiny to fulfil. Magic that can kill me — if my insane father does not get to me first. Ridiculous prophecies. You are going to be a priest. But, oh wait, you are also going to be a king. What is next? Do I have to save the world, too?"

Mikhandor made an apologetic gesture and looked at the floor.

"Zinnir's eleventh finger! No! I will not do it. You can all rot in the Pit of Doom with your stinking priest, king and saviour dung. I am not doing it, you hear me? You can go find some other poor sod to do that job. I shall be a priest, and nothing else."

CHAPTER TWENTY-SEVEN

Obscure

guardian
of sleep comforts
deprived mourner seeking
heir amongst the lost deprived of
honour

Finally came the day when my great-grandaunt and cousins arrived. Though Ammu Shadu assured me it was perfectly safe for me to accompany him to the drakenport, I was not so sure.

"The king and his men..." I began, then fell silent.

"What about them, lad?"

"They..." I took a deep breath, "they will be watching for me."

Ammu Shadu shook his head. "You worry too much. I can't think of any reason to assume they would."

"But he came looking for me." I cringed as the memory assaulted all my senses. His hand on my shoulder, strong, yet disturbingly gentle. His voice, so soft, and almost soothing. The anguish in those golden eyes. His sudden mood swings. The way my medallion had burned against my chest. It scared me.

"And he did not recognise you, so what exactly makes you think he would recognise you now?"

He sounded completely unperturbed. So rational, he almost had to be right, but my instincts told me he was wrong. The king was still looking for me, I knew this with absolute certainty.

"He won't make the same mistake twice." I emphasised every word. "He knows, or at least suspects, that you and the High Priest deceived him. He is still looking for me. I'm sure of it."

"The boy is right, Shadu." Mikhandor's voice was almost in my ear and I nearly jumped out of my skin. Always creeping up on us, that stealthy Erl. "It's not safe for him to go to the drakenport. Let me stay with him. Here. You know he will be safe with me."

"Mikhandor," I said as soon as Ammu Shadu had closed the front door behind him, "what do you know about the king?"

"A lot more than most people, young prince." He set up the pieces on the *Llulaba* board. "Giants versus Wizards?"

I nodded. I sat down across from him and waited for him to make the first move. "Tell me. I have the right to know."

Mikhandor didn't answer immediately. He stared at his pieces, as if he were contemplating how to win the entire game in just one move. Finally, he put his *kaliff* forward in a most unconventional opening manoeuvre.

"For one thing," he said, "I know he is still actively looking for you."

"I told Ammu Shadu so." It upset me more than I liked to admit that my great-granduncle acted as if I was just being paranoid.

Mikhandor nodded. "He has been just about everywhere, showing people that portrait one of these officers took at the drakenport, and he keeps asking if anyone has seen you. He still goes out every day, to ever more unlikely places, trying to locate you. The poor man seems desperate."

I studied the board and moved one of my pieces. "How do you know all that?"

I wasn't surprised. This simply confirmed what I had seen in my dreams already. But how did he know these things, when even the High Priest and Ammu Shadu had no idea?

"We have our people in the Royal Palace, young prince. You could have known that."

"Your people?" I echoed. "And how could I have known?"

"Your Highness, I told you we have been guarding every kind of royalty on every world since the creation of our All and its times. One of our men has been close to your father, ever since the day his mother birthed him."

"Right." My curiosity got the best of me, and I couldn't help but ask, "and who might that be? Your man?"

He laughed, and shook his head. "Sorry, young prince. I'm not at liberty to tell you."

"Then tell me more about my... about the king." Why did I even want to know? I hated the man, did I not?

He moved another piece, and I could tell I was already losing. I didn't even mind. "What is there to say? He is looking for you, and growing ever more distressed because he cannot find you. I don't think he is likely to give up any time soon."

"Neither do I."

From the dreams that troubled my sleep most nights, I knew this much: My father, the king, was a deeply disturbed man. I had seen him physically attack his brothers on several occasions, over the littlest of things. I had seen him weeping inconsolably over the deaths of his father, mother, siblings, nephews and nieces. I had seen him shouting at his staff, and heard him threaten to break their bones.

I had also seen him as a young man, wandering the District of the Poor, calling for my mother. "Lali, where are you?" or, "Lali, come back to me!" and, "Lali, I need you!" Seeing him like that ate away at my soul.

More worrisome, I had seen him going out in the streets, alone or accompanied by his eunuch, searching for me. Day or night, it didn't seem to matter to him. I could sense his desperate need to find me — a necessity larger than life itself — and I knew he would not stop. Not unless he found me.

I tried not to think of what would happen if he really did. A shiver ran down my spine and brought me back to the present again.

"Got a spider creeping up your leg, young prince?" A spider. Right. As if a spider ever scared me before. But if that was what he wanted to think, he had my blessings.

"Something like that." I got up. "I'm going to get me a drink. Shall I bring you something?"

"A cold beer would be nice." He yawned as he stretched his arms and legs. "No need to fuss with tankards, though."

"Too bad you finished Ammu Shadu's last beer yesterday. I could get you some dishwater, though. That should taste just about the same."

"I think I'll decline your kind offer. Just give me whatever you are having."

Before I reached the kitchen, I heard Ammu Shadu's karr pull up the driveway.

Up until that moment, I had thought I would run to the door to greet my cousins but now, inexplicably, my feet were nailed to the ground. An illusory fist clenched around my stomach and my breath caught in my throat.

I had imagined I would give them a grand tour of the house, and tell them all about our lives in Ebaru, but as they walked through the door, my tongue dried up in my mouth, and I could not utter a single syllable.

Here they were. Finally. My two best friends. My cousins. And none of us were moving or speaking. We just stood staring at each other, as if we were looking at some strange mirage.

"Well lads," Ammu Shadu broke the spell, "have you all lost your tongues?"

"Course not, Baba," Anur said in a hoarse voice. "It's just... Zinnir's beard, Niels! I sarding missed you, man."

Not a moment later he crushed me in a tight hug and pounded me on the back, while I tried to catch my breath. When he finally let go, Rasu gave me the same treatment.

"Who'd have thunk, eh?" He released me, took a step back and stood gaping at me once more. "Cousins. How cool is that?"

"Actually, he is our grandnephew, but yeah. Cousins sounds far better. And, to be honest, it feels more like we have a new brother now." Anur ran his hand through his hair. His voice still sounded funny. "Now, are you going to give us a tour of the house or what, Nie... uh... Moradin?"

"Right. Well. Follow me. This here is the kitchen. Your father had a dragonkiller's job fixing the plumbing, but you'll be pleased to know that everything is working the way it should now. No leakages, and no turds floating back into the privy. If you will come with me to the living room..." I led the way, "...you will have the honour of meeting—"

"Hey, I've seen you before!" Anur stared at Mikhandor. "You are... nah, you cannot be." He shook his head.

"My name is Mikhandor." A smile curled the corners of his mouth. "I have been assigned to shield and protect Prince Moradin, so I expect you will be seeing me around a lot. And yes, I did pose as Mig. That seemed like the most prudent course of action at the time."

"If you guys get your luggage, I will show you your room." My cousins trailed behind me into the hallway, where they picked up a large travel bag each. "I suggested you should have your own rooms, but your father said you would want to share a room."

"Baba is right. We like to be together."

"Where is he anyway?" I looked around in confusion. Only now did I realise I had been constantly aware of Ammu Shadu's presence, always very near, during these past few moons. Why had the medallion gone dormant now? Why could I not feel him? Had something happened to him? Something dreadful?

Anur shrugged. "He hasn't seen Mam in ages. I'll bet he's enjoying some private time with her."

"Definitely having a drawer conference." Rasu smirked. "You had better not show us the master bedroom, Niels."

"Moradin," I automatically corrected him. "The name my mother gave me."

"Sorry. I forgot, man. But I'm sure we'll all get used to it in no time at all. And now," he said as he threw his travel bag on one of the beds and opened it, "I got something for you." Smiling from ear to ear, he handed me a small parcel.

"Open it," Anur said. "It's from your parents. Your father brought it over to our place one night. Just before they left Dorhedde."

I swallowed. I had not been able to speak to them, or even write them a letter, once in the past three moons. It was too dangerous, not only for me, but for them as well.

"Left? What do you mean, left?" My hands were trembling as I tugged at the wrapping paper. The parcel contained a book, a framed picture of our family, and a small envelope with Papa's neat handwriting on it.

"Yes. Left. Dunno why or where." Rasu shrugged. "Some weird bloke took up residence in the house and put it up for sale, is all I know."

Tears stung behind my eyes as I ran off to my own room, where I tucked the letter away under my pillow. I didn't trust myself to read it just yet. Instead, I picked up the Holy Book and started reading from the prophecies. Not that I really understood them, but somehow trying to decipher the meaning of these cryptic statements calmed my senses.

Our first supper together in Ebaru should have been a happy one. I'd been looking forward to this meal for days — and it took just a few heartbeats to turn into a disaster when Ammu Shadu told my cousins about his plan to homeschool them.

Rasu put down his knife and fork. He leaned forward and glared at his father. "What do you mean, home educate?"

Ammu Shadu looked at him, his face unreadable.

"What if we want to go to school and make friends?"

"My son, you worry too much. You will have friends. Trust me."

"So you say, but tell me: How are we going to make friends if you keep us locked up in the house all day?"

"I cannot recall that I said anything about locking you up."

"You might as well. We'll be sitting at the kitchen table all day, everyday, with Mam teaching us history and our languages, you shoving the Holy Scriptures down our throats, and some hired tutor boring us to death with his maths- and science lessons." Rasu snorted.

"Now that you mention it... Yes, I suppose we could do that. You made some excellent suggestions there, son." Was he really suppressing a chuckle, or was I imagining things?

"You should have left us in Dorhedde. We were happy there." Rasu got up from the table.

"Rasu. Did I grant you permission to leave the table?" Ammu Shadu sounded calm, but through the medallion, I could feel his anger.

With a muttered curse Rasu sat down again. Then there was silence. An oppressive kind of silence that made me want to run away and hide. Ammu Shadu resumed eating his supper. Ameh Saryda pricked a few peas on her fork, but she seemed to have lost her appetite. Anur moved his food around on his plate.

When finally I could not take it any longer, I spoke up. "Please, can you not allow Anur and Rasu to go to school? They aren't in any real danger, are they?" I held my breath as I looked at him. I could only hope I hadn't angered him even more.

"Oh lad..." He shook his head, but seemed a little calmer now. He even smiled at me. "I appreciate your effort, but the answer is still no. Your cousins are in almost as much danger as you."

"You keep banging on about how dangerous Ebaru is," Rasu said in a low growl, "and how messed up this king Hanassan, and yet you decided we should all come and live here. I think that's insane."

"Enough, Rasu." Ameh Saryda sounded angry too, now. "Not another word. Your father did what he thought was best, and it is not for you to question his decisions."

After supper the three of us went upstairs to the twins' room.

"I don't know, Rasu," Anur said, "but maybe home education isn't going to be all that bad. School hasn't always been fun either."

Rasu sat cross-legged on his bed. He tossed a small ball from one hand to another and back again. "But I want to go to school. I want to make friends. I want to be able to... well, you know."

I knew what he meant. Unlike Anur and me, Rasu was an extroverted guy, who liked to be with others. The more, the merrier. He enjoyed playing pranks on people. His behaviour had got him into trouble numerous times, but he would just laugh and shrug it off.

"Life's to be lived, eh?" Anur winked at his twin. Those were the words Rasu used to say when he had earned himself yet another detention.

"Yeah. Besides, I really don't see how we'll ever get to know anyone worth knowing if we don't go to school."

If that was his problem, he should not worry. "Ebaru is not like Dorhedde. Not even a bit. Here, only the rich go to school."

Rasu inhaled sharply. He sat up straighter. "You are pissing in my boot, right?"

"No, I'm not. If you thought you had seen poverty back in Dorhedde, you are in for a nasty surprise. And I don't imagine things will improve, now that my... now that Hanassan has become king."

"What's up with this new king anyway?" Rasu leaned forward. "Is he really your father? Really?"

The all too familiar iron fist tightened around my stomach again. I nodded, and turned to look out of the window, so my cousins could not see my face. I didn't want them to see how miserable I felt.

"He is one sick excuse for a human being. Completely off his stones, and more dangerous than you can possibly imagine. That psycho has killed his entire family." A shiver went down my spine. "He would certainly kill me too, if he found me."

"Poor man," Anur sounded as sincere as ever, "I do hope he gets adequate treatment. He probably hates himself for what he has done."

I shuddered as a memory flashed through my mind. The memory of his hand on my shoulder, and the sorrow in his voice when he spoke of his nephew.

"I don't want to talk about him. I've got better things to do with my time. Did you know Mikhandor is going to teach me the ancient Sylphan language, so I will be able to read their Holy Books?"

"You. Don't. Say." For the first time that evening, Rasu sounded excited. He even smiled. "The Sylphan language?- As in, the Erlen language? Now that's something I'd like to learn."

Sleep eluded me that night. The reunion with my cousins, and all the emotions that came with the day's events, made my head spin. The house felt different now that we were all living together here. The sounds were different too. I heard my cousins talk in low voices until Ameh Saryda came and told them to be quiet. I then heard her fill the bath.

I took Papa's letter from under my pillow, ripped the envelope open and started to read.

My dearest Niels,

I hope this letter finds you safe and in good health. Due to the recent developments in Ebaru, we have been forced to evacuate. We'll be leaving tomorrow morning, but I don't know our destination.

Sadly, we will not be able to keep in touch. The risks are too great, or so we have been informed.

Though we hope for better times, and a speedy reunion, our reality is not that simple. But whatever the future may bring, you will be in our hearts forever.

All our love,

Papa, Mama, Rembrant, Kasper, and Machteld."

Soft footsteps on the stairs, probably half of an hour later, told me Ammu Shadu was coming upstairs. Next thing I knew, my medallion lost contact with him again, and when I heard muffled noises coming from the master bedroom, I hid my head under the pillow and plugged my ears with my fingers. I didn't even want to think about what they might be doing.

When sleep finally did come, the dreams came with it.

The king walked the dark streets of the city, followed by his eunuch. In his hand, he held a smudged, wrinkled piece of paper. My portrait, taken at the drakenport upon my arrival in Ebaru. He must have gone through dozens of these pictures by now, and I wondered how many more he would go through before he finally gave up. If he would ever give up.

"You!" He stopped a bone thin young woman. "Have you seen this boy?"

She looked at the picture through glazed eyes, and shook her head wordlessly.

"Have you seen him?" my father insisted.

"No sir." Her voice was hoarse and barely above a whisper. "Can't say that I have." She hopped from one foot to the other, and back again.

"But you must have!" His voice cracked. "I know he is here. Where did you hide him? Where? Tell me now!"

"Your Majesty." The eunuch placed a placating hand on his shoulder, which earned him an elbow in the stomach, but he did not budge. "The woman does not know. Let us not waste our time with her."

"Do you think so, Krys?" His eyes, narrowed to slits, darted from one end of the street to the other as the woman fled.

"I am positive, Your Majesty." Despite his ridiculously high voice, he managed to sound soothing, but my father was not having it.

"She stole my son!" he shrieked. "She stole him!" Spittle flew from his mouth. His eyes rolled up in their sockets, swerved from left to right and back again. He shuddered. "My son," he rasped. "I need him. I need..." He faltered, and big tears rolled into his beard. "Need to..."

Despite myself, I felt sorry for him as he sank to the ground and rolled up into a ball. In a barely audible voice, he kept repeating those two words, "my son, my son," as his body convulsed under the strain of his unravelled emotions.

The eunuch knelt down beside him. "Hanassan, light of my life." He cradled him in his arms and held him like a mother holds her baby. "We will find him, I promise you. We will."

I woke up gasping for breath and drenched in sweat, as usual. A knock on the door told me I woke Ammu Shadu again, too. I could feel his concern as he entered my room.

"Are you alright, lad?" He brushed a strand of wet, sticky hair out of my face. "Another of those dreams?"

Too shaken to talk, I just nodded.

"We need to talk about this in the morning. You, I and the high priest. It is beyond time we found a way to stop these dreams, don't you think?"

Again, I nodded. "He must not find me, Ammu Shadu," I whispered. "He must not."

"We won't let him, Moradin lad. We'll keep you safe." He gave me what was probably supposed to be a reassuring smile. "Our good Goddess herself will protect you. Go back to sleep now. We'll talk in the morning."

CHAPTER TWENTY-EIGHT

STAR

bringer
of gloom dispersed
when sunrise wakes the day
and sorrow's child cleanses the house
of kings

"Tell me about these dreams of yours, young man," the high priest said in that dispassionate voice of his. "How often do you have them?"

Ameh Saryda had gone to the library with my cousins and I sat on the sofa in the living room, flanked by Ammu Shadu and him. It made me feel like a prisoner. I could barely breathe. I couldn't think clearly, so I shrugged. "Most nights. Sometimes two or three a night. But some nights none at all."

"I see." He nodded. "What happens in these dreams?"

I shrugged again. "Just all sorts of random rot."

"Young man, I am a busy person. Stop wasting my time, and answer me."

Wasting *his* time? I could think of a thousand things I would rather do than being interrogated and lectured by this austere man, who smelled of dust and dried-up sweat. Why could he not just teach me what I needed to know and be done with it?

"I do not have to tell you what happens in my dreams. You only need to teach me how to sarding deal with them." I got up from the couch and went over to the window. A reluctant rain drizzled down from a sunny sky and I spotted no fewer than four rainbows. If only I could go outside, and let the gentle raindrops wash all my worries away.

"Your great-granduncle tells me these are no ordinary dreams. Do I need to remind you of the danger you are in?"

With difficulty, I swallowed some choice words. I wanted to kick his holy arse.

"Moradin." Ammu Shadu had got up behind me and laid a hand on my shoulder. "I know you don't like to talk about it, but Akdi needs to know."

"I fail to see why."

"Unless we know exactly what we're dealing with, we will not know how to fight it. And we do need to fight it, don't we, lad?"

I nodded. These dreams had to stop. They robbed both me and him of our sleep, and we were both near exhaustion. Dejected, I sat down again.

"It's the king. He is always in these dreams and I don't know, but I think..." I hesitated. What did I think? Were the dreams reality? Were they his dreams? His hallucinations? "I just don't know." I rested my head in my hands.

"Shadu?"

"I'm afraid I cannot be of much help, Ak. I don't get pulled into these dreams, the way I get pulled into his visions. I just feel my nephew's distress."

"That, at least, is something," the High Priest said. "This means we can rule out the possibility that we are dealing with visions of the past."

"No, we cannot," I said to my own surprise. "I believe these might be my... the king's memories of the recent past. Or something like that."

"The king's memories?" High Priest Ironheart actually managed to sound surprised. "That is unusual. What kind of memories?"

"All sorts of things." I got up and circled the room looking for something I could kick. Why could that inconsiderate man not leave me alone? "Just a whole lot of donkey dung." I sent the wastepaper basket flying. "Him fighting his brothers." I banged the door shut. "Shouting at his sisters." A small side table went down, and a vase of flowers with it. "Arguing with his staff."

Shadu seized me in a tight and unwelcome embrace just before I could attack the standing lightsphere. "Enough," he said. "You will clean this mess up before your great-grandaunt comes back home."

"Let go of me!" I struggled to free myself, but to no avail. "I don't want to talk about it. I hate him!"

"No more kicking innocent pieces of furniture, lad."

I kept struggling. "Let go of me! I hate you! Let. Me. Go!"

"Morad." His eyes bored into mine, and the resulting tightness in my chest and throat made me avert my gaze. "You will behave."

I winced. I gave up fighting. "Please," I begged. "Don't make me talk about it. Please."

He led me back to the couch and made me sit down. Only then did he release me.

"Moradin, lad." He shook his head, "I know this isn't easy for you, but you are not doing yourself any favours fighting us. We can't help you unless we know. You're a smart enough lad. I'm sure you understand this."

"Please, he's still looking for me. His behaviour scares me. He is always out there, with that creepy eunuch of his, looking for me, for Zinnir's sake. He will kill me. He will kill all of us."

"That is where you are wrong, young man," the High Priest said. "He may still be looking for you, but he will not kill you. The prophecies don't lie."

"The prophecies, my arse." I made a special point of not looking at him. "You and your piddling prophecies. How can you even be so sure that they are about me?"

"If you would finally give up fighting me hand and foot, and would agree to work with me, I could show you. There is so much you don't understand about the Scriptures yet. So much you need to learn."

"Ammu Shadu can teach me." I detested the High Priest, and in all honestly did not want to give up on hating him.

"Morad, I already told you. I cannot. Now, what to do about those dreams? Is there anything else you can tell us about them?"

I bowed my head. "Just that they scare me and I want them to stop."

"To recapitulate: Your father appears in your dreams, and you suspect we are dealing with his memories. You have seen him losing control when interacting with others, and you fear he is still looking for you." Ironheart's voice sounded as stoic and detached as ever. Sometimes I wondered if the man even had any feelings at all.

I nodded. "Yes. That about sums it up."

"And when did you say these dreams first started?"

When indeed? Had he not been in my dreams and visions for as long as I remembered? But no, the old dreams and visions, they were different. My mother had always been in them. These new dreams however, came directly from him.

"The first time," I tried to concentrate as hard as I could, "I think... you remember when he came looking for me?" A shiver ran down my spine as I felt his hand on my shoulder again, and the burning heat of the medallion against my chest. What had the king done to make that happen?

"I should have known." The high priest didn't even have the decency to sound surprised. "Still, this is highly unusual. A visit to the seminary's library seems called for. Come with me. Both of you."

He strode out of the room, and never even looked back to see if we were following his orders.

Situated high on a hilltop, about one hour's ride from the city, the seminary was larger and more magnificent than I could have imagined. The whitewashed walls reflected the sunlight, and the red roof tiles looked as if they had been touched by dragon's breath.

"Young man," Ironheart said as he parked his karr, "do I need to remind you to guard your tongue?"

I shook my head. "No sir." Fully aware of the danger, I would much rather have stayed home with Ammu Shadu, or even with Mikhandor, but the high priest would not hear of it. He seemed to think I needed to risk my skin coming to the seminary with him.

The eerie quiet in the long, broad corridors did nothing to ease my mind. The robed men that crossed our path and sometimes even stopped to look at us, made my skin crawl. Did they see the resemblance? Could they be trusted, or would the king have his spies even in this sacred building? And what if he came looking for me here? Today?

"Ammu Shadu," I said under my breath as we entered the library, "what are we looking for?"

"Books on dreams and visions, lad. They are over there." He pointed at a section near the far end of the enormous hall. As we walked by row upon row of bookshelves, our footsteps reverberated louder than thunder. A white-haired, bearded man who sat on the floor reading from a large tome, glared at us with watery eyes. Others looked up from their reading too, and I felt more miserable with each step I took. Someone would recognise me and go running for the king.

"Right here." The High Priest vanished between two rows of bookshelves and I had no choice but to follow him. "All the books in this section deal with the subject of dreams and visions. I suggest you find yourself a basic introduction. *A Guide to Dreams and Visions* by Saldyn Kemiri should suffice."

As I wandered down the aisle, I made a special point of not looking for that book. Why should I read anything he wanted me to? Most of the titles were dull and uninspiring. *An Introduction to Dreams. A First Look at Visions. Knowing your Dreams and Visions. Priestly Vision.* Like I was going to want to read that.

The Erlen books in goatskin binding — old, delicate and with yellowed pages — were much more interesting, but unfortunately my knowledge of the Sylphan language was still too limited, and I barely understood a word of what was written in them. Even so, I kept searching those shelves, hoping I would find a small, simple booklet. Something I would be able to study with Mikhandor.

"Morad." I felt Ammu Shadu's hand on my shoulder and turned round to look at him. "I think I may have found you something interesting here."

He handed me a black, leather bound volume with an incredibly realistic depiction of the priestly medallion. *Night's*

Reign, by Moradin Amari. Too astonished to say anything, I just took it from him and stood gaping at it for what felt like an eternity.

"Night's Reign," I whispered the words, almost reverently. "He... your brother wrote this?"

Shadu nodded.

"You knew, didn't you?"

"I had no idea, my boy. He never spoke about the turnings he worked at the seminary. He was a broken man who never spoke much any more, but he must have known."

"Known?" I looked up at him in confusion. "Known what?"

"We should go home," High Priest Ironheart cut in. "I found a few books that might be helpful. You can borrow that inconsequential little booklet for all I care."

"What in the names of all the gods got into you? Do you two want to lose your heads?" All the way back home he had not spoken a single word, but now the High Priest exploded. "What if the Ears overheard your conversation? You had better pray to all the gods that you'll still be alive come tomorrow morning."

"It was a stupid thing to do." Ammu Shadu sounded abashed. "I should have known better."

"I'm going home. I've seen quite enough stupidity for today."

Ammu Shadu sighed, but I was glad to see that windbag go. Humming a silly tune Papa used to sing to me when I was little, I started picking up the pieces of the broken vase. Ameh Saryda and my cousins should be home soon.

"I don't understand that man." I grabbed the wastepaper basket and began to collect the scattered rubbish. "What was he so worked up about?"

"The title of the book, lad. Night's Reign. You couldn't know this, but it is rather an ambiguous phrase, and the Ears, the king's spies, will certainly be aware of its deeper meaning."

I looked at him in confusion. He sat down on the sofa and, with a small gesture, invited me to join him.

"He had a brilliant mind, my brother, and when he was not with his people, he was studying the Scriptures. Most often, he would turn to the Prophecies of the Kings, which apparently were of particular interest to him. Night's reign, in the prophecies, refers to a dark time for the people, when the nation is being ruled by an incompetent king. The darkest time, the prophecies say, will be just before the sun returns."

He stood up, got the Holy Book from the bookcase and started leafing through it. Searching, I knew, for the passage that mentioned this 'Night's Reign'. It made me shiver. All these prophecies, and how the priests — and even Mikhandor — seemed to think they were alluding to me. That I should, somehow, be the Chosen One.

I felt an almost irrepressible urge to wreck the living room again, so I got up and went upstairs, where I locked myself up in my own room. I needed to be alone. Then, stupidly, I got my own copy of The Holy Book out and started studying. Scanning through the pages of the prophecies, searching for the words 'night's reign'.

I forgot the world around me. Forgot time, and didn't notice how dark it grew until I could not read any more and had to light a sphere. I did not notice my hunger, or my cousins calling my name until they were banging on my door, shouting, "Morad! Food!"

During supper I was caught up in my own thoughts, and paid no attention to the conversations of my relatives. After supper I went straight to my room again, opened the Holy Book once more, and read until finally I found a reference.

> *"And when the child of sorrows comes, darkness shall fall upon the land and night shall reign until the chosen one shall return and restore the house of the kings. Then, the sun shall rise, and a new day shall devour the night."*

It was even more obscure than some of the other prophecies, and I could not make much sense of it. This child of sorrows, honestly, could be anyone. This was Ebaru and, especially in the District of the Poor, there was sorrow beyond bounds. I had been there with Ammu Shadu quite a few times now, since he had taken on his brother's calling and become Priest of the Poor.

I had seen misery and poverty back in Dorhedde. Addicts living in the streets, picking through public waste baskets in search of food, sleeping under shrubbery or bridges. Even the street dogs seemed better off than them, because some people liked street dogs and would feed them, speak to them kindly or ruffle their fur. But nobody liked the homeless, and everyone avoided them.

Here, the poor were both worse and better off. Better, because they had each other and their ramshackle huts. Worse, because they had children and these children grew up in extreme poverty and, like me, were already addicted to alcohol and narcs before they were born. In a strange sense, I had been lucky that my mother died and I was cared for by the Maidens of Eylah until my adoption. Thanks to my mother's ill fate, I grew up relatively rich, and healthy.

As I thought about my mother, her memories washed over me again. They mingled with my own, and even with these new ones. My father's. Overwhelmed, I fell down on my bed, curled up in a ball and rocked myself to sleep.

When I woke up, the house was unsettlingly quiet, but my lightsphere was still glowing, and the Holy Book lay opened on my desk, exactly how I had left it. I was cold and stiff. It must have been well past midnight, but I was wide awake now, and decided to reread the prophecy.

This child of sorrows, and this chosen one — were they two different people, or were they one? And this time of darkness, night's reign, was that now? Who could tell? And how? These might be dark times, but how could anyone be sure these were indeed the days the prophecies were talking about?

And then there was that bit about restoring the house of the kings, which seemed pretty impossible to me. I might be the king's only living child, but I was by no means his heir. I also had absolutely no intention of ever becoming a king — if that were even possible. So, unless King Hanassan got married and fathered a legitimate child sometime soon, the House Dolanthi of Ebaru would cease to exist when he died. I did not really care either way. Or so I told myself.

CHAPTER TWENTY-NINE

Rise

> star shines
> golden by night
> staff and orb guide the hands
> of him assigned to lead humble
> mortals

"So this is it." I stared at the simple wooden slab in the dirt, unable to believe my eyes. This was worse than I had thought, and I didn't know what to think or feel.

"Yes." Ammu Shadu rested a hand on my shoulder. "This is how he wanted it."

He got down on his knees, picked up a handful of the black earth and let it slip through his fingers little by little.

"But he deserved better than this, Ammu Shadu. This isn't right."

Ammu Shadu got up slowly and I followed his gaze as it wandered over the grave site. There was no beauty here, in this pauper's field, with rubble, weeds and the odd tree or shrub scattered between the graves — some of them still fresh and bare, others overgrown with vines and only recognisable as burial monuments by their simple wooden markers.

"None of the poor souls that lie here deserved to be shoved under the ground like this, my dear Moradin. My brother chose to be one of them, in both life and death."

Angry with myself and my father's family, I turned and took a few steps away from my great-grandfather's final resting place. It was unfair. How was I supposed to ever come to terms with this injustice?

Ammu Shadu was watching me, but he didn't follow or try to stop me, so I did not really mind. As I roamed the grounds aimlessly, my feet getting stuck between the tangled creepers from time to time, I could feel the medallion burn against my chest. Instinctively, I reached for it and pulled it out.

"What is it now?" I snapped at it before realising how irrational my behaviour was.

I was about to tuck it back under my shirt when I noticed the warm glow that emanated from its centre. Still holding the golden ornament in my hand, I shook my head and shrugged. This was impossible. A trick of the light. It had to be, and yet I could not cast off the feeling that it wanted to show me something. Still sceptical, I followed its urging.

Hidden between the high grasses were the remnants of a lone wooden log. Bright yellow and orange fungi grew on its rotting surface, and I knew. This was the place where they had buried my mother. Just another nameless addict. Frantically, I pulled out the offending plants before I sank to the ground and let my tears flow.

It wasn't long before I heard him come up behind me, felt his hand on my shoulder, and smelled the familiar scent of incense; the incense he used to burn at daybreak, before he said the morning prayers. He held me in a silent embrace, and I cried even harder.

For how long we sat there, I didn't know, but my stomach was growling by the time we got up to leave the burial site. My legs felt heavy as we walked past one identical grave after another, and I felt like I could barely remain standing when Ammu Shadu halted by one of them, and said, "this one... Shirra, your grandmother, lies here with her little ones. Asra and Siana."

Again, he performed the little ritual with the dark earth, just like he had done at his brother's grave. Although I had no idea what it meant, I sensed that it gave him some kind of comfort, and on an impulse I followed his example and did the same.

Nothing happened. Not a single small change in my emotions.

"Why are we doing this?" In vain, I tried to keep the disappointment out of my voice.

"Tradition, my boy." He smiled a wan smile. "Tradition. It makes me feel better because I know I'm doing the exact same thing my fathers have been doing for generations before me."

I nodded, even though I was not sure that I really understood what he meant. My parents — my adoptive parents — believed in cold, hard science, not traditions, so I grew up without. Of course I had heard of some of the traditions of my ancestors, but I'd never really had the chance to incorporate them into my life. Not until now.

"I would like to see my great-grandfather's grave one more time before we leave, please."

My fatigue and hunger could wait. What might have seemed like but a trivial detail to others was, at that moment, the most important thing in my life. I wanted, needed to perform the ritual with the earth. I felt a deep longing to make this a part of who I was, and there was only one way to achieve that: by doing it each and every time I visited these graves.

Together we knelt down this time. Together we each picked up a handful of the black earth, and let it trickle down through our fingers. Together we got up and stood in solemn silence, watching my great-grandfather's final resting place, the stillness disturbed only by the mournful wail of a lonely bird.

Studying the Scriptures was easily the most important thing in my life. I was not interested in abstract mathematical formulae, the sciences or business studies. More than anything, I desired to understand the prophecies. What did they say? What was their true meaning? Were they really about me, or were the priests mistaken? I could not make my mind up. Just when I thought I had finally figured it all out, there was yet another prophecy that seemed to contradict the others and turned everything upside down again.

I wanted to learn about the history of Ebaru. And much more of it than I would ever be able to learn in school. I needed to know exactly what happened to the Dalanthian Empire. When did it fall apart into several smaller kingdoms? How did that happen, and what was the impact on the lives of my ancestors? Who were my ancestors? What kind of people had they been? What were their joys? Their struggles? Their values?

I genuinely enjoyed learning the old Sylphan language with Mikhandor. I was proud of myself when, after several moons of hard work, I could finally read a simple children's book. It was the first step towards reading the *Writings of the Sylphans* and finding out for myself what needed to be done to reverse the curse of the Erlen king.

Though I detested the high priest as a person, I learned to put my feelings aside and apply myself fully to my training sessions with him, when he taught me how to control the priestly medallion. It was during one of those sessions that I got an accidental glimpse into his inner being, and I was quite shocked to find out that he actually cared deeply. About me, Ammu Shadu, my cousins, the people of Ebaru, and even about the king. It was as if he carried the grief of the entire world inside his soul. No wonder he never showed his feelings. He could not afford to.

It lasted only a heartbeat. Then he was sealed up again, and apologised in his customary stoic voice. "Sorry about that."

He went on with the training as if nothing had happened, but the experience had a profound impact on me. It changed my attitude towards him. No longer did I secretly refer to him as Priest Ironheart. Now that I understood, I finally respected the high priest. He became one of the handful of people I felt I could confide in.

As moon after moon went by and nothing untoward happened — no more visits from King Hanassan, and no killings that we were aware of — I gradually relaxed. A knock on the door would not instantly turn me into a flailing, gibbering mess and, occasionally, I even braved the world and went to *The Barmy Bookworm* or *Fredo's Fat Fritters* with Tasim and my cousins — with Mikhandor lurking somewhere in the background, of course. These places were not the nicest ones around, but that was exactly what we wanted. I felt it was safer for me to go there than to the rich Sapphire Square Shoppes, which I only knew from hearsay.

In the sixth moon of Turning 9738, we went to the seminary together: Anur, Rasu, Tasim and I. Ammu Shadu and the high priest rented us a small house on campus. Under no circumstance would they allow us to live in a dorm. Not that I even would have wanted to, but Rasu was bitter about it. He said it felt like his life was put on hold yet again, and for a threat that he thought wasn't nearly as great as his father and the high priest assumed.

Anur, like me, preferred living in a house of our own, and so did Tasim. The three of us were convinced the priests were right. That the threat of King Hanassan finding out who I really was, was still as large as ever and we should not take any unnecessary risks.

On our first day at the seminary, all fathers had come with their sons, so moulds could be made of their medallions. The professor, a priest-goldsmith, told us how each family of priests had their own design, and showed us some different ones. Ours had three stars, a staff, and an orb, whereas the high priest's had a starbird with seven flames set atop its tail feathers.

Though I already had my own priestly medallion, none of the other new students had one, and our first lessons at the seminary were dedicated to the crafting of the amulets. Since I didn't need to make my own, I watched my cousins and Tasim as they made theirs. The process was fascinating, and I took turns with Anur and Rasu carving the wax moulds for their casts.

On the second day, each of the students was given an ingot of seventy-eight parts gold, twenty-one parts copper and one part eylarium, the Divine Element. The Divine Element, the professor told us, was extremely rare and could only be found in the Eylarian Peaks. Only priests of the Eylaurumi tribe, the goldsmiths, knew the exact location of the mines and could access them. They mined precisely the amount that was needed for religious purposes. Never more. Never less.

I watched from a safe distance as my cousins and Tasim melted their gold ingots and poured the molten gold into the casts, and secretly thanked Eylah that I didn't have to do the same. It was an awfully hot job, and certainly not without its risks, but we all wore protective gear and the goldsmith kept a close eye on us to make sure no accidents would happen.

Shortly after, my fellow students took their medallions out of the casts and I helped Tasim polishing his. By the end of the day they were ready to wear, but not activated yet. To activate, the student's father would have to wear the medallion with his own, on the same chain or string around his neck for a sevenday, so it could absorb its powers and memories. In the case of my cousins, Ammu Shadu would need to wear Anur's medallion for a sevenday first, because Anur was the oldest of the twins; after those seven days he would have to wear Rasu's, also for a sevenday. Apparently, wearing the two together with his own medallion would only dilute its powers, meaning he would have to wear them for up to a moon for the process to be completed.

Our turnings at the seminary were mostly uneventful. Where other students had all kinds of fun, for us there were no parties, no games, and no girls. We went to compulsory lectures only, and did all the rest of our studying at home. When we needed books or other resources, either Mikhandor or one of the priests got them for us.

We kept ourselves purposely apart. The only friends we had besides each other, were the guys we had got to know on our visits to the District of the Poor, before we went to the seminary; and I wasn't even sure we could really call them friends. Most of them were addicts, and in poor health, both mentally and physically. Like Ammu Shadu, we did what we could to make their lives more bearable, and yet it never felt like we did enough. Too many of them died before their time.

One of my professors, Ziubar Walani, appeared to have taken a liking to me, and rather too often for comfort, he would seek me out after his lectures. He would sit with me to chat idly, and as I stared at his aged hands and long white beard, I would wonder what had roused his interest in me. I worried he might be one of the king's Ears, until he let it slip that I reminded him so much of my great grandfather, it almost felt to him as if his friend Moradin had returned from the dead.

Later, he would even come over to our place once or twice a sevenday, because he was in the neighbourhood, or so he claimed. Ever more often, he would talk about his friendship with my great-grandfather, and how the two of them had studied the prophecies together. Meanwhile he would feed me bits of hidden knowledge about the prophecies. Things that he and Moradin had figured out all these turnings ago. Together, we read *Night's Reign*, which I had conveniently forgotten to ever return to the library, and thanks to him, I understood much more than I had ever thought possible. I began to see connections that Ammu Shadu and I had never made. Things even the high priest had never pointed out to me.

When the time came for us to choose our specialisations, I wanted to pick the prophecies, but Ammu Shadu, the high priest, and Ziubar all advised strongly against it, so I chose the priestly medallion instead. It seemed only natural for me to specialise in the workings of the medallion, they argued, because mine had such an exceptionally strong aura. All of the professors noticed it, and even most of the students.

During my specialisation I learned that the strength of a medallion's aura was directly related to the powers of the priest who wore it. Additionally, if an extraordinarily gifted priest, such as my great-grandfather, were to die young and one of his male descendants were to wear his medallion from birth, this boy would, as he grew up, be infused with his ancestor's strength. A strength that would increase his own innate strength vastly.

I finally had the answer to the question why my medallion was so much stronger than any other medallion, and why I was said to be the most gifted priestly student since the creation of mankind. Ziubar then told me that this tied in perfectly with some of the prophecies about the Chosen One, and warned me not to talk about that with anyone else. We could only hope none of the other professors or students would uncover that connection. Because, although we had no reason to distrust any of them, even one word spoken to the wrong person, or in the wrong place, could have disastrous consequences.

After that discovery we became even more reclusive, and more cautious than ever before. We only needed to hold out for a few more moons, until after our graduation. Then, we would leave Ebaru and each of us would move to a different part of the world.

All went well. We graduated with honours, which was not at all surprising. After all, we'd spent basically all of our time studying, these four turnings at the seminary. As requested, all four of us were offered positions in remote places.

Tasim would become a priest in Oks'Magdekk, in the Cru'Spahyns. Anur would go to Byarlara, in Vykaria, Rasu to Andrupol in the Antorian Highlands, and I would serve in Grummwell, Valkerland. I still couldn't believe we had actually made it, and although we were happy enough to leave the dangers of Ebaru behind, we were also saddened to become separated from each other. Of course, we promised to keep in touch, but we knew things would never be the same again.

CHAPTER THIRTY

Inferno

lightning
strikes in dark night
brings fatal destruction
mournful memories mingle with
present

It was two nights before our departures from Ebaru. Almost all of our belongings were packed, and we had gone to bed early. We were tired. Not just from all the work, but even more from the emotions.

Though I could usually block my father's dreams from entering my sleep — because that was what actually happened when I had these dreams in which he featured so vividly, I knew now — this night I was too tired, and his nightmare had free access to my already overworked mind.

It was horrid. Again, he was wandering the Hooker Zone, looking for me. He had run out of portraits some suns ago, but still he stopped several of the poor young women working there, and demanded to know where they had hidden me. "I need him," he repeated again and again. "My son, give him back to me."

But none of them had seen me, and they fled from the mad king's anger, while his eunuch tried to calm him. Yet, he would not be quieted and started calling out my name. "Niels! Niels! My son, where are you? Niels!" Louder and louder he screamed, until he collapsed. And still he sobbed, "Niels! I need..." He shuddered, and called out one more time. "Threat!" Then he cried uncontrollably, and the eunuch cradled the king's head in his lap and tried to comfort him, as he always did.

I woke up panting and sweating. I needed to do something to take my mind off my worries. Just two more nights before we would be gone from Ebaru. I could do this. I had just picked up my travel bag when I thought I heard something, but as I stood listening, all remained quiet. I was about to open my bag when I heard it again. A soft crackling. The sound of a campfire. Not even a heartbeat later I became aware of the smell. Petrol. The crackling swelled to a roar.

That was the moment I knew with absolute certainty that my father had finally found me, and sent his assassins to eliminate the threat, as he perceived it. Unable to comprehend how this could be happening, I stood nailed to the floor. Out of nowhere, Mikhandor appeared beside me. Without a moment's hesitation, he slung me over his shoulder, bag and all, and lunged forward.

I saw a flash of lightning so bright it hurt my eyes. A cold blue fireball exploded right in front of us. I heard some loud bangs, the ground shook, and a blistering heat scorched even the hairs on my arms. Then, there was nothing. Absolutely nothing. And we spent what felt like an eternity in this cold, dark, boundless nothing. I hated it.

Neither of us spoke. Apart from the clammy cold, I didn't feel a thing. I could not move. The air was so thick, it was almost impossible to breathe. My nightshirt hung from my body like a heavy, formless shroud. Time had lost its meaning. Was I dead?

We emerged from the void into what felt like cool morning air. The moment Mikhandor put me down, I threw up. Exhausted, I lay down in the bedewed grass and closed my eyes. I had no idea what had just happened, and frankly, I didn't even care. My head was pounding and I felt feverish. I only wanted to curl up and sleep.

Mikhandor dumped Anur down beside me. As Anur collapsed, Mikhandor disappeared, only to come back a heartbeat later, carrying an unconscious Rasu in his arms. Gently, he laid Rasu in the grass, and stepped back into nothingness for the third time. He returned just a moment later. Alone. He sat down a short distance away from us, and wept.

I sat up and looked around, trying to figure out where I was, and what had happened. We were on a patch of the greenest grass I had ever seen. Early morning sunlight seeped through a canopy of fan-shaped leaves and bathed the small clearing in a soft greenish glow. The air smelled of fruit and flowers, but that couldn't mask the acrid odour of fresh puke, or the smoky smell of burnt wood and textiles that still clung to me.

Memories slowly bled into my mind, as if through a thick fog. My father, King Hanassan, crying out for me and shouting "threat!" The popping, sizzling sound of a campfire that had intensified to a loud roar. The smell of petrol. Mikhandor appearing out of thin air, as he sometimes did, and picking me up as if I were a bag of potatoes. The sudden explosion followed by a trip through some kind of void.

Now we were here, but I had no idea where *here* was. Anur lay motionless in the grass, staring up at the sky. Rasu was coughing, and would probably come to soon. But where was Tasim? And why was Mikhandor so upset? A feeling of dread engulfed me as I pieced everything together.

Someone had purposely set our house on fire. In the middle of the night. Someone had meant to kill us. Not just me, but all four of us. And Tasim — I shook my head. Didn't want to believe it. This could not be true. Not Tasim. Not my best friend. They could not have killed him.

I scrambled to my feet and ran towards Mikhandor. "Why are you sitting here? Go find Tasim! You cannot let him die!" I grabbed him by the shoulders and shook him. "Go!"

But Mikhandor shook his head. Fresh tears rolled down his cheeks. "He is dead, Moradin." His voice sounded hoarse. "I could not save him. I failed."

I looked at him in disbelief. "You are mistaken," I insisted. "Go back and save him. Please!"

Again, Mikhandor shook his head. "There was nothing I could do, Niels."

Part of me knew then that it was true. He never called me Niels. Still, I could not believe it, and just like that, I was back at the Dr Lubinn Institution. Back in Sofieke's room, that pesky voice in the back of my mind taunting me. "Your fault. All your fault."

I shook my head. Balled my hands into fists. I was not going to give in to it. Not today. I was older and wiser now. That voice, it was just my subconscious playing tricks on me.

"Come with me, Moradin. We need to go." It was Rasælna. I hadn't heard or seen her coming, but she had probably been here for a while already.

"You need to come with me, Niels. There is nothing you can do here." Femke's voice. I could almost feel her presence. The medallion, I realised, throwing me back into a past I would much rather forget.

"Moradin." Rasælna again, sounding more insistent now.

"Niels!" Femke. There was urgency in her voice, but something else too. Something I had failed to notice all those turnings ago. I recognised it now. Insecurity. She was only a girl back then, eighteen or nineteen turnings, perhaps, and this was probably her first suicide. Poor lass.

"I understand how you must be feeling, Moradin, but..."

"No. You do not. You cannot. I just..." I clenched my jaws. I couldn't say it. That would make it real, and I didn't want it to be real. "Tasim..." I broke down.

When I had finally regained my composure and looked up, I was alone with Mikhandor. The sun stood high in the sky, but the trees filtered most of the sunlight and kept the clearing relatively cool.

"Where are we?" I asked, not even expecting Mikhandor to answer.

It didn't matter. Not now. "Your fault, the fire," the voice in the back of my mind sneered. I tried to ignore it, but it kept taunting me. "You should have used that fancy trinket of yours to cure the king. Some priest you are, with your puny magic."

"Thorf," Mikhandor said, apparently unaware of my inner turmoil. "My home world. You are safe here. Are you ready to come with me?"

I shrugged. I didn't care the least bit where I was, or where we went.

"Sure." I slowly heaved myself off the ground. My feet were heavy as I followed him to wherever he was leading me. I took no note of my surroundings, and would likely never be able to find my way back to this stretch of grass but that, too, did not matter. Nothing really mattered. My life had just been destroyed. Again. If I really were the Chosen One, then why were the gods constantly breaking me? Could they not at least have a little more compassion towards their instrument of choice?

Where the outdoors became indoors I never really noticed, but at some point I simply knew we were inside. The trees grew exceptionally close together, and their branches were interwoven in such a way as to form halls and rooms, or whatever these enclosed spaces were called here.

"In here," Mikhandor finally said, as he opened some sort of door and let me enter first. A carpet of purple moss lived on the floor of a spacious hall. At the end of the room was a dais, where a man with long white hair and an even longer white beard sat on a throne. The Erlen king, I presumed.

The walls of the hall were covered in blooming vines that infused the air with a delicate ambrosial scent. Beautiful exotic butterflies, ranging in size from smaller than a bumblebee to larger than a Goldfox Fleddermouse, darted from blossom to blossom. Though there was quite enough light in the room, I had no idea where it came from. There were no windows, or at least none that I could see.

Huddled together in a corner near the dais were Anur, Rasu, and Ammu Shadu. A feeling of dread crept up on me. If Ammu Shadu was here, then where was Ameh Saryda? And what had happened to the high priest and his family? I feared the answer would crush whatever part of my soul might still have been left unscathed.

A youngster, dressed in all white, stood talking to the ancient Erl. I stared at the old man in disbelief. He bore an uncanny resemblance to the legendary King Yumænor from the storybooks, and I could almost believe he was as old as the gods themselves. Donkey dung, of course. No man lived that long.

Rasælna was in the room too, and hurried towards me the moment she caught sight of me.

"Come with me for a moment, Moradin." She led the way into a small side room. "I need to do a quick health-check first, though I don't think you sustained any physical damage from the fire."

It did not take long, but when I put my stinky nightshirt back on, she looked at me gravely and took both my hands into hers. "I need to tell you something before you join your relatives." She took a deep breath. "There were several house fires last night. Our brothers did what they could, but we found out too late that your house wasn't the only one that was targeted. Your great-granduncle lives, but only because he wasn't home when his house was set on fire. The high priest might survive. If we are lucky."

I stared at her. "My great-grandaunt? Tulia? Navida?"

She shook her head. "I am so sorry." She still held my hands, and I felt she wanted to say more, though I could not imagine what more there was to say. Four of the people I loved, had been murdered. Because of me.

"The Maidens of Eylah." She bit her lip, and I could almost feel her struggle. "Their house was set alight as well and..." she breathed in and out several times before continuing, "they all..." she swallowed.

As my heart broke, the tears came anew. Farrah. Sweet Farrah, who had been like a mother to me when I was a baby, and again, when I just arrived back in Ebaru after my failed suicide. Who, during all the turnings I had been living in my native city, had continued to care for me, and treated me like the son she never had.

"Professor Ziubar Walani. They got him too. I am so very sorry." She brought her hands to her face and covered her eyes.

I wanted to scream, but my throat felt constricted and I couldn't utter a single sound. "Your fault," the voice in the back of my mind accused me again. "All your fault." I put my hands over my ears and, through my smothered sobs, started humming to myself. I did not have to listen to that stupid voice, and I would quiet it. No matter how much effort it took.

Niels leaned back in his chair and closed his eyes as the memories threatened to overcome him.

"Here, have a drink, brother." Niko thrust a warm goblet into his hand. "It will do you good."

He brought the chalice to his mouth, then realised it was filled with mulled wine. With a pang of regret, he handed it to Bel, who sat beside him. "I apologise, but I cannot drink wine. Not now."

"Why not?" Niko sounded befuddled. Or was that annoyance that came through in the man's voice?

"I... my mother was addicted to narcs. I was born an addict. Drinking to subdue my emotions is not a risk I am willing to take." He hoped Niko would understand. He needed the man's support. "I could do with a hot drink, though. Tea or a kaw brew would be nice."

He heard the clattering sounds of metal on earthenware, followed by the soft spluttering sound of water being poured into a vessel. A strong hand on his shoulder. A cup being pressed into his hand. Niko's deep bass, almost inside his ear. "Here, my man. Drink." Apparently, his brother-in-law did not hate him any more. That, at least, was a good thing.

As he drank, he slowly began to settle back into the present. He had lost friends. Good people who could never be replaced, but he had gained new friends, and he was reunited with his little sister. Not all was darkness and dread.

"You've been through some pretty rude things, mate," Niko said after a while. "I can't believe Mumi never told me that we are helping the prince overthrow his father. These are the fairytales!"

"You call it a fairytale," Niels held his now empty mug tighter, "but I think it is one big, unending nightmare. Also, I most definitely do not want to overthrow my father. I want to cure him so he can be a good king. I don't want his sarding throne."

"Suppose you were able to restore your father's health and miraculously turn him into a good king, who do you think will be on the throne after his death? Face it, brother. You are his only living child."

"He is not too old to marry a suitable woman and sire some legitimate children yet. It doesn't have to be me."

Niko laughed. Leks laughed too. Mikhandor and the women remained silent.

"Moradin, my friend," Leks said, "for a man your age, and with your life experience, you are remarkably naïve. Sometimes I think you don't understand people at all. And, morbid as it may sound, I cannot help but wonder what I would find if I were to have a look inside that extraordinary brain of yours. I'm pretty sure it would be fascinating."

Beside him, Bel gasped.

"You would probably find something comparable to what you found in this Zigman's brain." Niels put his mug down on the table. "Different wiring, so to say. Or is it too far-fetched to assume that all magic comes with a differently wired brain?"

"Do not tempt me, chum." Leks's voice took on a dark quality. "Do not tempt me. I am a scientist first, and a human being only way down the line."

Niels could not suppress a chuckle. He liked Leks and his insatiable thirst for knowledge. "I shall make you a promise. If I die during this quest, you can have my skull and do all the research you like."

CHAPTER THIRTY-ONE

Behold

<pre>
         dragon
      eyes are swirling
    blue and pink and golden
   alive with memories of days
          gone by
</pre>

Bel ploughed through the snow. It was hard work, and if her caster wheels didn't get stuck, her rear wheels would slip, but most of the time she managed to break free of the slush unassisted. She could, of course, use her magic to melt the snow if she ran out of options, but Guren had advised most strongly against it. "The Charm," he'd said, "is not a play-thing." Besides, where was the fun in that? Melting snow and ice was easy. Navigating it was a challenge that provided her with the opportunity to expand her wheelchair skills. A challenge she would not pass up.

Niels walked beside her, leaning on the walking stick Niko had crafted him. By the looks of it, he had a much harder time of it than she. He walked far more slowly than any man his age should, and he was panting and sweating, but his jaw was set, and he didn't complain.

"I need to pick up some provisions on the way back," Bel said, mainly to break the silence.

"Provisions? I thought the forest provided us with everything we need."

"Not for Returning Light, my love. Niko will never forgive us if we don't have a feast. And presents. Lori agreed to take care of the latter, and I promised to plan and supervise the preparations for the festive meal. Zera will help me in the kitchen, and Esh said she would take care of the decorations and stuff."

"Hmm. To be honest, I don't feel like celebrating at all."

"Neither do I. I only want to finally go to Ebaru and get this business with your father over with. But Niko and his people want to celebrate, and since the Aurora won't be back before most of the ice has melted, we're stuck here till spring anyway. We might as well humour them. I don't even want to think of what we'd do without them. Our chances of survival are pretty slim already. You do realise this, don't you?"

"Always." Niels heaved a sigh. "If there was any way we could avoid the upcoming confrontation, I would. But I've been studying the prophecies anew during all those days I've been a useless wreck. I hoped to find a loophole somewhere, somehow. But there is none."

He stood still for a moment, panting, then started walking again, leaning just a bit heavier on his stick.

"Through fire and ice, on mighty wings, he shall return to his father's house, to make the crooked straight — and should he fail, the worlds will pay in suffering tenfold," he recited.

The words sent a shiver down Bel's spine.

"I won't claim to understand all of this, but the implications are clear. We have to succeed. There is no other way. That's what gets me out of bed every morning, even when I still feel weak and exhausted. It's what makes me put one foot in front of the other, even when my legs feel like jelly."

"That's not a pretty prospect. The worlds falling under a curse if we mess this up." To be frank, it scared the Northern lights out of her, but Niels didn't need to know that. He was having a hard enough time already.

"Not pretty at all." Niels' voice sounded morose. "But the gods are on our side. We are going to Ebaru to lift that horrible curse. That should give our hearts courage."

They continued their trek through the woods in silence, and sooner than anticipated, they reached Valtstrom-Uer and the old school building Leks had rented and turned into a gym.

"Ready?" she asked.

"More than ready, Bel. I've missed this."

"Just wait till after our training. We have no mats."

"No mats?"

"That is correct." Mikhandor appeared out of nowhere, grinning from ear to ear. "But look at it this way. We have wooden floors. I'm sure they are far more comfortable than the rocks we're likely to encounter in a genuine combat situation."

Bel laughed as they entered the gym, but Niels had a scowl on his face. He'd probably be unpleasantly surprised to find out how much their little company had grown.

Janæla, who insisted on being called Jana now, had been the first new addition to their group. Like Mikhandor, she was a seasoned fighter. With Niko's arrival, six new members were added to their party. All six of them quite adept at street fights and tavern brawls, but only Flar a real fighter, which wasn't all that surprising. Bel was sure the tall man was Niko's Erlen guardian; and even the forgotten gods knew he needed one, her impulsive little brother.

As they were training, Bel couldn't help but notice Niels' struggle to keep up. His normally graceful movements were replaced by stiff, clumsy attempts at fending off the attacks of his partners. It was a good thing Mikhandor had secretly warned the others to go easy on him, for if they didn't, they might well beat him into yet another coma in no time flat. His reflexes were too slow. It was as if he'd completely forgotten how to fight.

When Pav came at him, wooden knife aimed at his neck, he barely managed to block the attack. Though the second time Niels fared a little better and got Pav in a wristlock, his technique looked sloppy, even too Bel's relatively untrained eye.

He didn't show his feelings, but Bel knew he hated it. How long would it take for him to get back to normal? Would he even regain all of his strength and endurance at all? Or had he done irreparable damage to himself? Bel tried not to feel guilty when she considered that possibility. He'd done this for her.

Every morning Bel and Niko went to their magic training at Guren's little house in the woods. Bel loved it, and easily gained ever more control over her fire, but too often, Niko lost his temper when yet again he failed at producing the kind of flame Guren wanted to see. Yellow instead of blue, wide and wavering instead of narrow and steady... Niko hardly ever got it right, and then he'd lose control completely and Guren had to snuff out his fire before it could do any real damage.

One morning, Niko managed to accidentally set their mentor's bread basket on fire. The silly look on his face had been hilarious. Guren's reaction not so much. The man had as foul a temper as Mumi and Niko together.

Guren. The old man intrigued her. There was something about him. Something familiar. Not because of the magic, which definitely created a bond, or because he was an Ingravian. Neither was it because she'd known him as Gerrolf Drachlieb when she was a child. It was something else, and Bel wanted to know what that was.

"Tell me," she said one morning as they entered Guren's little home, "who are you?"

"Beldenka *lief*, you know who it is I am. I am your Charm tutor and mentor Guren Fonvernum."

"Yes, and before that you posed as forester Gerrolf Drachlieb. You will forgive me if I tell you that I am convinced your real name isn't anything like Guren Fonvernum. That's not even an Ingravian name, for the love of the Dragonmother."

The old man sighed. "It is belike time then. Time for a special history lesson. 't Is quite a story, so I suggest you two make yourselves comfortable. I shall make tea."

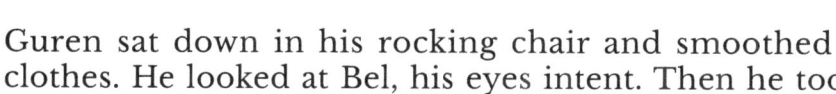

Guren sat down in his rocking chair and smoothed his clothes. He looked at Bel, his eyes intent. Then he took a deep breath and started talking.

"As I am sure you know, *Free Ingravia* rebels did shoot Emperor Bartomir's dragonet Saldriz with a poisoned arrow in the summer of Turning 9587. This enabled those folk to capture and depose him, because without Saldriz, his charm was reduced to almost nothing. These miscreants did touse the emperor's tongue first, then gouged out his eyes, and cut off his reproductive organs. After that, those knaves flayed him, starting at the toes. The emperor was long dead before they finally sliced the skin off his head and beheaded him. All before the eyes of his entire family."

Bel gasped. "Holy Dragonmother's teeth! That was in none of the history books I read."

"Nor in mine," Niko said. He looked pale. Paler than usual.

"That's because 't was never writ in the histories," Guren said, "but I have mine own resources."

He was silent for a moment and his eyes took on a far-away look. After a while he scraped his throat and resumed, "The rebels eke had killed the dragonets of Bartomir's son Arestim and daughter Olniya, who were eke captured and executed, as were the emperor's jointress, all his brothers, sisters and other relatives. Except for Arestim's oldest daughter Lillenka, who was expecting her seventh child.

"With the help of... her dragonet Shirza, Lillenka did manage to flee to the mountains, whither she lived with the dragons, and whither her son Nazradim was born. Like so many of his ancestors, Nazradim was blessed with the Dragon Charm, and his mother did teach him the art as most wondrous she could, but neither Lillenka, nor Nazradim were greatly gifted."

"How did Lillenka escape?" Niko asked the question that was playing through Bel's head as well. It wasn't the dragonet that helped her, she was sure of that.

"Ah..." Their mentor took a sip of his tea. And another one. Through the silence, Bel felt his reluctance to answer. "The lady, uh... was with a guardman's son. The one whose seed it was she carried.

"Nazradim was a wild and disagreeable sir, who scorned and despised people, and did misprise the prospect of ever having to live amongst those folk, even though this was Lillenka's wish for him. Instead of settling down in some obscure settlement, the young gent abducted a peasant's daughter and did force himself upon her. Then the degenerate did hold the poor wench captive for the rest of her life."

Guren clenched his hands into fists. He snorted.

"Some gent he was." He shook his head. "This mistress, whose name we don't right know, did bear Nazradim the twin brothers Viktomir and Dragomir. Once the boys were weaned, and Nazradim had nay more use for their mother, he skewered her gut as if she were but a mountain rat."

Again, their mentor fell silent. A shiver ran down Bel's spine. Those gruesome details... she'd never known them. What was the old man's mysterious source? She looked at him. Studied the deep lines of grief that were edged into his face. His suddenly insecure posture. He seemed so much older now.

"What a sick bastard," Niko said. "To think that scumbag is one of our ancestors." He growled, and hot steam rose from his nostrils.

"I can't quaint things up for you, young sir." Bel could have sworn she heard a slight quiver in Guren's voice, but when he resumed his story, it was already gone. "True to his nature, Nazradim never cared much for his get, and left the boys in their grandmother's care while he went out in the mountains chasing manewolves and northern bears. Every once in a while he would return home with meat. He then did stay for some few days, ere he would disappear again for moons on end.

"Finally came a time whither he simply did cease coming back. That was belike just as well. Lillenka did love her grandsons beyond measure and, although they did live simply, she made sure the boys never did want for anything."

Guren drizzled some more honey into his tea. His eyes took on that far-away look again. "Lillenka was gathered into the bitter cold embrace of Yat S'ber shortly after the boys did turn eighteen," he continued in a soft, sad voice, "at which hour the twins had decided to leave their home in the mountains and did settle in the village of Solrod. There they did take the name Ranovik for their last name. Two turnings anon, Viktomir did marry one of the village wenches. They had six children, four of whom survived into adulthood."

"You're one of them, aren't you?" Niko leaned in, an excited expression on his face.

"Not so hasty, young sir. Not so hasty." Guren waggled an admonishing finger at Niko, but Bel thought she detected a melancholy smile in his voice. "Dragomir took a while longer, but eventually had found himself a jointress too. The lady was a fiery redhead, with the clearest emerald eyes one can imagine. Zhelina was her name. Alas, she has passed hence giving birth to their daughter, Azabelya."

The old man let out an explosive breath. With lifeless eyes, he stared into the fire for what felt like ages, but Bel didn't dare interrupt his silent thoughts. Even Niko remained quiet, waiting for Guren to resume his narrative.

"Lyts Bel, as Dragomir called her, did have the same flaming red hair as her lady mother, and her father's violet eyes. Like her father, she was gifted with the Dragon Charm. She had a dragonet called Raznah, and the mischief they did get into together did bring precious moments of joy to her father's grieving heart."

Guren walked over to the window and stood looking at the blizzard that swept the snow across the small clearing in front of the house.

"Though the Charm had not been specifically outlawed in Ingravia yet, 't was not prudent to use it openly. As Solrod had grown from a tiny village into a bawbling town, Dragomir knew it had come time to move on, and he evacuated with his young daughter to a settlement so small it didn't even have a name.

"They had lived quiet lives in their tiny homestead, and didn't see many people, but eventually Bel had met Vykenti, a young architect from the North. They did get married, and at which hour his trade required him to live in the city, the young couple had moved to Moringarad."

Guren sighed. "More tea?" He turned around and, without waiting for an answer, refilled their cups.

Slowly, Bel started to piece everything together. Guren was no son of Viktomir. If he were, he'd be telling them Viktomir's story now, but he wasn't. And that left only one explanation. An impossible one, and yet...

"Dragomir, who did wish to remain close to his only child, had built himself a cabin in the dense woods just outside the city. By that hour, most people had forgotten about the connection between their previous emperor, the dragons, and the Charm, so the risks of living in a more populated area weren't too great.

"Bel and Vyk had one daughter, Zhelenka and two sons, Zigmandas and Bartoram. Of these three, only Zigmandas had the Charm, though, unlike his mother, he was not exceptionally gifted. He was, however, an extremely talented cellist."

Bel was barely listening. Her grandfather Zigman was long dead, and great-uncle Bart... She'd met him a few times. A kind old man with... with the same violet eyes as their mentor.

"Are you listening, Beldenka?" Guren's voice pulled her out of her reverie. "As I did just say, Zigman did marry fellow-cellist Rozanya Khroniev. They too, had three children. Three delightful girls, Mirtalya, Veralya, and Zitanya. Again, only one of their children was gifted with the Charm. Mirtalya who it is, with her gorgeous ginger hair and bright cornflower eyes did bear an uncanny likeness to her grandmother, mine own lyts Bel."

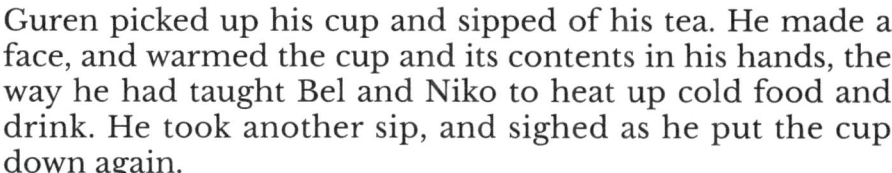

Guren picked up his cup and sipped of his tea. He made a face, and warmed the cup and its contents in his hands, the way he had taught Bel and Niko to heat up cold food and drink. He took another sip, and sighed as he put the cup down again.

"This is as much your history as 't is mine, and if it be true you did listen well, my lyts Bel, you at this hour know who it is I am. In truth, deep down you knew it all along, I bethink." The tenderness in his voice took Bel by surprise. Most of the time the old man hid his emotions behind that grumpy mask of his.

She stared at him, still unable to believe it. It couldn't be. Dragomir was born in Turning 9612, 140 turnings ago. He couldn't possibly be that old.

"Impossible," she said. "Nobody lives that long. No human, anyway. Besides, if this is true, then why haven't I seen your

Erlen guardian around? In all these turnings I've known you? Where is he? Or she?"

"My lyts Bel." He took her hands in his and looked her in the eyes. "Behold me. Behold me closely. What is it you see?"

The old man's violet eyes were swirling, like a dragon's eyes, and in those deep whirlpools she saw his memories. The people he had known, and the places he'd been. His laughter and his sorrows. All of it, captured in the depths of his eyes.

"But how?" she asked. She felt breathless, and dizzy. "How is this possible?"

"Our charm, Beldenka lief. It grants us longevity. If, and only if it be true, we have enough of it and use it wisely. Those of us who it is have only been gifted with a moderate amount of the charm or know not how to use it, shall have an average life span. But only if it be true they are lucky. At its worst, they'll belike die young. I bethink that might be what has happened to mine own father, though I did never care to find out. I've at each moment been better off without him." He warmed the contents of his cup again and took another sip of his tea.

Bel closed her eyes. A million thoughts ran through her mind, a million questions. Where was Guren's... no, Dragomir's Erlen guardian? They had to be around somewhere. What was their secret? A disguise of sorts? It almost had to be.

And then there was the matter of Nazradim's disappearance. His death wasn't recorded anywhere, and if even his own son didn't know what became of him... He might have been a scoundrel, but still. She needed to find out.

The clink of porcelain on porcelain made her open her eyes again. Just in time to avoid her great-great-grandfather's displeasure for not paying attention.

"What I know of the charm," the old man said, "I was taught not only by mine own grandmother, but most of it by the dragons themselves. Though those creatures may seem cavalier, they are mild and gallant towards those worthy of their trust."

"The dragons themselves?" That sounded exciting. "Would they..." probably not. She was just a beginner, after all, and botched it all the time. Maybe not quite as often as Niko, but still. Far too often. She was no good at all.

"They do speak of you. Already." The old man nodded, as if to add emphasis to his words. "As well they should."

Bel looked at him, her eyes wide. "Why?"

He laughed. "Why, the wench asks." He laughed even harder. "My lyts Bel, your dragon is the most majestic Ingravian Broadwing Dragon I ever beheld. What is more, the dragons themselves do say she be the Queen of All Dragons. They're but waiting for you to mature in your charm."

She? The Queen of All Dragons? It couldn't be. And yet, it made sense. The Ingravian Broadwing Dragon was the largest and most ferocious dragon that ever existed, and there were precious few of them left. Ordinary humans both feared and hated them. For centuries, they had hunted her beloved dragons and killed most of them. It wasn't as hard as most believed. Though their scaly skin protected them from most attacks, their furry chests were vulnerable. All it took was one well-aimed poisonous arrow.

Of course, back in imperial times, dragon hunting had been illegal, but with the fall of the Empire it had become a prestigious game for the new nobility, the so-called Lords. Minor, High or Grand, it made no difference. Usurpers and dragon killers. Bel had never wanted any part in that. If ever she became a King, or better yet, the new Ingravian Empress, she'd outlaw dragon hunting immediately, and make it punishable by death. Death by Dragonbreath.

She shook her head. She, a King. Or Empress, no less. What in all seven hells was she thinking? As if the other Lords would ever accept a Reject to rule beside them.

"Your daughter, Azabelya, what happened to her?" Could she still be alive, too? The stories said she was dead, but these same stories also claimed that Dragomir was long gone.

Dragomir bowed his head and folded his hands in his lap. "She was a daughter of nature and, like me, did misprise the city life. Oft, we'd wend to the Ingravian Peaks, to hunt rabbits and other bawbling prey. She was a splendid Copper Sweeptail Dragon, and did enjoy flying in the mountains. She did love the freedom of the wilds. She and I both."

He was silent for a moment, then continued, "T was in the summer of Turning 9696, and we was out hunting, when mine own lyts Bel was shot by a dragon hunter. One moment she was up in the air, a stout, vivacious dragon; the next she did lie on the ground." He coughed. Tears were glistening in his eyes and, with a violent shake of his head, he inhaled noisily. He rubbed his nose with the back of his hand.

"Mine own lyts Bel. A wounded, fragile mistress, convulsing as vast amounts of *thremble venom* did course through her bloodstream and did attack her nervous system. I could not do aught. I could not even be with mine own lyts wench and hold her as she did lie dying. Those knaves would have murdered me too."

He took a shuddering breath. "Mine own lyts Bel... 'T was the worst day of mine own entire life. Then, not even a sevenday anon, all charm was outlawed in Ingravia, and I knew time had come for me to leave the state. I did seek refuge in the Senkeberghe. Nay dragon hunters hither. I only would..." He fell silent again, and neither Bel, nor Niko spoke for a while.

"Well, I bethink I shall not need to tell you young ones what has happened to your grandfather Zigman. I told that gent to come with me, but he would not hark. He was in love. There's just nay reasoning with young lovers. All hormones and nay brain activity to speak of. One need only behold the two of you. Completely brain dead. Both of you."

Bel laughed, and even Niko chuckled. The old man was back to his old grumpy self again, and Bel liked him better that way. Grumpy old Guren, she could handle. Defeated old Dragomir — not so much. It was a side of him she'd never seen before, and it scared her. He was the strong one. Her mentor who had always known an answer to everything life threw at her.

He had been the one to teach her that being in a wheelchair wasn't the end of the world. He had taught her how to poke fun at life when life was beating you down. He had taught her not only the attitude, but also the skills to become an independent woman.

It was him who taught her how to work wood. How to fix stuff that was broken. And that had started when he had mended her heart, that was broken into a thousand pieces because her parents had sent her away and told her to never come back home again. He'd not just given her a new home, he had been her home.

My lyts Bel, he used to call her, and she'd seen the love in his eyes. Little had she known then just how much she really meant to him. In healing her broken heart, he had also allowed her to heal his.

But now, because of her questions, his old wounds had been rent open, and she thought she felt his pain almost as acutely as he himself did.

CHAPTER THIRTY-TWO

SLAYER

> baleful
> presence watches
> passing through bounds of time
> driven by thoughts of eternal
> ruin

Niels was impatient. Restless. They had been in the Senkeberghe for almost five moons now. That was longer than he had been a priest in the Barlows — and they were with too large a party. A strange party of unusual people.

They attracted attention. A merchant couple and their guards, who made no efforts to sell their wares, but instead chose to hibernate in the forest. A group of sailors who spent the winter in an insignificant inland town in an isolated Northern country.

The locals had seen them training in that old school, and were asking questions. Could they join? Why not? What were a woman in a wheelchair and an old man with a prosthetic leg doing in a combat training class? Niels could almost smell their suspicion. It would only be a matter of time before King Hanassan's spies tracked them down. All it took was one word spoken to the wrong person.

What was worse, they could not leave. Niko had, understandably, not wanted his ship to remain in the harbour all winter, so he had told his second in command to sail on to warmer countries and do some trading there. The Aurora would not be back until late spring, and they had nowhere to go if things went sour.

The only good thing was that he had ample time to recover from his embarrassing magic mishap. That, and having his sister back. Of course Bel and Niko needed their time with Guren, who turned out to be their great-great-grandfather Dragomir, to learn how to control their magic.

When the snows started to melt, Niels took to wandering the woods, mostly to distract himself from his worries, but also to work on his physical condition, which had plummeted during his moons of forced inactivity. Frequently, he would spot three dragons flying high in the sky and, as far as he could tell, having a great time.

Bel's brightly coloured Ingravian Broadwing Dragon was without a doubt the most magnificent of them. As delicate as she looked in human form, so impressive did she look when transformed into her dragon, Vindicia Feroxi. The name alone was enough to send awed shivers down his spine.

Dragomir's Green Firecrest Dragon, though advanced in age, was still an imposing presence, and Nikomir's fierce Horned Sharpclaw Dragon looked as elegant as the man himself, with its distinctive silver stripe on the top of its head.

It was during one of his long solitary walks, that Niels felt like he was being watched. His trained instincts kicked in instantly, and he stopped and sat at the foot of a tree, back propped against the trunk, as he pretended to rest. With unsteady hands he unstoppered the insulated flask he always carried with him on his hikes. He nipped at his hot kaw.

His unease notwithstanding, he managed to plaster a smile on his face. Made sure his breathing was slow, deep and regular. He needed to make it look as if he were just taking in the placid beauty of nature.

Niels let his gaze wander the still surroundings. Funereal trees cast long shadows on the scattered patches of half-melted snow. Here and there, shy new growth peered out from between the dead matter that lay strewn across the forest floor. A lone mouse scrambled through the jumble of pine cones and needles on that drab mossy carpet.

The apparent normalcy of the forest made him even more nervous. It was too peaceful. Too quiet. He wasn't alone. He could feel it. A dark, menacing presence. A presence he had felt before, he realised now, and the first time had been in Ebaru. Mere days before the fire. A baleful awareness, not his father's. King Hanassan's mind felt different. Disturbed. Confused. Angry at times, but not evil, like this thing.

He had felt it again when he was serving in Sern, a few days before his near-fatal accident. The third time had been several turnings later in Tan'Rabu, just before the virus escaped from the Laboratory of Pathology and Pharmacology and killed over half of the Askandu population.

He had been lucky so far. Mikhandor and Rasælna had saved his life these three times. But why wait and take unnecessary risks? Would it not be much better to evacuate now, before his adversary could strike again? He got up and ambled back to the cabin, well aware of the dark presence.

"We need to pull out. Tonight," he said as he put another log on the fire.

"What?" Bel sounded incredulous. Annoyed too, perhaps. He couldn't tell, and he dared not use the medallion to decipher her emotions. The risk was too great, especially now.

"There's something out there. A malevolent awareness. I am not sure exactly who or what, but I've felt it before. Three times. I cannot believe I didn't make the connection any sooner, but I see it clearly now. Mikhandor knows what I am talking about, I'm sure. We need to get our arses out of here. The sooner, the better. Dragomir too, if he values his life."

Mikhandor nodded. "You are right. We need to start packing now. Only the bare necessities. We have no time to lose."

"Dragonmother!" Sparks flew from Bel's mouth like spittle, and Niels held his breath.

Niko's eyes were dark, his eyebrows pulled together and the silver lock where his hair had been scorched, was glowing. "We cannot. Aurora will not return until the next moon yet."

"We have to." Mikhandor's voice sounded grim. "Beldenka, I need you to inform Dragomir. Nikomir, go get your people here. Now."

Niels hurried into the bedroom, and threw some clothes, the Holy Book and his memorabilia in his travel bag. When Bel entered their room, tiny swirls of smoke rising from her nostrils, he was already done.

"I hate this." Bel looked like she was about to spew fire. "I was happy here. I was happy in the Barlows too. I don't want this life. I never asked for any of this."

"I know. Neither did I, but this is the life we've got. As much as I hate it, I have a destiny to fulfil. And so have you — but someone does not want us to succeed. I've had a lot of time to study the prophecies anew here, and this I know with the utmost certainty: our destinies are tied together. If I fail, you fail. We're not going to let our enemy win, are we?"

Bel rubbed her eyes and took a deep breath. She shook her head. "But I still hate it." Her voice sounded small. "And I'm scared."

He went over to Bel, lifted her out of her chair and sat on the bed with her as he held her close and kissed her eyelids gently. "We can do this, my sweet. We have each other. We have our magic and, most importantly, we have the gods on our side."

"I need to pack." Bel transferred back into her chair. "You go pack us some food."

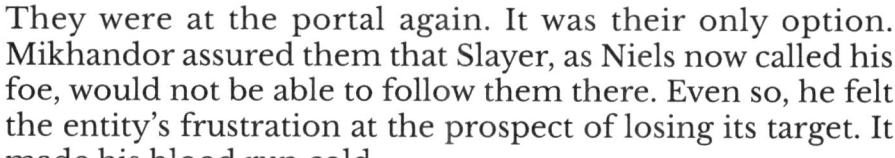

They were at the portal again. It was their only option. Mikhandor assured them that Slayer, as Niels now called his foe, would not be able to follow them there. Even so, he felt the entity's frustration at the prospect of losing its target. It made his blood run cold.

"Jana and I go in first, with Beldenka and her party, including Dragomir." Mikhandor spoke in a low voice. "Flar, you wait for a couple of heartbeats and then follow us with Nikomir and his Special Unit. We meet up at The Splice."

The Splice? Niels had never heard that name before. It didn't sound like any place on Thorf. Or on Sor.

"Ready?"

Their little group joined hands, Bel sat tied to her chair again, and before he knew it, they were inside, following not one of the seven smooth sandy paths, but an uneven grassy road, leading into a peaceful sylvan glade. They did not exit the portal, but instead Mikhandor let go of Leks's hand. "Sit down," he said. "We wait here for the others. As long as we stay in this glade, we will not need to hold hands."

"What is this?" Niels couldn't contain his curiosity.

"This, your Holiness, is The Splice. The place between worlds. There is no time here, which is why this is the perfect place to meet up with Nikomir and his people."

No sooner had he finished talking, than the others entered the glade. All six of them, and all of them wide-eyed, except for Flar, who had probably travelled the portals dozens, if not hundreds, of times already.

"What are our plans?" Flar asked. All were seated, but nobody seemed to be listening. Everyone was talking all at once, with Niko and his company asking one question after another.

"Humans." Mikhandor raised his voice just a little. "Calm down. Sit. And remain seated. For those of you who have never travelled a portal before, we are currently inside a portal in an in-between place, called the Splice. Flar can give you the specifics about portal travel later. For right now, it is enough for you to know that we are safe here. The portals are protected by Sylphan Magic, and evil cannot enter."

Niko snorted. "And we're running because Moradin sensed a ghost, right? Isn't that a little silly?" He studied his fingernails, as if they were the most interesting thing in the All.

"His instincts are quite a bit better than yours, young prince. I hear you have a habit of getting yourself into all kinds of trouble. Unnecessary trouble, I might add. That is not the best way to stay alive. Especially not when you are a descendant of Emperor Fedromir."

Niko opened his mouth again, but Flar held up a hand, and with that simple gesture compelled him to silence.

"We are fleeing because Prince Moradin correctly identified the presence of an antagonistic force. A force that found him three times before. All three times followed by attempts on his life, and the deaths of many others."

Mikhandor paused and turned his head towards Niko. "Am I correct in assuming that you don't currently have a manifest death wish, your Highness?"

"Plans?" Flar repeated, more urgently now.

"We have several options, and I like neither of them very much. No matter what we do, we are bound to lose precious time, and our enemy will increase his efforts to find and eliminate Prince Moradin and Princess Beldenka. And he is not particular about who else gets killed in the process."

Mikhandor paced the clearing. "Option one." He stood immobile. "We go to Thorf and wait there, for the gods only know how long, until it is relatively safe for us to return to Sor."

"A delay." Flar shook his head. "Not really an option. It achieves nothing."

Mikhandor nodded. "My thoughts exactly. Two: We all go straight to Ebaru, and deal with whatever we find there, or die trying."

Janæla laughed a joyless laugh. "Right. That is going to work. With a group as large as this, there is no way in all seven hells we are not going to get separated on our way there. Not even you are strong enough to keep all of us in the same time and place, and the gods only know when and where we would find each other back again. If we ever found each other back at all. Father would not be pleased with us."

Again, Mikhandor nodded. "So that leaves us with option number three. We separate on purpose. We go one way, and Flar another with his group. Not ideal, but I think it is the best we can do."

Niels sighed. Things never went as planned. They should have been in Ebaru about half a turning ago already.

"That ship of yours, Prince Nikomir, do you have any idea of its whereabouts now?"

Niko mumbled something unintelligible before he gave a slight nod. "Briscan Islands."

"Good." Mikhandor sounded pleased. "There is a portal near Sageharbour. Flar can take you there. You board your ship and sail for Ebaru. That should take you about two sevendays. Be extremely careful, and assume you are being watched. The enemy does not want any of us to reach our goal."

Two sevendays. A shiver ran down Niels' spine as he realised his party was probably going straight to Ebaru. Was there even a portal there?

"We are headed for Ebaru. No other choice. The portal in the Cahltaru Tops is far from ideal, but we shall have to make it work for us. We should be able to make it to Ebaru City in roughly two sevendays on foot. We may not feel like we are ready, but it seems our time has come."

"How are we going to find each other back?" It was the normally silent Pav who posed the question.

"Flar can contact me whenever he needs to," Mikhandor said. "Alternatively, we have several dragonets. We should have no trouble keeping in touch once we are out of the portals. Flar, let us try not to lose more than one day in here. Ready?"

Niko's group joined hands again, and Flar led them down the grassy road. When they were out of sight, Niels' group joined hands too.

"When we emerge in Ebaru, our adversary will probably already be watching the Cahltaru Portal. He may not be able to enter it, but he does know where to find it. And he knows the prophecies too. Expect the worst."

Niels shivered, and he saw Bel's face turn pale. He was by no means an expert at facial expressions, but even he could see the fear in her eyes. And the determined set of her jaw.

Too soon, they emerged from the portal. High up in the mountains, the air felt thin and relatively cool. Mikhandor gave each of them a handful of dried berries. The sweet, bright blue kind that only grew on Thorf. "Eat. I will not have you develop Mountain Sickness."

As he chomped down on his berries, Niels already felt his enemy's wrathful gaze.

INTERLUDE

INTERUDE 11

Tangle

<pre>
        hated
   for crimes his mind
  can't remember his heart
yearns for redemption and healing
       foretold
</pre>

King Hanassan of Ebaru sat in his private study. Alone, a luxury that was not often granted him. Always, there were people who needed to see him. Bureaucrats that needed him to approve and sign new laws or wanted his opinion on matters of state that, frankly, he barely understood at all.

Being a king was overrated. Hanassan hated his job, and had always been glad that he was the youngest of the brothers. In his naiveté he had assumed he would never have to ascend that oppressive throne, yet here he was. His entire family killed, and only him left to rule a nation that hated his guts.

He knew the rumours. Of course he did. Everyone knew them. And even now they grew. Tales of the crimes he had presumably committed. To hear the people tell it, he was the most promiscuous git ever to have desecrated the soil of Sor. A soulless villain who abused prostitutes and killed their children. According to the rumours, he had committed parricide on his entire family, simply because he was an inflated, power-hungry maniac who hated competition.

False tongues claimed that the engineering of the AsK-II-Nd virus, and its escape from that medical lab in Tan'Rabu had been by his design, and therefore he should be held personally accountable for the deaths of millions of people on the Southern Continent. And all that, simply because he had been abroad on a visit of state when the outbreak started and the entire continent was forced into a rigid and complete lockdown. He had been safe, while his subjects suffered and died their gruesome deaths.

Right now, the people believed that he was planning to kill off the entire priesthood and make himself head of the Church of the Goddess Eylah. Others claimed he was secretly planning a famine. It was ludicrous. Why would he do that? His entire reign, he had only tried to make life better in Ebaru. Though he could not eradicate poverty, he had made sure the hovels in the District of the Poor had been replaced by simple, but adequate homes. At no cost to the poor.

Yet people preferred to lend their ears to these malicious lies. Because of his mental affliction, they feared and hated him. What was worse, if he were entirely honest, sometimes he himself wondered if the slanderers might be right after all. They vilified him for a reason, and he knew that reason. He knew it all too well. History was against him, and even during his own lifetime, when bad things happened, circumstances had always been pointing an accusatory finger at him.

He should have been present at Yosan's birthday dinner where his entire family was poisoned. And he would have been there, had he not had one of his seizures late that afternoon and was still confined to his private chambers, recovering.

He knew, probably better than anyone else in Ebaru, about the curse that befell the House of Dalanthia, and still rested upon him and his only son. His family might have ruled the nation, but insanity ruled his family. He knew how the madness of some of his ancestors made them do horrible things, starting with Princess Dalenka killing her own firstborn child.

Everyone knew of Aleyshan's addiction, Shaldin's suicide, and Hashandor's epic losses in the war against Morynthia. Hashaldin's parricide and subsequent marriage to his own sister were well documented, as was Nabrissa's murder of her husband after the death of their infant son Brismandor. Nasrim's parricide followed by his suicide, only a hundred turnings ago, was still fresh in most people's minds. But Hanassan knew much more than that.

Not many people knew that Hashandor was not killed by the sword, but consumed by the fiery breath of an Ingravian Broadwing Dragon. They didn't know that Hashandor's son Arkim was often too depressed to get out of his bed. The history books only mentioned his wildly extravagant parties, and that he died from a hunting accident. They conveniently omitted the fact that he had deliberately thrown himself in front of an enraged longtusk boar.

People had precious little knowledge of all the other tragedies that befell the Royal House of Ebaru, and the grievous sufferings in each generation. The mental instability, the physical ailments, the addictions, the fears. They had no idea. But Hanassan knew. Every prince, and every princess of the Royal House of Ebaru had been taught this covert knowledge. They had also been taught that one day the Curse would be lifted, by a man who would be both priest and king.

The Erlen Curse, his subjects called it, but that was wrong. It was the Gloomfather's curse. High King Yumænor had never cursed them. In truth, he had tried to prevent King Haniman from calling down this horrible fate on his descendants. Sometimes Hanassan wondered how much better his life would have turned out, if only that stubborn Haniman would have listened to the Erlen king.

If only. But as his beloved father used to say, "when would have arrives, has is too late". A funny phrase, but it held a deep truth. If onlies were futile. Hanassan closed his eyes and took a shuddering breath. So often he had contemplated ending his life, but he could not. He would not let the Gloomfather win. He had to be strong and live. He also had to find his son and name him his heir. Only then could he surrender his spirit to Yat S'ber.

He went over to the bookcase and got his old diary out. He never wrote in it any more — not since the day Lali left and took a part of his soul with her — but often he would just sit and look at its yellowed pages, remembering happier days. He would look at the portraits he kept hidden away in it. One a portrait of Lali and him, taken by Krys, who at the time had been his best and only friend. The other was the portrait one of the city guards had taken at the drakenport. A portrait of his son, who had become a priest.

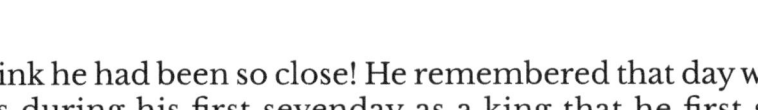

To think he had been so close! He remembered that day well. It was during his first sevenday as a king that he first saw that portrait, and he just knew. That face, those eyes, and the information on the boy's travel documents. Name: Niels Bosch; date of birth, 12-1-9720; place of birth, Ebaru City; country and place of residence, Darsrijck, Dorhedde. That said it all.

Fifteen long turnings had he wondered why Lali had left him, and what had become of her. So often, he'd gone out at night, trying to find her, and always in vain. This had to be the answer. In her farewell note she had written that she feared for her life, but not why. She must have thought his parents would kill her when they found out she was with child, and so she had fled from his parents. The boy, Niels Bosch, was her son. His son. His only child.

It hadn't been hard to find out where the young man was staying, and so he had gone to the house of High Priest Akdi Erumin. He'd been so sure he would find his son there, but then there were only the two priests, and that other priest's nephew. Long, braided hair, skin at least two shades darker than his own, and yet there was something familiar about him. So he went to see him. He had put a hand on his shoulder and looked into his eyes. Deep brown. Not the golden eyes he had so hoped to see. But he remembered the warm, tingly feeling that ran through his entire body the moment he touched the boy. He had often wondered about the meaning of that. It still puzzled him.

He hadn't known then, or even suspected, that the priests had deceived him. He had trusted them. They were priests, after all. How could they be anything but honest? And so he had continued the search for his son, until that day in Turning 9742, when Ardu showed him two sets of documents detailing the results of the DNA testing of a young man called Moradin Amari. One of them falsified.

Moradin Amari, the priest's nephew with his long braided hair. How they had managed to disguise him so completely, or why they had thought it necessary to deceive their king, he couldn't fathom, but the boy's terror at his touch had been unmistakable. Had someone threatened to take his life, too?

Together with Krys he had gone searching for his son again. He needed to find him, and warn him, before it was too late.

Then the city was plagued by fires that had destroyed the homes of both priests, and the dwelling of the Maidens of Eylah. Worse, there had been house fires on the campus of the Seminary too, and early the next morning he had been informed by Ardu that one of the victims of these fires had been his son, the newly graduated priest, Moradin Amari.

That had been the worst day of his life. Worse even than the day his family was murdered. Now he had lost his son, his only child, and he had never even been given the chance to get to know him.

Only, a little over a turning later, he had become aware that his son might still be alive after all. Strange though it seemed to him, he could feel the young man's presence. Somehow. And it occurred to him that this mysterious connection had been there ever since their paths first crossed, at the High Priest's residence.

It was a funny thing, that awareness. Sometimes it was incredibly strong, sometimes barely noticeable, and anything in between. Additionally, there were also times when he sensed nothing, and the connection appeared to have gone dead. Not today though. Just moments ago, he had felt it stronger than ever before. Almost as if his son were here, in this room, with him.

Maybe his son, Niels or Moradin or however he might call himself these days, had finally come to find his father. That would be the best day of his life. The day when he finally got to meet his son, the priest.

> "He shall be both priest and king, and he shall heal what was broken, protect the innocent, and bring redemption to the House of the Kings."

That was what the prophecies said. Could it be, that his son was the Chosen One? Could it really be?

EBARU

CHAPTER THIRTY-THREE

Track

mountain
peaks high its path
hazardous and narrow
plunges pilgrims into deathly
defile

Niels looked around, trying to get his bearings. Which way was Ebaru City? Although they were high up, the trees and surrounding peaks obscured his view.

"Let us find a path first." Mikhandor started walking. "This way."

"You're not going to sleep first?" Niels was surprised. Mikhandor always needed to sleep when they exited a portal.

"Today, there is no need. Portal travel is not nearly as exhausting when you don't hop worlds."

The terrain was rough, but Bel didn't seem to want or need any assistance yet. During their moons in Senkerland she had become remarkably adept at navigating uneven ground. Soon they reached a path. A narrow, uneven path close to the steep edge of the cliff. Too close for comfort. Though he took care not to look down, Niels felt dizzy and nauseous already. He did not look forward to the rest of their downward journey.

"You had better hold on to Beldenka's chair," Mikhandor said. "This is a treacherous path, and we would not want her to roll off and end up at the bottom of that ravine."

Niels looked at Bel, who was doing just fine. In fact, he could have sworn she was enjoying herself, but what did he know? Bel looked back at him, and nodded. "Yes, I think that's a good idea. It's rather a bumpy ride here, and my arms are tiring already."

Hold on to Beldenka's chair. That was easier said than done, seeing that the thing didn't even have push handles. Niels furrowed his brow as he grabbed the backrest as best he could. Bel's arms were strong. Far stronger than any ordinary woman's arms. And she had navigated worse terrain than this.

"You're not getting sick, are you, Bel?" He couldn't think of any other reason why she would need his assistance.

"I'm fine, dear. Just tired from training so much over the last couple of days."

"Of course." Niels was not convinced. He hoped that really was the reason. They couldn't afford for Bel to get sick now.

He was still pondering, and maybe just not paying enough attention to his surroundings when he felt his feet slip. As he cried out, the startled cries of the others echoed around him as well, and they were all hurtling down, speeding towards their deaths in that cold, dark abyss. His eyes snapped shut, and he dared not open them again.

His arms and legs were flailing. His hands reached for something to hold on to, but found only empty air. The wind whooshed, and pulled at his clothes, his hair. It lashed at his face. The heady scent of tropical forest flowers assaulted his nostrils. He heard his blood pumping through his veins, pounding on his eardrums. A large bird of prey screeched. He could even hear its enormous wings flapping.

He landed on something soft, rolled a little more downwards, and finally came to a stop on a hard, scaly surface. As he did not seem to be dead, or even dying, he opened his eyes again. A warm wind stroked his face and played with his hair. To his surprise he sat, rather clumsily, on a huge dragon's back. A blood-red Ingravian Broadwing Dragon. Vindicia Feroxi. Mikhandor sat behind him, a stupid grin on his face. A second dragon flew beside them, with Janæla and Leks on his back. He recognised the dragon as Iorthen Priscii. Dragomir.

"Sit back and enjoy your flight," Bel's thoughts sounded inside his mind. "I'm taking you straight to your destination." She seemed happy, and excited. Niels had been relieved for one moment, but now his sense of dread increased again. He was not ready yet. Not nearly.

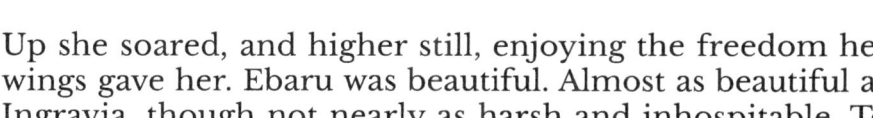

Up she soared, and higher still, enjoying the freedom her wings gave her. Ebaru was beautiful. Almost as beautiful as Ingravia, though not nearly as harsh and inhospitable. To most people, harsh and inhospitable equalled depressing and disconsolate. To her, it meant home. A home she had lost and would never see again.

Compared to the Ingravian Peaks, the Cahltaru Tops seemed more like friendly little hills. Then again, the cave-in of their path had been anything but kind, and for a moment she had feared she'd lost them all. Her husband and their friends. She'd had to do a quick, steep dive to catch Niels and Mig, and Iorthen had done the same to save Leks and Janæla. Her chair and travel bag lay at the bottom of the ravine, ruined beyond repair, but she didn't want to think about that just yet.

Vindicia looked around, curious. Such a lush, green country! Most of the land was covered in broad-leaved trees, not unlike the vegetation she'd seen on Thorf. The mountaintops were blanketed in a layer of snow that shone blindingly bright in the sunlight. Beyond the golden beach that curved like a ribbon along the coast, the azure ocean stretched as far as the eye reached, until it met the horizon and became one with the sky.

Ebaru City lay like a random mythical city dropped in the middle of a tropical forest. Dazzling white and gold, with touches of red and blue. Vindicia felt as if she had been cast into a real-life fairytale. The hot, humid air only added to her feelings of wonder.

In the distance, the three dragonets were dancing in the air. They marvelled as much at their surroundings as Vindicia herself did. She looked at Iorthen, whose eyes sparkled with delight. He looked younger, somehow, and stronger than she'd ever seen him.

"Don't fly too high," his thoughts came to her. "Your passengers might not like it."

Reluctantly, she dropped a few hundred feet. He was right. The way Niels sat on her back, so rigidly, he couldn't possibly be enjoying the ride. It was as if he were afraid he might fall off any moment. Mikhandor, on the other hand, seemed completely at ease. They were an odd pair, these two. So different, it was hard to understand how they could be such close friends.

"Relax, husband," she sent to Niels. "You are perfectly safe on my back. I'm a good flyer."

"I know, my dearest," his thoughts came back to her. "It is not about you. It is... I don't think I am ready to face the king yet. Up there, we still had two sevendays. Now we have probably, what? Two hours?"

She looked in the distance. Two hours? Ebaru City didn't look all that far away. "Most likely sooner," she sent back. "It's not far. I'm sorry."

For a moment Vindicia entertained the thought of doing some sightseeing. She would like that. But it would be unwise. That presence that Niels had felt... she felt it too. It was watching them, and it was furious that its wicked ploy hadn't worked. It would do anything to prevent them from reaching their goal. It was her job to get them safely to the Royal Palace. As soon as possible.

"Quit worrying so much, husband. I am with you. Our friends are with us. You are not alone."

The people in the streets of Ebaru City stopped and stared at the sky. They pointed upwards, and alerted others to the dragons. Niels heard their cries of wonder, and cries of alarm. Guards rushed towards the Royal Palace. Their footfalls rang loudly on the gold-paved streets, but the dragons were faster.

They landed in the courtyard. Vindicia had long perfected the art of landing on her behind without rolling over on her side. Nothing showed of her disability. She just sat there, looking as imposing as ever.

Soft pink roses climbed up the marble pillars that surrounded the courtyard. Their delicate fragrance, mingled with the fruity scent of citrus trees permeated the air. The susurration of the water feature in the centre of the courtyard reminded Niels of the House of Prayer. Home. It calmed his nerves.

Dressed in spotless white, the king stepped out of the archway, his eunuch by his side. Back straight, head tilted slightly forward, he smiled widely. As Niels took one cautious step in his direction, the king rushed towards him, arms opened wide.

"My son!" he exclaimed. "Finally we meet."

Niels shrunk back. His breath caught in his throat. He held up his hands, in an attempt to ward off the almost inevitable embrace. Beads of sweat sprang on his brow. This was worse than threats. Thankfully, amazingly, the king stopped in his tracks and stood waiting for Niels to speak.

For what felt like an eternity, they stood like that. Niels struggling to overcome his panic, and the king watching. Waiting. Like a spider in its web.

Niels breathed slowly. Deeply. The way Mikhandor had taught him.

"Yes," he said when he had regained his composure. "We meet. And we need to talk. I need answers." Strange, how completely calm and in control he felt now. But he knew, the gods were on his side. His father might be a king, and a very disturbed man, but still just a man.

"Come inside, you and your friends, and I will gladly answer all your questions."

Come inside? Was he completely off his stones? What made that psycho assume he would want to do that?

"Not like that, your Majesty. Why did you try to kill me?"

"Kill you?" The king sounded incredulous. He shook his head. "I never did such a thing. Why would I want to kill my own flesh and blood?"

"Why indeed? That is exactly what I need to know. And while we are at it, why did you murder your parents? Your brothers and sisters, their spouses, and their children? Why?"

He sat on the couch in the high priest's living room again, with Tasim, watching the funeral of the Royal Family. Twenty beautiful white coffins. An almost peaceful scene, and a stark contrast to the atrocities that had so recently been committed by a cruelly disturbed mind.

"Oh, my son." The king's voice sounded subdued. "I had hoped that you at least would not believe those malicious lies. I had nothing to do with any of that." He was silent for a moment, then said, "I know the rumours. I know the circumstances. I cannot change those. There is nothing I can do to convince you of my innocence. I can't even force you to believe me when I tell you I will not harm you. Ever."

Niels looked at Hanassan. Scrutinised his face. He even looked into the king's eyes. Briefly. He saw no deceit there, but rather something that could probably best be described as grief. The man looked as bereft as he had on the day of the funeral. He seemed honest. As honest as a psychotic could be.

Maybe he should give him the benefit of the doubt. It was a risk. But was this not why he had come to Ebaru in the first place? To meet his deranged father and deal with the attempts on his life?

He nodded slowly. Wiped his sweaty palms on his pantaloons. "I shall come inside with you. Do you have a sedan chair?"

"Of course I have one. Why do you ask?"

"My wife lost her wheelchair on our way here."

"She can use mine. I only need it when I am recovering from an exceptionally bad seizure." The king nodded at his eunuch, who went inside. "So..." he seemed awkward. "Could you perhaps introduce me to your wife and friends? And what is your name? Your real name?"

Niels shifted his weight from his heels to his toes and back again. Back and forth, back and forth, in a slow rocking motion. The sudden pressure on his bladder worsened his discomfort. "My mother named me Moradin, but my adoptive parents called me Niels. I have been using both names since I first came to Ebaru."

"If my Lali named you Moradin, then that will be your name. Prince Moradin Dolanthi of Ebaru. I shall make an official statement that you are my son and heir. I intended to do that eighteen turnings ago already, when I first found out that I had a son, but..." He made a defeated gesture.

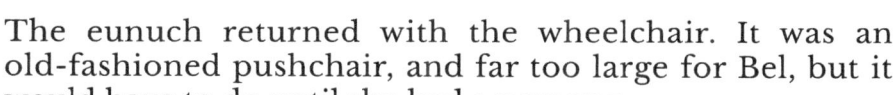

The eunuch returned with the wheelchair. It was an old-fashioned pushchair, and far too large for Bel, but it would have to do until she had a new one.

"Young lady." The eunuch placed the chair in front of Janæla, opened his mouth and closed it again. He looked around, and scratched his bald head in obvious confusion. "You are not... Where is the prince's wife?"

Niels looked at Vindicia and Iorthen before he turned to look at the king again. What if Bel's transformation triggered one of his outbursts? Or something even worse? "Don't be alarmed," he said. "My wife has the Dragon Magic."

In an instant, Vindicia became Bel again, and Iorthen turned back into Dragomir; both of them completely naked. As Niels helped Bel up from the ground and wrapped her in his cloak, the eunuch hurried towards them with the chair. From out of the corner of his eye, he saw Janæla offering Dragomir her cloak, which was far too large to fit the old man properly, but it was the best they could do for now.

"Thank you, your Majesty," Bel said in her clear, confident voice. "I appreciate this very much, and hope it does not inconvenience you."

"Not at all, young lady. And might I ask... With whom do I have the pleasure?" Strangely, the king didn't seem the least bit daunted.

"My name is Beldenka Nadinov, your Majesty. It's an honour to meet you."

On their way inside one of the guards strode up to the king. "Your Majesty." He sounded flustered. "Is all well? Do you need our assistance?"

Niels held his breath. Was this going to be the moment where the king would show his true colours?

"I need to make an official announcement to the people, and I want it transmitted on the vidisphere. Live. As soon as possible."

"Of course, your Majesty. I'll see to it. Anything else?"

"I shall be in my private chambers with my guests, and do not wish to be disturbed. Not until everything is set up and ready so I can make my announcement."

"Certainly, your Majesty. I'll post guards at the entrance to your chambers." He saluted and withdrew.

"Beldenka Nadinov," the king said as he sank down in one of the plush armchairs in what must be the drawing room, "and you have the Dragon Magic, just like my favourite violinist, the High Lord Mirtalya Grigonov."

"She is my mother, your Majesty. As I'm sure you already guessed."

Hanassan nodded. "Please, be seated, all." He looked at his eunuch. "Krys, my guests will undoubtedly be hungry and thirsty after their journey. Would you provide them with refreshments, please?"

Niels sat down in one of the opulent sofas and, unable to relax, let his gaze travel through the room. Two large portraits hung on either side of the hearth. One of King Ishvat, the other of Queen Adella. On the mantle stood a fair collection of smaller portraits of the king's brothers and sisters and their families. Surprisingly, there were no portraits of the king himself.

One entire wall was devoted to the king's bookcases. They were beautifully crafted, reaching from floor to ceiling, but not overly ornate. Much like Niels' own bookcases, they looked tidy and organised.

A thick, red woollen carpet lay on the floor, and long golden yellow drapes adorned the oriel windows. A few simple lightspheres, some candles and several large plants in copper pots completed the interior.

Niels didn't know what he had expected, but certainly not this. The room, though by no means inadequate, seemed too simple. Too ordinary for the king of Ebaru.

"My mother," Niels said. He couldn't help himself. He had to know. "What was she to you?"

"She was my all," King Hanassan answered immediately, and he sounded so sincere, it was hard to believe he would be lying. The king got up from his chair, went over to the bookcases and took a book out.

Part of the bookcase slid in front of the shelves next to it and revealed a study. "Just a moment," the king said over his shoulder as he went in and disappeared from view. Within three breaths, he came back carrying a leather-bound notebook.

"Lali, I called her, because she was such a delicate flower." He retrieved a small portrait from the notebook and handed it to Niels.

Niels' sight fogged up as he looked at it. It was a picture of his mother and the young Prince Hanassan, and they looked happy. He remembered the visions in which he had seen the two of them together. Talking, eating, and having fun. Behaving just like an ordinary couple. He remembered his mother's last words. "Cold. Naz... Naz."

"She..." Niels swallowed the lump in his throat. "She called you Naz, didn't she?"

"Yes." The king sounded surprised. "How do you know?"

"My priestly medallion." On an impulse, Niels pulled it out from under his shirt. "Do you recognise it?"

"That..." He came closer, and bent over, his face uncomfortably close to Niels' chest. "That is..." He froze as the double doors flew open and two guards came tumbling in, iron rods protruding from their eyes.

A man clad in black jumped over them, agile as a cat. He was followed by more men. All clad in black. All equally agile. And all of them carrying scimitars.

CHAPTER THIRTY-FOUR

Thrust

<pre>
         men scream
       as flesh burns and
    blood flows from fatal wounds
   when the broken beat tyrant's trained
            killers
</pre>

No time to think. Bel shrugged Niels' cloak off and did a forward roll out of her borrowed chair. That thing would only hinder her. Transforming into Vindicia was out of the question. The room wasn't nearly large enough, which was a real shame. Vindicia could have taken all ten of them on at once. Easily. She would have roasted them alive before gorging on their charred remains.

She scanned the room. Niels was holding his own. Barely. He made some defensive moves, but nothing more than that. Dragomir fended a man off with a shimmering, spark-spewing stick. Leks grimaced as he whacked one of the assassins on the head with his baton. With their dancelike moves, the Erls mowed their attackers down with the same ease a scythe cut through high grass. But the king! That poor man looked like he was going to faint any moment. Another forward roll and she grabbed the king's attacker by the ankles and pulled his feet out from under him, so he fell flat on his face. Just a heartbeat later, Leks's throwing knife landed neatly between the assassin's ribs.

Then the eunuch was back. He brought no refreshments, but carried a drawn rapier instead. His jaw was set, and his eyes were ablaze as he drove his weapon deep into Hanassan's second attacker's chest. Bel looked away, only to see Dragomir burning the skin off his foe's face. The man fell to the floor screaming and clutching at his scorched skull — which only made him scream even louder.

Leks was having far too much fun with his daggers, and had already killed two more assassins. Mikhandor looked glum as he snapped his assailant's neck, and Janæla growled like an angry manewolf as she bare-handedly broke a man's leg first, and both his arms next.

Niels however, wouldn't hold out much longer against the two savages that seemed all too eager to chop off his head. He only just narrowly evaded one strike when the next man swung his scimitar at shoulder level, and all he could think to do was dropping to the floor and rolling backwards. It bought him hardly any time. Why was he not at least trying to eliminate them? Dumb harehead of a man! High time for her to step in and save his stupid arse. One forward roll, and—

The last of the three remaining assassins put his booted foot on her bare stomach. Though she couldn't see his expression behind the mask, she knew he was smirking as he swung his sword in a showy manner, probably thinking he had already won. Furious, Bel breathed a huge flame and aimed it at the man's eyes. He doubled over, howling in agony, and dropped his sword as both his hands flew towards his face. With a soft clink, his weapon landed beside Bel on the carpet, so she picked it up and skewered his gut. He reared backwards and fell, the blade still stuck in his belly.

Bel rolled over her shoulder and sat up to survey the situation. Niels' attackers had just been neutralised by Leks and Mikhandor. Pity. She would have liked to take another of those murderous swine out herself. Niels stood looking at the mess, rocking back and forth on his heels. A tortured expression on his face. Bel doubted he was ever going to be a real fighter.

Leks was grinning from ear to ear, but Bel knew he would feel bad about all of this later. He might love the rush of the fight, but deep down, he was a gentle man, who hated violence and death. Mikhandor and Janæla looked grim. Bel had no idea what was going on in their minds. Erls were hard to read.

Dragomir drew Janæla's cloak tighter around himself. He shook his head slowly, clearly saddened by what had just passed. His tough outer shell was just that. An outward appearance. He was really just a sweet old man, who had seen far too many deaths in his lifetime.

Finally, she looked at the king again, and was shocked by what she saw. King Hanassan lay on the floor. Unconscious, convulsing, and frothing from the mouth. His eunuch sat hunched over him, his body protecting him from further attacks. Another roll, and she was beside them.

"It's over," she said in a hushed voice. "Will the king be alright?"

"I don't know." The eunuch's voice sounded tormented. "We can hope."

"You're his guardian, aren't you?"

He nodded. "A bit more than that, actually, but that should better not become common knowledge."

For a moment Bel wondered what he meant, then she understood. Lovers. "Oh," she said. "I see. Then why are you telling me this?"

He shrugged. "I don't know. I guess..." He left it hanging. "He will need his medicine. Would you stay with him, while I go get it?"

"One moment, please." She rolled over to her chair and grabbed Niels' cloak. No need to remain naked.

Before the eunuch returned, Niels' healer — what was her name again? Zelma? — entered and knelt down by the king's side. She pressed her fingertips gently against Hanassan's temples and closed her eyes in concentration.

"Oh gods," she said as she opened her eyes and pulled her hands away from him. "Oh holy gods. I'm going to need... do not give him that, Krystandor!"

The eunuch stared at her, the king's pills in his hand. "What is wrong?"

"The king is being poisoned. Slowly. It might well be in his medicine. What better way to poison a man, than by tampering with his medication?" She rummaged in the velvet bag she wore on a leather strap around her waist, muttering curses under her breath.

"I am deeply sorry, Rasælna," the eunuch said. His high voice took on an almost child-like quality. "I should have noticed."

"Yes, you should." Selna's voice dripped acidity. "And you failed. I shall have to report this, and you will have to answer to the Supreme Council for your negligence. We are extremely lucky the king isn't dead yet."

She got a silver vial out of her bag, gently turned the king's head sideways and carefully dropped some greenish liquid in his mouth. She held his head and watched him intently until his convulsions subsided and finally stopped entirely.

"Get his doctor here. I need to speak to..." She hesitated. "Him? Her?"

"Him," Krystandor said. He hurried out of the king's private chambers. The poor man was probably glad to be away from Selna for a while.

"Incompetent idiot," Bel heard the healer grumble. "Should never..." She quieted as the king stirred. Once again, she took his head between her hands and closed her eyes.

Her methods fascinated Bel. Obviously, the woman used magic to heal. But what kind of magic? It was different from hers and Niels'. Probably different from Mikhandor's too, which made her wonder. How many different kinds of magic existed on Thorf? And how did Sylphan magic compare to Human magic?

"Padr," Niels whispered as he took the king's hand in his. He looked at King Hanassan as he lay on the floor. Frail and utterly vulnerable. He had seen it before of course, in his visions, but this was different. This was real, and it was happening right now, in front of him. He was not just an onlooker. Not this time.

He'd never thought he would call the king Padr. All these turnings, he had feared and hated this man. An innocent man. Now, he felt ashamed of himself.

He had accused his father of crimes he never committed. That much was quite clear now. Not only had the assassins gone for the king first, but someone had also been poisoning him for the gods only knew how long already. Slowly but steadily. And they would have succeeded too, if Mikhandor hadn't summoned Rasælna.

His seizures, Rasælna explained, were induced by a rare poison, made from a plant that only grew on Zilcon, Chey's world. It was a slow-acting poison that built up over time until, after a certain threshold had been exceeded, it killed the victim.

The moment he saw the king lying on the floor, convulsing, Niels had wanted to rush towards him and heal him, but Mikhandor had physically restrained him until his sister arrived. Then, Rasælna's stare alone had been enough to keep him from using the medallion on his father and quite probably killing himself in the process.

For a moment, he had been angry with Mikhandor and his sister. Was this not exactly the reason why he was here? To heal what was broken? Was that not what the prophecies said?

Rasælna had initiated Hanassan's healing. She had neutralised the poison, and stopped the seizures. Only then had she allowed Niels to approach.

He studied his father's clean-shaven face. Though his hair was starting to show some grey, he was still a handsome man. His skin was smooth, his jaw strong, and his lips full. He looked... Happy? Peaceful? Niels couldn't really tell.

"Padr," Niels said again as the king opened his eyes. Eyes as golden as his own. "Let me heal you." For the second time that day he pulled his pendant out from under his shirt.

"This is a priestly medallion, the same one my mother wore." Hanassan nodded, and Niels could see he recognised it. "It is imbued with a tiny element of the divine. I am going to press it on your bare chest. It will feel warm, and it will help me cure your body. Will you consent to that?"

The king nodded again, and pressed Niels' hand weakly.

Mother of mankind, Niels sent his silent prayer to the goddess, *guide my hands, my heart and my mind. Let your love and healing flow, and help me end this dark night's reign.*

He took a deep breath. Tried to steady his trembling hands. This had better work. He hadn't gone through all these hardships to have this end in failure. He needed his father to be well. Needed him to be a good king, so he wouldn't have to take his place. Not yet. Even ten or twenty turnings from now would be too soon.

The moment the medallion touched his father's skin, it reacted. It was unlike anything Niels had ever experienced before. It recognised Hanassan, started glowing, and began to sing. That same rippling tide of power that had overwhelmed his already overwrought senses the first time the king had touched him, coursed through his body again — but far more intense now. Though it felt warmer than ever, it didn't burn him.

Without him putting in any conscious effort, the amulet's energy travelled through Hanassan's limp body and repaired the damage to his internal organs. Scar tissue untangled and smoothed itself. Lesions regenerated. Even the brain's structure altered ever so slightly. Grey matter formed where there was none. Cavities in the brain shrunk. Would it be enough? Niels could only hope so. What did he know about the brain and how it functioned? He was just an ordinary priest.

Memories surfaced. Him, healing little Tulia after her fall from that tree, and how his efforts had nearly killed him that day. Zia, unconscious on the floor of her flat... He pushed his sombre thoughts away. He couldn't afford to get sidetracked now. He needed to keep his wits together and heal his father. His homeland. The world.

Please, good goddess, help me. I can't do this alone. Help me fulfil the prophecies as has always been my destiny.

When the process was complete, the king blinked several times. A tenuous smile appeared on his face before it broke through in full splendour. Slowly, carefully, he sat up and looked at Niels, his eyes shining. He brought his hands to his cheeks and from there moved them upwards in a gentle, controlled movement. He examined his chest, his arms, his legs — and all the while, his elation seemed to grow. "Well, that was something. Quite something indeed." There was wonder in his voice. Awe, even. "I... thank you, my son. I feel like a new man."

"It is nothing." Niels' hands were still quivering and he struggled to tuck the ornament back under his shirt. "I was..." He stopped himself. What was he doing? Why was he lying? He wasn't just doing his duty, as he'd been about to say. And it definitely wasn't nothing. It was the single most important thing he had ever done. If this had gone as well as he hoped, the curse was now lifted, and better times lay ahead.

"This was what I came to do," he said. That sounded lame — even to his own ears. Why couldn't he be more like Bel, who always knew the right words to say? "I had been wanting to heal you ever since... since my first sevenday in Ebaru. When you came looking for me, and put your hand on my shoulder."

"And yet it took you eighteen turnings to finally come to me. Why, my son?"

The pain in his father's voice made him wince. "I was afraid. I thought, like most people, that you were the criminal mastermind behind the assassination. That you were behind the killings of all these children that might be yours. I feared you would kill me too. Then the assassins came for me and my friends and relatives. They killed..." He swallowed the lump in his throat and shook his head. He should not be thinking of that now. Today had seen more than enough suffering. No use dwelling on the past.

"We have much to talk about, Moradin. But first I will want to make my announcement that you are my son." He turned towards Krystandor. "Is the throne room ready?"

"Yes, your Majesty," the eunuch said formally. He looked at the floor, apparently unable to face the king. Could it be he was still smarting from Rasælna's scolding?

"With all due respect, your Majesty," Rasælna said, "you are not going anywhere. Not right now. We need to talk to your doctor first. What is taking that man so long?"

Just then, a scrawny, rat-faced man appeared in the doorway, where he stood panting before he entered. Niels knew that man. That arrogant mug! He would recognise it any time. Anywhere. Little weasel.

"My apologies," the insidious snake said, still a little out of breath. "I was with a patient when I received your message. I came as fast as I could."

"And you are?" Rasælna's voice sounded icy. She raised an eyebrow.

"Sebben Dansinger, his Majesty Hanassan's physician and psychiatrist." His voice was still the same too. It still had that thin, emasculate quality that had always grated on Niels' nerves.

"You prescribed him these medicines?" Rasælna showed him the pills Krystandor had been about to give the king. How his father would have been able to swallow them during his seizure, Niels could not even fathom.

Sebben took a pill out of Rasælna's cupped hand, held it between thumb and index finger and peered at it intently. Finally he shrugged. "Hard to tell. Usually, my clients get their medicines from the pharmacy. This one here seems to be handmade, probably by a private pharmacist who works exclusively for the nobility."

"How safe would you say that is?"

"Not. Not at all." He shook his head vehemently. "There is zero control. Absolutely none. That pharmacist might as well be giving him crushed chicken feather pills mixed with donkey droppings."

"Or some deadly poison?"

Sebben cringed. "I would hope not, but it would certainly be a possibility."

"What if I told you the king was being poisoned? Slowly, over a long period of time?"

Sebben took a faltering step backwards. "That is horrible. Horrible." He shook his head, then squared his shoulders and reverted back into the same inscrutable man Niels had always hated. Gods-accursed psychiatrists. Always so sarding in control of their emotions. "That's exactly the reason why those quacks should be stopped. How bad is it?"

"It was extremely bad. If I hadn't come, the king would probably have had less than one moon." She stopped and stared at Sebben. "I neutralised the poison. Prince Moradin was able to repair the damage to the king's system, and probably even a bit more than that."

"Prince Moradin?" Sebben sounded confused.

Niels' hands balled into tight fists. His muscles tightened. He most decidedly did not want to engage with Sebben, but now he had to. "That would be me. Prince Moradin Dolanthi of Ebaru. I also happen to be a priest, which allowed me to heal my father. Hopefully completely."

Sebben stared at him, his mouth agape. "I... I didn't know," he stammered. "I mean, I thought..." He shook his head.

"You mean you thought I was just a figment of my father's imagination, eh? You head shrinkers are all the same. Paranoid to the extreme." Niels knew he shouldn't allow his mouth to run away with him like that, but he couldn't help himself. Sebben still got on his nerves, just like all those turnings ago. What was he doing here in Ebaru anyway? He should have remained at the Dr Lubinn Institution.

"Your Highness?" Sebben asked in his silky voice. Then his eyes went wide. "Do... do we know each other?"

"We sarding well do. You used to know me as Niels Bosch. Back in Dorhedde."

"Ah, Niels Bosch. Yes, I remember. You didn't like me very much back then either. Some things never change." He sounded perfectly unperturbed, maybe even amused, which infuriated Niels all the more.

"With some luck, my father will not be needing your services any longer."

Bel rode up behind him and grasped his hand. "Calm down," her thoughts whispered inside his mind. He tried to shut her off, but she wouldn't let him. Little dragon!

"I would not be too sure of that, your Highness. Even if you did manage to cure him of his psychotic disorder, he might still need my care for a while longer. Besides, I want to know exactly what went wrong with his medication. That was my responsibility."

"Do what you like, but stay out of my way."

"Gentlemen." The king laid an amazingly firm hand on Niels' shoulder. "Has it not occurred to the two of you that I might wish to have a say in this?"

Sebben bowed his head and apologised, but Niels felt like the angry, rebellious teenage boy he once was. If his father thought he was going to put up with that invertebrate, he was mistaken. He wanted Sebben with his effeminate demeanour gone. Preferably to another world.

"As you wish, Padr," he said, "but I don't want that man anywhere near me ever again."

He stalked away, into his father's hidden study and picked up a random book. He didn't even open it. Instead, he just brushed the lambskin cover, and ran his fingertips delicately across the gilded title. He brought the volume up to his face and took in the wonderful scent of aged leather, and ink on brittling paper.

For how long he stood there, cherishing the book, he couldn't tell, but after a while he felt Bel's presence. Very near.

"Moradin, my love, it is time. We're going to the throne room now. Are you coming?"

CHAPTER THIRTY-FIVE

Reveal

golden
box enclosing
bittersweet memories
of budding love and shattered dreams
opens

They had been fussed over in the dressing room. Perfumed ladies had dusted his face with scented powder, and fiddled with his new clothes, making him itchy all over, and now the vidisphere crew were bustling around like a small army of crazy ants.

His father sat on his gilded throne, and Niels on a slightly smaller throne to his right. Bel was seated on yet another throne to the king's left. Though she wore but a simple kaftan, she looked as beautiful and confident as always.

Several recording devices stood facing them from a number of different angles. Small but powerful acoustic sensors hung suspended from the ceiling, barely visible to the casual observer's eye.

The excited buzz of the people that had gathered in the throne room made Niels want to cover his ears with his hands, but he knew he couldn't do that. Much to his chagrin, he was a prince now, and had to appear calm and dignified, no matter how agitated he felt.

A young woman stood on the dais, reporting about the attempted assassination. She disclosed that most of the assassins had been killed in the fight that ensued, and only one of them, though seriously wounded, had survived. This man was now in custody. He had received medical treatment and would be questioned as soon as the doctors thought it medically permissible.

"Our good king, may he live forever, survived the attack unscathed, and will speak to the people now."

The woman withdrew, and Hanassan rose from his throne.

"People of Ebaru," he addressed the crowd. "Today, the twelfth day of the fourth moon of Turning 9753 after the creation of mankind, arrived at my palace, on dragonback, priest Moradin Amari, with his wife, Grand Lord Beldenka Nadinov of Ingravia, and their companions, the Lords Yeleksim Bogrovik and Dragomir Ranovik."

He made no mention of either Mikhandor or Janæla, which was most likely intentional. Politics were a strange, and often dangerous, thing.

"For those of you who remember the fires in the eighth moon of Turning 9742, which took the lives of too many people. A man named Moradin Amari was amongst those who were presumed dead. This was a great personal loss to me. I had learnt only days prior that this promising young priest was, in fact, my son. My only child, the fruit of my loins. This had been confirmed by advanced DNA-testing.

"It is with great joy, that today I may present to you, my son and heir, previously known as Moradin Amari."

The king extended a hand towards Niels, indicating that he should join him. Whispers. People were whispering. Was that a good thing, or bad? They had so many reasons not to trust their king. So many reasons not to trust any of them. A shiver ran down Niels' spine. He tried to ignore it.

"No longer shall you be called Moradin Amari. From this day on, my son, your name shall be Moradin Dolanthi."

He took Niels' left hand in his right, raised both their hands and proclaimed in a sonorous voice, "People of Ebaru, I present to you, my son and heir, Prince Moradin Dolanthi of Ebaru. May our good Goddess grant him life eternal and good health."

A thundering applause rumbled, and shouts of joy — or so Niels hoped — reverberated in the hall. Again, the din made him want to run and hide, but he pushed his feelings of overwhelm back, and smiled through gritted teeth as a roar of "Long live the prince! Long live Prince Moradin!" went up and resonated ever louder in the throne room.

Would this be his life now? Trying to survive these horrendous gatherings? Being a prince already proved to be *stone-squeezingly* awful. How much worse would his life be, once he had to assume that dreaded throne? If only his father could live forever!

Bel's thoughts rang inside his mind: "You can sit down again, Moradin. Go. Sit on your throne." Dazed, he did as Bel instructed him. He hoped nobody had noticed his absent-mindedness.

When he looked up, Bel sat in her borrowed chair on the dais beside the king, who still stood talking to the crowd. "... grant her the title Princess of Ebaru. People of Ebaru, welcome your princess and future queen, Princess Beldenka Nadinov of Ebaru."

Applause again, and all that other dreadful clangour. It took Niels all his self-control to keep his face straight. This was torture. He closed his eyes, then forced himself to open them again as he realised that, as a prince, he couldn't even do that. Not in public.

Bel took him by the hand as she rolled past. "Come," she whispered. "It is done."

As in a haze, he stood up and walked alongside Bel. Away from the noise, the light, and the smells. Now, all he wanted was a long soak in a hot bath, to wash that foul scented powder off, and let the tension drain from his aching body.

They were in the king's parlour again. The blood-soaked carpet had been replaced, and the messes cleaned up. The scimitars were either with the investigators, or in the armoury, save for the one Leks had confiscated.

"You were going to tell me about my mother, when we were interrupted." Niels took a sip of his iced tea and looked at his father.

"Yes." His father's voice sounded soft and warm. "My Lali. We were both little more than children when we met. I was seventeen turnings old, and she only fifteen. I had never had any interest in girls, and thought something was wrong with me, so my brother Yosan suggested I should go to the Hooker Zone, pick up a girl and take her home with me. That was quite the adventure, of course, as we didn't wish for our parents to find out. We were sure they would disapprove, but my brothers helped me sneak those girls in and out of the palace. I, in turn, was expected to help them when they wanted to spend the night with a girl of their choosing.

"I cannot vouch for the chastity of my brothers, but every time I took a girl home, she and I would end up talking all evening. We might play a game of Llulaba, watch a show on the vidisphere, or I would read her some poems. I would let her sleep in my bed, and make sure she had a good breakfast the next morning. Then I would give her a pouch filled with gold coins and my brothers and I would smuggle her out of the palace again." He smiled.

"So, one night I took Lali back home with me. I'd only seen her around two or three times before, but always another man took her with him first. I was uncharacteristically excited when finally I did manage to get to her first. By then, the girls all knew that I treated them well, and most were happy enough to come with me. No work, all play, and good pay. That was what they told each other.

"Like all other girls, she was only going to be with me for one night, but the next morning I had to admit to myself that I didn't want her to leave. I liked her. Liked her more than any of the other girls. She was special. So I asked her to stay with me for a few more days, to which she agreed.

"It only took my parents until that evening to find out that I was hiding a girl in my chambers, but to my surprise they didn't mind at all. They told me I had to make sure I wouldn't get her with child, but if she were to get pregnant, they would deal with it.

"I was fine with that. I didn't think we would be bedding each other anyway. And at first, this was true. But I liked her more than I thought I could ever like any girl, and from one thing came another. Of course, we were not careful at all. Like I said, we were mere children and naïvely didn't think she was old enough to conceive yet. We loved each other as passionately as only the very young can.

"We lived as in a dream, until one morning I woke up and found her gone. The presents I had given her, the beautiful clothes... She had left them all behind. The only things she had taken with her were the golden earrings and bracelet I had given to her the day after we had first become one. I bought them back from a shifty street vendor several sevendays later.

"I kept them, with the note she left me that morning, in my memory box, where I also kept some of my other presents to her. I've still got all of them. But my Lali... I never found her back."

He fell silent then, and stared at his fingernails. Exactly the same way Niels himself did so often when he felt uncomfortable. He heaved a deep sigh, then got up and went into his study, where Niels heard him rummaging in one of his bookcases, or maybe his desk.

Moments later he was back, carrying a gilded box, inset with precious jewels.

"My memory box." He sat down on the sofa beside Niels and opened it. He retrieved a yellowed scrap of paper, and handed it to Niels. "Here, read this. I still can barely understand how this could have happened. I thought we were happy together."

My beloved Naz,

My sun and stars, as I'm writing this, my heart is heavy with sorrow. Your parents will not tolerate my presence for much longer, and I am in fear of my life. I have no choice but to leave you.

Please, don't try to find me. I cherish the time we spent together, but our love was not meant to be. May the Lady bless you with true happiness, long life and good health. You will be in my heart for as long as our good Goddess gives me life.

Your Lali.

Niels read and reread the note. He scratched the nape of his neck. Clearly, his parents had loved each other intensely. She had never been a one-night stand for him. They had been together for several moons, Niels now understood. His father had loved his mother as passionately as he himself had loved Sofieke.

He handed the note back to his father. "I have misjudged you, Padr. I used to think you were a disgraceful man. A scoundrel and a pervert, who would use women, just because he could. I have done you wrong. Forgive me."

"Do not chastise yourself over your mistake, my son. I know what it looks like. I know what people think of me. A whore hopper and a booze beast. The irony is, I don't drink. Not a droplet. I've seen what alcohol can do to a man. My beloved father, may he rest peacefully in the arms of A'harat, he... It was not pretty." He closed his eyes and shook his head.

"As for my alleged promiscuity... The only woman I have ever been intimate with, was your mother."

This was getting ever more confusing. All those children that had been murdered, presumably on his father's orders, couldn't even have been his. It made absolutely no sense. Unless his father was lying, but Niels didn't think he was. He sounded sincere. What was more, his mother's memories, as preserved by the medallion, corroborated his story.

"You never loved another woman?" Still, Niels could barely believe it.

"No. As I said, I never had any interest in girls, and I still cannot understand how I developed such strong feelings for Lali." He sounded bemused.

"But all those other children you presumably sired?"

"Moradin." His father shook his head and smiled. "And here I thought I was clueless. Did I not just tell you my brothers took girls home with them as well? Sandor probably stopped doing that once he got married, but Yosse... I have no illusions about him. He always said his heart was far too big for just one woman to fill it."

He walked over to the mantle and stood looking at the portraits of his brothers for a while, apparently deep in thought.

"I was only fourteen when I first set eyes on Krystandor," he resumed. "He was the most gorgeous boy I had ever seen. Those eyes, that face! We became friends and I think we both knew the attraction was mutual, but neither of us wanted to admit it.

"It was not until I had finally accepted that Lali had left me and would never be coming back, that our camaraderie developed into more than just friendship. By then, I was twenty.

"We have been together ever since. He was never supposed to be my guardian. That had always been his father's job. But when our relationship became ever more serious, I pleaded for Krys to be allowed to take over from his father and be my guardian. It seemed only natural. We were, and still are, inseparable."

The king looked up at Krystandor, who stood behind him now, hands loosely on his partner's shoulders.

"Zinnir's beard!" Niels couldn't hide his astonishment. "This is..." he burst out laughing. "And all these people think you are a lady's man and spread your seed all over Ebaru City. Do you still go to the Hooker Zone?"

"Of course. These girls have such hard lives. This is just one little thing I can do to make things a tiny bit better for them. Even if only for just one night."

Niels looked at him. "Forgive me for saying so, but I from what I have seen in my visions, they are actually scared of you."

"That is, unfortunately, not completely beside the truth. Some nights, my mind deserts me, and though I personally have only sketchy memories of those nights, Krys fills in those voids. Always. I have no excuse for yelling at these poor girls, and I'm ashamed of my barbaric behaviour on those occasions."

He shifted in his chair and stared at his hands for a while before he continued his narrative.

"Once or twice a sevenday, Krys and I both pick up a girl. We take them home with us, and give them a night of innocent fun. Music, games, reading... whatever they like. We give them a nice bed to sleep in for that one night, and a good breakfast the next morning. And more money than they usually earn in a sevenday."

"But," Niels said, "that way, you perpetuate the lie. People will keep saying you are a wanton cave cork."

His father shrugged. "Let them. They can think whatever they want. It won't stop me from doing good." He sat down in his comfortable chair again. "Your turn now, son. How did you survive the fire? And how has your life been since?"

"You are not the only one with a Sylphan guardian, as I'm sure you know. Mikhandor has been watching over me since before I was born, he told me back when I was... uh... fifteen. So, when the fire broke out, he was there. Appeared out of nowhere, created a vortex and teleported me to Thorf. He went back to save my cousins but, sadly, was unable to save my best friend's life."

Niels buried his head in his hands as the memories sprang back to life, and grief overcame him. Thankfully, nobody spoke as he sat there, like the sentimental fool he was, until he regained his composure. Then he continued his story.

"My great-granduncle, priest Shadu Amari, was safe. High priest Akdi Erumin, too, although he was severely injured and never regained his good health. He lives, if one can even call it that, in a tiny home on Thorf, where he remains completely dependent on the constant care of his Sylphan caretaker. He can speak, but with difficulty, and is unable to feed himself.

"Ten of my friends and relatives died that night. I blamed you, Padr, and hated you even more than I did before. I thought you had finally found me and sent your assassins to eliminate me, the man you perceived to be a threat to your throne."

His father shook his head. "I knew nothing of it. Not until the morning after. And you are most welcome to my stinking throne, but I have this feeling you aren't exactly eager to take my place." He played with his signet ring.

"It is ironic, isn't it? Asandor was looking forward to one day becoming king, and I am fairly certain he would have made a fine monarch, too. I had always been happy to live in the shadows of my older brothers. I felt secure in the knowledge that I would never have to be king. Yet here I am. Life does not care about our wishes, son, and we have to do our duties as best we can."

"What I still do not understand," Niels said, "... your parents, your brothers and sisters... surely, they had guardians of their own? Why did they not save them?"

"I wondered about that too. The only thing Krys and I can think of, is that the poison the assassin used — if it was indeed poison, because that has never been confirmed — was undetectable. Their guardians, Krys's father amongst them, died too. It was far, far worse than the official news reports disclosed."

"Zinnir's teeth! That is awful."

"Yes. I still have nightmares about it."

Niels nodded. "I know. I sometimes get to ride along in them. The priestly medallion. It can do that kind of thing. Usually, I am able to block your subconscious from entering mine, but when I am too tired, my defences fail. Then some of your memories, dreams and nightmares can freely cross over into my mind as well."

"That is unpleasant. For both of us. I hope..." The king broke off. He started fiddling with his signet ring again. "So, tell me, what happened next?"

"Next?" What did he mean?

"Yes. After the fire."

"We stayed on Thorf for..." Niels sat back and tried to relax, but he couldn't. All these deaths. All the grief. The suffering and pain. He took a few deep, calming breaths and tried again.

CHAPTER THIRTY-SIX

Annihilation

> lethal
> sickness unleashed
> upon faultless victims
> of slayer's voracious thirst for
> power

We stayed on Thorf for a little longer than one turning. Those of us who had survived, needed time to heal. That, and Mikhandor had to find us new positions on Sor. He also provided us with new identities, since we were supposed to be dead.

I became Farradin Tahiri, priest of Sern, a small town in Glelland. For a time, all was well. I had a nice, fully furnished little flat not far from the House of Prayer. A cleaner came in once every sevenday, and the local greengrocer delivered my groceries right on my doorstep.

I inherited a little *barkmouse* that had been named Blof by its previous owner, an old lady who had died shortly before my arrival in Sern. With its bat-like snout and short legs, it looked ridiculous, but as far as barkmice go, Blof was alright. He didn't bark overly much, hardly ever tried to nip at people's ankles, and got me out of the house several times a day.

Although I never made any real friends in Sern, I got along with most people well enough, and went to combat training three times a sevenday with Mikhandor and four other guys. We formed a harmonious group, with all six of us rather serious about the sport. Often, we practised with the staff, wooden sword, or dagger.

Four winters turned into spring, and those springs became summers, and the worst things that happened in those turnings, were people dying of old age. Life was finally good to me. My father, the king, had forgotten about me, and the assassins would never even think to come looking for me. For the first time in many turnings, I thought I was safe.

And I was wrong.

It was a beautiful morning in the early autumn of 9747, and I was on my way to the park with my little barkmouse. The loamy scent of damp earth was so potent, I could almost taste it. Dappled sunshine fell on my face, a soft breeze cooled my skin, and the first fallen leaves crunched under my feet. I was about to turn the last corner and enter the park, when something heavy smashed into my side and threw me off balance. With a dull thud, I hit the ground.

A slate grey karr with blinded windows tore through the place where I had been only a heartbeat ago. It had no identification plate, but I recognised Ebaru's royal mascot on the gravel shield. Half dazed, I sat up. A young woman lay a few feet away from me, her head at an impossible angle, blood seeping from her mouth. Further on, more people lay on the ground. Blof had run off and was nowhere to be seen.

A cloaked, hooded figure stood bent over me. "Looks like they found you," Mikhandor's familiar voice said. "I need to get you somewhere safe. Fast. Come with me."

He led me through a maze of narrow streets to a dodgy-looking drinking establishment. "I have a room here." He pushed me inside. "Through here. Wait, I'll tell Master Vlas to send Lina up with their best mulled wine. You look like you need a good drink."

"No, I don't." Surely, he knew better than that by now. "I was born an addict, remember?"

He slapped his palm against his forehead. "Right. A kaw brew then."

I looked around the room. It was tiny, dirty and smelly. And were that rat droppings, in that corner? What on all seven worlds possessed Mikhandor to live here?

"We need to leave Sern, you understand that, don't you?" Silent as always, he had come back in. "Do you have any possessions that you absolutely need to take with you?"

"Just the things I brought with me to Thorf the first time. You are taking me there again, aren't you?"

"Yes. We'll use the portal if we have enough time. Best hurry up."

After a timid knock on the door, a young lass entered, carrying a wooden tray with two steaming mugs of kaw.

"Thank you, my lovely." Mikhandor winked at the girl, whose cheeks turned a pretty pink. She retreated almost immediately.

"Why do you live in a place like this?"

He shrugged. "I don't know that I would call it that," he said. "Living, I mean. I sleep here some nights. I sleep in other places on other nights. Serves me well enough. But after today, the innkeepers will find out that I'm not coming back. Pity. I liked them. I'll leave old Vlas some extra silvers."

He gulped his brew down, and I did the same.

"You ready?"

We were on Thorf. For the second time in my life. We had, indeed, been able to use the Rakkon Portal, and I was glad for it. This wasn't nearly as taxing on my physique as vortex travel, though it clearly drained Mikhandor, who fell asleep the moment we exited the portal.

When Mikhandor was rested, he took me straight to High King Yumænor's palace, just like the first time I visited Thorf.

"Welcome back, young prince," the high king said. "I understand you need to disappear for a while again."

"Unfortunately, yes." My life in Sern had been good, until that morning. I hated being uprooted like that and, once more, with no time to prepare. "So, what happens now?"

"Now we eat, of course." Yumænor gestured at the table, which was already set for an informal meal. I was not hungry.

It was almost like an ordinary meal, with ordinary people. The food and wine were good, but not fanciful. The table conversations were exactly what the word implied. Dumb, useless small talk.

After dinner I took a bath and put on the clean, new clothes the Erls had provided me with. Wonderfully soft robes, without the nasty seams of the ordinary clothes I wore on Sor. It was one of the things I loved most about my stay with the Erls.

Since I knew we weren't going to talk about the accident and my current situation yet, I decided to go and see Akdi.

It was a nice walk to Akdi's little home, and I enjoyed being out in the beautiful Thorf nature, with its brilliant colours, delicate scents and elegant forest animals. For once, I was really alone. On Thorf there was no need for Mikhandor to keep a close watch on me. I was truly safe.

Akdi had just woken up from his afternoon nap, and still looked a bit dishevelled but, as always, seemed pleased to see me. We did not speak much. Talk was exhausting to him and, through our medallions, we understood each other well enough without words, so most of the time I just sat by his bedside and held his hand. That was enough.

I left with a heavy heart, yet happy to have been with him for a short while. I shook my head as I remembered how intensely I had resented him as a boy, and how convinced I had been that he detested me even more. How could I have been so wrong? He was one of the most caring people I had ever known, and I hated what had become of him. All of his current suffering was because of me. Because someone had wanted me dead.

This time we only remained on Thorf for several moons. When High King Yumænor deemed it safe for me to return to Sor, Mikhandor found me a position in Tan'Rabu. I was worried about that, and would much rather have gone to another small town or even better, a tiny village somewhere in the middle of nowhere. The Erls disagreed. The assassins would never expect me to take up residence in the capital of Askandu, right on Ebaru's doorstep. It seemed like a foolhardy thing to do, and that made it actually safer than any other option.

I became priest Bilkim Shirtokhi, one of the many priests in Tan'Rabu. Indeed, I was such a common sight, nobody looked at me twice. I had almost complete freedom. Just another priest. Most people didn't even know my name, and that suited me fine.

Tan'Rabu offered me the opportunity to live a normal life. I could go to the library, any library, and spend an entire day there, amongst all these other people. I could be studying, and there would be at least ten other priests, looking just like me, doing the exact same thing. I could go for a walk in one of the many parks, like hundreds of others, and never get noticed in the crowds. It was pure bliss.

Again, and far sooner than in Sern, I felt safe. I started to take risks, and did things I had never done before. I asked a woman out for a drink. A cup of kaw. Such an ordinary thing, yet it was monumental to me. And it didn't stop there. I asked her out for dinner. We started dating.

Zia was her name. Ziatara Soltani. She was a calm and soft-spoken woman. Intelligent, and well-read. She worked as a junior scientist at Tan'Rabu University, and was writing a research paper on the human genome and infectious diseases.

Our little romance lasted only a few moons.

We were going to the theatre, but that night something was wrong. I knew it the moment she answered the door. She didn't open it all the way, like she normally did, but only a crack.

"Go away." Her voice sounded scratchy, and her face was so blotchy, even I could see she'd been crying.

"What is wrong?" I took a step forward, but she tried to close the door on me. I held it and attempted to squeeze through.

"Moradin, no!" She tried even harder to push the door closed. Pinkish tears came running down her cheeks. "Go. You can't come in. It's..." She fainted.

I opened the door further and entered her flat. Knelt by her side and felt her pulse. It was racing. Beads of bloody sweat stood on her brow. Her breathing was rapid and shallow. I peeled one of her eyes open. It was bloodshot, and the pupil was dilated.

Without hesitation, I pulled my priestly medallion out from under my robes, tore her blouse open, and pressed the amulet on her bare chest. I closed my eyes and channelled healing and strength into her failing body. For a moment it seemed to work, but then she started coughing up blood mixed with foul smelling greenish phlegm.

"Moradin," she rasped between coughs, "go. Flee."

Then it registered. She had called me Moradin. Not once, but twice. I was Bilkim. Nobody in Tan'Rabu had ever known me as Moradin. The assassins were onto me again, and Zia had been their weapon. Now she was dying. Because of me. I doubled my efforts to save her.

I was being a fool. I was killing myself in an attempt to save the enemy. I knew this full well. Logic demanded that I should let her die, but I could not. As a priest and a human being, it was my duty to try and save her life, her treachery notwithstanding.

She stopped coughing. She stopped breathing and went limp. The medallion went cold.

"Zia," I whispered. "Wake up."

I cradled her in my arms, held her against my chest and kissed her hair. "Zia, please!"

"Your fault!" The voice in the back of my mind was there again. Mocking me like those other times. That morning when I found Sofieke dead in her room. The night Tasim had died in the flames. "Your fault. You didn't try hard enough."

"Niels." Mikhandor stood before me, and he looked larger than ever. "We need to go." He grabbed my hand and tugged at me.

"Niels, come with me." Femke. She took me by the hand. Would these memories keep haunting me? Forever?

"I cannot." I refused to let go of Zia's immobile body. Refused to get up. "We need your sister here, to cure Zia."

Mikhandor shook his head. "She is dead, Niels. And if we don't leave now, you will be dead too. You may already be infected with whatever nasty bug this is."

"No. I will not leave her." I clutched Zia to my heart even closer. Pressed the medallion against her chest anew and began channelling even more of my strength into her. I could not accept her death. I was going to bring her back to life again.

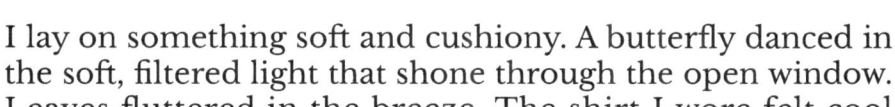

I lay on something soft and cushiony. A butterfly danced in the soft, filtered light that shone through the open window. Leaves fluttered in the breeze. The shirt I wore felt cool against my burning skin.

"When will you ever learn, Moradin?" Rasælna looked down on me, her face grave.

"That was the stupidest stunt you pulled so far, my friend." Mikhandor's voice sounded strange. Hoarse. Smothered.

"Zia," I said. "Is she…"

Rasælna shook her head. "She was already dead, your Highness. You know this."

I wiped the sudden tears from my eyes. I had hoped, against all reason, that she had somehow survived.

"She was doing research on some infectious disease, and how it affected the human genome." I closed my eyes as I tried to catch my breath and get the dizziness under control. "Does that… mean…" I coughed a dry, raspy cough, "… engineered?"

"Yes, Moradin. The AsK-II-Nd virus, from which Miss Soltani suffered, is a man-made virus. It is extremely contagious, and lethal. The official reports say one of the researchers got accidentally infected, and unbeknownst to herself and her colleagues, carried it with her into the world. The entire Southern Continent is currently in lockdown to prevent the virus from spreading to the rest of the world until a cure has been found."

"Then why are you not ill? And how am I still alive?" I closed my eyes again.

"The virus only affects humans and, thankfully, I was able to cure you. Your fever has already subsided significantly, and will continue to drop, but the cough may linger for a while longer. And you weakened yourself. As usual. But I managed to drive the virus from your body. Not that you deserve it. Now sleep."

I wanted to stay awake and ask more questions. Why were her people not on Sor, healing those who had been infected? What was going to happen now? How long before I could go back? Yet, my body decided differently, and I drifted off to sleep.

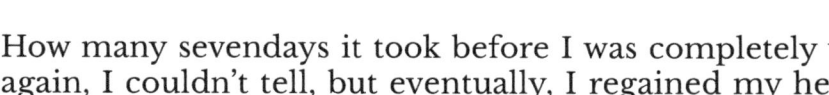

How many sevendays it took before I was completely well again, I couldn't tell, but eventually, I regained my health and strength. All of it. Mikhandor and Rasælna made it quite clear that they were not happy with me. Even High King Yumænor expressed his displeasure in his own gentle way. Once. And that was more than enough.

Mikhandor's grumblings and Rasælna's stern looks I could deal with. They always griped and fussed when I got myself into trouble. They would get over it, and so would I. But the high king's gentle rebuke made me want to hide in the inner depths of Sor, and never show my face again. I had disappointed him, and that hurt.

Ever more often, I went to see Akdi. Because of his delicate condition, the Erls sheltered him from bad news, so he didn't know about my latest run-in with Yat S'ber, and how I had, once again, managed to dodge death. Through no merit of my own.

Seeing Akdi, however, was both a blessing and a curse. I still blamed myself for his cruel fate and, on top of that, I felt guilty over my obstinate behaviour towards him when I was younger. I knew he was aware that something had happened.

He was frail. Not stupid. He probably would have wanted to know what went wrong this time, but I kept it from him.

My silence lasted until one afternoon he looked at me, his eyes intent, and said, "Boy, why don't you just tell me?"

Boy. Funny, how he still thought of me as a boy. For a moment, it confused me. Then I realised that he, in his own way, still felt responsible for me.

"I am not as fragile as everyone here thinks, young man. Tell me."

And I did. I told him everything, and he simply listened. Without interruption. Without judgement. It was healing. Rasælna might have cured my body, but he mended my tormented soul.

When I was done, we sat in silence for a while, until he said, "I used to be like you. I felt that everything that went wrong in the world was my fault."

I remembered that afternoon, that training session, where his ward had slipped for the shortest moment and I got a glimpse into his soul. He was right. I was doing the exact same thing. I was carrying the grief of the entire world on my shoulders.

"That burden, Moradin, was not mine to carry, and neither is it yours. Ask your medallion to take it from you."

I looked at him in utter surprise. "It can do that?"

He nodded. "I never knew until after I arrived here. Do you want me to guide you through the process?"

CHAPTER THIRTY-SEVEN

Restoration

*past meets
presence and life
moves towards new futures
where old sins are forgiven and
wounds healed*

Sooner than expected, the AsK-II-Nd virus was eliminated, and the Southern Continent was opened up again. I was not surprised. The assassins would never have set a deathly virus loose in the world if they didn't know beforehand they could quench it once it had done its nefarious job.

It had failed at doing what it was designed to do, and I was sure my enemy was aware of that fact. He would also know I would not be coming back until the virus was erased, so it only made sense that he should do that as soon as possible. He had nothing to gain from leaving it out there, making victims left and right, while I was safe and out of his reach.

I longed to go back to my home world. With the virus gone, I could think of no manifest reason to stay on Thorf for a prolonged period of time, and lingering there would not magically solve my problems on Sor. No matter how much I feared and loathed it, I still had a destiny to fulfil. Sooner or later, I had to come face to face with the man who sought my death, and I had finally decided sooner would be better. It had been too long already.

I was not afraid to die, but I mourned the people who had died for me. Each and every one of them. That was what scared me. The prospect of more people dying because of me. It was also my motivation to go back. This was the one thing I had to stop.

Mikhandor found another position for me, and I had to take on yet another fake identity, but I was done with the histrionics and subterfuge. It didn't even work, so why bother? And so I went to the Barlows as myself. Niels Bosch. That name, the name my adoptive parents had given me, came closest to who I felt I really was.

I lived in a quaint cottage with a beautiful garden in which I grew fragrant herbs, and some vegetables. I had three adorable hens, and a cocky rooster. But best of all, I worked closely together with a cantor who was not only the most beautiful woman I knew, but also very talented. I would have been content to stay there for the rest of my life. With my cantor.

"Quit flattering me, you charmer." Bel snuggled up to Niels, and he draped an arm around her shoulders.

"Well, you know what happened next. I came here to confront you, Padr, and found out that things weren't at all what they seemed. Now we have to find out who the real mastermind behind all these assassinations is."

Hanassan nodded. "With some luck, Sebben will be able to get closer to the truth when he speaks to my pharmacist."

Sebben. Even the name left a bitter taste in Niels' mouth. He bent forwards and peered at his father. "Do you honestly trust that man? Who says he didn't secretly instruct your pharmacist to tamper with your medication?"

"Easy enough," Krys said. "He has only been your father's physician for a little over a turning. Only since the previous one died."

"His predecessor died? How?"

"Traffic accident." Again, it was Krys who answered the question. "Being your father's doctor seems to be a dangerous job. They all die. One after another. We were lucky to find Sebben willing to risk his life."

"Zinnir's teeth!" He might dislike the man, but that was no reason to wish him dead. "What are you doing to protect him?"

Krys stared at the floor. "Not much, I'm afraid. We offered him a bodyguard but he declined."

"That's it?" Mikhandor sounded indignant. "You could at least have the man shadowed, for the sake of all the gods. How did you ever become a guardian? I shall have to ask the council to relieve you from your duties."

"Yes sir." Krystandor sounded timid. "Of course. As long as I can stay with Hanassan."

Mikhandor nodded. "That should not be an issue. He is your partner. Which is actually another reason why you should never have become his guardian."

Niels furrowed his brow. This was a part of Mikhandor he had never seen before, and for the first time in his life, he wondered just how old his friend and guardian really was. He had to be quite senior, to be carrying such weight.

It made a strange kind of sense, though. The Erls had suspected he was the Chosen One even before he was born. They would not have wanted to take any unnecessary risks with him.

"But..." His father's voice sounded anxious. "A new guardian? I don't want anyone but Krys. I don't want some strange new guy prying into my life, following me around wherever I go."

Mikhandor shrugged. "That's unfortunate for you, your Majesty, but you are royalty. You have no choice. But with some luck you won't even notice the change. Now get someone to tail... oh, never mind. I shall take care of it myself. We can't afford to lose Sebben. Right now, he is our best chance to find out who's behind all these killings."

"So, what do we do now?" Niels fidgeted with his uncomfortable clothes. "Are we just going to sit around and do nothing?" That did not seem useful to him, or even likely.

"Several things," Mikhandor said. "Beldenka needs to contact her mother and brother, if she hasn't already done so, and tell them to join us as soon as possible. We can use all the help we can get. Although the guys we took out today will not be bothering us any longer, there will be others. And Moradin, you are a pathetic fighter. You should take a leaf out of your wife's book."

As if he didn't know. But he was a priest. How could he ever take a life?

"First, you cannot forever hide behind the priesthood. Unless, of course, you like being prey, and because of you see the friends and family die," Toni's words came back to him.

Was it true? Was that what he was doing? Hiding behind his priesthood? He most certainly did not enjoy having his loved ones killed because of him, yet he still shirked from striking back. Why? Was he really using his priesthood as an excuse? Was he simply too soft?

He got up from the sofa and went over to the window. His back turned to the others, he said, "How much more fighting will there be?"

He didn't really expect an answer.

"Probably a lot."

"Suppose we kill them all, and we win. Then what?" Niels looked at the guards walking their rounds. "Will we then live happily ever after?" The thought alone was so ridiculous, it barely even deserved to be spoken aloud.

"Hardly." It was his father, who spoke. "Being royalty is a rotten job. You have absolutely no privacy, and everyone has an opinion on you. Usually an unfavourable one. No matter what you do, it is never good enough." He sounded bitter. "Even with my incredible clumsiness, I think I would much rather be a carpenter."

His father's words were like a dagger in his stomach. How could he have misjudged him so? If only he could have seen the real Hanassan, back when he was a boy. All those lost turnings. He could have been with his father, and healed him so much sooner, if only he hadn't been so quick to believe these malicious whispers. If only he had given his father a fair chance.

Because of his anger and stubbornness, his father had suffered for far longer than necessary. And even though now his illnesses had been cured, his suffering wasn't over yet. The effects of a lifetime of iniquity could not be undone in mere moments. The people of Ebaru hated their king still, and would not mourn his demise if he were to be assassinated.

Niels turned to face his father. "As a king, what do you want to do for your people, and what have you achieved so far?"

"What I want, my son, are the impossible dreams of a man who needs to get his head out of the clouds. I want to eradicate poverty. I want good and free healthcare for everyone. No hunger. No pain. No fear. I want to root out all crime. I want to extinguish the flames of hatred. I want only happiness for all." The fervour in his voice died as he added, "and I know all of this is totally unrealistic and will never happen."

He joined Niels by the window and laid a gentle hand on his shoulder. "I managed to have simple homes built in the District of the Poor. I appointed a health practitioner to care for the poor one day out of every seven. I urged the new high priest to keep the position of priest of the poor filled, but so far, he has failed to do so, and I can't force him. As a king, I am not allowed to meddle in matters of the priesthood. You know that even better than I do, I'm sure."

Niels nodded. "I might be able to persuade the high priest. I am a priest, after all. I could offer to be Priest of the Poor until I become king, which I wholeheartedly hope is still a long way off."

"You would?" The king sounded surprised.

"Absolutely. It's a bit of a family tradition, actually. My great-grandfather, Moradin Amari, was Priest of the Poor. So was my great-granduncle Shadu Amari. I feel I should be following in their footsteps."

"I liked him. Your great-granduncle. Despite the fact that he deceived me. But of course, I didn't know that at the time. Is he well?"

Niels felt his throat constrict. "I don't know. One of the worst things about pretending to be dead is that you cannot contact your loved ones from your previous life. Ever. No matter the circumstances, and no matter how much you might want to. I was not even allowed to know my cousins' and great-granduncle's new names, or where they were going to, when we went back to Sor."

His father looked incredulous, but remained silent. Like Niels himself, he stood staring out of the window, fumbling with his fingers.

"I read a small booklet, once," he finally said. "It was written by Moradin Amari. *Night's Reign*. I should have it somewhere still. In my study, I think. Do you know it?"

"I read it front to cover, and cover to front. Not once, but many times over. I still know parts of it by heart, even though I lost my own copy in the house fire." If his father had tried to distract him from his sombre thoughts, he had failed miserably.

Tasim. His best friend. Eaten by the flames. He remembered when he first came to Ebaru, how they had shared a room for a couple of moons. He remembered their whispered conversations during those long first nights, when everyone else was sleeping. How he had confided in Tasim, when he was being plagued by his father's nightmares.

He remembered the discussions they'd had during their time as students. Discussions about the prophecies, the histories, politics, crime. There had been nothing the two of them couldn't talk about, and he would give anything to be able to speak with his friend just once more.

He sat down, head in hands, and sighed deeply. Then Bel's hand was on his thigh. Strong, yet gentle and comforting.

He woke up in a comfortable bed, between soft silken sheets. Bel lay cuddled up to him, sleeping peacefully. He moved his head closer to her and took in her scent. Love. It was the smell of their sweet love the night before. The memory quickened his heartbeat. He wanted to kiss her and do it all over again, but then he would have to wake her, and he didn't want to do that. So he contented himself just looking at her, and listening to her deep, regular breathing. He still couldn't understand how he, awkward fumbler that he was, had gained the love of this precious, wonderful woman.

For how long he lay there, staring at her, he could not tell, but eventually she opened her eyes and smiled at him. "Have you been awake for long?"

"I couldn't possibly tell." He played with a lock of her hair. "But I don't think so. It feels like only a moment."

She put a hand on the back of his head and pulled him closer to her. He didn't need any urging. He was about to kiss her when a knock on their door disturbed their intimate moment. He sighed.

"I already hate being a prince," he said in a low voice before he called, "enter!"

A young lady in a simple but elegant azure dress entered. Niels recognised her clothing as the royal livery.

"Good morning, Your Royal Highnesses, ma'am, sir."

She opened the curtains and windows before she walked up to the bed.

"My name is Gulzhar. I am Princess Beldenka's lakaì." She addressed Bel then, "I shall ready your bath, ma'am. We have a busy day ahead of us."

Bel nodded wordlessly. Niels looked at her. She did not seem happy, but before he could ask her what was wrong, there was another knock on the door.

It was a male liveried servant this time, and quite a bit older than Bel's cute lady in waiting.

"Good morning, Royal Highnesses. Sir, ma'am. Name is Nikdel. Prince Moradin's lakaì. Sir, bath is ready. If you will come with me, please." He held up a white cotton bathing robe and averted his gaze discreetly as Niels shrugged into it.

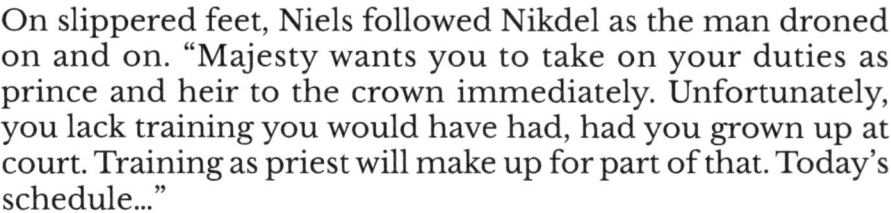

On slippered feet, Niels followed Nikdel as the man droned on and on. "Majesty wants you to take on your duties as prince and heir to the crown immediately. Unfortunately, you lack training you would have had, had you grown up at court. Training as priest will make up for part of that. Today's schedule..."

Niels was not listening any more. He sat in the tub, eyes closed, trying his hardest to not freak out completely. He concentrated on his breathing, the hot water, the feel of the suds on his skin, the sweet fragrance of the steam he inhaled. Nikdel's voice became a distant murmur.

A cough.

"Your Royal Highness?"

Another cough, and the same phrase repeated, more insistently this time, "Your Royal Highness?"

Niels looked up. His lakaì stood with the white robe at the ready.

"I apologise," Niels said. "My mind drifted for a moment."

Nikdel helped him into a suit. A sarding suit! And it felt horrible. Stiff, itchy, and restrictive.

"I shall need to buy me some robes today," he said. "I cannot wear these... these monkey suits."

"Monkey suits as you call them, sir, are what prince is expected to wear when performing royal duties. No choice, I fear. Also, royalty cannot buy own clothes. All clothes be custom made. Appointment with royal seamstress scheduled before lunch."

So this was his life now. Being fussed over by a sarding servant, who seemed unable to speak in complete sentences. Not allowed to bathe and dress himself. Would he even be allowed to think for himself, or was he supposed to let others do all the thinking for him as well? As he followed his manservant, he wondered where they were going. His stomach was rumbling, and he felt a headache coming on. Already.

CHAPTER THIRTY-EIGHT

Counting

> pages
> unspoilt by ink
> denote new beginnings
> and lessons to be learnt before
> time's up

The morning sun cast long shadows on the marble floor tiles of the royal office, a spacious room with too many windows and a desk the size of a small ship. As he took his place behind that desk, Niels suppressed a shiver.

They were four, their Erlen guardians not counting. Padr and Niels. Niels' lakai, and Padr's vizier, a man in his seventies, who had a service record dating back to the last turnings of King Hazzid's reign. Ardu was the man's name. Ardu Bakhmandi. Despite his age, he stood as straight as any younger man, and moved with a grace and confidence that was rarely seen in the elderly. Niels did not think for even a moment that the scimitar he wore tucked into his belt was there for purely decorative purposes either.

"Moradin," his father said, "you need to learn how to be a prince, and your job starts today. For, make no mistake, it is a real job, and the work is hard and unappealing."

Niels picked up the lambskin notebook that had apparently been put on the desk for him to use. He opened it, and caressed the pages. Not only did it look beautiful, it also smelled good.

"We have breakfast together every morning. You, Princess Beldenka, and I. After breakfast we meet here, in this study to discuss our day. Ardu will brief us on the political situation in Ebaru, and what world affairs we need to be aware of, and he will help us prepare our workdays."

That sounded tedious. Niels picked up the silver stylo that lay beside the notebook. It felt cool and heavy in his hand. Just the way he liked it. He jotted down: *meeting with Padr after breakfast.*

"I may need to discuss new laws with my advisors," Hanassan continued, "and I shall probably have audiences. Most of the time you won't be needed there yet, but you will need to start training with my guards every morning. And you will be wearing a scimitar at all times."

"A scimitar?" That was an unpleasant surprise.

"Yes, Moradin. I understand you are not very proficient with the sword, and I need you to be an excellent swordsman. So you will wear your scimitar at all times. You need to get accustomed to the feel of it. To always be prepared. And to project a powerful and confident impression. In this line of work, looks are everything."

Niels stared at the almost empty page of his notebook. He should probably write this down, but he did not want to. "Yes, Padr."

"And you cannot look down like that. You'll keep your head high, no matter how uneasy you might be feeling. The confident bearing, son."

With a suppressed sigh he looked up, past his father, at the map of the Southern Continent that adorned the wall behind him. "Yes, Padr." He felt like a schoolboy. And not a particularly clever one, at that.

"Good. Much better. Now, after your combat training you'll either have appointments in the palace — today you will be seeing the seamstress — or you'll be studying Royal etiquette, Ebari law, history, and other relevant subjects."

Combat training, scimitar, royal duties, Niels scribbled down. That vizier, Ardu. He was looking at him. Niels could feel his gaze resting on him and it made his stomach cramp.

"During the afternoons, you are free to perform your priestly duties. Go speak to the high priest today, and see how you can be of service."

"Thank you. I will." He would convince the high priest of the need to fill the vacancy of Priest of the Poor.

"I expect you to report to me just before sundown every day. After that, we'll have supper as a family. You will typically have the evenings to yourself unless, of course, we have official obligations to attend to. Concerts, banquets with other political leaders, that kind of thing. Questions?"

Niels picked up his stylo again and played with it as he thought. He had so many questions, he wouldn't even know where to start. Again, he felt Ardu's eyes on him. What was up with that man? What did he want?

"No." He closed his notebook. "Not at the moment."

His father nodded. "You can go now. I'll see you before supper."

For a moment, Niels hesitated. How should he behave? Did he have to say something? Bow? Then Nikdel stood by his side, ready to escort him to the training grounds.

"I need a moment with His Royal Highness the prince," Mikhandor said as they were about to enter the training grounds.

Nikdel stepped back politely, and Mikhandor took Niels by the arm and pulled him even further away from his lakai. "Do not show them what you can do with a sword," he said under his breath. "Show them the clumsy, overwhelmed Moradin of yesterday. We don't know yet whom we can trust. There's bound to be some assassins around, and we want them to think you are an easy victim."

"Do you want me to cut myself on my sword as well?" Niels felt the heat of the anger rise to his cheeks.

"That wouldn't be a bad idea." Sarding Erl wasn't even joking. "Mind you, just a scratch. We would not want you to get really hurt."

Niels snorted. "You are so droll."

"Your Royal Highness." A short, muscular man in uniform looked up at him and saluted. "Daroz Khelat, head of the guards. At your service, sir."

Niels inclined his head, but didn't know what to say, so he remained silent.

"His Majesty your father the king has directed me to instruct you in the Art of the Sword. I do not doubt that he'll order the armourer to make you a custom scimitar, but for now a practice sword from the arsenal might be more prudent. Follow me, please."

And off they went to the weaponry depot. Daroz picked up a sword, looked at it with a critical eye, and put it back again. The same happened several times more, until at last he handed him a blade that seemed a little rusty, and dulled with age.

Remembering Mikhandor's words, he held it as clumsily as he could, and Daroz corrected him immediately. "Not like that, sir. Look, this is how you hold a sword." He drew his own sword and showed Niels how it should be done.

"How does that feel?" Daroz said when he was finally satisfied with Niels' grip.

"Strange." He was not lying. Until this day he had only ever trained with straight, wooden weapons. This was a metal blade. Curved. And blunted, Niels hoped.

"Never held one of these darlings, eh?" Daroz smiled, and there was a tenderness in his voice as if he spoke of his one true love. "You'll get used to it soon enough." He scrutinised Niels, took a step back, and studied him again. Then he nodded.

"Yes," he said. "Yes, I think this one will do fine. It looks right on you. Now I'll teach you how to care for your blade. We'll make her shine. Come with me."

Niels was on his way to the Grand House of Prayer. Though he could easily have walked the short distance, he had been told he would be driven there. By his private chauffeur, who doubled as his personal bodyguard. As if Mikhandor alone were not far better than ten human bodyguards could ever hope to be. Then again, it was probably all about appearances again.

He closed his eyes. That was perhaps the only good thing about being driven around in a royal karr with blinded windows. He could close his eyes and shut the world out, even if just for a moment.

His appointment with the royal seamstress, a buxom woman in her forties, blond, and with a rather too-easy smile, had been exhausting. The woman had chattered almost incessantly as she took his measurements. His neck, shoulders, chest, waist, hips, arms, legs, and feet. Even his head circumference. It had taken forever, and Niels could not fathom what she would need all those measurements for.

"Do you have any special requests, sir?" she had asked when she was finally done.

He had been tempted to tell her to stick the titles and other courtesies some place dark and smelly but, unfortunately, as a prince, he could not do that.

"I hate a close fit, and need all my seams to be enclosed, and as flat as possible. Also, I cannot stand rough fabrics, and wool scratches my skin and makes it bleed. I will not wear it under any circumstance."

"No problem, sir. Just for reference, how do you like the shape of your current suit?"

"Not. Not at all. It is too tight. I would rip it off right now, if I could." He had not been exaggerating.

"I'll make sure your new suits don't cause any inconvenience, sir. I understand you also need the priestly robes?"

"Yes. Two blue, one black and one brown. That should suffice." An idea sparked in his mind. "Come to think of it, do not make me any suits. I will only be wearing robes. I'm sure my paternal ancestors did the same. You can base my royal robes off of theirs."

Although she had looked doubtful, the seamstress had nodded anyway. She probably thought she wasn't allowed to contradict a prince.

The karr came to a standstill. As Niels reached for the door, Mikhandor shook his head at him, so he sighed and withdrew his hand. What kind of life was this, where he was not even allowed to open his own door?

Ramshur Eldani, Akdi's successor, walked up to Niels and bowed so deeply, his nose almost touched the floor. "Your Royal Highness, welcome."

"Please, Honourable Brother, I come to you as a priest, not a prince." He was sick of being addressed by these stupid titles.

"Even so, sir... brother, you are my prince, and I should pay you all due respect."

"You respect me more by calling me brother, or even better, Moradin. I am a person, not a title. And do not bow down for me ever again. I am not a god." That came out fiercer than he intended.

The high priest took a step back. "If you insist. But then I'll have to request politely that you call me Ramshur, Your Roy— uh, brother."

Niels nodded. "Ramshur. We need to talk. In private."

"Certainly. Follow me, please."

The high priest led them to the little room behind the main hall. The priest's lair, Akdi used to call it. It had not changed much. The walls were lined with simple bookcases. There were a few armchairs, and a low wooden table. Instead of Akdi's family portraits, pictures of Ramshur's wife and children now graced the mantle. Children the same age as Tasim and Tulia had been when Niels first arrived in Ebaru.

The chauffeur — Niels had forgotten his name — took up his post just outside the room, by the door. Mikhandor, on the other hand, followed him inside and took a seat in the largest, most comfortable chair.

"Mikhandor accompanies me at all times," Niels said. "There have been too many attempts on my life."

"So," Ramshur said, "yesterday wasn't the first time, then?"

"The first time was almost eleven turnings ago. The house fires that killed your predecessor's entire family. Akdi himself was beaten up so severely, he never completely recovered. He lives, but cannot even feed himself." Niels felt his blood boil.

The high priest nodded, as if he were not at all surprised. "I'm sorry," he said in a soft voice. "Pretty much every Ebari citizen suspected foul play, but the investigations never yielded any results. Most of us believed — and I hate to say it, but you must be aware of this too — that the king was behind it all. Frankly, I was not happy at all when I learned that I was to be the next high priest."

"I myself suspected my father, too. And I have certainly been in no hurry to come back to Ebaru, but my wife and her parents convinced me that it was the best thing to do."

"You say you take your responsibilities very serious. And yet you allow your father's killers to destroy those who are dear to you. This seems irrational," Mir's words echoed in his mind.

"It wasn't until yesterday that I discovered things were not what they seemed. I am convinced now that my father is a victim too, and although I have no idea who is behind all this wickedness, I intend to find out and deal with it." He meant every word he said, and that surprised him. He had not realised how angry he was, and how determined.

"But enough of that." He had not come to talk about politics. "As I said, I came here as a priest. I last served in a small village in Briscona, and I long to serve again. I hear the position of Priest of the Poor has not been filled yet. Might I ask why?"

"Priest of the Poor. As you probably know, there have only ever been two of them. Your ancestor Moradin Amari, and his brother Shadu." He stroked his beard. "I have asked around, but nobody seems keen to follow in their footsteps. Most think the Amari family is as cursed as our royal family, and they fear the curse extends to that function as well."

What a load of donkey dung. "Considering that I am already affected by these curses, I have no such qualms. With your approval, I would like to become Priest of the Poor. I am expected to fulfil my royal obligations in the mornings, so I can dedicate myself to my priestly duties in the afternoons."

"When can you start?"

"Right now, of course." Niels couldn't understand why Ramshur even needed to ask. Was it not obvious?

"Wearing these clothes?"

Niels shrugged. "I cannot see why not, although I would have preferred to wear my travelling clothes, but my father would not hear of it. He might even have ordered his vizier to have them burnt."

"The Poor might be reluctant to speak to you, though, when you are wearing your princely attire."

"I do not intend to talk to anyone just yet. I need to inspect the Ancient Temple. We cleaned it up when my great-granduncle was Priest of the Poor, but since the poor haven't had their own priest these last eleven turnings, I fear I shall find all sorts of things in the building that do not belong in a House of Prayer."

Eighteen turnings ago, the place had been grimy, and littered with refuse. The kind of waste addicts left behind. Cleaning it up had not been a pleasant job. It wouldn't be any more agreeable now, but it was the first thing that needed to be done.

"But you are a..." Ramshur began, but Niels interrupted him.

"A priest," he said. "I am a priest, and this is just a part of my job. I do not want or need any special considerations just because I happen to be a prince."

Before he left the House of Prayer, he said the blessings over the Sacred Candles and the Holy Water. Then, he recited his prayers. All this time, ever since he left the Barlows, he had not been inside a House of Prayer or, indeed, even seen one on his travels, and he had missed it. As a priest, he could not truly be whole if he did not say the blessings, and recite the prayers at least once a day.

He left feeling a lot better and more at peace than when he arrived. Yet, he dreaded his visit to the Ancient Temple. He already knew what he would find there. Syringes, needles, empty bottles, dubious contraceptive contraptions, dirt and grime. That was not what he feared.

The Ancient Temple. It was the place where he was born. A place of memories. Could he handle them at this time?

CHAPTER THIRTY-NINE

Encumbered

<pre>
       courtly
      obligations
   clutter empty pockets
  of time invading intimate
         moments
</pre>

Bel was happy only moments ago. Until Gulzhar came in and spoiled their early morning cuddle. The girl couldn't help it, of course. She was only doing her job, but really! She'd been hoping to spend some quality time with her handsome husband before being thrown into the day's duties.

She'd better put on her dressing gown before Gulzhar came back. Her lakaì — how perfectly awful to even have one — should immediately be disabused of the notion that she was in any way needy. She was not going to give up all her freedoms. She'd worked hard enough to obtain them.

By the time her little servant re-entered the room, she sat in the king's monster of a wheelchair. "Your bath is ready, ma'am." She was already reaching for the push handles.

"None of that, young lady. I am perfectly capable of wheeling myself around."

For just a moment, the girl looked taken aback. Then she regained her composure and smiled politely. "Of course, ma'am. I'll be sure to remember that. Please, follow me."

They were in a torching palace, and their chambers didn't even have their own bathroom. What kind of folly was that? She had to roll down a long hallway to get to the baths. The guards, the scullery boys, the cleaners... everyone could see their future queen riding down that hall, dressed in nothing but a bathing robe. That simply would not do, and should be addressed as soon as possible.

"Will you be needing any assistance getting into the bath, ma'am?" At least the girl seemed to be a quick learner.

Bel shook her head. "No, thank you. I can manage on my own." She'd done it a thousand times back at home, in the Barlows. Another home she would never see again. "Turn around." A small degree of privacy couldn't hurt.

She dropped the robe and heaved herself out of the chair, into the bath. "What's my schedule for today?" She closed her eyes and tried to relax.

"Breakfast with His Majesty the King and His Royal Highness Prince Moradin first, an appointment with the royal seamstress immediately after, and instruction in Royal Etiquette next. You will have the afternoon and evening to yourself."

Well, at least she did still get some free time, though she was well aware that might change soon enough. This was exactly one of the reasons why she hated her titles. They brought obligations with them. She'd seen that with Papi and Mumi, neither of them even Grand Lords, but people always knew where to find them for all sorts of official dung.

Yet here she was. A torching Royal Princess. What was worse, she had only herself to blame for it. If she hadn't married Niels... but that was inconceivable. She loved that man, awkwardness and all. Loved him so much, she had chosen to be his queen when the time came for him to be king. She'd known her marriage to him would end her anonymity and severely curb her free will once and for all. No use complaining now.

Too soon, she had to get out of the bath. Gulzhar helped her into a gorgeous but hopelessly impractical dress, with a skirt so wide she couldn't possibly ride her chair without the thing getting caught in the wheels. She would have to tell the seamstress she needed breeches. Lots of them.

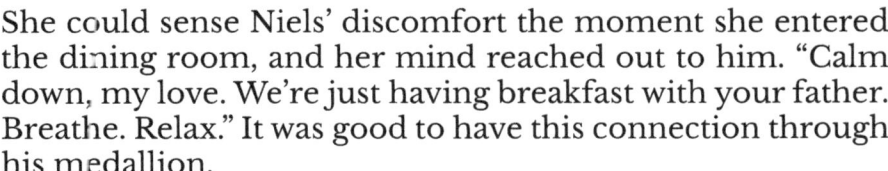

She could sense Niels' discomfort the moment she entered the dining room, and her mind reached out to him. "Calm down, my love. We're just having breakfast with your father. Breathe. Relax." It was good to have this connection through his medallion.

He turned his head and looked at her. "You look absolutely stunning, Bel," he said in his rich baritone; that amazing voice, that never failed to send shivers of joy down her spine. He probably wasn't even aware of it, but he would have been an incredible singer, had he chosen that path. She still intended to teach him.

"So do you." That tight fitting suit not only showed off his strong torso, but the cream-coloured fabric contrasted beautifully with his skin, and the elaborate golden loop fastenings of his tailcoat drew the attention to his ravishing eyes. She had to force herself to look away from him, and greet his father.

"Good morning, your Majesty. I hope you slept well."

"Please, Beldenka, let us dispense with the formalities in here. It is just the three of us, after all, and I loathe all these titles. Call me Hanassan."

Three? She counted ten persons. Besides the three of them, there were Mikhandor, Krys, Janæla, Niels' lakaì — what was his name again? — Gulzhar and some old bloke, whose function wasn't immediately clear to her. Then there were the two guards by the door. Apparently, none of them counted. Being royalty was certainly going to take some getting used to, and she already understood the need for her to be educated in the subject of royal etiquette.

"Then maybe you could just call me Bel?" She gave him her sweetest smile, and his answering grimace looked every bit as awkward as Niels' smiles so often did.

"Of course. I hope your chambers are to your liking? Also, I was thinking, since you lost your chair, you will need a new one. Mine is far too large and heavy for you."

"It will do for now, and I was hoping Mikhandor's man might get me a new one." She looked at the Erl.

"Certainly, my dear Princess. I have already contacted him. You should receive your new chair shortly."

That brightened her mood. The king's chair was, of course, far better than the alternative of having to be carried around in a sedan chair, but it was still cumbersome. She had truly loved her new chair, and the prospect of having it replaced by a similar one made her happier than anyone with two good legs could possibly understand.

Their breakfast was better than any of the meals they'd eaten in the past nine moons, ever since they embarked on their quest. It consisted of quail eggs, freshly baked flatbread, the richest, creamiest butter Bel could imagine, several cheeses and spreads, and a varied selection of fresh fruits. There was kaw brew, tea and fruit juice. Truly a breakfast for a king. And Bel was ravenous.

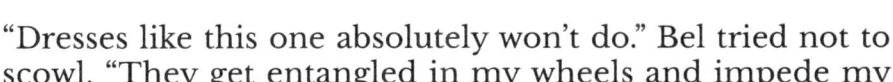

"Dresses like this one absolutely won't do." Bel tried not to scowl. "They get entangled in my wheels and impede my movements. I need breeches. Made for sitting."

The seamstress stared at her. "Breeches, ma'am?" Her already protruding eyes seemed about to pop out of their sockets.

"Yes, breeches." She glared back at the woman.

"But that is men's clothing."

"No, it is not. Not in my book. It is practical wear for a woman in a wheelchair. Would you like trying to ride around in a silly dress like this one? You can borrow this chair. It is wide enough to fit you. I could break your legs, if you like." The words were out before she knew it, and she bit her lip as she realised this was totally inappropriate. As a princess, she couldn't afford to be that sarcastic to her staff, no matter how annoying they were.

"That won't be necessary, ma'am." The poor woman had turned an amazingly white shade of pale. "If you need breeches, I make you breeches. But can I politely advise that you will also want to have one or two dresses for special occasions? I could make them fit tighter around the legs, so they won't interfere with riding your chair."

So she did at least have a minor degree of common sense. And just as well. "You know how Ingravian merchant women dress?"

"Of course. I am Antorian, ma'am. And the seamstress. My job is to know these things."

"Good. I like those dresses. They work well for me."

"I'm sure they do, but there is one problem with those dresses, ma'am."

If only the woman would stop ma'aming her every other word! It drove her up the wall. "And that is?"

"These are merchant's dresses, and you are a royal princess. They are sending the wrong message."

Two whole sentences, and not a single ma'am! "So you make some changes. A lower neckline. An open back. Shorter sleeves. Use your imagination. Draw people's attention away from my useless legs, and up towards my upper body."

"Even lower neckline, ma'am? But that would mean..."

"Yes, I know what that would mean. My husband would love it, I'm sure." Bel couldn't suppress an impish grin.

"Just like other men, ma'am, and your husband may not like that very much."

The torching woman could well be right about that. "Look, you are the royal seamstress, so you have to be good at your craft. As long as you ensure a tight fit around the legs, some extra room in the shoulders, and a seated fit, you should be alright."

"I can do it, no problem, ma'am." She held up a tape measure. "I will like to take your measurements now."

The seamstress took more measurements than Bel thought possible, but she trusted the woman knew what she was doing.

"Do you like to select your choice of fabrics now, ma'am?" She laid the tape measure and notebook on her desk, and gestured at the shelved wall behind her.

The shelves stored more bolts of fabric than Bel had seen in her entire life. Beautiful fabrics, too. Fine cottons, soft silks, and cool linens in an astonishing variety of colours and designs. She certainly wouldn't mind taking a good long look at those.

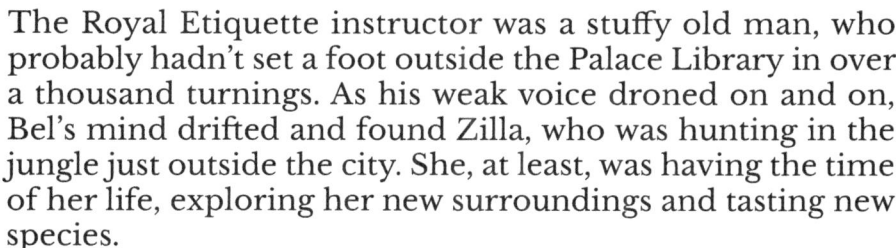

The Royal Etiquette instructor was a stuffy old man, who probably hadn't set a foot outside the Palace Library in over a thousand turnings. As his weak voice droned on and on, Bel's mind drifted and found Zilla, who was hunting in the jungle just outside the city. She, at least, was having the time of her life, exploring her new surroundings and tasting new species.

"Your Royal Highness?"

Dragon's dung! For how long had the old fogey been trying to get her attention?

"My apologies, sir. I'm still a bit wearied from my travels." A small white lie was probably the best course of action right now. Most people assumed the wheelchair meant she was feeble anyway, and at times like these it seemed silly not to take advantage of their ignorance.

"Of course," the man wheezed, "of course." He fumbled a bit with his stack of yellowed papers, then seemed lost in thought for a while. Was he sick? Senile? Why was he still working? The poor chap didn't look fit at all.

"Are you well, sir?" She bit her lip. Why had she paid so little attention? Now she couldn't even remember her tutor's name.

"Yes, yes." He wheezed even harder. "It's nothing. Just my asthma. Now where is my puffer?"

He checked his pockets but apparently found nothing there, then shuffled aimlessly around until finally he returned to his desk, and found an inhaler in one of its drawers. It made Bel even more concerned. She would talk it over with Gulzhar. The girl might know what to do.

"I think we should end this lesson now. I really need to rest." Another little lie, but she couldn't bear to make the old man even more uncomfortable, and she was pretty sure he really did need some rest.

"Yes, yes..." He erupted into a coughing fit, and waved at her to go.

"He needs a doctor," she said to her lakai as soon as they were outside of the man's hearing. "He looks really ill to me."

Gulzhar nodded. "I'll see to it, ma'am."

Bel hoped it was about time for lunch yet. She was starving, which was probably Zilla's doing, with all her hunting and gorging. The little thing was going to be bloated and good for absolutely nothing by the time she got back to the palace, which in all likelihood wouldn't be any time soon.

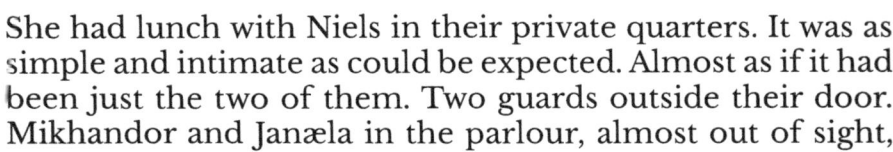

She had lunch with Niels in their private quarters. It was as simple and intimate as could be expected. Almost as if it had been just the two of them. Two guards outside their door. Mikhandor and Janæla in the parlour, almost out of sight, and their lakais on lunch break. Probably in the kitchen with the other servants.

She was about to ask Niels about his morning when her mother's thoughts came to her. "Little Sparkle, we're on our way."

"On your way?" Bel sent back, "so soon already?"

"Of course, dear. We want to catch this killer. It would be so embarrassing if someone else found and destroyed this bag of dragon's droppings."

Bel smiled. "Don't worry, Mumi. We haven't found him yet. But where are you now, and when will you be here?"

"Papi and I are aboard a draken, flight EB 9623, which has just departed from Moringarad Drakenport. It is zero hour, and I think it will be around noon in Ebaru?"

"Yes, Mumi. In fact, we just sat down for lunch, Moradin and I. So, how long will your flight take?"

"On schedule, that should be eight hours."

"So your flight would land just after supper." That was unfortunate. They'd probably be hungry, tired and cranky. Mumi worse than Papi. "Any word from Niko?"

"No, but I'm sure he will contact you directly."

Bel nodded, though she knew her mother could not see her. "I was rather hoping he would be taking a draken too."

"Knowing him, he probably will. He, too, was looking forward to killing some bad guys."

That made Bel chuckle, and Niels gave her a questioning look. She would tell him later. Maybe. He was such an innocent sweetheart, he might prefer not to know.

"I'll make sure someone is at Ebaru Drakenport to pick you up tonight. Have a safe flight, Mumi."

"Thank you, Sparkle. See you later."

She was still smiling, when Niels — really, she should go back to thinking of him as Moradin again — interrupted her thoughts.

"You were conversing with your mother?"

"Yes. Papi and she are on their way. Their draken should land here tonight, just after supper. I'd like to go pick them up." With effort, she resisted the urge to nibble the nail of her index finger. Would the king provide them with a karr? Would he even allow them to go, or would he just want to send a chauffeur?

Nie— Moradin nodded as he helped himself to some rice. "And what was so funny?"

"They were looking forward to, uh... the adventure."

Moradin raised an eyebrow. "I don't understand why that should be so amusing."

"It's not something you would appreciate, my love. You are..." She didn't get the chance to finish her sentence, as just then, Niko contacted her.

"Hey sis!"

"Nikomir. What news have you got for me?"

"We will be landing at Ebaru Royal Drakenport in about two hours."

"What?" She could barely believe it. "So soon already? How on all seven worlds did you do that?"

"Simple enough. I told Felnar that he was in command of the Aurora again, and then paid some Briscan officials to book me on the next flight to Ebaru. Me, Lori, and Flar, who insisted that he should come with us. In fact, all of my Elite Force wanted to come with me, but I had to demand that they stay aboard the ship. They will join us later."

"Pity. I would have enjoyed having them around."

"I know, but it was simply impossible. This flight was already fully booked, so some passengers had to be persuaded to take a later flight."

"That must have cost you a load of silvers."

She could almost see her brother's nonchalant shrug. "This is what they are for, eh? Anyway, it would be nice if you could send someone for us. I hear it's a long walk from the drakenport to your humble abode."

CHAPTER FORTY

SACRILEGE

*past and
present collide
in nightmarish display
of contempt for decency and
honour*

The street was cleaner than Niels had ever seen it before. The Poor used to hang around here, smoking, and drinking. Littering. Now, there was no sign of them. The only living being besides themselves was a stray cat basking in the warmth of the afternoon sun. She lifted her head lazily when they passed, blinked once, and went back to sleep.

Curious dark vines with thick, velvety leaves grew against the walls of the temple. They were dotted with red, heart-shaped flowers that oozed a slimy, pungent smelling liquid. Niels was about to push the heavy door open, when he noticed the strange symbol that was carved into it. He looked up at Mikhandor. Though he wouldn't admit it openly, he was nervous, and that wasn't just because of the ghosts of the past. It was something else. Something evil.

"Allow me to enter first, Your Holiness," his friend and guardian said in a hushed voice. "I'm not fond of surprises."

Niels nodded. "Neither am I."

No sooner had they entered the temple, than Mikhandor gasped. He stood still so abruptly, Niels bumped into him. "Wait here with Bardil."

Bardil. The chauffeur. Could he even trust the man? His father and Mikhandor seemed to think so, but he had his doubts. Yesterday's events had proven, once more, that trust could be lethal.

As Mikhandor walked cautiously further into the building, Niels became aware of the strange odour. He'd expected the Abandoned Temple to smell musty, but it didn't. Instead, it smelled more like a bar after closing time. It was the sour, sweaty stench of people who'd had a few drinks too many. And something else. Something he couldn't define.

The moment his eyes had grown accustomed to the semi-darkness inside, he saw her. Naked, and bound on the altar. Legs apart. Without a moment's thought he rushed forward, past Mikhandor, towards the unfortunate woman. He pulled off his tailcoat and covered her with it the moment he reached her.

"What happened, woman? Who did this to you?"

She looked at him with wide eyes, but didn't say a word. His chest tightened. This was hardly a woman. So young. His mother's age when she gave birth to him. Perhaps even younger than that. Poor child.

"Don't be afraid. We will not harm you." As he tugged at the knots, trying to undo them, the realisation struck him. That strange smell — it was sperm, mingled with vaginal fluid. How utterly disgusting, to desecrate the temple like this. Small wonder the girl was too scared to speak. He increased his efforts to free her from her bonds, but his hands were shaking and he couldn't think clearly.

"Allow me, Your Holiness." Bardil stood beside him. The thin streak of sunlight that crept in through a crack in the wood of the door glinted off something metallic in the man's hand. In a reflex, Niels caught his hand around the wrist and twisted it. In one fluent motion he spun around to face the man, and kneed him in the groin. The knife clattered to the floor, and Bardil went down beside it. Knees pulled to his chest, hands cradling his manhood, he rolled from side to side, moaning in agony.

Too late, Niels realised his chauffeur had probably only meant to use his knife to cut the young lady loose. Momentarily befuddled, he looked from Bardil to the girl on the altar and back again. He should apologise but in his current state Bardil probably wouldn't even hear him. He sighed, picked up the knife and cut the ropes. Strangely, the girl just remained lying there, completely motionless. Now what?

"They're gone." Mikhandor's voice was charged with vexation. "And if you had waited, like I instructed you to, this would not have happened." He looked down at Bardil, then bent over to help him up.

"My apologies," Niels said to his hapless chauffeur. "I panicked."

"No need, Your Holiness." The man still sounded a little out of breath. "This was entirely my own fault. I let my emotions cloud my judgement."

What was wrong with all these people? First Ramshur acting as if he were a god, and now this. He hurt the man, and yet he wasn't even allowed to apologise? What was going to be next? Would they expect him to urinate in a cup so they could drink his pee as if it were some divine potion?

Involuntarily, he balled his hands into stiff fists. He turned and took a few steps away. He wanted to bang his head against the wall. He wanted to... No! He couldn't afford to have a meltdown.

He took a few deep breaths. Looked around. What had they, whoever 'they' were, done to his temple? The headless statue of the goddess was smeared with— he came closer, scrutinised it. Was that blood?

The fountain. Where had they taken it? He peered through the gloom. In that corner over there? His tread leaden, he drew nearer. It was some other object, similar in shape to the fountain, but startlingly different in function. Several long, sharp, metal objects hung from hooks that were inserted into the marble foot of the thing. On top sat a bronze, lidded bowl. When he took the lid off, the stench of decay assaulted his nostrils, so he quickly replaced it. He had no desire to find out what was inside. Mikhandor could deal with that.

As his eyes roamed the hall once more, he finally located the statue's head, or rather what was left of it. He edged towards it, his head tolling with so many emotions he couldn't possibly tell one from another. With every step he took, the tension inside his body increased. When finally he stood over it, ready to pick it up, the overwhelm pulled him down. He sank to the floor, doubled over, and wept.

---⋅◆○◆⋅---

It lasted for only a moment. It lasted an eternity. Then Mikhandor's hand was on his shoulder.

"We should go."

Niels took a deep breath. Tried to steady himself. Sat up feebly. "The woman?"

"We'll take her with us."

There was more to say. More to be done. So much more. But it would have to wait. This was not the time for it. He needed to go home now, to Bel, who always knew how to make him feel better.

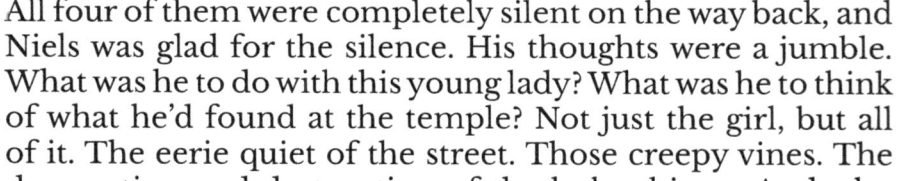

All four of them were completely silent on the way back, and Niels was glad for the silence. His thoughts were a jumble. What was he to do with this young lady? What was he to think of what he'd found at the temple? Not just the girl, but all of it. The eerie quiet of the street. Those creepy vines. The desecration and destruction of the holy objects. And who were those 'they' Mikhandor had referred to?

As they entered the palace, Niels had made up his mind. He would take the girl to Bel. She'd know what to do. Bel understood people. Relieved, he hurried through the long corridors, and only became aware of the fact that he'd lost the others when he had already reached his chambers.

Great. He rested his head against the door. Why was he such an oblivious cabbage head? He turned and walked slowly back, head bowed and shoulders drooping. Soon, he bumped into Mikhandor. For the second time that day.

"My apologies," he said. "I got ahead of myself."

"Your chambers, I assume?" Mikhandor knew him so well by now, it often seemed like the Erl could read his mind.

"Yes. I thought Bel would know what to do."

"Good thinking, Your Royal Highness."

"Do you really have to do that? With those titles?"

Mikhandor chuckled. "It irks you, doesn't it?"

"Yes."

"Well, there's your answer, Your Royal Highness."

"You... you're doing this on purpose? To annoy me?" Never in all those turnings had he suspected his friend could be that cruel. "That is no way to treat your friends."

He opened the door to his parlour, where another unpleasant surprise awaited him. Bel was not alone. Lori, Niko, and Flar were with her, chatting, and laughing, and he would have loved sitting with them and enjoying a cup of kaw and some of those delicious biscuits he saw on the table, but not right now.

Just when he was about to close the door again, Bel looked at him, and her voice sounded in his mind. "Breathe, my love."

She excused herself and wheeled towards him.

"I hadn't expected you back yet. What happened?"

"The temple. It..." He stepped aside, so Bel could see the girl. "I don't know what's going on there, but it's bad. Could you...?"

"Of course. I'll take her with me to Niko's rooms. Could you ask Lori to join us there? Just Lori. No-one else."

"But I need to be alone."

"Oh, Morad." She pulled him closer, so he had to bend over, and kissed him lightly on his forehead. "Wait here then. I'll go back inside and tell Niko and Flar to go for a walk or something. Just a moment."

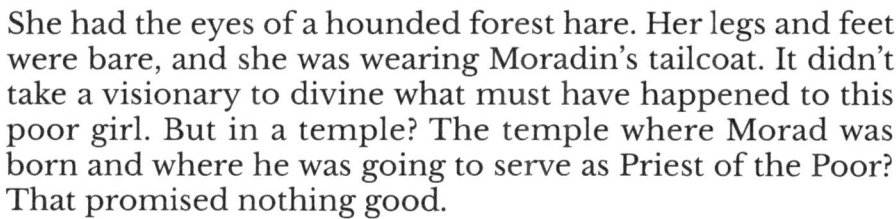

She had the eyes of a hounded forest hare. Her legs and feet were bare, and she was wearing Moradin's tailcoat. It didn't take a visionary to divine what must have happened to this poor girl. But in a temple? The temple where Morad was born and where he was going to serve as Priest of the Poor? That promised nothing good.

"Would you like a drink?"

The girl stared at the floor. Her hands cramped around her knees.

"And some food, perhaps?"

A very slight nod was the only reaction Bel got out of her, but it was a start. She couldn't expect the poor thing to trust her immediately. Not after whatever ordeal it was she'd just gone through.

She looked at Lori. "Would you mind...?"

"Of course. I'll be right back."

That young lady was a marvel, and Niko a lucky man to have gained her love. He'd better treat her well.

She eased herself out of her chair onto the sofa, next to the girl. Could she chance laying a hand on her arm? Or would that be too soon? She didn't want to mess this up.

"I'm Bel. What's your name?"

The girl's fingers moved almost imperceptibly before they regained their iron grip on her knees again. "Numisia," she whispered.

"Tell me, Numisia, is there anything I can do to make you more comfortable? A nice, comfy blanket, perhaps?"

Where that idea had come from, Bel couldn't tell, but apparently it was exactly what the girl needed. The death-grip on her knees loosened a little, and she sat up a bit straighter. "Yes please." Even her whisper was a fraction louder.

As Bel transferred back into her chair, Lori entered carrying a silver tray with three glasses of cold pineapple juice, and several bowls filled with fruits, nuts and other small delicacies.

For a while they sat quietly munching on their snacks and sipping from their drinks — Numisia snuggled up safely under her blanket — but then Bel decided the question had to be asked.

"What happened to you, sweetheart?"

Numisia tightened her grip on the blanket. She bit her lower lip. Her eyelashes glistened with unshed tears. "They..." Her voice was hoarse. "They said they were priests, but they weren't like them other priests. They wore masks, and red robes. Red like blood."

She sniffled. A few tears fell on the blanket. "They took my clothes and... and..." She wrapped herself more tightly in the blanket. Violent sobs shook her body as the tears streamed down her face.

Bel stroked her hair gently. "You're safe here, sweetheart. Nobody will hurt you now. I'll personally make sure of that." She meant every word she said. Anyone stupid enough to even look at Numisia wrong, would meet with her wrath. Hers, and Vindicia's.

CHAPTER FORTY-ONE

Deluge

> piercing
> stare unsettles
> sensitive awareness
> till sight and sound and smell mingle
> and strike

The last few sevendays had been crazy. Life at court was unlike anything else, and although it had some perks, Niels didn't think he would ever really like it. He was never alone.

No matter where he went, he was followed around by his lakaì, one or more guards, and Mikhandor — but the Erl at least knew how to be subtle about it. Even the privy was not exempt, although his well-meaning stalkers did have the decency to wait outside the door while he was relieving himself.

His princely duties drove him insane, especially when he was required to sit in on his father's audiences, or accompany him to concerts, banquets and the likes. Everyone recognised him. Everyone wanted to talk to him. Touch him.

It freaked him out, but he was never allowed to show how much it hurt him, both physically and mentally. What was worse, he could never completely hide his discomfort. No matter how hard he tried, some of it always broke through.

He would start chewing the insides of his cheeks, which felt continually raw now, or run his tongue along the back of his teeth, wriggle his toes inside his shoes, or something like that. Always something seemingly insignificant, and invisible to the casual observer.

Though these little things helped him carry on as if nothing were wrong, the tension would still build up. Just slower. Then, when finally he was back in his own chambers, he would shut down completely, and not even Bel could reach him.

Now he had to sit through another of Padr's dinners, and entertain their foreign guests. Swivian emissaries this time. They looked at him as if they had never seen a prince before, which he knew was absolute nonsense, and treated him as if he were some kind of divinity. What was wrong with all these people?

And then there was Ardu. Staring at him as always. Staring. His piercing blue eyes weighing him. What did he want?

The heat of the day that lingered in the room became ever more oppressive. The buzz of the insects swelled into a roar. The smells of the food overpowered and nauseated him. The drone of the voices, the smacking of lips, human sweat, flickering candlelight... it was too much.

Their weird guests. Ardu. Food. Smells. Sounds.

He should go, before it was too late.

As he got up, his chair clattered to the floor. "My apologies. I need to go."

"Moradin?"

"I feel unwell." He all but bolted.

He fled to his own chambers, and made the guards jump in alarm as he threw himself at the heavy double doors, and plunged heels over head inside. When one of them made to come inside and help him up, he picked up the nearest object, a heavy bronze vase, and hurled it at the woman's head.

Shouting, screaming, and yelling curses at the top of his lungs, he burst into the parlour. He kicked a lightsphere down. Sent a crystal decanter with red wine flying. A ceramic bowl filled with fruit and nuts went after it. A golden candelabra. An unoffending book. Nothing was safe from the madness that had taken possession of his entire being. Though he wanted to stop his violent behaviour, he was unable to.

On and on it went, until his knees buckled and he sank to the cool marble floor, where he lay down, weeping uncontrollably until finally, that too, passed. Too exhausted to get up, or even talk, he just remained lying in his foetal position, rocking himself gently.

Then Bel was by his side. She lowered herself out of her chair and sat down beside him. When she reached out as if to touch him, he flinched and drew in a sharp breath. Immediately, she withdrew her hand. He saw her lips move, heard sounds coming from her mouth, but was unable to make sense of her words. In the end, she left him, and he was alone. Blessedly alone.

Moments later, Sebben entered the room. Of all people, they had to get that bleeding heart in. As if things weren't bad enough already.

"Moradin? Can you talk?" His voice was softer than usual, yet strangely more commanding. This was the psychiatrist he had trusted once, for just a mere moment. And, irrational though it might be, he trusted him again.

"Yes." It took all his strength, and still came out a whisper.

"What happened?"

Last time Sebben had been quick to inject him with that nasty medicine, and Niels worried the same would happen now.

"No Tempaz," he said. His voice sounded strange. Gravelly.

"That was a long time ago, Moradin, and this is a completely different situation. So far, I've seen no indication that you need it. Not this time."

Niels grunted his approval. He needed nothing. Just a good night's sleep.

"What happened?" Sebben didn't seem likely to give up just yet.

Niels wanted to shrug, but his body refused to function properly. "Just... these people... that vizier."

The moment he said it, he knew. That had been the trigger. Ardu. Padr's vizier. Something had been bothering him about Ardu ever since that first morning in the Royal Office. He hadn't realised it then, but his medallion had been responding to the vizier's presence whenever he was near. Now he knew why.

Dinner with the Swivian ambassadors. He had felt Ardu's eyes on him again, and looked up at him. Looked straight into his eyes. Eyes as blue as the ocean. His mother's eyes.

"What about him?" the psychiatrist asked.

"He is... my grandfather." He closed his eyes again, and tried to focus on his breathing.

"Are you sure?"

Ardu. The name had sounded familiar because it was. Ammu Shadu had mentioned it. Ardu had been his grandmother Shirra's husband. His mother's father, who went missing when she was a little girl.

How had Ardu not recognised his own daughter, during those moons she had been staying with Padr? Or, even worse, had he just not wanted to recognise her? Had he chosen to ignore her?

What was wrong with this man, that he hadn't taken care of his own wife and children when he had found a job at the Royal Palace? When he had become King Hazzid's vizier? They would never have needed to live in poverty. His mother could still have been alive today.

It was not right that this wretch should have such an influential position at court. How could a man who cared so little for his own family possibly care much for his ruler? Or his country? A sudden panic took hold of him. What if Ardu was his true adversary?

He started rocking slowly. Almost imperceptibly. Sebben noticed it nevertheless.

"Why does that upset you so?"

Those blue eyes staring at him. Weighing him. Following him. He needed to talk about it, but not here. It wasn't safe. Not if his suspicions were true. He was about to communicate his misgivings to Bel through his medallion, when he reconsidered. If the medallion had a link with Ardu, which it obviously had, that might not be prudent either.

"Zilla," he said, and looked at Bel, his eyes pleading. He hoped she understood. Hoped it would work.

Then Zilla sat by his side, her keen eyes seeming to read into his soul, and he tried to convey his thoughts and fears to her, though he had no idea how. The dragon magic was too different from his own powers.

Bel looked at her dragonet intently. "I see," she said, "thank you, Zilla."

The dragonet flew back to her and perched on her shoulder again. She rubbed her head against Bel's cheek, and Bel scratched the creature's soft chest.

"Moradin needs to sleep now," she said to Sebben. Her voice sounded flat, and tired. "Thank you for coming in. That was most helpful."

When Sebben had left, Mikhandor helped him to his feet. Niels leaned on him as he slowly walked to the bedroom.

"Sleep now, my love," Bel said when he lay in bed. "I'll go and tell your father you'll be needing the day off tomorrow."

For once, they had breakfast with Padr in their own private chambers. It was more intimate than Niels had thought possible. No vizier, no lakais, no other servants. No guards inside either. Just the two outside their door. The Erls were there, of course, but not in the same room, with the notable exception of Krys, who was after all, Padr's partner.

"Beldenka told me you weren't well last night. How are you now, son?"

Niels shrugged. How would he know? Feelings were such fleeting, immaterial things. It was hard to name them, unless they were truly overpowering. "Well, I guess."

Padr nodded. "Life at court can be overwhelming. I've always had trouble dealing with that, too." He took a sip of his kaw. "I suggest you and Bel get out of the city today. Find a nice spot in nature. Unwind. You may take one of my private karrs, and go with just your Erlen guardians."

Niels didn't know what to say. He had known he would have the day off, but he certainly had not expected his father to send him away. It made sense, of course, but Niels worried. If Ardu really was their enemy, then leaving Padr alone could be extremely dangerous.

"Would you come with us, Padr?"

"Come with you," his father echoed. He seemed hesitant, and Niels nudged his emotions just a little bit with his medallion. "Yes, I think I would like that. I could do with a day off, too."

They took one of Padr's private vehicles, an unremarkable beige karr, like hundreds others, soon after breakfast. They wore the dull, colourless clothing of common workers. Their faces were smudged, and their hair was greasy and untidy. Nobody would recognise the royal family.

As soon as they were out of the city, Niels said to Mikhandor, "I need you to take us to the Splice."

Mikhandor nodded curtly. "I thought as much. But be warned: It's a six-hour drive, and the terrain is rough. We'll also have to somehow avoid that cave-in, and I don't really know how yet."

"Six hours?"

"Yes, Your Royal Highness."

"Erl's balls!" Too late, he realised how his guardian felt about that particular curse. "My apologies, Mikhandor. I didn't mean to..."

"Just shut up and let me drive, yes?"

Niels looked at Mikhandor in bewilderment. His choice of words, the terseness in his voice... none of that sounded like him at all.

"I could do the driving, if you prefer?" Janæla offered. "And I could take us there in about half that time."

"Be my guest." Mikhandor brought the karr to an abrupt halt.

In less than no time, Bel's guardian sat behind the steering wheel, humming a cheerful tune as she sped the karr up. "Hold on tight." She all but purred. "I'm going into boost now."

Going into boost? Whatever that was supposed to mean, it was probably bad. He didn't have to wait long to find out. The karr lurched forward, and Niels almost threw up. After that, their vehicle moved more smoothly than any karr should, yet so fast the world whizzed by in a blur of motion. He settled back and closed his eyes. No need to watch the world fly by.

He must have dozed off then, as it seemed only moments later when Janæla parked the karr in the woods, just off the mountain road. He vaguely remembered being shaken awake a little while ago and offered a handful of Mikhandor's dried berries. The ones against Mountain Sickness. He must have managed to eat them before drowsing off again. He felt fine.

Mikhandor and Krys were talking to Padr, so Niels probably wouldn't have any explaining to do with regards to the portal and how it worked. For that, he was grateful. He was going to have more than enough talking to do anyway.

"Now tell me, son. You did not bring us all the way here for no reason, did you?" At least his father didn't waste words on pleasantries.

"Yesterday, at the dinner..." Niels began, then broke off. He took a deep breath, and started again. "Your vizier, he..." Gods! How was he going to be able to tell Padr? He picked up a small twig and started fiddling with it.

"You became unwell, excused yourself, and left. I remember. But what did that have to do with my vizier?"

"He... you may not have noticed this, but he has been watching me, like an eagle watching its prey. He was watching me again, at the dinner, and when I looked up at him..." He felt his heart rate accelerate, and had to swallow down the lump in his throat. "His eyes... have you ever looked into his eyes, Padr?"

His father shook his head. "I prefer not to look people in the eyes. Why?"

"He has my mother's eyes."

"Your mother's eyes? My Lali's eyes?"

"Has she... did she not tell you her father went missing when she was little?"

"She never spoke much about her life before she met me, and I didn't prod her. I assumed she didn't want to talk about it." Hanassan scratched his neck. "She told me once that her mother and younger sisters had died. I cannot remember that she ever mentioned her father, but I always assumed he had died, too."

"Her father's name was Ardu. He left his wife and children when my mother was little. And if that is not enough of a coincidence, my medallion has been responding to his presence ever since I first saw him."

"So," Padr said slowly, "let me see if I understand this correctly. My vizier is your grandfather?"

"Yes." He snapped the twig in two and let the two halves fall from between his fingers.

"But you don't seem happy. Why?"

"Think about it. He was your father's vizier when my mother lived with you, right?"

"That is correct." His father fell silent, and seemed lost in thought for a moment. Then, he nodded. "Ah, I see. He must have seen and recognised her. But he never acknowledged her. His own daughter. He could have saved her life. Easily."

"Exactly. And he chose not to." Niels couldn't keep the indignation out of his voice. "What father does that?"

His father nodded again. "Strange. Very strange indeed. I fear you are right to worry about that. It might be nothing, but then again... Did I tell you my pharmacist died before Sebben Dansinger ever got the chance to talk to him?"

"No."

"And do you know how many people knew Sebben was going to pay him a visit?"

Niels' heart skipped a beat. "Not a whole lot of people, I would think. But Ardu would certainly have known, right? Is that not his job?"

"Correct, son. This worries me. Him possibly being the driving force behind..." He choked up. Then he shook his head. "To think I trusted him. Trusted him with my life. With the lives of..." He got up and walked to the edge of the glade, where he remained standing with his back towards the others.

Niels looked at him and felt sorrow squeeze his throat shut. He would have to confront Ardu. His own grandfather. The sooner the better.

They remained in the Splice for some hours, and rested. The Erls picked leaves, nuts and berries, and served them a simple but delicious meal. When it came time for them to return to Sor, Niels regretted not being able to stay in the peaceful glade for a little while longer.

Janæla took her place behind the steering wheel again, but didn't seem nearly as cheerful now. In fact, everyone's moods appeared to be subdued. Nobody talked, and when night fell and the stars came out, even their light looked dulled. As if the entire world suffered under the burden of what was to come.

Too soon, they entered the city. Too soon, Niels saw the contours of the Royal Palace rise up in the distance, their white walls gleaming threateningly in the pale moonlight. The closer they came, the stronger grew his sense of foreboding. His medallion throbbed.

Something was wrong. Terribly wrong.

CHAPTER FORTY-TWO

Damage

> blood like
> crimson trail of
> tears flows from innocent
> victims' wounds despoiling sacred
> substance

It was eerily quiet in the palace, and the long, broad hallways were deserted. No voices but their own. No footfalls but their own. Where were their friends and relatives? The guards? Niels dared hardly breathe. He felt both anger and fear coming from his medallion. What was going on? Intuitively, his hand went to the hilt of his scimitar. It was comforting to know it was there. Just in case he needed it.

He glanced at Bel, in her new chair. She rode it with ease and confidence. Though he could feel her unease building up, nothing in her posture betrayed her inner turmoil. Not for the first time, he wished he had the same fortitude.

The three Erls walked with firm treads, and their faces wore grim, determined expressions. Although they carried no weapons, they looked ready for whatever might be coming their way.

Even Padr seemed more in command of his feelings than Niels himself. Blessedly, his father had not experienced even one psychotic episode since the medallion had released its healing powers on him, and Niels began to believe he had somehow really been able to cure Padr's mental affliction.

Two guardsmen stood watch by the entrance to the Royal Office. They remained immobile when Mikhandor pushed the heavy doors open.

Ardu sat in Padr's chair, behind Padr's writing table, two guards posted prominently behind him. More guards were posted to either side of each and every one of the arched windows. Hands behind his neck, feet resting on the polished wooden surface of the desk, Ardu was the perfect portrayal of insolence.

He didn't bother to get up when they entered. He just looked at them through half closed eyes. One corner of his mouth was lifted as if in a slight smile as he picked some imaginary dust particles off his waistcoat. What was his game?

"Your Majesty. Your Royal Highnesses. I hope you enjoyed your day out. Please, make yourselves comfortable." He raised the king's golden goblet. "A most excellent wine, indeed. I shall drink to my own continued good health."

He rose from his seat and ambled up to Niels.

"Grandson." He laid a heavy hand on Niels' shoulder, and Niels staggered backwards at the vizier's touch.

"Ardu, what is this supposed to mean?" Padr's voice sounded cold. "What in the name of all the gods do you think you are doing?"

"I am doing the will of my God, your Majesty. The will of the One and Only true God, F'der Gloumben. His prophet Isabi gave me his personal blessing, and the blessing of my Illimitable God, may His holy name be praised."

Niels shuddered. F'der Gloumben. The name Mirk's followers gave their god. Things were worse than he thought. Far worse.

"Yes, grandson," Ardu said in a deceptively mellifluous voice, "my God is the one you *Unsighted* call Mirk. The great and righteous ruler of the All. He who was before the beginning of times."

He grabbed the front of Niels' shirt and pulled him closer, till their noses almost touched. His breath stank of rotting meat. "Your mother, your grandmother, your great-grandfather... Unsighted, like you. I tried to reason with them, tried so hard to make them see the magnificence of the One and Only. If only they could have understood. But they would not listen." He shook his head. "They left me no choice. I had to leave them behind. They made their own doom. Even so, it pained me. It still does."

He let go of Niels and took a few steps back. "But you, grandson, you are F'der Gloumben's Chosen One. Not me. Nor your mother or father, but you. I am just the *Lodestar*. Appointed to prepare the way. To deal with the lawlessness and corruption of this world.

"Yes, it was I who made sure the unworthy royals died. Though I took no pleasure in it, it was imperative that only your father remained. The right man in the right place. Then, exactly as foretold by the great prophet Isabi, you arrived the next day. *Carried by resplendent wings the Chosen One shall come to deal justice and restore the rule of righteousness.*"

Ardu paused. Were his eyes really glowing, or was that just an illusion? A trick of the light?

"But then you disappeared. Had I been wrong? Had I misinterpreted the prophecies? I almost despaired, but Isabi reassured me. You had not left Ebaru, and I would eventually find you. I only needed to watch the comings and goings of your great-granduncle. Sooner or later he would lead me to your hiding place. That gave me hope and strength.

"Little did I know you were hiding in plain sight. Studying at the Seminary even, under the tutelage of some of my God's most devout believers. It was not until the day you graduated that I finally found out, and by then it was almost too late. Too much damage had been done, and the time for gentle extrication was past. We had to take quick, decisive action.

"The plan was to dispose of all your infidel friends and relatives whilst saving you at the very last moment, so your miraculous survival would prove to all people — faithful and faithless alike, yes even to you — that you are, indeed, F'der Gloumben's Chosen One. The Heir of Greatness."

Niels shuddered. Mirk's chosen one? That fiend's heir of greatness? Gods help him! Being chosen by Eylah was one thing. He'd made a reluctant peace with that. But being Mirk's chosen one was of a completely different order. He wanted no part in that.

"Does that surprise you, grandson? You didn't really think we would let you die, did you? You are so much more important than you think. But your friends, your family... they are dispensable. All of them but one." Ardu unsheathed his dagger and stroked it carefully, almost lovingly.

"With Isabi's help, we set those fires. To serve as a light and reminder to the people, that F'der Gloumben is great, and his wrath consumes the infidels but saves the righteous." His voice thundered and he pumped a fist in the air.

"Unfortunately, the evil Daxens came and ruined everything. Before our *Holy Iaktor* could save you, that savage of yours took you away to his home world. You, your cousins, their father, and that traitorous high priest. Still, not all was lost. We made sure everyone believed you were dead, all of you. Then, we waited.

"Several times you came back. Several times we attempted to bring you into our fold in such a way that everyone would see F'der Gloumben's greatness and believe. More and more people had to be sacrificed for the greater good of the world. Yet every time you were taken from us, to Dax, the only world we cannot enter. Nor would we if we could. It's the world where the Master of Evil resides."

Dax, Daxens, Drussa... It was Thorf, Erls or Sylphans, and Doruya. Why did Ardu have to use those weird, offensive names? Why? It confused the blazes out of Niels. And what on all seven worlds was a iaktor? Some kind of priest?

"Now finally — finally! — you are here. And yet still we have not been able to get through to you. Still you serve the immaculate goddess Eylah, whose rose has never tasted the gardener's compelling touch. What shall I do with you, grandson? What shall I do?"

Ardu placed the tip of his dagger in the hollow of Niels' throat, just above the sternum, and Niels dared hardly breathe.

"I shall teach you a little lesson." He withdrew his dagger, but not before he nicked Niels' skin. "I shall teach you the ways of men. Real men, who know their place in the hierarchy. Who serve the One and Only with confidence and pride."

He sat down in Padr's chair again, and began cleaning his nails with his dagger.

Niels looked at his grandfather. Anger clouded his vision. He felt the warm blood tickle his skin before it trickled into his shirt. It might seem like a mere scratch, but it meant much more than that. It was a badly veiled threat, and that angered Niels even more.

"I denounce you. You are not my grandfather. You sired my mother, but you are no blood of mine. Your heart has been defiled by the enemy of light and life. I abhor the darkness that inhabits your soul and made you do all these terrible things."

Ardu remained silent and looked at him. Looked until Niels wanted the ground to open up and swallow him. The silence stretched.

Finally, Ardu spoke again, his voice too soft. Too gentle. "I am sorry to hear you speak those words. However, I cannot say I'm surprised. Unfortunately, I expected you to react this way. Hence, I have already prepared your first lesson for you." He paused for a moment, then continued, "surely, you have noticed how quiet it is in here, and how deserted the halls of the palace are."

Niels' hands balled into fists as he took an involuntary step forward. "What have you done?"

"Nothing too drastic. I am not a cruel man. I only convinced cook to add a little something to the food, so all your Northern friends are asleep. The guards and all other staff members too, by the way, except for those who have already given their hearts to F'der Gloumben, the Great and Illimitable God."

He sounded the bronze gong. "Let the ceremony begin."

Niels' heart sank. What had that degenerate in store for him? He looked at Mikhandor, wishing he could somehow communicate with him without the need for words. He wanted to tell him to do something. Anything.

Mikhandor looked back at him, seemingly unperturbed. Niels let out a long breath. Maybe his Erlen guardian already had a plan. He was a resourceful man. It would not be the first time he surprised Niels.

The echoing sound of approaching footsteps drew his eyes towards the entrance. A loud knock on the door made him want to cover his ears.

"Enter," Ardu said in a carrying voice.

The double doors swung open, and in came a guard. He wore Daroz's uniform. A uniform this pretender had no right to wear. Niels balled his hands into fists again. He clenched his jaws.

"Ready?" Ardu prompted.

"Yes, your Honour." The guard made an elaborate bow before he approached the vizier and handed him a lidded bronze bowl.

"Bring the Pledged in." Ardu placed the bowl almost reverently on the desk before he sat down again.

The guard left the Royal Office backwards, bowing to Ardu three more times as he retreated. Niels stood motionless and held his breath as he heard the man's footfalls fade, until there was complete silence. A silence even more unsettling than his grandfather's insults.

Then he heard the rattle of chains. Distant at first, but coming closer at a slow, steady pace. When it stopped, another firm knock sent Niels' heart racing. Ardu's voice cracked with what Niels assumed was excitement as he called, "Enter!"

The massive doors opened again and there, exposed in the doorway, stood Machteld, wearing nothing but the iron chains that bound her. Her face was tear-stained and swollen, and blood seeped down the insides of her legs.

Niels' hand went to his scimitar as one of the guards pushed Machteld inside. Then he withdrew his hand again. There was nothing he could do. Not yet. Getting his sword out now would be suicide.

"Your enticing sister. Adoptive sister. Remember that. She doesn't share in your ancestry." Ardu trailed a finger down Machteld's left cheek which, Niels now noticed, was also bleeding. "Look at her. Young, blonde, and blue-eyed. A luscious flower from the North. That creamy skin! So tasty. Don't tell me your member doesn't swell with delight at the sight of her."

"You disgust me." Niels wanted to beat Ardu's foul mouth shut. Seeing his sister humiliated like that only aroused his anger.

Ardu shrugged. "It may take some harsh lessons, but you'll learn to speak differently, grandson. And your delicious little sister will learn to love me, her lord and master."

"Never," Machteld said in a choked voice. "You can rape me. You can kill my husband and make me your possession. But you can never make me love you, you filthy ferret fondler!"

"I shall fondle your little ferret, my darling." A small trail of drool dripped down Ardu's chin. Niels was sure that was intentional, and he loathed his grandfather even more for it.

"Unchain her ankles," Ardu ordered the guards. "Get her up on the desk and spread her legs. She needs a lesson in humility, and my grandson needs to see how real men treat women."

Niels reached for his scimitar again, but Mikhandor shook his head almost imperceptibly and held him back with whatever magic it was that he used on him. He looked Niels in the eye, as if he wanted to tell him something, but Niels looked away. He could not take it. Soon, he was going to have another melt-down. He could feel it in the lightness of his head, and in the tightness of his chest. It was building up rapidly.

"Look at that nice, ripe peach." Ardu pawed Machteld's private parts. More drool dripped from his mouth. "Ready for the eating." He buried his head between her legs. "Aaaaah," he murmured as Machteld screamed her defiance. "Not even the nectar of a spring blossom is as sweet as her feminine juices."

When, after what felt like an eternity, Machteld's body spasmed, he stood upright again, his now blood-smeared face triumphant. He reached for the lidded bowl that still stood on the desk, only a few handspans removed from Machteld's head. He held it high, admired it, then placed it back again.

Niels felt sick to his stomach. If only he could do something, but Mikhandor still would not release him. Why was nobody doing anything to make that vile vizier stop?

He could feel Bel's anger, but she neither spoke nor acted. One look at her answered his unspoken question. She sat rigidly in her chair, apparently fighting the invisible bonds with which Janæla must be keeping her from acting.

He looked at his father then, who also seemed to be struggling against an invisible force. Was Krystandor holding him back? But why? Why would they not allow them to fight?

"Tell the priest to enter."

So, he had a priest at his bidding. He should have known. Yet as Ardu's priest entered, masked, and dressed in a blood-red robe, Niels could not hide his shock. He would recognise that man any time. Anywhere, mask notwithstanding. "You!"

"I am sorry, Moradin," Ramshur said. "I truly am. Let me assure you, it is nothing personal. I did not mean to deceive you, but the time wasn't right yet to reveal my true status. But now, let us reacquaint. I am Ramshur Eldani, High Priest of the Illimitable F'der Gloumben. It is my pleasure to welcome you into our fold. Unwilling though you are, you belong with us."

The traitor priest strode up to Ardu, took his outstretched hand, and kissed it deferentially. "Your Honour."

"Your Holiness, I have the required offering for our Great God." He picked up the bowl, took the lid off, and got something out. Something that resembled... Niels averted his gaze. This had better not be what he thought it was.

"Grandson. Over here," Ardu said, and Niels had no choice but to obey. "You will want to see this. It was going to be the love child of your sister and that wild Dragonboy. Hold it."

Aghast, Niels took a step backwards, but Ramshur poked him in the back and made him step forward again.

"Your hand, grandson," Ardu said, and though every cell inside his body revolted against it, Niels held out his hand.

"Now open it." Again, he obeyed. He hated himself for it, but he could feel Mikhandor's eyes burning in his back.

Willing him to do as he was being told. For now. It took him all his self-restraint not to fight both Mikhandor and his grandfather. He was beyond caring.

Ardu dropped the foetus in Niels' hand. So beautiful. So perfect. So tiny. And so dead.

"You swine," Niels growled through gritted teeth. "I vow, I'll..." he sank to the floor, weeping. Yet as he lay rolling back and forth, he whispered "... make you pay for this."

And again, to the rhythm of his rocking. "Make. You. Pay." Again, and again. And there was nothing anyone could do to stop it.

Amidst the clangour of steel on steel, and the shouts of angry voices, Niels slowly came to his senses. Strong arms were holding him, and someone was rocking with him in a slow, steady rhythm. Like Papa used to do when he was little. It felt good. Familiar.

He opened his eyes. "Padr?"

His father nodded reassuringly, even though there was nothing reassuring about their situation. "Are you well now?"

"Well enough." Niels got up and drew his sword. "I've got an egg to crack with that depraved creature." He scanned the Royal Office.

Their little troupe had grown. Leks was there, fighting like a true combat master. If he hadn't known, Niels would never have guessed the old man only had one leg. Dragomir was breathing fire. So were Bel and Mirtalya. Toni wielded his sword like an expert swordsman. The members of Niko's Elite Force were handling themselves well. The Erls were unstoppable. Guards stood against other guards.

A bare-chested Niko was with Machteld, who was wrapped up in a man's tailcoat that came almost to her knees. Gently, carefully, he guided Machteld through the chaos, towards the doors, where Rasælna stood waiting.

But where was Ardu? He should not be allowed to get away with his horrible crimes. Niels wanted to make sure the man got what he deserved.

Someone swung his sword at Niels, and he dodged, then struck back without thinking. His attacker's sword flew through the air, and his hand with it. Momentarily befuddled, Niels shook his head. He had no idea how he'd done that, but it was effective enough. He continued his search for Ardu.

Another of his grandfather's men came at him, sword at the ready, but Niels was prepared now and parried the attack easily. The guard swung his sword again in a clumsy, barely controlled movement. With one well-aimed strike of his own weapon he disarmed the young man and cut him across the face. The guard dropped to the floor instantly. A howling, gibbering mess. Just a lad.

Another of Ardu's men advanced on him, ready to cut his throat, and Niels barely had time to block the strike. Instinctively, he swung his own blade at his attacker's neck, then watched in horror as the man's head landed on the floor a small distance away. At his feet, a fountain of blood spurted from the guard's headless body.

Sick to his stomach, he turned round and found himself face to face with Ardu. For a moment, his mind went blank. Then he steeled himself. He was ready.

CHAPTER FORTY-THREE

Aftermath

<pre>
       wailing
   shatters dead air
 as young lives waste away
in stifling stench of somatic
        discharge
</pre>

"You," he said under his breath, "have forgotten what it means to be human. You have no shame, no compassion, and clearly don't know what love is."

He had his sword at the ready, but didn't use it yet. Irrationally, he still hoped he wouldn't need to. "Do you even have a heart?"

"Do you even have nuts, grandson? Or are you as emasculated as your father's pathetic excuse for a boyfriend? At least Dragonboy got his lovely little wench with child. You don't seem to have been able to fill your woman's belly yet."

"Is that all you can think of?" He struck at the vizier, but Ardu evaded his blow easily, struck back and drew blood. It was just a scratch, but Niels knew that was exactly what he had meant to do. He was taunting him.

Niels concentrated on his posture. His breathing. The way he held his scimitar. The way he moved. He wasn't going to let Ardu provoke him. He was going to subdue him. Kill him if he had to.

"Ran out of words, grandson? Are you soiling yourself yet? You, the Heir of Greatness. F'der Gloumben's ways are a mystery to me. You're such a deplorable milksop."

That hurt. Worse than the scratch on his arm. Far worse. He had been shamed and ridiculed for his weird behaviour his entire life, and no matter how hard he tried to change, he just could not. It was truly beyond his control.

Don't let him get to you. Breathing. Posture. He molested your sister. He humiliated her. Killed her child.

Somehow, reminding himself of that depraved creature's crimes renewed his strength. He lashed out again.

For Machteld. And again, for her child. For Tasim. Farrah. Ameh Saryda. Tulia. Navida. Ziubar. Ziatara. With each name he recited inside his head, he dealt Ardu another blow.

It wasn't easy and, as far as Niels could tell, Ardu was actually enjoying the fight. That deprecating smile never left his face as he moved nimbly from one stance into another. The vizier's scimitar cut through the air in a smooth, elegant dance, biting into Niels' unprotected arms, leaving one small gash after another. Ardu wasn't trying to kill him; he couldn't afford to. He was only toying with him, like a cat playing with its prey. Trying to wear him out. But he couldn't let Ardu win.

He began reciting names again. King Ishvat. Queen Adella. Asandor. Yosan. Niabella. Shadira. Each next blow he delivered was fiercer than the previous one. Emmali. Odella. Ishi. His sword swung to the rhythm of the names. Karoli. Aziya. Nelfi. Alina. There was no stopping him now. Arkesh. Elmin. Belina. Diara. Noria. His arms were bleeding from countless small cuts, but it barely even registered. Arando. Aramo.

He hated this man, who was responsible for the deaths of almost his entire family.

"Shirra," he yelled, as he sliced his opponent's left ear off. Ardu didn't even seem to notice. "Asra." Ardu faltered for a moment. "Siana." The vizier stopped mid-swing, then came at Niels again, screeching profanities at the top of his lungs.

"Shansi!" Niels roared. Ardu's sword flew through the air, and the fingers of his sword hand with it.

"You killed my mother." Niels held his grandfather at sword point. "You murdered almost my entire family. You poisoned my father. You brutalised and violated my sister.

You killed her unborn child. You deserve to die a thousand deaths."

Still, Ardu was defiant, and seemingly unaffected by his wounds. "I regret nothing," he said through clenched teeth. "Nothing. And I would do it all over again. For the glory of F'der Gloumben, the One True God, may his Holy Name forever be praised."

"I will hand you over to my brother in law, to do with you as he pleases." He turned his head to where he'd last seen his father's head of the guards. "Daroz, take him away. I cannot bear to look at this wretch any longer. The sight of him sickens me."

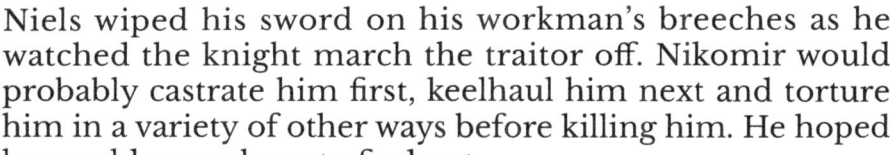

Niels wiped his sword on his workman's breeches as he watched the knight march the traitor off. Nikomir would probably castrate him first, keelhaul him next and torture him in a variety of other ways before killing him. He hoped he would never have to find out.

He turned around and surveyed the situation. Bodies lay on the floor, sprawled in blood, entrails and severed body parts. Several of the bodies were still moving feebly, while some others were convulsing violently. The stench of sweat, urine, faeces, and vomit made his stomach heave. The wails of the wounded tormented both his hearing and his soul.

Bel pulled herself up in her chair. Although she was dirty, and covered in blood, she didn't seem to be badly wounded. Leks retrieved a throwing knife from the guard that lay at Bel's feet. His usual grin had been replaced by a frown. Mikhandor looked like a savage as he snapped a man's neck. Dragomir shook his head as he observed the carnage. He seemed older, and more haggard than ever.

Padr pulled his blade out of a corpse, shook his head and scanned his surroundings. Gradually, his posture relaxed. With slow, tired motions, he wiped his sword clean and tucked it back in his belt.

Just when Niels thought it was finally over, he saw a movement out of the corner of his eye. He turned his head, and looked right at Ramshur who stood to the side, in the semi-dark, half hidden by a large bookcase. With dragging feet Niels went over to him. His voice thick with emotion, he said, "I wish things could have been different, Ramshur, but I have to relieve you of your duties as a high priest. Please, take your medallion off."

For a moment it looked as if Ramshur would oblige. He reached under his robes and pulled his medallion out. Then, instead of taking it off, he held it in his open hands and fixed his gaze on it. The medallion started to glow, until it became incandescent, and sparks flew everywhere. Niels took an involuntary step back and shielded his face with his arms, just before a white-hot flame shot up out of the religious ornament and burned not only the medallion itself, but also its wearer. Nothing remained of the former high priest but a pile of ashes.

Niels stood staring at Ramshur's remains, still in shock, when Bel took his hand.

"Come," she said. "We should go." Gently, she pulled him away. The Royal Office was still a heart-rending mess of wounded, dead and dying men and women, but there was nothing he could do. The fight was over.

She took him to the cisterns, and ordered a frightened servant to draw them a bath. When the bath was ready, she sent the servant away and told Niels to undress. He was still fiddling with the unwilling buttons of his stinky, sweat soaked shirt when Bel had already discarded her clothes. He didn't object when she started tugging at his clothes and helped him undress.

The lavender-scented bathwater, neither too hot, nor too cold, felt good on his burning, itchy skin. He inhaled deeply, closed his eyes and tried to relax. Bel sagged against him, and as he looked at her, he saw tears in her eyes.

"It's alright now," he whispered, not knowing what else to say. "It is over." He drew her closer to him and kissed her eyelids.

They sat huddled together in Padr's parlour. Despite the late hour, it was still hot. The air was humid and suffocating. The food on the table remained untouched. Candlelight reflected from the crystal decanters filled with wine and fruit juice, but none of them were drinking. Nobody spoke.

Young Pav was dead. Zera too. Toni had lost an arm, but Rasælna had patched him up as best she could. He would probably survive. Nikdel had taken a dagger to the gut. Though Rasælna had taken care of his wound as well, he might still die.

She had given Machteld a special herbal cocktail to help her sleep. It was too soon to say how well she would recover from the trauma. If ever. Loathe as he was to admit it, it was probably a good thing that Sebben was still around. Rasælna was a healer, not a psychiatrist and, as she herself once told him, not very skilled with human emotions.

Then again, maybe Niko should take Machteld home, to Ingravia. Ebaru might not be the best place for her to be right now. Or maybe...

"Padr," Niels said, "I would like to invite my parents over, from Ingravia."

His father nodded slowly. "That would be a good idea, I think. After all that you've been through, it seems only natural that you should want them here with you. Your sister will need them, too. And I would like to get to know them, and thank them. They raised you well. Better than I myself could have done, truth be told."

"And," Niels looked at Mikhandor, "my great-granduncle. If he still lives."

The day his parents arrived, Niels couldn't stop pacing the study, until finally Padr said, "This isn't working, son. Go to the training grounds and practice your forms with Daroz."

"Yes, Padr." He fumbled with the sash he wore around his waist. "I... I apologise."

"No need. I understand. Now go."

Niels was already on his way out, when he heard Hanassan's voice behind him. "In fact, I'll come with you. I could do with some exercise as well."

They sparred until lunch time, the king dancing through the forms as if he were a young man, and Niels had to keep his wits together if he didn't want to get hurt. It felt good. No time to ruminate.

Then his parents were there, looking older than Niels had envisioned. For the longest time, he just stood gaping at them like the total turnip he was. Unable to move or even speak, until finally Mama took a step forward and broke the spell.

"Niels," she said in a barely audible voice. She took another step forward, and now Niels saw tears blinking in her eyes. Instinctively, he averted his gaze as he swallowed the lump that had lodged itself in his throat.

"Mama." He took her in his arms and pressed her tight against his chest. She felt different than he remembered. Not as soft and rounded. Had she lost weight? She smelled different, too, but that was probably just her perfume. Women were like that. Changing scents almost as frequently as they changed clothes.

He released her from his grip and held her at arm's length. Studied the contours of her face. "Mama," he said again. "I missed you."

"I missed you too, Niels. More than you could possibly imagine. But it's alright now." She took a step back, and Papa took her place.

"My son." His voice sounded muffled, and his movements seemed awkward as he drew Niels into a solid hug.

"Papa."

Then, there was nothing more to say. No words to express the myriad of emotions that crowded Niels' mind and heart. But for just a little while, all was well.

Later that day, Ammu Shadu arrived. Alone. Grief had etched deep lines into his face, and he walked with heavy steps and bent shoulders, like a man carrying a heavy burden. Again, Niels didn't know what to do or say.

The same pattern repeated several times more over the next few days, when his brothers and cousins arrived with their families.

Niels felt stupid and useless, until Rasu grabbed him around the neck and wrestled him to the floor, the way he used to do when they were boys.

"You utter cabbagehead," Rasu said as they both sat up, still holding each other. Then, they laughed, and the others with them. "What have you been up to then, all these turnings? Look at you, all fancy!"

"I've been running around the world a bit, dodging assassins, but we dealt with them now." Or so he hoped. After all these turnings of constantly looking over his shoulder, it was almost impossible to believe he was really safe now. "But how about you? What have you been doing?" Much better to steer the conversation in a different direction. Away from himself.

"Can't you see? I learned how to hide from my wife and children." Again, everyone laughed.

"You don't really hide from them, do you?"

Rasu punched him playfully on the shoulder. "Still no sense of humour, eh? Course I don't." He picked his youngest son up and sat the little lad on his shoulders. "But I did teach them not to disturb me when I'm in my study. Otherwise, I'd never get any work done."

Life slowly normalised. What used to be the Royal Office, had been converted into the Memorial Hall, which might best be described as a private museum. It displayed portraits of Niels' royal ancestors, dating back hundreds of turnings, to King Haniman and his wife Queen Kiora. Ancient royal artefacts were on display, most of them placed inside glass cabinets, to protect them from dust, humidity, and insects.

Though most of the items were everyday articles — silverware, bowls, drinking horns and goblets — some objects were more sinister. Like the dagger King Shaldin supposedly used to take his own life.

The Royal Office was now located in the Royal Library. The giant desk, that had been so grossly abused by Ardu, had been chopped up into firewood and was replaced by a much smaller desk, that was still twice as large as any ordinary desk.

The biggest change, however, was yet to come. Much to Niels' chagrin, his father had decided to abdicate.

"Moradin," he said one morning during their customary meeting, "as much as I hate to admit it, Ardu was right about one thing. I should abdicate. I have not been a good king, and the people of Ebaru distrust me. I need you to step up and wear that crown."

"I cannot," Niels objected. "I am not ready. Besides, you can make it up to the people now. You can still gain their trust." He was grasping at straws, and he knew it.

His father shook his head. "No, son. Too much has happened. Guided by Ardu, I made too many wrong decisions. I wrote too many questionable laws. The best thing I can do for my people is to step down now."

Stubborn, Niels repeated his objection. "No, Padr. I am not ready. I can't do it. I will mess up. I will..."

Hanassan held up a hand. "Enough, Moradin. Do you think I was ready when I assumed the throne? When my entire family had just been assassinated?"

That drove his point home. Ashamed, Niels bowed his head. "I apologise, Padr. You are right. Being a king is not about being ready. It's about honouring your obligations, whether you are ready or not. How long do I have to prepare?"

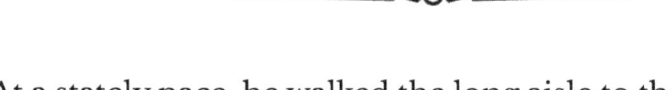

At a stately pace, he walked the long aisle to the podium. Bel rode by his side. She wore a splendid blueish green dress that left her shoulders and most of her back bare, but covered her front appropriately. She looked truly regal. Niels himself wore a long silken robe, the colour of clotted cream.

Though he nodded to the left and the right, as per his instructions, he tried not to look at all those faces that were turned towards him. Most of these faces belonged to strangers. Rulers and other high officials of other countries. People he could well do without.

Only when he passed the front rows, did he venture a quick glance at his guests. Papa and Mama. Rem and Kas, and their families. Mir and Toni. Bel's three sisters. Ammu Shadu. Anur and Rasu with their families. Dragomir, Leks, the Erls. Even High King Yumænor, and Akdi, with his Erlen carer.

Niels tried not to think of all the missing faces. Machteld and Niko, who had taken a draken to Ingravia as soon as Machteld was well enough to travel. Tasim. Ameh Saryda. Farrah. Ziubar. Pav, Zera, and all these others who had died. For him.

He ignored the steps leading up to the podium, but instead accompanied Bel on the ramp, and only let go of her hand when they took their places. He on his throne, Bel in her own chair, which was in all likelihood far more comfortable than those straight, hard wooden thrones, coated in a thin layer of gilding.

Padr rose from his throne and stepped forward.

"People of Ebaru." He paused for a moment, and took a deep breath before he continued. "Today is a historical day. That which has never before been done in the long history of our kingdom, is happening today."

Again, he paused. Through his medallion, Niels could feel his father's emotions. His pain and sadness. His regret.

"A little over eighteen turnings ago, I became your king. I promised to be a good king, and a faithful servant to you, my people. A promise I have not been able to keep. It is for this reason that I have decided to abdicate. From this day forward, my son Moradin will be your king."

He stood in silence for a moment longer, visibly struggling to contain his emotions, then stepped back and sat on his throne again. The throne to Niels' left.

The new high priest, a man Niels' own age and most likely one of his fellow students at the Seminary all those turnings ago, climbed the stairs to the podium. He spoke at length to the people, but Niels didn't even hear half of what he said.

The words seemed just that. Loose, unconnected words, with no meaning.

Moradin! Bel's thought inside his mind felt urgent. *Vows.*

He got up and walked the few paces towards the lectern, where the high priest — what was his name again? — stood waiting for him. He knelt down on a thick red velvet cushion. The same cushion on which his father had sat kneeling when he made his vows almost twenty turnings ago.

"Moradin Dolanthi of Ebaru, do you promise to be a good king, and a faithful servant to your people, for as long as our good Goddess grants you to reign?"

"Yes, Holy Brother. Let all those gathered here be my witnesses. I will do everything within my power to be a good and fair ruler, guided and governed by our good Goddess Eylah herself."

The crown, the same simple golden circlet with the seven rubies that had adorned his father's head before, was now placed on his own head. Though it weighed next to nothing, he felt pressed down by the enormous weight of the responsibilities it placed on his shoulders.

"May our good Goddess bless your reign, and our country with prosperity," the high priest recited. "May the Lady's wisdom guide your decisions, and may she bless our gracious king with life eternal and good health."

He took Niels' right hand, raised him to his feet and presented him to the crowds; both those inside the Hall of the Kings, and those watching the ceremony outside on the screens, as well as the people witnessing it at home, on their vidispheres.

"Long live King Moradin! Long live the King."

A loud applause went up, and shouts. Shouts of joy, Niels hoped. The whirring of the crowd hurt all his senses, and the only thing he wanted was to flee. Yet he remained standing on the podium, as was his duty, and pretended to face the people. His people. Then, Bel was by his side and took his hand in hers. He felt her calm. A calm she somehow managed to transfer to him without losing her own share of it.

People flocked towards him. His father, now Prince Hanassan again, Mama and Papa, his brothers, Mir and Toni. He was hugged, and worse, kissed. He shook hands. He smiled and spoke friendly words to complete strangers, all the while screaming inside.

Finally, it was over. Back in the palace, he had a moment of solitude whilst taking a bath. These days, bathing had nothing to do with hygiene any more. Not to him. It was a much-needed break from the endless stream of social engagements. One of the few things that helped keep him sane.

The festivities that night were horrendous. Loud music, dancing, fireworks, and worst of all, people. Everywhere. And they all wanted to see him, talk to him, touch him. As if he were some kind of deity.

It was well past midnight when finally he lay in his bed, his head still spinning with all of the day's emotions.

> *"He shall be both priest and king, and he shall heal what was broken, protect the innocent, and bring redemption to the House of the Kings."*

That was what the prophecies said. Part of them had been fulfilled, but even more work remained to be done. This was not the end. It was just the beginning.

Bel placed a hand on his chest. "King Moradin Dolanthi of Ebaru," she murmured before she pressed her lips on his.

"Queen Beldenka Nadinov of Ebaru," he whispered between kisses. "We need an heir."

GLOSSARY

Gods, Religion, and Folklore

Zinnir: He who watches, the Fathergod
Oummi: She who hears, the Mothergoddess
The Seven Siblings: Ona, Chey, N'kell, Eylah, H'hos, P'ther, Doruya
Mirk, F'der Gloumben: Lord of the Night; also called the Gloomfather
Yat S'ber: Death
A'harat: Goddess of the Afterlife
The forgotten gods: Forgotten, but still honoured
Eyades and Kradim: Malignant folklore figures in human mythology
Erls: Mischievous but benign folklore figures in human mythology
Maidens of Eylah: Religious order of women devoting their lives to the care of the poor and needy.

Time and Festivals

Turning: The amount of time Sor takes to complete one cycle around its sun
Sevenday: A seven-day period
Moon: The amount of time the moon takes to complete one cycle around Sor

Names of the sevenday days: Elday, Druday, Cheyday, Kellsday, Hosday, Therday, Onday

Overmorrow: The day after tomorrow

Festival of Returning Light: Seven-day festival, celebrated around the winter equinox

Festival of New Life: Ten-day festival, celebrated around the spring equinox

Festival of Abundance: Three-day festival, celebrated around the autumn equinox

Words and phrases

All, the: The seven known worlds and their suns, moons and stars

Ameh: Aunt

Ammu: Uncle

AsK-II-nd: Genetically engineered virus that claimed the lives of millions of people on the Southern Continent during the reign of King Hanassan of Ebaru

Barkmouse: Popular pet, esp. Amongst older ladies, that looks like a hybrid between dog, bat and mouse

Blackdrop thistle: Thorf herb that renders men temporarily infertile

B'radar: Brother, informal form of address for a male friend

Brozka: A clear distilled alcoholic beverage

Datamarble: Device on which data can be preserved digitally and accessed again later using a logatome or other compatible device

Datori: Species of people created by the god P'ther; also called Hunters

Ded: Grandfather, old man

Dragonet: Parrot-sized animal with telepathic powers, related to dragons

Draken: Vehicle designed for air travel

Drakenport: Stretch of land where drakens take off and land

Drawers: Underwear for women

Erl: Mischievous folklore figure in the Human mythology; See also Sylphan

Firecrest Dragon: A smaller sized dragon, but no less imposing than its larger cousins
Flour Dust: Illegal powdery drug for inhalation
Gi: Uniform worn when engaging in one of the martial arts
Giggle of children, a: A few children (three or more)
Goldfox Fleddermouse: Largest existing bat on Sor, with a wingspan of 1.5 m
Hog Flare: Illegal injectable drug
Horned Sharpclaw Dragon: Elegant, fierce dragon
Humans: Species of people created by the goddess Eylah
Hunters: See Datori
Ikorn: Cat-sized squirrel-like omnivorous animal with two tails
Ikorn Pestilence: Epidemic, affecting the entire Southern Continent, during the Reign of King Ishvat of Ebaru
Ingravian Broadwing Dragon: A fearsome, highly aggressive beast. The female is larger and more aggressive than the male, esp. when she has eggs or hatchlings to protect. Rumoured to also eat humans
Intemporal: Semi-immortal being
Kaw, kaw brew, perk: Bitter, dark liquid made from the roasted bark of the kaw tree
Kaliff: Playing piece in the game Llulaba
Karr: Egg-shaped high velocity vehicle, powered by magnetic forces, with two antennae on top at the front
Karrosse: Vehicle for hire, with driver
Kooler: Insulated cabinet that keeps food cool by means of evaporation
Korli: Closest and dearest friend
Lightsphere: Lamp, working on magnetic power or earth current
Lief: Dear, sweet
Logatome: Digital multi-purpose book, with can be used for creative, recreational and professional purposes. Usually voice-operated
Llulaba: Strategy board game
Lyts: Little
Marble: See Datamarble
Manewolf: wolf-lions, enormous beasts with a wolf's body, tail and hind legs, shaggy fur, and a lion's manes, poisonous fangs and sharp front claws

Mouldywarp: Subspecies of mole
Mountain ape: Fierce ape, twice the size of a man
Mountain misk: Middle-sized feline, living in mountainous areas
Multikarr: Powered vehicle for public transportation, shaped like an elongated egg, with four antennae sprouting from its caterpillar-like head
Naa: Grandfather
Narcs: Illegal drugs
Northern Bear: Huge bear that can easily measure 3 m standing on its hind feet and weigh around 1200 kg
Okular: prosthetic eye with built-in camera, often used by spies who have one eye purposely removed so it can be replaced by an okular
Ophidian Death: See Swivian Reptichitis
Oracle: Illegal psychedelic drug
Otherlander: Foreigner
Pickle and onions: Vulgar term for the male genitals
Pizzle: Vulgar term for phallus
Portadire: Silvery disk about the size of a person's hand, used to make voice calls to people in other parts of the world, taking portraits, etc.
Prowlfox: Ferocious carnivorous fox the size of a wolf. Used in executions in Tirona
Rainbow Crush: Illegal powdery drug for inhalation
Reject: A person who is unacceptable and/or unwelcome
Saffire Tease: Illegal injectable drug
Sard, sarding: Vulgar term for sexual intercourse, most commonly used as an expletive
Sensei: Martial arts teacher
Smallclothes, smalls: Underwear for men
Snakefish: Large, snake-like fish
Sor: World created by the goddess Eylah, inhabited by Humans
Sphere: See Lightsphere
Starbird: Mythical bird that is born from the dust of a falling star
Stones: Vulgar term for scrotum (to be off one's stones: to be delusional)
Stone-squeezing, (adj: stone-squeezingly): Excruciating
Stylo: Writing implement, usually made of gold or silver

Swivian Reptichitis: Pandemic, originating from Ba Swaru, that wiped out entire families on the Southern Continent during the reign of King Hazzid of Ebaru; also Ophidian Death

Sylphan: Species of people created by the goddess Doruya; also called Erl

Tempaz: Strong, injectable prescription-only tranquiliser

Thremble venom: Poison that attacks nervous system and causes convulsions first, and complete paralysis soon after

Thorf: World created by the goddess Doruya, inhabited by Sylphans

Transient: Someone who travels between worlds, also called Traveller

Tunnelrider: Powered vehicle for public transportation using an underground rapid transit system which is inaccessible to other traffic

Velo: Two-wheeled high velocity vehicle, powered by magnetic forces

Vidisphere (vidi): Circular metal device with a silver screen on which one can watch optically transmitted shows and events that are happening elsewhere in the world

Wedding orb: Object given to a couple at their marriage, symbolising their eternal love and devotion to each other

Zinnir's eleventh finger: A semi-polite profanity referring to the father-god's phallus

A Word of Thanks

My Heart-Felt Thanks

To my daughter Lisa for the many hours we spent talking about the story, and for the beautiful artwork she created for me. I love you more than words could ever express.

To Anat, for reading my first draft and providing me with more valuable feedback than I could have ever hoped for. Also for being a wonderful friend and a listening ear when I needed one.

To Michael and Jenni, who went above and beyond their obligations as beta readers. Thank you for all the time you spent answering my never-ending questions and for helping me polish my manuscript. I feel privileged to call you my friends.

To Gyppo and Jo, for their encouragement and expert advice on so many things writing-related. I couldn't have done this without your help.

To Nina Gracia, my weird and wonderful friend, for always believing in me, and being my greatest fan.

And last but not least, to my parents and grandparents for instilling a love of stories and the written word in me from a very young age.

ABOUT THE AUTHOR

Author and poet Daan Katz was born in 1963 in The Hague, the Netherlands, where he also spent the first fifteen years of his life.

From a very young age, Daan has been enchanted by stories. When immersed in his books, Daan would forget everything else. The real world would cease to exist, and there was only the imaginary world, with his imaginary friends, who would continue to speak to him long after he'd finished reading the book.

Given his love for stories, it was only natural for him to start writing his own as soon as he realised that he could.

Daan's characters are real people. Not people who exist on Earth, but real all the same. They all have good and bad inside of them. They all face their own struggles in life. They come in all colours and sizes, with their own sexual preferences and gender identities. And several of them are disabled.

Daan is a wheelchair user, diagnosed with Hypermobile Ehlers-Danlos Syndrome and Autism. This makes him the perfect man to write disabled characters — and make them shine. Because who wants a pitiful wretch of a main character, when they can have one that kicks arse?

As for Daan's private life, that is just that. Private.

BY DAAN KATZ

Poetry

NIGHT SONG - SONGS OF REDEMPTION, BOOK I:
A collection of fantasy-themed cinquains

MEWSINGS OF A CAT LOVER:
An exclusive E-book for new subscribers to Daan's Official Newsletter only.

Fantasy

NIGHT'S REIGN - CURSE OF THE FATHERS, BOOK I

DEATH AND THE MAIDEN (Publication in late 2022)

ACCURSED KINGDOM (Publication in early 2023)

STEP INTO DAAN'S WORLDS

AND LET THE MAGIC BEGIN!

Subscribe to Daan Katz's official mailing list at https://daankatz.com/newsletter and receive an exclusive, free short story with each newsletter as well as updates on new and upcoming books.

You'll also get a free copy of Daan's exclusive E-book "Mewsings of a Cat Lover"

Last, but not Least

Your Feedback Matters

Thank you for reading Night's Reign.

I spent countless (mostly) enjoyable hours crafting this story for you, and hope you enjoyed reading it as much as I did writing it. Now, I would like to ask you a small favour.

Could you please leave a review?

Reviews are incredibly important to Indie authors like myself. Not only do they help with our rankings and improve our sales, but they can help us authors to improve our craft, and help other readers to determine if the book is right for them.

Leaving a review need not be hard. It can be as simple as giving a rating (1 star: I hated it; 2 stars: I did not like it; 3 stars: It was OK, 4 stars: It was good; 5 stars: It was amazing) and a quick comment explaining why you gave that rating. E.g. "The characters felt real", "I liked how X did Y", or maybe you could just add a favourite quote from the book.

On a related note, despite several rounds of thorough editing and proofreading, it is quite possible for the occasional typo to have slipped through. This happens even with traditionally published books, and I have no illusions about mine.

If you happen to find one of them, I would be thankful if you could let me know about them — either via my website, facebook, or instagram — so I can fix them in the next edition.

I would be grateful for your feedback.

DAAN KATZ

https://daankatz.com
https://www.facebook.com/DaanKatzAuthor
https://www.instagram.com/katzdaan

Lightning Source UK Ltd.
Milton Keynes UK
UKHW010627250422
402014UK00001B/3